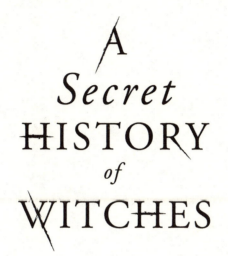

A
Secret
HISTORY
of
WITCHES

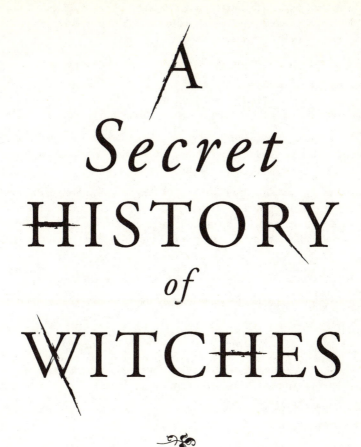

A Secret HISTORY of WITCHES

Louisa Morgan

REDHOOK

www.redhookbooks.com

Cover design by Lisa Marie Pompilio
Cover art by Arcangel Images and Shutterstock
Cover copyright © 2017 by Hachette Book Group, Inc.

Redhook Books/Orbit
Hachette Book Group
1290 Avenue of the Americas
New York, NY 10104
hachettebookgroup.com

First Edition: September 2017

Redhook is an imprint of Orbit, a division of Hachette Book Group.
The Redhook name and logo are trademarks of Hachette Book Group, Inc.

The publisher is not responsible for websites (or their content) that are not owned by the publisher.

The Hachette Speakers Bureau provides a wide range of authors for speaking events. To find out more, go to www.hachettespeakersbureau.com or call (866) 376-6591.

Library of Congress Cataloging-in-Publication Data:

Names: Morgan, Louisa, 1952– author.
Title: A secret history of witches / Louisa Morgan.
Description: New York : Redhook, 2017.
Identifiers: LCCN 2017011477 | ISBN 9780316508551 (hardback) |
    ISBN 9780316508582 (trade paperback) | ISBN 9780316508568 (ebook) |
    ISBN 9781478977025 (audio book downloadable)
Subjects: LCSH: Witches—Fiction. | Mothers and daughters—Fiction. |
    Families—Fiction. | Magic—Fiction. | Brittany (France)—Fiction. |
    London (England)—Fiction. | BISAC: FICTION / Occult & Supernatural. |
    FICTION / Fantasy / Historical. | FICTION / Family Life. | FICTION /
    Historical. | FICTION / Literary. | GSAFD: Fantasy fiction.
Classification: LCC PS3563.A6732 S43 2017 | DDC 813/.54—dc23
LC record available at https://lccn.loc.gov/2017011477

ISBNs: 978-0-316-50855-1 (hardcover), 978-0-316-50856-8 (ebook)

Printed in the United States of America

LSC-C

10 9 8 7 6 5 4 3 2 1

In loving memory of my mother,
June Margaret Bishop Campbell.
May your line continue forever.

1821

The layered clouds, gray as cold charcoal, shifted this way and that, mirroring the waves below. They obscured both stars and moon, and darkened the beach and the lane running alongside. Beyond the lane, in the field of standing stones, a handful of caravans circled a small fire. Firelight glimmered on the uneasy faces of the people gathered there, and reflected in the eyes of their restive horses. The invisible sea splashed and hissed, the only sound except for the crackle of burning wood. The flames cast their wavering light over the menhirs, making the stones appear to move out of their centuries-old alignment, to sway and tremble like ghosts in the night. The child Nanette whimpered and buried her face in her sister Louisette's rough skirts. The older Orchiéres glanced nervously over their shoulders, and at one another.

Two of the stones, collapsed on their sides in some unremembered era, formed a pit for the fire where a brace of rabbits had roasted, sizzling and spitting into the embers. The rabbits were gone now, their meat eaten, their bones buried in the ashes. One of the women stoked the fire, then stood back to make way for her grandmother.

Grand-mère Ursule, carrying a stone jar of salted water, walked a circle around the pit. She muttered to herself as she sprinkled the ground. When that was done, she brandished her oaken walking stick at the sky and whispered a rush of words. The clan watched in tense silence as she laid down her stick and reached into a canvas bag for her scrying stone. She carried it with both hands into the blessed circle, and lifted it into the firelight.

The stone was a chunk of crystal that had been dug out of a riverbank by the *grand-mère* of the *grand-mère* of Grand-mère. Its top had been rubbed and polished until it was nearly spherical. Its base was uncut granite, in the same rugged shape as when it emerged from the mud.

The scrying stone glowed red, flaring with light as if it burned within. It was a light reminiscent of the hellfire the Christians feared, and it reflected off Grand-mère Ursule's seamed face and glittered in her black eyes. Nanette lifted her head from her sister's skirts for a peek, then hid her eyes again, sure the blazing stone would burn her grandmother's hands.

Ursule crooned as she turned the stone, seeking the best view into the crystal. Her eerie voice made gooseflesh prickle on the necks of the watchers. She was the greatest of the witches, inheritor of the full power of the Orchiére line, and watching her work struck awe into the hearts of even those closest to her.

The men shifted in their places and worriedly eyed the lane leading from the village of Carnac. The women clicked their tongues and drew their children close in the darkness.

All the clan were fearful this night. Word of another burning had come to the ears of the men when they went into Carnac-Ville to buy beans and lentils. Nanette had heard them tell the tale, though she didn't fully understand it until she was older.

It had taken place in the nearby city of Vannes. It was said that one Bernard, a young and ambitious priest, had tracked down the witch. He took it upon himself to examine her for the signs before he denounced her in the public square. The archbishop, eager to be known as a burner of witches, had set the torch to the pyre with his own hand.

There was great excitement over the news of this burning in Carnac-Ville. The Carnacois applauded when Father Bernard, a man with sparse red hair and eyes too small for his face, appeared in the marketplace. Nanette wanted to cover her ears when Claude, having returned in haste from the town, told the story, but Louisette pulled her hands away. "You need to hear," she said. "You need to know."

"They say he hates witches because of his mother," Claude said.

"Why?" Louisette asked.

"She had a growth in her breast, and died in pain. Bernard accused the neighbor—a crone who could barely see or hear—of putting a curse on her."

Grimly, Louisette said, "There was no one to protect her."

"No one. They held one of their trials, and convicted her in an hour."

"Did they burn the poor thing?" Anne-Marie asked in a low voice.

Claude gave a bitter laugh. "Meant to. Bernard had the pyre laid. Stake ready. The old woman died in her cell the night before."

"She probably wasn't a witch at all." Louisette pulled little Nanette closer, absently patting her shoulder. "But he feels cheated."

"Been hunting witches ever since."

A grim silence settled around the circled caravans. The day was already far gone. The salt-scented dusk hid the ruts and holes of the lane, making it unsafe to travel before morning.

It wasn't safe to stay, either. They were only three men and five women, with a handful of children and one grandmother. There would be little they could do against a bloodthirsty mob.

The Romani had always been targets, and were always wary. When the blood fever came upon the people, when they were overcome by lust for the smell of burning flesh and the dying screams of accused witches, there was neither law nor reason in the land.

"We should leave," Paul, Anne-Marie's husband, said. "Move south."

"Too dark," Claude growled.

Louisette nodded. "Not safe for the horses."

They all understood. There was nothing left for them but to rely on Grand-mère.

The old woman swayed in the firelight. Her cloud of gray hair fluttered about her head. Her wrinkled eyelids narrowed as she gazed into the scrying stone. She resembled a menhir herself, craggy, timeless, inscrutable. Her thin lips worked, and her voice rose and fell as she recited her spell. The gathered clan shivered in fear.

After a time Grand-mère's chant died away. She stopped swaying and lowered the crystal with arms that shook. In a voice like a violin string about to break, she said, "There is a house."

"A house?" Nanette lifted her head to see who was speaking. It was Isabelle, the most easily frightened of the six sisters.

Louisette put up her hand to shush her. "Where, Grand-mère?"

"Beyond the sea," Ursule said. "Above a cliff. Long and low, with a thatched roof and broken shutters. A fence that needs mending. A hill behind it, and a rising moor." Her eyelids fluttered closed, then opened again to look around at the faces in the firelight. Her voice grew thinner. "You must go there. All of you."

"But Grand-mère," Florence said. "How will we find it?"

"There is an island, with a castle on it. It looks like Mont St. Michel, but it isn't. You will pass the island. You must go in a boat."

The clan sighed, accepting. When Ursule scried, there was no arguing. Even four-year-old Nanette knew that.

The old woman sagged back on her heels, then to her knees. Her head dropped toward her breast. Nanette stirred anxiously against Louisette's side, and her eldest sister shushed her. They waited in the chill darkness, listening to the murmur of the ocean and the occasional stamping of one of the horses hobbled among the stones.

Sometime near midnight the clouds above the beach drifted apart, admitting a narrow beam of moonlight that fell directly onto the circled caravans. It gleamed on painted canvas and hanging pots and tools, and shone on the clan's tired faces. Grand-mère shot upright with a noisy intake of breath, and glared at the break in the cloud cover.

She commanded, "Put out the fire!"

One of the men hurried to obey, dousing the flames with a bucket of seawater kept handy for the purpose. When a child's voice rose to ask why, Grand-mère said, "Be still, Louis. Everyone. Silence." She reached for her canvas bag and covered the scrying stone with it. She got stiffly to her feet and bent to pick up her stick. She held it with both hands, pointing at the slit that had opened in the clouds. She murmured something, a single emphatic phrase that sounded to Nanette like "Hide us!"

Everyone, child and adult, gazed upward. For a long moment there was no response to Grand-mère's command, but then, lazily, the clouds began to shift. They folded together, layer over layer, healing the break as if it were a wound to be closed. No one moved, or spoke, as the light faded from the painted canvas of the wagons. The fire was nothing but a mound of ash smoking faintly in the darkness.

As the Orchiéres' eyes adjusted, their ears sharpened. The sea grew quiet as the tide receded from the beach. The wind died away. Not even the horses seemed to breathe. Gradually their straining ears caught the muffled tramp of feet on the packed dirt of the lane, and the voices of people approaching.

"Grand-mère," one of the sisters murmured. Nanette thought it was Anne-Marie, but she sometimes got them confused. She was by far the youngest of the six sisters, and the only one who had never known their mother, who had died giving birth to her. "Shouldn't we—"

"Quiet!"

Grand-mère Ursule was tiny and bent, like a doll made of leather and wood, but everyone knew her fierceness. She gripped her stick in her gnarled hands and whispered something under her breath, words so soft only those closest to her could hear. One last spell.

Mother Goddess, hear my plea:
Hide us so that none can see.
Let my belovèd people be.

Louisette clamped a hand over Nanette's mouth so she would not cry out as a deep shadow, more dense than any natural darkness, enfolded the campground. The footfalls of the approaching people grew louder. Some cursed when they stumbled. Some prayed in monotonous voices. One or two laughed. They reached the curve in the lane that curled past the field of menhirs, and the Orchiéres froze. The older children huddled close to the ground. The men braced themselves for violence.

The townspeople in the lane trudged along in an untidy crowd. They drew even with the campsite, with the dark sea to their left and the standing stones to their right, and walked on. Their steps didn't falter, nor their voices lower. They marched forward, a mindless, hungry mob in search of a victim, all unaware of the caravans resting among the menhirs, and the people crouching around a cold fire pit. It took five full minutes for the Carnacois to pass beyond the hearing of the clan.

Not till they were well and truly gone did the Orchiéres breathe freely again. In careful silence they signaled to one another and retreated to their caravans to rest while they could. The men murmured in one another's ears, arranging a watch. The women tucked their children into their beds and lay down themselves, exhausted.

But Grand-mère Ursule remained where she was, her stick in her hands, her eyes turned upward to the sky. She stood guard until the moon set behind the clouds. She held steady while the slow dawn broke over the rows of standing stones.

No one heard the sigh of her last breath when she crumpled to the ground. The man whose turn it was to watch was focused on the lane. The women, her granddaughters, slept on beside their children, and didn't know she had left them until they rose in the chilly morning.

It was Nanette who found Ursule's old bones curled near the fire pit, her hair tumbled over her face. The little girl shook her *grand-mère*'s shoulder, but there was no response. Nanette put out her small hand and brushed aside the mist-dampened mass of gray curls.

Ursule's eyes were closed, her mouth slightly open. Nanette touched her cheek with a tentative palm. It felt cold as old wax. Nanette sucked in a breath to cry out, but Louisette appeared beside her, catching her hand and pressing it.

"*Chut, chut*, Nanette. We have to be quiet."

"But Grand-mère!" Nanette wailed, in a small voice that died against the surrounding stones. "We have to wake her!"

Louisette bent over the still figure, then straightened with a heart-deep sigh. "No, *ma petite*. We can't wake her. Grand-mère is gone."

"Where did she go?"

"I can't say that, Nanette. None of us can."

"I want to go with her!"

"No, no, *ma petite*. You can't do that. You have to go with us."

Louisette signaled to her husband, and he came to stand beside her, looking down at Ursule's frail body. Her stick lay beside her in the damp grass. The scrying stone was cupped against her with one arm, as if she had died holding it.

"We'll have to bury her here," Louisette said.

"Hurry," her husband said. "We need to go."

"Oui. D'accord."

Nanette watched them wrap Ursule in a quilt from her caravan. Her *grand-mère* never complained, or tried to push them away, even when they covered her face. The other two men brought shovels and began to dig in a space between two of the menhirs. Louisette called Florence to take Nanette away to her caravan to pack her things. When they emerged again into the brightening day, Ursule and her quilt had disappeared. A mound of gray dirt marked the place between the stones.

Nanette turned to Louisette to ask what had happened, but her eldest sister's face was forbiddingly grim. The question died on her lips. She clutched her bundle of clothes, blinking away tears of confusion and loss.

The clan unhobbled the horses and smacked their hindquarters to send them running. They abandoned the caravans where they were, leaving them in their colorful circle in the field of standing stones. With their most precious possessions packed into bags and stuffed into baskets, they started away on foot. Louisette had charge of the crystal, and had packed Ursule's grimoire along with her own things. Nanette would learn later that her grandmother's staff had been buried with her, because no one else had the power to use it.

The Orchiéres left their grandmother, the great witch Ursule, resting alone with none but the deathless menhirs to guard her shabby grave.

THE BOOK OF NANETTE

1

Nanette shook the pony's reins and clucked at him. He sped into a trot, but not for long. He soon settled back into his usual walk. The jingle, empty now of the vegetables and cheeses Nanette had sold at the Saturday market, rattled against the stones of the cliff road. Nanette shifted anxiously on the bench seat, chafing at the slowness of the journey, but she didn't reach for the whip. She had trained this pony herself. Whipping only made him rebellious. To pass the time she recited the major and minor Sabbats. The pony's ears twitched with interest as he plodded on.

By the time the thatched roofs of Orchard Farm came into view, the sun had begun its descent beyond the peak of St. Michael's Mount. The Cornish wind bit through Nanette's coat and homespun dress. She was cold, tired, and worried. When Claude emerged from the byre to take the pony's reins, she could barely manage to nod to him.

"Good day?" he asked, speaking French as always.

In irritation she answered in English. "The priest was there."

He lifted his brows at her. *"Prêtre?"*

"Priest. Priest! I know you understand that much English!" She jumped down from the jingle and stamped around to the back to unload the empty baskets and folded bags.

"Seventeen years old you are, to my forty. Show some respect."

She sighed and switched to French. "Yes. The priest was there. *That* priest. Bernard."

Claude didn't answer, but his customary scowl deepened as he led the pony away.

Nanette hurried up through the garden and let herself into the porch. She stacked the baskets beside the door and went on into the kitchen. The house was warm, and the scents of pottage and fresh bread made her stomach contract with hunger, but she hardly noticed.

Anne-Marie was bent over the stone sink, scrubbing a pot. She glanced up, saying, as Claude had, "Good day?"

"No." Nanette sagged into a chair, feeling as if she had carried home the weight of the world.

"What's wrong?" Louisette came to the door of the pantry, a dish of butter in her hands. She was the eldest and the tallest of all the clan, even the men. She had a man's voice, and she often spoke like one. She frowned at Nanette.

Nanette propped her chin on her fist and glared back. "Aside from the fact that I'm the only one of this family who speaks the language of this country?"

Anne-Marie said in her mild way, "Pierre speaks English."

"He's gone, though, isn't he? And George, and Louis. Left as soon as they could get away, and left it all to me." No one responded, and Nanette wished she could snatch back the words. Her older sisters had mourned their children's leaving, as she knew very well. Their sons had fled, one to Scotland, one to Ireland, and one back to Brittany, which had proved disastrous.

Fleurette brought a bowl of pottage and set it before Nanette. She rarely spoke—sometimes Nanette wondered if she still had a voice—but she touched her little sister's shoulder with a forgiving hand. Nanette gave her a wan smile. "*Désolée*," she murmured. It wasn't fair to be cross, though she was exhausted. Her sisters had been both mother and father to her for as long as she could remember. She knew they were afraid, and they had reason. She had grown up hearing the stories of the burning times.

Louisette said, "Nanette. Tell us what happened."

"The witch hunter was in Marazion."

The sisters glanced at one another, and tension filled the room with darkness, as if the wood stove had belched a gout of smoke.

The Orchiéres had found the farm Ursule had prophesied, every detail just as she had described. The voyage had been a misery, but the boat had deposited them on a rocky beach within sight of St. Michael's Mount, a miniature imitation of Mont St. Michel. They found the farmhouse nestled at the foot of a boulder-littered tor, with a moor stretching beyond it. The place was in such poor repair as to be uninhabitable, and no one objected when they took possession. They spent months making the farmhouse livable, the garden productive, and the byre safe for livestock.

It had been a sacrifice, settling down. The Orchiéres preferred the road, new scenery every season, hidden places where they could practice the old ways undisturbed. In Cornwall the older Orchiéres left it to the younger ones to learn English, and such bits of Cornish as they needed. For the first ten years, the clan had felt safe in Cornwall.

Then, three years before, Bernard had appeared. He put it about that he had been sent to establish a Catholic parish in Penzance, but the truth was that the priest was still hunting witches. The clan had no need of Ursule's scrying to tell them so, and that was a blessing. Ursule's magic was lost to them.

"You need to eat," Louisette said to Nanette. "Then you can tell us." She pulled up a chair on the other side of the table, and rested her elbows on the scarred wood.

Nanette obediently took a spoonful of pottage, and then another. Despite everything, she was hungry, and the soup was good, flavored with summer sage and pepper. She knew Fleurette had dipped out the largest chunks of meat she could find, and she smiled at her again. Florence carved a slice of bread off the loaf and slid the butter dish close to her hand. While Nanette was eating, the men came in, and the women served them. No one spoke until they had all finished.

"Enough?" Louisette asked.

Nanette sat back. "Yes, thanks."

"Well, then."

Nanette brushed bread crumbs from her fingers. "He spoke to me."

"Did he?" This was Anne-Marie, the second eldest of the sisters. She was the calm one, but even her face was tight with alarm.

"He watched me all day, even when I was chatting with my friend Meegan. When I was harnessing the pony, he walked right up to me, in front of everyone."

All of Marazion knew that the Orchiéres never attended the Anglican service at St. Hilary Church. Everyone would have noticed Bernard, in his rusty black cassock and flat-brimmed hat, speaking to someone from Orchard Farm.

"What did he say?"

"He quoted Scripture."

"'Thou shalt not suffer a witch to live,'" Louisette said in a toneless voice.

"No. It was different." Nanette rubbed her windburned face. "He said something about 'a man or woman with a familiar spirit, or who is a witch, shall be put to death.'"

Florence said, "We don't keep familiars."

No one responded. It was pointless, because the witch hunter wouldn't care. When Louis, Isabelle's only child, had returned to

Brittany, Bernard had found him and beaten the clan's location out of him. Isabelle didn't know if Louis had lived or died.

"He knows our farm," Nanette said. "He said we should take care on the cliff road, since we don't have God's protection."

"A threat," Louisette said.

The rest sat in silence, absorbing Nanette's grave tidings.

Nanette sipped at the mug of honeyed goat's milk Fleurette brought to her. She could have said more. She could have told them how the witch hunter's empty eyes made her stomach clench, how his sour breath reminded her of the very devils he prated about. She could have said she would just as soon convert and get it over with. That would make Meegan happy, and she might make other friends.

But she was tired, and, now that her stomach was full, sleepy. She didn't want to talk anymore. She longed only to take off her heavy boots and close her burning eyes.

The wick of the oil lamp was trimmed short, and the kitchen was comfortingly dim. One of the men lit his pipe, sending the sweetness of applewood curling to the rafters. The low ceiling of the farmhouse, with its thickly thatched roof, felt as cozy as an old quilt. Nanette wanted to go to her bed, to bury her face in her pillow of goose feathers, to forget all about the man who hated them so much he had pursued them across the Channel. Who had thrown a string of beads at her, daring her to pick it up, hoping it would burn her fingers.

She should, of course, have ignored it, but she hadn't. She had picked up the string and dropped it into her pocket, just to prove she could.

She drank off the milk, murmured her thanks to Fleurette, and rose from the table. She said, "*Bonne nuit,*" to the room in general.

Claude put up a weathered hand. "*Attendez.* You women," he said. "No more rites."

Louisette turned to her husband. *"Pourquoi?"*

"He spies on us. He and that other priest, the one from St. Hilary. Not safe."

"No one sees us when we climb the tor."

"A peddler might ride by. A neighbor come to call."

"Pfft! Neighbors never come to call."

Claude's rocky features didn't change. "Don't argue."

Louisette pursed her lips, stood up, and left the table in a stony silence. The others, Anne-Marie, Isabelle, the spinster twins Florence and Fleurette, dropped their eyes.

Nanette shrugged, too tired to care. She plodded off to her bedroom at the back of the house, where she closed her door, kicked off her boots, and stripped off her clothes, letting them lie in a pile on the floor. The beads were still in the pocket of her skirt, forgotten in her exhaustion. She was half-asleep before she slipped her nightdress over her head.

When Louisette's hard hand shook her, she was in the midst of a nightmare. She was driving the jingle along the cliff road, with the sea on her right, and the lethal drop to the rocky beach below. On her left was only the empty moor, and behind her, coming up fast, was the witch hunter. She couldn't see him, but she knew he was there. She couldn't get the pony to run. Her hands ached with gripping the reins, and her legs twitched with the need to hurry, while the pony plodded on and the witch hunter came closer and closer. In her dream Louisette's hand became the hand of the priest falling on her shoulder. She startled awake on a shriek of terror.

Louisette clamped her fingers over her mouth. "Quiet!" she hissed. "They'll hear you."

With a shudder Nanette came fully awake. Louisette's grip loosened, and Nanette whispered, "Who? Who will hear me?"

"Claude. Paul. Jean."

"What's happening?"

Louisette plucked Nanette's dress from the floor and thrust it at her. "We're going to the temple. If Claude knows, he'll stop us."

Nanette sat up. Beyond her window, stars glittered in a wind-swept sky. The early frost of approaching Samhain rimed the edges of the glass. Nanette shivered as she wriggled out of her nightdress and back into her clothes. Louisette found a pair of stockings and held them for her. In the darkness her eyes were like black stones.

Nanette shivered again and whispered, "Why, Louisette?"

"We're going to try a spell of diversion."

"But Claude—"

"*Pfft!* Men know nothing of the craft."

With her boots in her hand, Nanette padded after her sister, down the dark hallway and out through the kitchen. On the porch they found the others waiting, so shrouded in scarves and coats Nanette could barely tell them apart. She thrust her feet into her boots and chose a coat at random from the rack of pegs. Someone—she thought it was Isabelle—pushed a woolen scarf into her hands, and she wound it about her neck as the sisters filed silently out through the side door and into the garden.

The climb up the tor that was so familiar in daylight was treacherous in the dark. The stars' uneven light glistened deceptively on the stones of the path. The brambles that curled beside it were all but invisible, and threatened to trip the marching women. Anne-Marie led the way, with the twins behind her. Isabelle, carrying a basket with the new candle and jar of salted water, walked in the middle. Nanette came after Louisette. She trudged wearily upward. The goats would be bleating to be milked in only a few hours. She wanted to complain that she didn't see the point of doing this, or that it could have waited for Samhain, but she kept those thoughts to herself. When Louisette set her mind on something, arguing was a waste of energy.

Louisette was the one, when they took possession of Orchard Farm, who had found the cave at the top of the tor. It was an echoing space with a narrow entrance, well hidden by towering chunks of tumbled granite. The sisters had swept away the feathers and bones and gravel that littered the floor, and appropriated a three-foot stalagmite that erupted from the center for their altar. They used rock outcroppings as shelves for their supplies. Ursule's crystal rested on the altar, covered with a piece of homespun linen.

For years they had observed the Sabbats in the cave, which they called their temple. They followed the rites Ursule had taught them, referring to the ancient grimoire for simples and potions. They lit a new candle, sprinkled salted water, burned the proper herbs. They wore ceremonial scarves, and stood in a swaying circle around the scrying crystal.

Not once, since her initiation into the craft, had Nanette seen the crystal respond in any way. She doubted tonight would be any different.

2

When Nanette was still small, she had begged her older sisters to be allowed to climb the tor with them. Louisette said, over and over, "Not yet. Not yet," refusing to explain. Nanette even tried once asking Claude, but he growled at her, as if he were a dog and she were a bothersome kitten. It was his only answer.

Fleurette had found her voice that day. "Men don't understand," she said, with a touch of her hand, but she offered no other explanation.

Nanette eyed the tor from time to time, wondering if she dared climb its twisting path alone, if she could find the temple by herself. She could have, she supposed, but she was busy from dawn to dusk with chores, or the market, or having to translate for her family with the farrier, or the ragman, or the men who came to buy ponies. It remained a mystery as she grew to be ten years old, twelve, fourteen. Then, on the day of her first blood, Louisette gave her a wolfish grin across the kitchen table. *"Aujourd'hui,"* she said. Today.

"Today what?" Nanette asked plaintively. Her belly hurt, and the sight of her own dark blood on her clothes when she rose that morning had made her feel queasy. Florence had fitted her out with a homemade clout of homespun. She hated it. It chafed her thighs and caught on her skirt when she sat down.

Louisette leaned forward. "Today you can go to the temple."

Nanette stared at her. *"Aujourd'hui? Pourquoi?"*

"Because now you're a woman!"

"This was what I was waiting for, all this time?"

"Exactly."

"Couldn't you have told me?"

"And argue about it? No. This is what the craft teaches." Louisette pushed up from the table. "We'll go as soon as the sun sets."

Despite feeling unwell, Nanette was thrilled when she first set foot inside the temple. The climb up the tor had been chilly, but the boulders that marked the entrance to the cave blocked the wind. Suddenly much warmer, she stood gazing in wonder at the granite walls, the niches here and there holding stoppered jars and lumpy baskets. In the center of the cave an upthrust cylinder of granite held something covered with cloth so old it was crumbling to bits. When she caught sight of it, a shape both mysterious and promising, her neck prickled and her aching belly quivered.

"Ursule's crystal," she murmured.

Anne-Marie, a broom in her hand, nodded. "We'll uncover it in a moment."

"I remember it," Nanette said.

"I don't think you could. You were only four."

"I do, though. I remember. It glowed in her hands, and I thought it must burn her."

Anne-Marie began to sweep, shaking her head with a sadness Nanette didn't understand.

Her older sisters draped her in a scarf. They invoked the Goddess. They circled the scrying stone, their scarves rippling in the candlelight like starlit waterfalls. Isabelle's candle emitted a pure light that pushed the shadows far back into the stony recesses of the cave. The crystal glimmered, but only with reflected light. The bloody glow Nanette remembered never appeared.

It was full dark by the time they began their descent from the temple. Louisette and Anne-Marie carried oil lamps to illuminate the path. The men had left a light burning in the farmhouse, a beacon in the darkness. When they reached home, the men had gone to their beds, and the sisters gathered in the kitchen. Fleurette set about warming fresh goat's milk and stirring it with honey while the rest divested themselves of hats and boots and coats.

When they were seated, Nanette asked, "Am I a witch now?"

"You always were," Anne-Marie said. "But now you're an initiate in the craft."

"You have a lot to learn," Louisette reminded her.

Isabelle offered, "We'll teach you what we can," making Nanette raise her eyebrows.

A stiff silence stretched around the table as Fleurette poured mugs of warm milk and handed them around. When it seemed no one was going to explain what Isabelle had left unsaid, Nanette spoke up. "What did that mean? Didn't Grand-mère teach you the craft?"

"She taught us the three parts," Florence said. "Simples, potions, and spells. Spells are beyond us now. We are left with only the minor talents."

"I thought the power was passed down from mother to daughter."

"It should be," Louisette said. "But our mother had no gift, other than for producing daughters." She sounded irritated, but Nanette knew that was because she was unhappy. "Anne-Marie has a small gift for charms, which is why her soaps sell well at the market. Fleurette is good at simples—things to help you sleep, or ease your back when it aches."

Isabelle said, "And sometimes I dream things that are true."

"Aren't those things part of the craft?"

"Oui, oui." Louisette cradled the mug between her big hands. "But none of us have the power Ursule had. Florence and I have nothing at all. The crystal doesn't respond to any of us. None of us can work spells."

Nanette said, with the innocence of a fourteen-year-old, "Have you tried?"

Every eye turned to her, and she saw the bitter truth in their faces. They had tried, and tried again. They had done all the ceremonial things she had just witnessed. They had followed their *grand-mère's* path as best they could. Profound disappointment clouded the atmosphere in the kitchen and reflected in the dark eyes of the sisters.

"Why do you keep on?" Nanette asked.

"It is our heritage," Anne-Marie said. "Our birthright."

Isabelle sighed. "We thought it might be different for you."

"You were our last hope," Anne-Marie said.

"Yes," Louisette said. "But now our line will die out. We have only sons, of course. If you have no gift, either…" Her deep voice cracked, and this evidence of emotion shocked Nanette more than anything.

"You hoped the crystal would respond to me."

No one spoke, but she understood. They had tried to do everything right, waiting for the right time, saying the right words, following the traditions. They were disappointed in her, and as she realized it, the thrill of her first rite in the temple evaporated.

The years passed, and the sisters persisted. They celebrated all the Sabbats. They chanted to, and praised, and occasionally pleaded with the Mother Goddess. Anne-Marie blessed the little soaps she made in the vat in the laundry shed. Fleurette perused the grimoire afresh each season for recipes for the simples she stored in colored jars in the pantry. But the crystal, despite their last hopes for Nanette, remained dark and lifeless.

Florence said once, after one of the minor Sabbats, "It's our punishment."

Her twin gasped, but Anne-Marie shook her head. "I don't believe it."

Florence clicked her tongue. "We left her there. Just—put her in the ground, with no proper ceremony to speed her on her way."

Louisette snapped, "It's what she would have wanted! There was nothing we could do."

Isabelle said, "Our ceremonies aren't much good, in any case." No one argued with her.

Now, despite the men's objections, and with the witch hunter threatening them, the sisters gathered around their altar one more time. They uncovered Ursule's scrying stone, and began their preparations as always, but there was a heaviness in the air, and desperation in their demeanor. Fleurette had tears in her eyes. Her twin stayed close by her, as if afraid she might break down. Isabelle set the fat white candle next to the stone, and Anne-Marie laid their offering of dried thyme and rosemary beside it. Louisette finished the sprinkling and stood gazing into the dark stone, her expression as hard as the granite walls around them. The others watched her, waiting for her to begin the rite.

The long silence of the night was broken only by the whistle of the wind around the tor. Nanette breathed in the scents of thyme and rosemary and melting wax. She closed her eyes, comforted by the familiarity of it all, the protection of the cave, the presence of her sisters, even the solidity of the dormant crystal at the center of their circle. There was magic just in this, she thought, in this company, in this ritual, in their history.

Louisette still didn't speak. Nanette opened her eyes to see her staring at the stone, her narrow lips pressed tight. Anne-Marie whispered, "Is something wrong?"

Louisette gave a shake of her head, not in the negative way, but in the way a person does when she can't find words.

Isabelle said, "Do you want one of us to begin?"

Louisette expelled a breath and pushed back her scarf. "We have to do something different," she said in a harsh tone. "Something has to change, or we are lost."

"Goddess help us," Fleurette said, her little-used voice only a thread of sound.

At that very instant a sensation began in Nanette's belly. It reminded her of the way she had felt on the day of her first blood, achy and hot.

Her belly began to throb. The feeling swelled and rose, filling her chest, warming her cheeks, rushing into her brain. Her breathing quickened, and her hands, without her volition, extended toward the crystal. One of the sisters made a sound, but someone else shushed her.

Nanette stepped forward and laid her palms on the smooth quartz. She spread her fingers and looked between them into the depths.

The circle around her tightened, the sisters moving closer, leaning forward, pressing shoulder to shoulder.

Nanette didn't know where the words came from. She had listened to Louisette, and sometimes Anne-Marie, reciting prayers for nearly four years. She had always believed they came from the grimoire, that they were written down, but now...

Now words sprang into her mind, and she heard herself speak them in a steady voice.

Mother of All, your daughters pray
That you will lead the man astray.
Confuse his path and cloud his mind,
Make him as one fully blind.

She reached into her pocket and drew out the string of beads the priest had tossed at her. Her friend Meegan had one like it, a rosary, wooden beads and a clumsy cross strung together with cotton thread. Nanette was vague about its purpose, but she thought it must be some sort of ritual object, like the candles and herbs and scarves she and her sisters used. She clumped the beads in her palm and dropped them onto the flame of the candle.

The flame billowed up, twice the height of the candle, then three times. The beads blackened and burned, drowning in wax. The cross was consumed by the unnatural flame. Nanette's hands still hovered above the crystal, and as the beads burned, a glimmer of light shone in its depths, a shimmering spark that laughed up at her as if it had been awaiting this moment.

She watched the spark dance within the stone as the surface of the candle turned dark with ash, and the wick collapsed. Rapt, Nanette gazed into the crystal—the great Ursule's scrying stone—and felt its power surge through her body. The light faded slowly, reluctantly, but the tingle in her fingertips and her toes remained, as did the slight ache in her belly, the ache of energy and strength and purpose.

The ache of magic.

No one moved or spoke until Nanette drew a noisy breath, breaking the spell that mesmerized them. She stepped back from the stone and looked up at her sisters.

Louisette's head was thrown high, her eyes blazing with triumph. Anne-Marie's features were soft with wonder, and Isabelle pressed her two hands to her mouth. Fleurette's tears had fallen and were shining on her cheeks as they dried.

Florence blurted, "What was that?"

Nanette said, "A spell of diversion, as Louisette wanted. To turn the priest's attention away from us."

"That spell is not in the grimoire!"

Fleurette whispered, "Neither were many of Grand-mère's."

"But—but how did you know what to say? What to do?"

"She was inspired," Louisette pronounced, her baritone ringing against the granite walls. "As Grand-mère was." She regarded
them all with blazing eyes. "The Orchiére line continues after all!"

The sisters made their stealthy way down the tor and into the
house. They had to forgo their usual honeyed milk for fear of
waking the men. Each of them crept to her bed in silence.

Nanette, though she went to her bedroom, couldn't fall asleep.
The goats would begin to bleat all too soon, but she lay wakeful in her bed, body and soul thrumming with excitement over
what had happened. She was a witch. She was truly a witch,
like her *grand-mère* Ursule, like Ursule's *grand-mère*, like all the
Orchiére *grand-mères* who had gone before. The crystal, having
lain dormant for so long, had come to life for *her*. She felt as if
she could do anything, make anything happen, work any spell in
the grimoire.

Louisette had whispered to her, just as they came into the house.
"Be warned, Nanette. The spell may not work, even though the
stone responded to you. Magic has its own rules."

But Nanette was bursting with confidence. She was seventeen,
a woman grown, a proven witch. She was sure, in her bones, that
the Goddess had heard her.

She lay with her cheek pillowed on her arm and watched the
stars fade over the sea until her nannies began to bleat.

Yawning and dry eyed, she went down through the garden to
the byre, a bucket in each hand. Tired though she was, she smiled
as the she-goats crowded around her, and she breathed in their
sweet, strong scent with new appreciation. She milked without

hurrying, savoring the sound of the pail filling and the warmth of the nannies in the cool morning. She relished the sense of being more fully alive than she had ever been.

She had just finished, and released the she-goats out into the pasture, when she heard a faint mewling. She paused to listen, but it didn't come again. No doubt it was one of the byre cats scratching through the hay in the loft, searching for mice. She covered her buckets and set them on a workbench while she scraped the byre floor clean. As she hung her shovel on its peg, she heard the sound again. It was definitely the sound of a cat, but high and fragile.

A kitten! One of the cats must have gone into the loft to have a litter.

The cats were usually Isabelle's charge. She was fond of cats, but Claude forbade animals in the house. She hadn't mentioned a litter. Nanette wondered if she knew about it.

She left her buckets where they were and climbed into the hayloft. The mewing grew louder as she ascended, and she was met at the top of the ladder by the tiniest, most pitiful kitten she had ever seen.

Cats had never been Nanette's favorite beast. She loved the ponies, and the goats, and the birds that wheeled above Mount's Bay. Cats were useful, to keep the mice out of the goats' feed, but otherwise they held little appeal for her.

But this one, scrawny and gray, with one lopsided ear and eyes running with pus, called to her newly invigorated spirit. She climbed the last rung of the ladder and crouched down for a closer look at the little creature. "Where is your *maman*?"

It pressed itself against her ankles and mewed again. She wasn't sure she should pick it up. It could be lousy, or full of fleas. It crawled over one of her feet, and then, with one more sad cry, it fell to its side as if it hadn't strength enough to stand. A male, she saw, a tiny tomcat with nothing to recommend it. Still, she couldn't leave it there.

She took off her apron and wrapped the kitten in it. She scanned the loft and checked behind the mounds of hay the men had piled there at the end of summer, but she found no other cats. If there was a litter somewhere, it wasn't in the loft.

With the kitten to manage, she needed two trips to get the milk to the cold cellar and handed off to Anne-Marie. When that was done she went in search of Isabelle, and found her pinning laundry to the clothesline.

Isabelle smiled when she saw her. "Did you sleep?"

"No. I couldn't. But Isabelle—look." She held out her folded apron and opened it to reveal the kitten. It looked like a scrap of gray rag lying nearly lifeless on the figured cotton.

"Oh!" Isabelle whispered. "The poor little tyke! Where was he?"

"He was in the loft. I couldn't find the cat. I don't even know if he'll live."

Isabelle gently lifted the kitten and turned him this way and that. "He doesn't look like much. He's been abandoned, I think."

"Claude would say we should drown him."

"We won't tell Claude. Let's feed the little thing, and clean him."

"His eyes look bad."

"Yes, I see. He might be blind, but still..." Isabelle cuddled the kitten to her chest, with no evident thought for fleas or lice. "Can you get some milk? Or cream, if there's extra."

When the kitten was washed and rubbed dry, and had lapped up an astonishing amount of cream skimmed from the butter churn, Isabelle held him up on her two hands. "He's not blind," she said. "See how his eyes are following you?"

"Following me?" Nanette peered at him and saw that it was true. The kitten's eyes were an odd sort of yellow, and they were fastened on her face. "Homely little thing, isn't he?"

"Beauty isn't everything."

"What do we do with him now? He's too small to stay in the byre alone."

Isabelle held him out, and when Nanette accepted him, though with some reluctance, the kitten curled up against her chest and promptly fell asleep.

"You," Isabelle said with a smile, "now have a cat."

"But I can't! What about Claude?"

"Keep him in your bedroom. Claude never goes there."

"What if he mews?"

"Claude's half-deaf. Louisette has to say everything three times before he hears."

Nanette suspected that wasn't about Claude's hearing, but she let it pass. He and the other men were scything hay in the farthest pasture, so she carried the kitten into the house. She still wasn't at all certain about actually keeping it, but she couldn't think what else to do.

She found an old basket that had lost its handle and lined it with a bit of cotton. She set the basket beside her bed and nestled the kitten into it. He opened his yellow eyes once to blink at her, then closed them again. She stood, arms folded, looking down at him. "You are the most unprepossessing creature I've ever seen, but it seems you're mine, at least for now."

All at once the sleeplessness of the previous night caught up with her. She yawned so hard her jaw cracked, and she sank onto the edge of her bed, rubbing her burning eyes. She lay down on her unmade bed, clothes and all, and settled onto her pillow. In moments she was as deeply asleep as if it were midnight instead of midmorning.

When she woke, the gray kitten was curled beside her, its head tucked under her chin.

On the next market day Nanette, in defiance of the witch hunter's threats, wore her brightest headscarf and parked the jingle in the center of the green, where everyone would see her. It was a clear, cold October day, one of the last markets of the season. She arranged her wares as appealingly as she could and began a brisk trade, all the while keeping an eye out for the redheaded priest.

The Orchiéres were regarded as foreigners by the citizens of Marazion, but Nanette was accepted, for the most part, by the other vendors at the weekly market. Her wares were known to be of good quality. She dressed plainly, as they did, and spoke unaccented English and even a good bit of Cornish.

Her friend Meegan, another farmwife, lived on a tiny holding on the eastern edge of the moor. She left her own wagon, where she sold eggs and freshly plucked chickens, and came to Nanette at midday in search of a cheese for her lunch. Nanette gave her a cake of Anne-Marie's soap just to be friendly, and invited her to sit on the open gate of the jingle to eat.

They chatted a bit, and Nanette asked after Meegan's brood. "Five of them now!" Meegan said, "And me not yet twenty-three. Take my advice. Don't go rushing into a wedding!"

"Oh no," Nanette said, shaking her head. "That's not likely to happen. I never meet anyone. I think I'm meant to be lonely."

"A pretty thing like you? Someone will come along and sweep you right off your feet. You'll see!"

"Is that what happened to you?"

"Hmmm," Meegan said, breaking off another piece of cheese. "I wouldn't quite say my Bert swept me off my feet. Not much of a sweeper!" Her laugh was easy, and she elbowed Nanette as she said, "He tumbled me, though, that's for certain sure."

"So then you were married."

"Not much choice, really. There was a bun in the oven—I should have stopped right then!" She laughed again, a burbling sound that made the pony's ears twitch. Nanette smiled to hear it. No one at Orchard Farm laughed very much.

"Best to marry first, my girl," Meegan said comfortably. "My father was none too happy with me. And Father Maddock told us if we didn't marry up quick, he'd put us out of the church."

"Could he do that?"

"Oh aye. He could indeed. I expect that Catholic priest—the mean-looking one, with the red hair—he could put you out of your church, too. Then it's straight to hell with you, and you wouldn't like that!"

Nanette understood the assumption that if she wasn't Church of England, she must be Catholic. She filled her mouth with bread and cheese so she wouldn't have to lie to Meegan, or admit she wasn't a member of any church. Wasn't anything, indeed, that Meegan would recognize.

"Of course, that priest is gone now," Meegan said, brushing crumbs from her generous bosom. "Good riddance if you ask me, hoping you won't take offense. He gave me the shivers, with those little eyes peering around all the time."

Nanette's mouth fell open, and she had to press her palm over her mouth to keep from spitting bread crumbs. Her heart began to thud so hard she thought Meegan must hear it.

When she had managed to swallow, she said in a choked voice, "He's gone?"

"You didn't know that?" Nanette shook her head. Meegan's eyes widened. "Fancy that. Well, Father Maddock said his archbishop called him back. Something about the work not going well here."

"The work?"

"He was supposed to collect money to build a Catholic church in Marazion, but no one wants that popery here, begging your pardon again. No one gave him any money, not even His Lordship across the water there." She gestured with her chin in the general direction of St. Michael's Mount.

Nanette hardly dared speak. She wanted to dance, or turn somersaults. Gone! The witch hunter gone! It was everything she had asked for.

A customer approached the jingle then, and Nanette jumped up to help her. She sold her a packet of *fines herbes*, one of Anne-Marie's specialties, which always brought a good price. When her customer walked away, Meegan also was on her feet.

"Thank you for the soap," she said. "I'd best get back. I still have eggs to sell." She paused, pointing into the half-empty bed of the jingle. "What's that, then?"

Nanette followed her gaze. "It's a kitten," she said.

"What's it doing there?"

"It was a stray, and it's adopted me, I guess. It goes everywhere I do."

"You like cats?"

Nanette shrugged. "They're all right. It wasn't my decision, I'm afraid."

"I could use a cat. There are always mice around a henhouse. I'll take it if you don't want it."

The kitten, which had been dozing in the sunshine, sprang to its feet. Its yellow eyes narrowed to slits. Its bony spine arched, and it hissed at Meegan as if she had tried to pinch it.

Meegan started and leaned back, away from the angry little creature. "Ho! There's a cat that knows its own mind."

"It's a strange one, isn't it?"

Meegan laughed and turned away. "That's the way it is with cats sometimes. Well, I'm off to my own work. See you soon."

Nanette nodded and waved and turned to rearrange the depleted assortment of cheeses. She smiled to herself, feeling as if the sun had grown brighter, the breeze more gentle, even the voices around her sweeter.

She surveyed the housewives strolling past. She willed them to turn to her, to buy, to take the rest of her produce so she could harness up the pony and start home along the cliff road. She could hardly wait to carry her good news to Orchard Farm.

3

The success of Nanette's spell energized all the sisters. Anne-Marie created a new batch of soaps, scented with lavender, and the entire stock sold in one day. Fleurette concocted some simples for influenza, and after Nanette mentioned them to Meegan, four of their neighbors rode up in their wagons to buy them against the illnesses of the coming winter, and not one of them haggled over the price. Isabelle saw a missing trowel in a dream, and Florence found it right where she'd said it would be, though Florence told Paul she'd found it by chance.

They were careful to hide their rites from the men, but it was difficult not to be excited. The mood around the kitchen table grew hopeful. Even the farmhouse itself seemed less gloomy, as if the lamps burned more brightly. Claude and Paul and Jean gave the sisters suspicious looks, but Louisette quelled them with her own dismissive ones.

Isabelle, the morning after the last market day of the season, followed Nanette to the byre when she went to do the milking. Nanette glanced over her shoulder, and waited when she saw her sister on the path through the garden. "I thought you were going to make bread."

"I need to tell you something."

Isabelle was the smallest of all six of the Orchiére sisters. She had the dark eyes and thick black curls they all did, but there was something fragile about her. Though Nanette was a decade younger, she often felt an urge to shield her from the things that frightened her. She said now, with the milk pail banging against her knee, "Why not talk to me while I milk the goats?"

"*D'accord.*"

The nannies waited at the half door to the byre, their breath misting in the icy November air. Nanette opened the door, and they brushed past her in an eager crowd of warm bodies and cheerful bleating. The gray kitten, grown leggy now, skittered out of their way, then followed at Nanette's heels as she forked hay into the manger and opened the stanchion.

Nanette pulled a stool close to the first she-goat and positioned the bucket. Isabelle stood on the other side, one hand on the ridge of the goat's spine. "I had a dream about you."

Nanette's forehead was braced against the nanny's flank, but something in her sister's tone made her lift her head. "One of your true dreams?"

"It's always hard to tell, but I think so. It seemed real."

"Good or bad?"

"Good *and* bad."

Nanette chuckled. "Best tell me, Isabelle. So I can be prepared."

Isabelle looked away, gazing up into the dusty hayloft. "It's a man," she whispered. "A beautiful man. And he's coming here."

❧

His name was Michael.

He was what the Cornishmen called Black Irish, with straight dark hair falling past his chin and vivid blue eyes set in a thicket of black lashes. He appeared at Orchard Farm the day after the Sabbat of Ostara.

The sisters had observed the vernal equinox the night before, and Nanette was heavy eyed and sleepy. His wagon, fitted out with a portable forge and racks of tools and horseshoes, rattled up the cliff road with Michael seated high on the bench, a king on his throne, a flat workman's cap for his crown. Nanette's fatigue evaporated the moment she saw him.

He was a farrier, a man who spent his life roaming the countryside in search of farms with horses. The Orchiéres never shod their beasts, but they had six ponies in the paddock, and trimming and cleaning their hooves made them look better for the horse sales. It was Louisette who first spied the wagon bumping along their lane, with a thin mare in the traces. She called to Nanette to go out and speak to him in whatever language he preferred.

Louisette didn't know about Isabelle's dream. Nanette had made her swear to tell no one, but when they celebrated in the temple—Yule, then Imbolc, then Ostara—Nanette held the promise of her sister's dream in her mind. She whispered a private prayer when no one could hear, begging the Mother of All to make Isabelle's dream a true one. She was just eighteen, and she longed for someone to love her.

She knew, despite Isabelle's prophecy, how unlikely it was. The villagers in Marazion were happy to buy the Orchiéres' produce and ponies and soaps. They might tolerate Nanette's place at the market, even her friendship with Meegan. They would never ride out along the cliff road to Orchard Farm to pay her a visit. They would never invite Nanette to their weddings or christenings or funerals.

And they would never, ever consider her a suitable bride for one of their sons.

When she pulled back the curtain of the kitchen window and saw Michael climbing down from his wagon, his hair rippling in the spring breeze, wonder stopped her breath. For long seconds she stared, and her belly began to ache as it always did in the presence of magic.

"Nanette, don't just stand there! Go see how much he wants to do the ponies," Louisette commanded. "Hurry, before he decides no one is home."

Nanette let the curtain drop and put her hands to her hair. She had been churning butter in the pantry with her hair tied up in a threadbare kerchief. Her apron was splashed with buttermilk. "Louisette," she began, "I can't go out like—"

"What does it matter how you look? He's just a farrier, and we can use his services. If he doesn't charge too much, that is. Hurry! He doesn't look Cornish. Probably speaks English."

Nanette took one more peek past the curtain. The man looped the mare's reins over the front panel of his wagon, then brushed dust and leaves from his trousers. He was young, with narrow hips, and the thick arms of a man who worked with iron.

Isabelle left off peeling potatoes over the stone sink and came to stand beside her. When she leaned forward to see what Nanette saw, she sucked in one sharp breath, then clamped a hand over her mouth.

"Nanette!" Louisette snapped.

"I'm going," Nanette said. She avoided looking at Isabelle as she turned toward the kitchen door, pausing before opening it to pull off her apron. She undid the kerchief so her hair spilled over her shoulders, and then, conscious of Louisette's impatient frown, went out to meet the man Isabelle had prophesied.

He touched the brim of his flat cap as she came out through the gate. "Now here's a nice surprise," he said. His smile was all white teeth and deep dimples. "They told me this farm was full of old women and even older men. Sure, and I never expected a *cailín* just out of the schoolroom!"

Nanette tossed her head and said as tartly as she could, "School-room? Hardly."

"Well," he said, snatching off his cap and making a slight bow. "Michael Kilduff, at your service, miss. Might you be needing a farrier? They told me in Marazion that Orchard Farm keeps ponies."

"We do." Nanette nodded toward his horse. "Your mare could use some water, I expect, sir."

"Michael, please, miss. And yes, my Pansy would be grateful for a drink."

Nanette cast a swift glance over her shoulder. Louisette was peering out from behind the curtain. Nanette gave her a shake of the head before she turned back to Michael Kilduff. "Can you turn your wagon, and move it down to the byre? The trough is just inside the paddock."

It was no simple matter, in the narrow lane, to back and turn the heavy wagon, but the farrier managed it without much fuss. In moments he was leading Pansy by a drop rope under her chin. Nanette walked beside him. The gray cat trotted happily behind them.

"You haven't told me your name," he said. "So we can be properly introduced."

"Nanette is my name," she said. "Nanette Orchiére."

"Nanette," he repeated. His voice was sweet, with a lilt to it that promised music and laughter. Her heartbeat sped so she felt it pulsing in her throat, and she felt a betraying heat in her cheeks. "Nanette. That, Miss Orchiére, is the prettiest name I've ever heard."

They reached the paddock, and the ponies, clustered at the far end, threw up their heads with interest at the sight of the mare. Michael freed Pansy from the shafts of the wagon, and she put her head over the stone fence and began to drink from the trough.

Nanette stroked her smooth shoulder. "She's a gentle soul," she said to Michael.

"Aye. More gentle than any of your lot, I think. Ponies can be contrary when they've a mind for it."

Nanette smiled up at him. "That's why none of us wants to trim their hooves."

He grinned at her across Pansy's bent neck. "You have work for me, then."

"If it doesn't come too dear, we do."

"Miss Orchiére, with the charming name of Nanette, I will let you set the price." His impossibly blue eyes twinkled at her. When Pansy had drunk her fill, he backed her up and settled her in the shade of the byre. "Shall I fetch your rascals, or will they come when you call?"

"They'll come when I shake the oats bucket," she said. "But my sisters will want to know the charge first, Mr. Kilduff. For all I know, you could demand an entire guinea!"

"Come now," he said, dimpling at her. "Am I a lord, to be talking about guineas? Not at all, not at all. And please. Mr. Kilduff is my da. I'm Michael."

Nanette smiled back at him. "*Bon*. Michael it is."

He winked and released Pansy's lead so she could crop the moor grass sprouting at the foot of the wall. "Will you be wanting shoes for that lot, then?"

"No. Cleaned and trimmed is what we need. We don't shoe moor ponies."

"Right. Let's say a shilling for the lot, then. And a cup of tea when I've finished." His dimples flashed again. Nanette's heart fluttered unevenly beneath her breastbone.

"Fair enough, but I'll have to bring the tea to you," Nanette said regretfully. "My sisters—the family—they don't meet people. They couldn't speak with you in any case."

He had turned to his wagon, and was unloading a wooden box of tools with a wide leather strap. He slung it over his shoulder and turned to her, his thick eyebrows arching. "Whyever not, then?"

"They only speak French."

"Ah, French. That explains your charming accent, Miss Nanette."

"Just Nanette." She couldn't help the giggle that escaped her. "An ordinary farm girl."

Halfway through the paddock gate, he paused to look back at her. "There's nothing ordinary about you, Nanette Orchiére. Nothing in all the wide world, I tell you sure. While I'm dealing with these little beasts, I'll be dreaming of taking tea beside you."

Nanette ducked her head as she went to fetch the oats bucket. Isabelle had dreamed true. He *was* beautiful. He was perfect. She thanked the Goddess in her heart.

Michael was deft with the ponies, and patient with their antics. Nanette stayed close, helping him to tie up a hoof when it was needed, passing him a tool when he asked. While he clipped and picked and filed, she watched his broad back bent over the work, the ripple of muscle along his thighs where he braced the ponies' feet. When he reached the last one, she left him to it, and went up through the garden to the farmhouse. By the time she returned with a tray laden with cups, a small plate, and the teapot under a knitted cozy, he had finished. The ponies were munching a flake of hay he had tossed down for them, and he was packing up his gear.

Pansy had a feed of hay, too. Michael pointed to it and said, "I thought you wouldn't mind if Pansy had a bite."

Nanette set the tray down and turned the cups over in their

saucers. "Of course not," she said. "And there's a pasty for yourself, Michael. Your shilling is under the plate."

"No pasty for you?" He straddled the milking stool she set for him, and picked up the teapot to pour for them both.

"It's almost time for *souper*. Supper, that is."

Michael took a huge bite of the pasty and spoke around it as he chewed. "How many languages do you speak, lassie? You seem to shift back and forth with no trouble."

"Only three," she said, reaching for one of the brimming teacups. "French, *bien sûr*. English, as you've heard. Some Cornish, though most don't use it anymore." She sipped and regarded him over the edge of the cup. "And you, Michael? What languages do you speak?"

"English, after a fashion." They both grinned. "Irish. Welsh. A bit of Cornish, as a traveling man must, but it's hard, isn't it?"

"I don't know. I learned it when I was small."

"You can take my word, then, lass." He picked up his own teacup. "Hard as the rocks on the tor. That old gray cat never lets you out of his sight, does he?"

"He's not so old, actually. He just looks that way."

"He's not pretty, but he looks wise."

"He was wise enough to find me when he was abandoned, at least."

"Does he have a name?"

Nanette laughed. "I keep meaning to think of one. For now he's just the cat."

They chatted on while the sun settled into the horizon and the sea beyond the cliff darkened. The wind rose and ruffled Pansy's fluff of mane where she stood, head down, drowsing in the twilight. Through the byre's small window, Nanette saw the window of the kitchen begin to glow as the lamp was lighted. A few minutes later someone struck the gong beside the kitchen door, calling the clan to their evening meal.

"I'll have to go in, Michael," Nanette said ruefully. She rose and arranged the cups and plate so she could balance the tray. "I'm sorry we can't offer you a bed inside, but you can sleep in the hayloft if you like."

He jumped to his feet. "I'll carry that up the path."

She shook her head. "No, they'll be watching. I can manage."

"But will I see you, Nanette?"

She paused, the tray balanced against her hip, and looked up into his eyes. She felt a tug between them, as if they were tethered together, the rope pulling tighter and tighter with each breath. The feeling of ease she had enjoyed faded, and was replaced by something more intense, far less comfortable, utterly irresistible. Nanette said, through a mouth gone suddenly dry, "Are you going to sleep here, in the byre?"

"If I can put Pansy in that loose box," he said, indicating it with his chin. His eyes didn't leave hers, and though he didn't touch her, she felt as if he caressed her somehow, drew her to him with some mysterious force.

The Goddess, she thought. The Goddess had sent him to her. It would be wrong to turn down Her gift, no matter the consequences. In any case, she couldn't bear to do it.

She whispered, "Yes."

"Yes to what?" He dimpled, and her bones tingled.

"Pansy," she said. "The loose box."

He chuckled and bent close to murmur in her ear. "Come back after your *souper*, lassie. When your French-speaking family have gone to their beds."

She gazed at him, her lower lip caught between her teeth, for a long, considering moment. She knew what he meant. She knew what her family would have thought, but she didn't care. At this moment nothing mattered but the masculine, miraculous presence of Michael Kilduff.

She breathed. *"Oui. D'accord."*

The night Nanette spent with Michael was dense with magic, a magic she had never known existed. The cold stars shone through the hayloft's unglazed window to sparkle on his ebony hair and in his wonderful eyes. His skin, smooth and pale where it was untouched by the sun, gleamed in the starlight, and the touch of his hands caused her to shudder with delight and desire. Her belly ached no longer with blood and mystery, but with longing. She felt, when she opened her arms, that she could encompass the world in her embrace. When Michael held her she trembled like a bird, knowing she could fly away at any moment, wanting only to remain where she was forever.

As she wept beneath him, sobbing with the intensity of the magic, Nanette felt as if she were truly alive for the first time. They clung together as the stars wheeled above the cliff, breathing in synchrony, listening to the distant wash of the sea, and Nanette thought that if the world could stop now, right at this moment, she would be content.

When the stars began to dim over Orchard Farm, she stirred against Michael's shoulder. The cat, who had perched near the window of the loft all night, was on his feet. His yellow eyes burned through the gloom, and his ragged tail switched back and forth.

"I must go," Nanette whispered.

Michael's strong arm pulled her closer to him, and he nuzzled her neck. "I will remember you, Nanette Orchiére." He didn't ask her to go with him. He didn't promise to return.

The meaning of those omissions chilled her as surely as the wintry air biting at her bare skin. She made no answer, but wriggled free of his grasp. She adjusted her clothes, did her best to brush the straw from her skirt and her hair. She avoided his gaze until she was ready, and then she took one last look at his beautiful face in the dawn shadows. She said, hurriedly, before her tightening throat betrayed her, *"Au revoir, Michel."*

Before he could respond she whirled away from him, climbed as fast as she dared down the ladder into the byre, and scampered up through the garden to the farmhouse, her skirts in her hands. The slow dawn was breaking as she tiptoed to her bedroom. She heard her sisters and their husbands beginning to stir, and the clank of ewer against basin as the twins washed.

Nanette slipped into her room and collapsed onto the edge of her bed. She stared blindly at the small round mirror above her bureau, not seeing her own tangled hair or pale cheeks, but a pair of dimples and two blue, blue eyes. Her body was sore in the hidden places. Her thighs burned, and her lips felt bruised, but the ache in her heart overwhelmed those small hurts.

When she went down for the milking, Michael and his big wagon and skinny mare were gone. He had driven down the lane to the cliff road, setting off for his next destination, no doubt his next encounter with a lonely farm girl.

The magic of the night was over. Come and gone in the space of a breath.

She wondered if there was any left.

4

At the breakfast table Louisette spoke to Claude in a strong voice. "The witch hunter is gone, and tonight is the eve of Beltane. We want to go to the temple."

He didn't bother looking at her. *"Non."*

Anne-Marie said, "No one will know."

"That redheaded devil is not the only priest in Cornwall, nor is he likely the only witch hunter. Why risk us all?"

Paul said, "You heard Claude, Anne-Marie. Leave the craft in the past, where it belongs."

Louisette set her cup down with a bang. "We will never abandon the craft. It's what brought us here."

Florence said, "It's what sustains us."

Claude's *"Pfffff-fft!"* sent spittle over the pottage in his bowl. "Sustains you!" he growled. "Your line is dead. Why don't you see that?"

"What do you mean?" Louisette demanded.

Her husband turned on her, his face suffused with resentment. "Not a one of the six of you could produce a daughter, despite your ceremonies and potions. Ursule was able to do anything she set her hand to, but not a one of her granddaughters can work the plainest spell!"

Nanette had been listening with her head down, her hands

linked tight in her lap. At Claude's pronouncement she lifted her head. In a level voice she said, "*Ce n'est pas vrai.*"

"How is it not true?" Paul snapped. "Soaps and simples!"

Louisette threw her youngest sister a warning glance, but Nanette ignored it. "I," she announced in a strong voice, "worked a spell of diversion."

Claude's voice rose in confusion and anger. "You lie!"

Nanette lifted her chin. "Why do you think the priest left Marazion, Claude? After all this time, you think the witch hunter just gave up?"

"*Oui!*"

"*Non!*" Nanette laid her two palms flat on the table and pushed herself up. She leaned a little forward, holding her brother-in-law's black-eyed gaze with her own. "You know nothing of the craft, or of the power of Ursule's blood. Of *my* blood." Her temper rose, and her words spilled out of her like boiling water from a kettle. "You see a girl good only for milking goats and speaking English and driving the jingle to market. *Pffft!*" She pushed away from the table and turned her head to hide the furious tears burning her eyes. "You men! You all go on about Ursule this and Ursule that and you don't see what's right in front of you!"

Nanette stamped out of the kitchen and through the porch. Without pausing for a coat or even a scarf, she ran through the garden and out the gate, then across the lane to jump the ditch beyond. She ran for ten minutes or so, the winds tugging at her hair and clumps of heather tangling her skirt. She didn't know she was weeping until, ribs aching and lungs afire, she collapsed on a hillock and buried her face in her hands.

She had always hated tears. Of the Orchiére sisters only Fleurette wept easily, the soft tears sliding down her cheeks like raindrops. When any of the others cried, it was ugly to see, distorted lips, swollen eyes, sobs that tore at the throat. Of course the men never shed tears. Nanette thought of them as too dried up to cry. She doubted they had tears to spare.

She would have liked to cry over Michael, to sit by her window and look out over the sea, sorrowing for her lost love. She felt Isabelle's eyes on her sometimes, the knowing look that invited confidences, but Nanette refused to indulge herself, or to talk about him. She was a witch. She had power Michael couldn't guess at. She would not give in to girlish weakness.

But now Claude's clumsy accusation had tipped her over the edge, like one of the boulders losing its balance to roll over the cliff and crash to the rocks beneath. She wept loudly, wetly. Her face felt raw, and she supposed her cheeks would be chapped. Her whole body felt as tender and vulnerable as a newborn kid's. She wrapped her arms around herself against the whirling wind, tucking her hands into her armpits. Her breasts ached under the pressure.

Slowly she opened her arms and stared down at herself. Her tears dried as she gazed in alarm at the expanded shape of her bosom beneath her bodice. It seemed her breasts had swollen to twice their size. That couldn't be. Surely she had finished growing these three years past?

She got to her feet, not with her usual lithe ease, but gingerly. Every bone and muscle felt fragile, as if she had been ill with a fever. She turned away from the distant sea view and gazed up at the moor, greening now with spring. Beltane, known to Marazion as May Day. Michael had come at Ostara. If she'd had a calendar, she could have counted exactly how many weeks that was, but she knew, all at once, that there was no point in doing it. There was nothing to be gained by trying to remember her last monthlies.

She was breeding.

The clan would be furious.

❧

"How?" Claude demanded.

A week had passed since Nanette recognized her condition. Isabelle had noticed the changes in her, and they had decided together it was best to tell them all at once.

"Oh, for pity's sake!" Louisette snapped. "How do you think? You do know how it's done, Claude!"

"But she knows no one! Goes nowhere!"

Anne-Marie, usually the peacemaker, had been leaning on the cold stove. Now she straightened and glared at her brother-in-law. "You like it that way, don't you?"

"What do you mean by that?" he spit. They were gathered in the kitchen, but there was neither food nor drink on the table. They stood or sat about the room, postponing the workday as they took in Nanette's shocking news.

The window was open to the spring air, redolent already with the sweet smells of freshly turned earth and heather yearning to bloom. By contrast, especially to Nanette, the kitchen reeked of rendered fat and oil smoke, and it turned her stomach. Isabelle had promised her it wouldn't last. "Three months for that," she said. "One month from now, you'll feel better."

Isabelle stepped forward now. "She means," she said to Claude, and included the other men in her gaze, "that you're all content for Nanette to be at your service, year in, year out. For her to have no friends, no time for herself—no fun."

"Fun?" Paul said. He was sitting across the table from Claude, their dark, grim faces nearly mirror images of one another. "When did any of us have fun?"

"She's eighteen years old," Anne-Marie said.

"You had Louis when you were eighteen," Paul said.

"That was before we came here. We were able to meet people, make friends—"

"Obviously Nanette had one friend," Claude said sourly.

Nanette, leaning against the wall beside the window, pressed her hands over her queasy stomach as the talk swirled around her. It was disorienting, hearing the kitchen, usually so silent, resound with voices growing louder every moment. She stopped listening and closed her eyes against the angry faces. She let her mind drift out to the moor, where the wild ponies would be wandering down from the high country to nibble the new grass, and the foxes would be peeking out from beneath the brambles. She didn't notice when the family stopped arguing.

She felt a hand on her shoulder, then around her waist, and opened her eyes. It was Florence, guiding her to the table. The men had gone off about their chores, and only the sisters remained. Fleurette emerged from the pantry with one of her small dark bottles. She uncorked it and poured a measure of its contents into a clay tumbler.

"Drink," Florence said quietly. "A simple to ease your stomach."

Obediently Nanette downed the sour liquid, wrinkling her nose at its taste, then sighing with relief as her nausea receded.

"Better?" Isabelle came to sit beside her, taking her hand. Nanette nodded.

Florence busied herself putting wood in the stove, filling a kettle, setting out cups. Fleurette went down the hall, and when she returned, she carried the homespun sack they kept the grimoire in. She set it in the center of the table and pulled out the ancient book, taking care with its cracked leather cover. She opened it and turned the leaves of parchment. Some were clearly marked in sharp script. On others the ink had begun to fade, the handwriting to grow spidery and faint. She pulled the oil lamp nearer and bent to squint at the page.

"What are you going to do?" Nanette asked.

"That depends on you." Fleurette's disused voice creaked. "Your babe. Your choice."

"I don't understand."

Isabelle patted her hand and released it. The copper kettle began to boil, and Florence prepared the tea and covered the pot with a cozy while Fleurette brought each of them a cup.

The twins settled across from Nanette and Isabelle, and the four sisters sat in a gentle silence. Tears glistened in Fleurette's eyes. It was Florence who put their thought into words.

"Nanette, you don't have to bear the child."

"I—What?" Nanette's head jerked up. At the same moment she felt the cat's weight on her toes, his warmth winding around her ankles. He had learned to avoid the men, and demonstrated an uncanny knack for knowing when they left the farmhouse. The sisters ignored him, for the most part, except for Isabelle. She made sure there was always something for him to eat in the pantry, where Claude and the others wouldn't see.

Florence said, "There is a potion. You would miscarry."

"It would hurt," Fleurette whispered.

"Childbirth hurts," Isabelle said.

Nanette stared at each of them in turn. She saw no judgment in their faces, nor anger. They gazed back at her, waiting.

Deep in her belly Nanette felt the stirrings of fresh magic, the energy of new life flickering through her bloodstream, speaking to the future. "I want to keep her," she whispered.

"You won't be able to hide it from people," Florence said.

"Who will care?"

"Claude. Paul. Jean."

"Why? They never see anyone."

"Because," Isabelle said, "they want us to quit the craft. A baby means—maybe—the Orchiére line continues."

"I thought Claude might send me away from Orchard Farm."

"He would if he could," Florence said. "We would never allow it. You're an Orchiére. He is not."

"Orchard Farm belongs to us," Isabelle said. "Ursule made it so."

"Is that why he is always angry?"

"That's part of it," Florence said.

"They hate it that their own names are forgotten," Isabelle said.

"After all this time?"

She lifted one shoulder. "While Ursule was alive, there was no question of taking their names and giving up our own. Our father knew that, and never complained once. But since Grand-mère is gone—and the power with her—"

"But *I* have the power."

"Do you have enough?" Florence asked.

Nanette looked past her sisters' faces to the freshening sky, and gave a tired sigh. "I didn't have enough to keep Michael, though I would have liked to. But I have enough to keep his babe, and I will."

"Perhaps the babe will have the power," Isabelle said.

No one answered, because none of them knew.

∽ঙ৯

As Nanette's condition grew obvious, the citizens of Marazion began to look askance at her when she went to the market. The housewives whispered as she passed. The men scowled and stepped aside, as if her swelling belly might contaminate them. Only Meegan, her own belly increasing once again, gave her friendly greetings as always, and chose the Orchard Farm cheeses over any others.

"You could claim to be wed," she told Nanette one day, as the two of them rested side by side, perspiring in the unseasonal October heat. "Or widowed."

"Why should I? I don't care what they think," Nanette said. "As long as they buy."

Meegan sighed at that. "Your things are the best, or they wouldn't. For sure and certain, you're not going to sell that one anything." She nodded toward a fat farmwife standing beside a wagon piled high with unsold vegetables. The red-faced woman had tucked her hands under her apron and was glaring at the two of them.

Nanette glanced at her and then away. "That one? No, not even if she was desperate. She's making the sign against the evil eye."

"The cow," Meegan said. "She doesn't even know you."

Nanette smiled, grateful for her loyalty. "She can't hurt me, Meegan."

"I hope you're right about that."

Nanette suffered no doubts. She brimmed with confidence these days, just as her body brimmed with the miracle of new life. Her babe was growing apace, her wares selling better than ever. It was no wonder other farmers resented her.

Of course, Meegan wouldn't know of the spells she had cast over her wares, the charms Anne-Marie had created and hidden in the corners of the jingle, nor the protective amulet Fleurette had made for Nanette to wear around her neck. When the amulet moved against her breast, she felt an answering stir in her womb. Magic surrounded her. She felt invulnerable.

Even at home, though Claude had stopped speaking to her altogether, and though the men who came to look at the famous Orchard Farm ponies looked over her head to pretend they didn't see, she wore her pregnancy proudly.

"It's not," she said to Isabelle one morning, "as if I'm the first unmarried Cornish girl to conceive a child." She squirmed on the milking stool, trying to ease the weight of her stomach onto her thighs.

"They don't see you as Cornish, Nanette."

"I've lived here since I was four!" She grunted a little as she reached for the nanny's teats. "I speak their languages, I talk to them, I do business with them..."

"It's because of us. We're foreign to them, and you're one of us."

"That's hardly my fault," Nanette said pettishly, and then clicked her tongue. "Sorry, Isabelle. I didn't mean that the way it sounded."

"I know, *ma chère.*"

"I'm just out of sorts. It's hard to catch my breath."

"Let me finish the milking. You go and rest in the kitchen."

Samhain was well past, and Yule coming up swiftly. There was a long list of things to be done before winter closed in. Nanette hated to give in to her weakness, but the thought of putting up her swollen feet and resting beside the warm stove was irresistible. "You don't mind, Isabelle?"

"*Non, bien sûr.* I remember how it is. By the time George was born I could barely walk."

"*Merci.*" Nanette handed her sister the milk bucket and walked out of the byre and up through the garden. She felt like a waddling duck, and she was sure her face was as swollen as her breasts. She yearned for one of Fleurette's simples, especially the one she made with lemon balm to rub on her feet and her distended belly.

She was halfway to the house when she heard the clatter of wagon wheels on the cliff road. It wasn't a particularly remarkable occurrence, but the moment the sound reached her ears, a slow ache began in her belly. It spread swiftly, between her hip bones, up into her diaphragm, sharpening to a near pain. She touched Fleurette's amulet beneath her bodice, and the ache intensified. A warning, then. Something was wrong.

The appearance of the cat, awaiting her at the door to the porch, convinced her. He was arched and spitting, his patchy gray fur standing up, his tail whipping back and forth so fast she could barely see it. The hoofbeats slowed as they reached the lane, and drew close.

She tried to hurry her steps, to reach the farmhouse before whatever it was reached her.

"Mademoiselle!"

Too late. Feeling ponderous and awkward, she turned.

He had changed in the year and more he had been gone from Cornwall. His gingery hair had begun to fade, and his thin cheeks had grown thinner, making his eyes look pinched together above his drooping nose. He was driving a pony cart. He reined in the pony and jumped down from the seat in one movement.

Evil glittered in the witch hunter's eyes as if a devil hid behind them, a devil born of hate, and fear, and fanaticism. Instinctively Nanette covered her swollen belly with her hands.

As he drew close to the garden gate and leaned over it, her nostrils twitched at the miasma of rotten eggs that clung to his dirty black cassock. When he spoke his breath was even more foul, surely the smell of true brimstone. He addressed her in French. "I see you are paying for your sin, *mademoiselle*."

Nanette drew herself up, straightening her spine as much as her belly allowed. The ache began to ease, and she made herself look directly into his face. She realized for the first time that one of his eyes wandered wildly, first looking into her face, then rolling away. "Did you drive your poor pony all this way in the cold just to tell me that, sir?"

"Call me Father."

"You are not my father, and I am not one of your flock. You have no power over me."

His sneer revealed gaps in his rotten teeth, and his rolling eye found her face once again. "You are mistaken," he said.

"You don't have a church here," she said. She felt better for facing him, for speaking her mind. Her womb quivered, reminding her of the power she held. "You have no authority."

"I have God's authority," he said. "And Father Maddock and his congregants are God-fearing Christians, upright soldiers of the Lord. They know what is right."

She moved her hands to her hips, knowing the posture made her belly more prominent, and not caring. "What do you think is right, sir? What is it you want of me?"

He pointed at her swollen stomach. "That child," he said flatly.

"My child? Why?"

"An innocent child should be raised in a Christian home, with a mother and a father, not in this immoral nest of *witches*!" He hissed the last word, and the sulfurous odor increased.

She thought he must stand at the doorway to hell itself, the hell he put so much faith in. She gritted her teeth and turned her back on him to go into the farmhouse.

"We will come for the babe the moment it's born," he shouted at her.

She paused and looked back over her shoulder. He stood pressed against the garden gate, his rusty cassock blowing in the icy wind, his flat hat gripped in one bony hand. He was the ugliest human being she had ever beheld, inside and out. Her belly began to ache, but with power now. As she whirled to face him, she felt as if the Mother Goddess herself spoke through her. "Go to hell, Monsieur Bernard! You will never set foot on Orchard Farm again!"

He reached across the gate with his free hand, undid the latch, and stepped through. His bad eye rolled wildly as he strode toward her, his hand outstretched. He was muttering something, Scripture, prayer, perhaps just curses. Nanette couldn't help taking a step backward. She could almost feel the grip of his bony fingers around her throat.

The cat at her feet began to squall with a sound like a child screaming. The priest's face turned the color of ashes, and he hissed, "Demon!" He seized the brim of his hat and spun it toward the cat, who yowled afresh when it hit him. The witch hunter snarled, "You will do as I say, whore," as he reached for Nanette with both red-spotted hands.

A harsh voice sounded from inside the porch. "Touch her, priest, and you die!"

The witch hunter jerked to a stop, looking past Nanette to the porch. The door slammed, and Nanette felt Claude's bulk at her shoulder. She cast him a sidelong glance. He had an ax in his hand, the same he used to split wood for the stove. He hadn't stopped to put on his boots, but even in his stockings he was a daunting figure, tall, dark, muscled from years of farm work.

The priest's face contorted. "I'll have that child!" he swore. "You'll see!" He turned sharply away, his long black robe swirling about his boots, and banged through the gate, leaving his black hat lying in the dirt.

Neither Nanette nor Claude budged as he hauled himself up onto the bench seat of his cart. Nanette winced as he yanked at the pony's reins, jerking the poor creature to the left to turn the cart in the narrow lane. He looked back at them once, when the cart had bumped in a semicircle and was facing the road. Claude lifted the ax to shoulder height without speaking a word. The witch hunter shook a fist as he drove away.

"He means it," Claude growled, standing at Nanette's shoulder.

"I won't give her up."

"We won't be able to protect you."

"You just did." She inclined her head to him. "I thank you. He meant to hurt me."

"He will bring others," Claude said. He lowered the ax at last and ran his palm over the flat of the blade. "He will bring that other priest, the one from Marazion."

"Father Maddock."

"And other men. Your babe is just their excuse. What they want is to drive us out."

Nanette's head pounded with the pressure of her bloodstream, and her belly still cramped with the deep ache of magic. She whispered, "Then I will get rid of him."

"How? What can you do?" Claude asked, but she was already on her way.

She hurried out through the gate and set off up the tor as fast as her ungainly body could manage. The cat preceded her at a sinuous lope. Her sisters came after, drawn as if she had rung a bell to summon them. Isabelle left the milking half-finished. Florence and Fleurette walked away from the house with the breakfast dishes still unwashed. Louisette abandoned the cheese she was wrapping in the cold cellar. Anne-Marie emerged from the steamy washhouse, leaving a pile of smallclothes soaking in the wooden tub. She gathered a few things from the pantry and started up the path to the temple behind her sisters.

Despite the cold, Nanette was perspiring by the time she reached the boulders that crowned the tor. Awkward as she was, her pace was slow, and her sisters had caught her up by the time she stepped into the dimness of the cave. There was no need for anyone to speak, to ask questions or give orders. The magic drove them, and its power was in full spate.

There was also no time to lose.

5

The candle was not new, but it was white as milk and nearly intact, with a stout wick. It burned with a steady light as the sisters took their places.

Nanette felt the need to hurry, but though the power sang through her, she moved slowly, her misshapen body more of a hindrance than a help. She had trouble drawing a deep breath, difficulty even staying on her feet as she faced the crystal. She held out her hands, her palms grazing the cool stone. The words were in her mind before she touched it, and the conjoined strength of the sisters infused every syllable.

Mother Goddess, through your power
Come to me in this black hour.
Send the devil into the sea.
Protect my babe, my family, and me.

It was a good spell. A strong one, more specific than usual, uttered swiftly out of necessity. She spoke it three times three times, her words spilling over one another, and before she finished, the crystal began to burn. A light flared within the stone, red as fury. Nanette's sisters gasped to see it. Nanette closed her eyes and the crimson light glowed through her eyelids, answering her, promising her.

As she finished the rite, a new pain began deep in her body. This was not the ache of magic. This, she knew, was the beginning of her daughter's life.

She struggled to stand, to hold her place in the circle until the crystal's fiery glow began to dim. Then, with a rending groan, she sank to her knees. The stone floor beneath her turned shiny with her broken waters, and her womb cramped, hard.

Florence and Fleurette, the spinster twins, cried out in alarm. Anne-Marie admonished them not to frighten Nanette. "It's just her time," she said calmly.

"No!" Nanette grunted. "Not until Yule—"

"We can't predict such things."

They let the first pain pass before they lifted her between them, Anne-Marie on one side, Louisette on the other. Isabelle said, "We have to get her down the tor."

"*D'accord.*" Louisette spoke calmly, too, as if women went into labor in a cave high on a hilltop every day. "Florence and Fleurette, you gather the things. Isabelle, will you go ahead? Make sure there's nothing Nanette could trip on?"

"*Bien sûr.*"

Moments later Nanette found herself staggering out of the cave on shaking legs. The pain was gone as if it had never been. Only her sodden skirts and dripping thighs, cooling unpleasantly now, reminded her something was happening.

"There will be more pains," Anne-Marie said. "We're going to get you down to your bed. It's going to be hard, but you can do it. We'll stop whenever the pains come."

Louisette said, "Tell us when you feel one beginning."

Clumsily they inched their way down the steep path, able to move forward only for short distances before Nanette was forced to cry out, "*Maintenant, maintenant.*" Each time, her sisters helped her down to her knees, holding her as she rode out the contraction. The pains that followed that first one lacked the element of surprise, but still, the intensity of them shocked her. Her body had taken control, and there was nothing she could do but submit to its will.

The descent from the tor to Orchard Farm usually took thirty minutes or so. On this day it seemed it might take thirty hours. Florence and Fleurette soon caught up with their sisters, and Louisette sent them ahead to make preparations. Anne-Marie murmured comforting phrases into Nanette's ear, and Isabelle walked ahead, keeping watch for loose stones or brambles that might cause Nanette to fall. Slowly, slowly they made their way down, following the twists and turns of the path.

Halfway to the bottom they stopped again, at a point where the path broadened and straightened, opening up a view of the road to Marazion as it wound along the cliff. The sea beyond stretched to the horizon in a sheet of dull silver. As she groaned through a long, deep pain, Nanette yearned toward the water. She was no longer thinking of the witch hunter. The straining of her body, the heat of her labor, occupied her fully.

But Isabelle had not forgotten. She had been peering down toward the gray winter sea, and now she exclaimed, "Look there! The priest!"

As her pain began to ease, Nanette, panting, lifted her head. She followed Anne-Marie's pointing finger, squinting through droplets of sweat. "I don't see him," she said hoarsely.

"Not him. His cart."

As her breath returned and the contraction receded, Nanette felt strong enough to struggle to her feet, careful of her balance on the icy path. Leaning on Anne-Marie, she looked along the road as it curled along the rocky cliff. "Oh!" she breathed, at last. "I see it! The pony, standing there in the cold—but where's the priest?"

"I don't see him," Anne-Marie said.

Isabelle asked, "Could he climb down the cliff from that point?"

"I don't think so," Louisette said.

Nanette drove the road often. "No," she said hoarsely. "It's nearly straight down to the rocks. That's where people throw things over when they want them gone for good."

"Goddess will it, the witch hunter's gone for good, too," Louisette growled.

"He's not there," Isabelle said with certainty. "I don't see him anywhere."

This time when the pain seized Nanette's belly, it was the babe and the magic together, a great swell of pain and power and triumph, rising and cresting over her like an ocean wave, leaving her drenched and panting and weak with gratitude.

The labor went on into the night. Fleurette had a simple waiting to help, and Florence, though she had never borne a child herself, seemed to know precisely what to do. They walked with Nanette through the dark hours, between the pains. They rubbed her back and massaged her belly and held her when she cried. Not until the very end did she call Michael's name.

Florence clicked her tongue at that, but Fleurette whispered, in her hesitant way, "It's a job of work to do on your own, Nanette. No choice about it." Nanette was too far gone in her labor to understand in the moment, but she was to remember it later. Being born, giving birth, facing death—work to be done alone.

The infant girl came into the world as the sun rose the next day, an Orchiére from her little head to her perfect toes. She was born with damp black curls and eyes dark as night. She protested mightily at the indignity of the cold air, the harsh light, the rough cotton Fleurette swaddled her in. Not till Nanette put her to the breast did she quiet, but by that time she had woken the house.

One by one they came to see her, Louisette grimly proud, Anne-Marie smiling, Isabelle rapt. Even the men came to view the babe, though none made any show of emotion. Only Claude spoke, gruffly. "Another Orchiére girl."

"Yes, Claude," Louisette said. "The line continues."

"Don't know that yet."

"I do know it," Nanette said. "I know it very well. And her name is Ursule."

⁓≈⁓

Louisette made Claude and Paul go along the cliff road to rescue the priest's abandoned pony, left standing in its traces at the cliff's edge all through the winter's night. As the men told the sisters later, they recognized the cart, and drove it along to the stable where it belonged. With their broken English, they managed to make the stableman understand where they had found the rig, and men from the town followed them back to search for the priest.

If the tide had been in, they might never have discovered what had happened to Father Bernard. Since the tide had only just turned and begun to cover the causeway between the mainland and St. Michael's Mount, the corpse of the witch hunter lay fully exposed, broken and bloody, on the rocks at the foot of the cliff.

"They think he stopped for a piss and slipped over the edge." Paul spoke with grim relish. "Hauled him up with ropes. Bones broken right through the skin, and his skull smashed like an eggshell. Those little eyes staring, like they used to stare at us, but now—"

"Hush, Paul," Anne-Marie said. "Nanette is nursing her baby."

Nanette, seated beside the woodstove with her babe at her

breast, said, "I want to hear it. I want to be certain the witch hunter is dead. I want to know we're safe at last."

Fleurette spun around at that, and the cup in her hands slipped, falling to the flagstone floor with a great crack.

Her twin was at her side in a moment. "Are you all right?" she asked in a low voice. "What is it?"

Fleurette only shook her head, but she had gone pale as fog, and her empty hands trembled. Florence encircled her with an arm to lead her out of the kitchen to their bedroom.

Louisette tutted as she brought a broom to clear up the shards of pottery. Anne-Marie said, "Paul, you've upset Fleurette."

Nanette shuddered and cuddled tiny Ursule closer. "No, Anne-Marie, it wasn't Paul who upset Fleurette. It was me." She looked down at the nursing infant, at her little rosebud mouth sweetly suckling, her eyelashes like the wings of a blackbird against her tender cheeks. "I was wrong, and Fleurette knows it. Evil is never vanquished." She put her head back against the high back of her chair, careful not to disturb the infant. "We all have to face it. Even my poor child won't escape." She closed her eyes with a weary sigh. "So long as the Orchiére line persists, I fear, the struggle will never end."

The family cosseted Nanette for several days. Even Claude treated her gently. When little Ursule was five days old, he presented Nanette with a cradle he had constructed in secret, working behind the byre with his saw and hammer, polishing it so no slivers would scratch the infant, waxing its hinges so they swung smoothly to rock the child to sleep. Nanette thanked him, and praised him to Louisette, wringing a rare smile from her eldest sister.

Isabelle took over the goats for a time, too, and that meant that when Father Maddock came from Marazion to visit Orchard Farm, Nanette was alone in the farmhouse with her babe.

Above the howl of wind from the sea, she heard the clop of hooves on the road, and the softer sounds they made in the dirt lane. She had just laid Ursule in the cradle. She went to the kitchen window and lifted the curtain in time to see the priest tethering a brown gelding to a fencepost and brushing dust from his cassock. His garb was so similar to that of the dead priest that her heart missed a beat, thinking the witch hunter had returned from the dead. She half expected, when Father Maddock came through the gate, to see a ghoul with a smashed skull and protruding bloody bones.

He walked to the front door of the farmhouse, a door that was never used, and pounded on it with the butt of his whip.

Nanette hesitated, tempted to ignore the summons, but then decided that behaving normally, perhaps as Meegan would, was a better idea. She wiped her hands on her apron and tidied her hair with her fingers as she walked through the hallway to the door. It screeched on its rusty hinges, resisting her efforts to push it open. She succeeded, though it took three tries, and it scraped fiercely on the sill when it finally swung free. He raised his thin eyebrows at her.

"Apologies, sir," she said. "This door is never used."

"You never have guests?"

As a greeting, it was hardly courteous. She lifted her chin, which put her head on a level with his. She said, in her best English, "You are the first in a very long time."

He was a fat man, with sparse brown hair and weak eyes. He held his flat-brimmed hat before his protruding belly, as if to hide it. "I am not here to pay a call," he said.

Her temper began to rise, and she folded her arms, striving to hold it in. "Well, then. You must have some other reason for coming all this way."

"I believe Father Bernard, before his untimely death, spoke to you about your bastard."

Nanette gritted her teeth, afraid she would say something disastrous.

He sniffed. "I see that I'm right. I should tell you that I agreed with him. Though we serve different churches, our principles are the same."

"If you think," Nanette said tightly, "that I would hand over my child to him or to you or to anyone, you've taken leave of your senses."

"I suppose the father refuses to marry you."

She unfolded her arms and put her hand on the latch of the door, ready to pull it to. "I prefer not to marry." She thought she sounded a great deal like Louisette at that moment.

His face reddened. "You should at least christen the poor thing. Save it from purgatory!"

Nanette couldn't help herself. She spit in the dirt at his feet.

His face grew even darker, and his lips worked before he shouted, "For shame! Godless, the whole lot of you Orchards! Your child will be doomed for all eternity!"

As if she had heard, Ursule began to cry. Nanette felt the instant response of her breasts, and she knew without glancing down that her bodice was soaked with milk. "Leave us alone," she snapped, and with an earsplitting squeal of hinges, she closed the door in the priest's face.

She thought he had gone, and had settled into a chair to suckle the babe when she heard the fat priest's tread on the back porch. She started at the sound, and the infant began to wail when the nipple slipped from her mouth. Nanette scrambled to her feet, her babe screaming in disappointment. The priest, his hat on his head and his whip in one hand, stamped into the kitchen without bothering to knock. Nanette hastily tried to cover herself.

She thought of shrinking back into the pantry and locking the door, but her temper was higher than ever. "What do you want?" she demanded. Little Ursule cried harder, and she lifted her to her shoulder.

For answer, Maddock held up a battered and filthy object in his free hand.

For a few seconds Nanette stared at it, uncomprehending. When she realized what it was, a chill spread through her chest, damping her temper. The babe's tears drenched her shoulder, and the little body shook with sobs as Nanette sank back into her chair. She covered the child's soft head with her hand, as if the priest might bite her. She said in a shaking voice, "What is that?"

But she knew.

He had dropped it when he fled. It must have lain there ever since that ugly day, its shape dissolving under the weight of the weather, its color faded by the mud, but it was still recognizable. Especially to one who wore one so much like it.

The witch hunter's hat.

She felt the blood drain from her face. "You can see I have a babe to feed, sir! I pray you leave me to it!"

"He was here," Father Maddock said. He shook the object in his hand, spattering the flagstones with crumbs of dirt. "He was here the day he died!"

"I don't—"

"I know it!" he shrilled. "He told me he was coming, and he did, but he never made it back!" He leaned forward, fat cheeks quivering with anger. His bad eyes seemed to find their focus as he brought his face much too close to hers. "What did you do to him—" He spit the last word, as if it was the foulest thing he could say: "*witch*?"

Nanette, with a wet and weeping babe in her arms, drew one

deep, steadying breath. She had nothing to fight him with but her power. She drew it around her like a shield. A weapon.

Deliberately she came to her feet. The blood returned to her face, and the ache of magic began deep in her body, where her womb was still tender from childbirth. As if she felt what was building in her mother, little Ursule ceased sobbing.

"Listen to me, priest." Nanette took a step around the end of the table. Maddock fell back, the dilapidated hat dangling from his fingers. "We are an old and honorable clan, and we protect our own." She felt the words charged with her power, her body singing with it. It was a building wave, gathering strength and volume, rising to a crest. "If you threaten us, priest—" She took another step, and she could see he felt it. Her magic was a comfort to her babe, but it struck terror into the heart of her enemy. "If you threaten us—if you threaten my child—we will destroy you."

From nowhere, as it seemed, the gray cat appeared, his tail slashing back and forth, his yellow eyes fixed on Father Maddock. The priest paled when he saw it.

"How—you can't—" he tried to cry, but his voice strangled in his throat. His hand, holding the dilapidated hat, shook wildly.

She reached for it. "Give me that thing."

His mouth opened and closed like that of a gasping fish. He released the hat, and it fell into her waiting hand. The cat arched and hissed, and the priest's face grew even whiter, until it looked like one of Isabelle's batches of bread dough.

Nanette tossed the hat toward the open hearth, where it landed in the half-burned coals, limp and defeated. The ache in her belly swelled and rose into her chest. She could have sworn she grew taller and broader, and the register of her voice dropped to match. "Go, priest," she intoned. "Before something happens to you, too."

The hat improbably caught fire, blazing up to fill the room with acrid smoke.

Father Maddock gasped and backed toward the door, crossing himself as he went. The cat followed him on mincing paws, snarling. "Harlot!" the priest croaked. "Jezebel!"

The cat pounced at him.

The priest gave a wordless cry as he crashed through the door and onto the porch. He scrambled out into the garden, nearly falling, staggering toward the gate with his whip flailing beside him.

The moment the gate swung shut behind the priest, the cat turned back with his tail high. He walked calmly to the hearth and lay down on the warm bricks. The smoke that had billowed out from the fire a moment before shrank and disappeared up the chimney, leaving the air as clean as if the winter breeze had blown right through the house. Nanette stood where she was for a few moments, feeling the power subside around her.

Ursule stirred against her shoulder and mewled. Nanette blew out a breath, went back to her chair, and settled in it to give her babe the breast once again.

She felt victorious, and she savored the feeling, but she knew it was a treacherous emotion. It was not over. It would never be over while women like her wielded their power over men like that.

She looked down at Ursule's face, savoring the line of her tiny nose, the curve of her downy cheek. "I would die for you, Daughter," she whispered.

On the hearth, the cat's tail switched an irritated rhythm.

THE BOOK OF URSULE

1

1847

Ursule Orchiére loved growing up on the Cornish coast. She had a paddock full of moor ponies to ride, a henhouse busy with chickens, and a flock of goats who crowded around her whenever she appeared, eager to be scratched under their chins.

The only animal who wouldn't come near her was the ancient gray cat who slept in her mother's room. When she asked why that might be, Nanette shrugged, and said that was a cat who did just what he wanted and no more.

Ursule understood that. Animals had their own reasons for doing the things they did. She did, too.

"Maman," she asked once, when she was still small, "why won't Tante Louisette and Tante Anne-Marie and the others speak English? No one in Marazion speaks French."

"Shhh," Nanette said. "They'll hear you."

"That makes no difference! They won't understand me anyway."

"You'd be surprised. They understand more than you think." Nanette flashed her little daughter a look, then seized her up to tickle her. She was the only one of the Orchiére sisters little Ursule had ever heard laugh.

Ursule's curiosity grew as she grew older. "What's the matter with the family, Maman? They never leave the farm if they can help it. They hide when people come to look at the ponies or buy cheese. They're like—like *ermites*!"

"You mean *hermits*, Ursule. Don't mix your languages."

Ursule put her small fists on her hips and tilted her head, a gesture she had learned from Nanette herself. She demanded in her childish voice, "Well?"

Nanette tweaked one of her curls. "Be respectful of your elders, Ursule. That includes your mother!" Ursule wrinkled her nose in answer, and Nanette gave in. "I think they wish they were still in France, sweetheart. None of them—not Louisette or any of them, including the uncles—wanted to leave."

"Why did they, then?"

"It's a sad story."

"Tell it to me."

They were in the garden, where Nanette was hoeing a row of potatoes. She paused and leaned on the hoe as she gazed out beyond the cliff to the uneasy gray sea. The silhouette of St. Michael's Mount lifted above the horizon, separated from the mainland now by the high tide of midday. "I was only four years old when we fled," she said. "But I was old enough to understand that everyone was afraid."

"Of what?"

"People. Angry people." Nanette took up the hoe again. "We were Romani. Gypsies. The people didn't like that."

"Why?"

Nanette shrugged. "People take notions."

"That's not an answer!"

"There aren't always answers, sweetheart," Nanette said, serene now. She moved down the row, chopping at the soil. Ursule followed her, bending now and then to pull a weed from the softened ground. From time to time she piped another question, but her mother didn't answer.

When Nanette reached the end of the long row, she straight-ened, one hand on her back. "Well, at least that's done. I'm tired, but it's milking time."

"*Non, non, Maman!* The goats are mine. I'll milk them."

Nanette smiled behind her hand. Ursule knew she had been tricked, but she didn't mind. By the time she was ten she had taken charge of the little herd of goats, milking them, guiding them up to the moor to graze, seeing to their hay and mash through the cold winter months. More than once she'd spent a night in the byre, helping one of the she-goats deliver a kid.

Unlike her aunts and uncles, Ursule thought of herself as Cor-nish. She loved their old farmhouse, with its long, low roofline and her cramped bedroom tucked under the eaves. She spent hours rambling across the moor, trying to coax the wild ponies to come to her. She dug clams from the rocky beach below the cliff, carrying them up the steep path in a bucket for the aunts to boil for dinner. She rode along in the jingle when Nanette took cheese and soaps and vegetables to the markets in Marazion, and there she chattered away with housewives and farmers, speaking English or Cornish as they preferred. She played with the other children who came, especially Meegan's, and sometimes she went to Mass with Meegan and her family.

Nanette smiled at all of this, except on the day she saw the priest of St. Hilary Church put a hand on Ursule's shoulder and speak to her, wagging his finger in her face. On that occasion Nanette called her daughter abruptly away.

"Why did you do that?" Ursule cried, when they were back at the jingle. "That's just Father Maddock, from the church."

"Stay away from him," Nanette said.

"But I like going to church with Meegan. They have sweets after."

"That's fine. Meegan will look out for you. But don't be alone with him."

"Why?"

"He doesn't care for our kind."

"What kind is that? You mean Gypsies?"

"For once, just do as you're told, Ursule," Nanette said, in a tight voice Ursule barely recognized. "Father Maddock is danger-ous to us. Trust me." She would say no more, and Ursule, in time, gave up.

Ursule was even better at bartering and business than her mother was. Each time they returned home from the market, she would pour out her earnings onto the kitchen table and stand with arms akimbo, awaiting the praise of the clan. She was certain, young though she was, that one day she would make Orchard Farm the most prosperous in the county.

The aunts and uncles were Nanette's older sisters and their hus-bands, but they seemed so ancient to Ursule that she thought of them as her mother's aunts and uncles, too. The women were tall and gaunt, especially the eldest. Tante Louisette wore a habitual scowl, something her next sister, Anne-Marie, chided her for. Isa-belle was smaller than her sisters, and softer hearted. Florence was fussy and prim, and often spoke for Fleurette, her twin, who could go days without saying a word. The uncles, tall and bony like their wives, spoke in monosyllables. To Ursule the three men seemed interchangeable, though when Claude, Louisette's husband, decreed something would or would not be done, everyone obeyed him.

One of the uncles startled Ursule, one night after supper, by putting down his pipe and fixing her with a muddy gaze. "How old are you now, girl?"

"Twelve, Uncle Jean."

"Huh. Twelve. Natural farmer, you are." He thrust his pipe back between his teeth, and around its stem he grated, "Vaga-bonds, the rest of us. Not our choice to be here. But you—you're at home."

2

Ursule was thirteen when she began to change. She felt that she was shedding the innocence of childhood the way a garden snake might wriggle out of its old skin and leave it behind. She wondered if the snake sensed things differently, if its new skin felt raw and sensitive, if the ground beneath it seemed rougher, the sun above it more intense.

That was the way she felt, especially after her monthlies began. The taste of food was more layered. The scent of her goats was sweet and subtle, but the smell of barn soil repelled her. The homespun clothes she had always worn scraped at her so she felt itchy and hot. She was impatient with everyone, even her mother. She looked about her with harder eyes, and saw, with surprise and some sadness, that her clan was aging.

Her uncles were much like other old men, with swollen joints, drooping shoulders, grizzled hair. They appeared to be wearing away a bit more each year, as if the endless work of the farm carved away their substance, much as the wind and rain sculpted the granite boulders on the tor. Her aunts seemed stronger, their hands not so gnarled, their skin not so weathered. Their hair was gray—even Nanette's black curls were frosted now with silver—but their eyes remained the same shining black they had always been.

They behaved strangely, though. Ursule couldn't think why she had never noticed before. The aunts whispered together when the men were outside. They slipped one another small objects when the uncles weren't looking, tucking them into apron pockets or hiding them in sleeves. When Ursule caught glimpses of these things, they seemed unremarkable—a candle, a sprig of thyme or rosemary, a paper twist of salt—nothing that needed to be kept secret. These bits of furtiveness irritated Ursule, and she found herself stamping away with unnecessarily loud footsteps whenever it happened.

Her attic room had a small window tucked under the slanting ceiling. It faced north, to the rising flank of the tor and the changing colors of the moor beyond. She was in the habit of kneeling beside the sill for a last look at the stars before she got into bed, or savoring the wash of silver moonlight on the tor.

One spring night, when the heather had just begun to green, she settled beside her window in her nightdress. She meant to try to catch a glimpse of the new moon, but she saw instead the six Orchiére sisters creeping through the dark garden, tiptoeing past the washhouse.

Mystified, Ursule stared after them. There was no sound in the house but the distant growl of one of the uncles snoring. The swaying figures of the aunts and her mother faded into the darkness, shadows into shadows, and disappeared. Ursule pulled a blanket around her and stayed where she was, watching for the women to come back.

After an hour, as the stars moved and the new moon climbed the sky, there was still no sign of them. Her knees ached on the cold floor. Her eyelids grew heavy, and she rested her chin on her fists, half-asleep.

She gave up at last, and went to bed. She told herself she would listen for their returning footsteps, but sleep was a deep, enveloping thing for the young Ursule. Once it took hold of her, she heard nothing until the cock crowed at daylight.

She startled awake when she heard him, and sat up. Everything seemed as it always did in the mornings, a murmur of voices downstairs, the bleating of the goats from the byre. She hurried to wash her face and hands and tie back her hair. With her boots in one hand, she slipped barefoot down the narrow staircase, glancing around her for some clue as to what had taken place in the night. She saw nothing. When she reached the kitchen, she found all the adults at the table, eating bread and cheese in silence, just as they did every day.

Ursule waited, on that morning, for her mother to be alone in the garden, pulling weeds from a patch of lettuces. Nanette heard her footsteps and glanced up. "Oh, Ursule, good. Fetch a hoe, will you? Some of these have stubborn roots."

Ursule stood where she was, gazing down at her mother. When Nanette raised an inquiring eyebrow, Ursule put her hands on her hips. "Where did you go, Maman?"

Nanette sank back on her heels. "I don't know what you mean."

"*Oui*, you do!"

"Ursule," Nanette said sternly. "One language at a time."

"Tell me where you went. You and Tante Louisette, and Anne-Marie, and the rest."

"How interesting," her mother said, tilting her head. "You remember your aunts' names."

"Maman!"

Nanette clicked her tongue, and rocked forward to her knees again. She seized a weed and pulled on it, but it wouldn't loosen its hold on the earth. "A hoe, Ursule. If you please."

"I'm not going until you tell me."

"I'm not telling you until you bring a hoe."

Ursule blew out a frustrated breath, but she spun on her toes to dash to the garden shed. She knew her mother well. When Nanette said a thing, she meant it.

She pulled the shed door wide to let a shaft of sunlight brighten the dim interior. She found the hoe on its peg, hanging among the mattocks and sickles. She carried it back to her mother, who was tossing weeds into a wicker basket with an air of unconcern.

Ursule held out the hoe. *"Voilà."*

"English, Ursule. Or Cornish. Or French. Not a bit of this, a bit of that." Nanette took the hoe and used it to help herself stand. She grimaced and put a hand to the small of her back.

Ursule suffered a pang of guilt, which she tried to assuage by taking back the hoe and beginning on the weed that had resisted her mother's efforts. "I want to know where you went. All of you, in the dark, when the uncles were asleep."

"You were supposed to be asleep as well."

"Where did you go?" Ursule repeated, even as she wielded the hoe in one smooth motion, cleaving the root of the weed in two. She bent to retrieve the severed head of the plant and tossed it into Nanette's basket.

Nanette sighed and touched the basket with the toe of her dirt-encrusted boot. "I'll tell you one day, Ursule. When you're old enough."

"How old is that, Maman?"

"Well...I learned of it when I was just your age, but that was a different time..."

"Bon. I mean good. You can tell me now."

Nanette sighed again and pointed to another weed. Deftly, with the ease of young muscles, Ursule chopped it out of the ground. Nanette picked up the remnant and tossed it into the basket. She pointed to another weed, but Ursule leaned on the hoe, shaking her head. "Not till you tell me."

"I can't, sweetheart," Nanette said. "In any case, it's better to show you."

"You'll show me where you and the others went, then?"

"Yes, but not now. When the time is right." Her mother turned to gaze beyond the cliff to the sea. Wind-whipped white-caps glinted in the sunshine. Ursule's hair blew about her face, and Nanette pulled her wool jacket tighter. "And you will have to promise, *ma fille*, that you will never speak of it to a living soul. It is a matter of life and death."

Ursule refrained from commenting on her mother's mix of French and English. "Life and death? Aren't you being dramatic?"

"*Non.* I am not."

"It's just one of your stories you're going to tell me."

Nanette took back the hoe and leaned on it. "Ursule," she said, in a voice unlike any Ursule could remember her using. It was both sharp and cold, like the blade of the scythe hanging in the garden shed. "You must listen to me. Your Tante Louisette thought we should not tell you at all, for your own sake. I think ignorance is dangerous, and I insisted you know, but you have to understand how perilous this knowledge will be."

Ursule's skin prickled. "You're frightening me," she whispered.

"*Bon.*"

❧

Ursule had to curb her curiosity through an entire month. During those weeks Nanette refused to say anything further. Her aunts cast warning glances at her, but also kept their silence. They whispered together, as before, falling silent whenever Ursule or one of the men appeared. They still gathered things. Ursule saw Anne-Marie cutting sprigs of lavender from the garden, tying them together with a bit of string. She watched Florence and Fleurette clean a block of beeswax from the honey harvest of the year before, and pour a beautiful new candle. Louisette set a stone

jar on a stump one rainy day, and went to check it often as the
rain fell, bringing it in when it brimmed with clear rainwater.
She stoppered it and set it beside the candle.

All these things were done while the men were out of the
farmhouse. Each afternoon, before the uncles returned from the
fields, Isabelle stowed everything in a cupboard. Ursule saw that
the hidey-hole was full of things, including a thick book with a
cracked leather binding. She didn't ask about it. It had been three
weeks since her talk with Nanette in the garden, and she was getting used to the admonishing fingers, the whispered "*Chut, chut,
ma fille,*" and the pressed lips and shake of the head, the turning
away as if Ursule had done something offensive.

"What are we waiting for?" she hissed at her mother, when
they were once again working in the kitchen garden.

"For the Sabbat," Nanette said shortly, stabbing at a hillock of
weeds with her spade.

"What's a Sabbat?"

"*O, mon Dieu, ma fille!*"

Neither of them had seen Louisette come up the row of potatoes. She spit into the turned soil. "The child knows nothing,
Nanette! Better to leave it that way."

Ursule bit her lip, afraid she would be denied after all, but her
mother said, "Innocence is no protection, Louisette. We were
innocent enough, when we traveled through Brittany. He pursued us anyway."

"*Pffft!* It's hardly the same."

"Who? Who pursued you?" Ursule asked, but Louisette turned
away, and Nanette would say nothing more.

At times Ursule thought she would go mad with waiting to
understand the mystery. Her aunts and her *maman* went on behaving much as usual. The uncles were silent as always, working,
eating, smoking their pipes in the evenings. Ursule dug the gar-

den and milked the she-goats. When her chores were done she wandered the cliff edge, restless as one of the pony colts galloping around the paddock just to burn off energy. It seemed to Ursule that a minute had become an hour and an hour a day, when at last, on the final day of April, her mother whispered in her ear.

"Tonight. Go to your bed after supper, but don't undress. I'll fetch you."

Ursule barely noticed what she ate that evening, or what anyone said. She hurried up the narrow staircase to her bedroom under the eaves. She didn't go to bed, but knelt in her customary place beside the window, wondering what the night held in store.

Her mother whispered at her door an hour before midnight. Ursule opened it, careful of its betraying creak. Nanette crooked a finger at her, then started down the stairs.

When they had put on their coats and boots, and wound scarves around their heads against the wind, they let themselves out through the kitchen door. The other women were already on the porch, similarly wrapped. They looked like ghosts, tall and shapeless. Ursule, aflame with curiosity, followed them through the garden and past the washhouse to the gate. They crossed the lane and set their feet on the goat path that wound up the tor.

There was no moon, but Ursule knew the path well. She trod it often, herding the goats up to the moor to graze. This time, though, the women pressed on past the roll of brambles where Ursule usually turned out onto the moor, with the goats pattering beside her. They climbed steadily upward, breathing harder as the way grew steeper.

The path was still familiar to Ursule, although she had not climbed the tor since high summer. It grew narrow as it rose, and the wind—blowing, in Cornish fashion, from every direction at once—made their scarves snap like sheets on a line. No one had breath to speak, but then no one had spoken a word since they left the farmhouse.

Ursule had never climbed so high on the flank of the tor. In the starlit darkness the jumbled blocks of granite topping the hill looked like the towers of a tumbledown castle. In nearby brambles she heard the whirring, rhythmic call of a nightjar, intensifying her impression of a castle's ramparts, with guards calling the hours, perhaps a moat meant to drown intruders. The silence of the women, the clutch of the wind at her clothes, the shadowed boulders and fading path gave her the shivers. "Maman! Where are we going?"

Her mother put out a hand to her. "We're almost there. A few more steps."

"It's too dark. And freezing!"

"There will be light soon. Have patience," her mother said softly. She released her hand and turned to follow the swaying silhouettes of her sisters.

Ursule hurried after her, but her steps slowed and her mouth hung open as she saw her aunts disappear, one by one, as if swallowed up by the hill. Nanette followed them without hesitation. Ursule inched forward with her hands out, sure she was about to bash herself to insensibility on the cold granite.

Nanette reached back to take one of her outstretched hands, and led her around what looked like a blank wall of stone, but that she discovered was the outer wall of a cave. The beating of the wind ceased on the instant. Someone struck a sulfur match and set its flame to three tall candles waiting in niches of stone. Flickering yellow light flared up to waver on the faces of the women.

Ursule gazed about her in wonder at the high-ceilinged chamber. It was surprisingly warm, insulated by rock and soil against the chill of the night. The candles gave uncertain light, but enough for Ursule to see the crevices filled with cloth bags, a few bottles, one or two baskets. A broom leaned against one wall.

In the center of the space, a granite pedestal thrust up from the floor, and on it rested a stone, almost spherical on the top, the granite beneath left rough. It gleamed with reflected candlelight.

Ursule put out a finger to touch it, and Tante Louisette slapped her hand away. *"Tsst!"* she hissed. "That belonged to Grand-mère. You don't yet have the right."

Ursule drew her hand back and thrust it under her opposite arm. She threw Nanette a hurt look, and her mother sighed. "Louisette, Ursule barely knows who Grand-mère was, except that she bears her name. Give her time."

Louisette sniffed. She lowered her basket to the floor and began to remove items and arrange them on a shelf.

Nanette murmured to Ursule, "That—" She pointed to the pedestal. "That is our altar." She tugged Ursule to one side of the chamber, where the candlelight barely reached. Ursule's boots crunched on the detritus of the birds and animals that must use the cave. Only the center was swept clean, and here the five older sisters clustered, brushing crumbs of dirt and dried leaves from the floor with the broom, wiping down the polished surface of the pedestal, setting out twigs of lavender and heather and gorse. No one touched the crystal.

Nanette said, "Tonight is the eve of Beltane, the Sabbat of spring. The heather and gorse are returning, symbolizing the rebirth of the world. The Goddess has lain dormant through the winter, and now labors to bring forth new life."

Ursule turned her head to try to read her mother's expression in the dim light. She expected a look of amusement, sure that Nanette had spoken in irony. Instead her mother's face was rapt as she gazed at what she called the altar.

"Maman, what is this? What are you all doing?"

Nanette turned to look her full in the face. They were so close that the daughter could feel her mother's breath on her cheeks. Nanette said solemnly, "This is who we are, Ursule. We are

Grand-mère's descendants. We are Orchiéres, and we practice the old ways."

"The old ways..." Ursule's voice trailed off in confusion.

"We are sisters in the craft."

"What craft?" Nanette turned her face away without answering. Ursule caught her breath in a gasp. "Maman! Not—not *witchcraft!*"

They were speaking French, and the word *sorcellerie* rang through the cavern with its sibilant consonants and sharp ending vowel. Louisette, in the act of sprinkling salt from a twist of paper into a tiny pottery pitcher, threw Ursule an angry glance. "*Chut!* There will be no *sorcellerie* tonight. There will be only worship."

"Worship! Worship of what? Who?"

"The Goddess, of course," Louisette snapped. "The Mother of Earth, and of us all."

Ursule gazed, openmouthed, at her aunt. Her mother patted her shoulder. "Never mind," Nanette whispered, when Louisette had turned back to her task. "She's only worried we will be discovered. The more people who know, the more danger we're in. This is why we come in secret. Your uncles have forbidden it because of the risk of discovery, but we—"

"Why should we be in danger?" Ursule interrupted. She looked from one to the other of the wrinkled, familiar faces, meeting scowls and frowns.

"I told you we should leave her out of it," Louisette pronounced. She had the pitcher in one hand now, poised above the altar of stone. "She is too young to understand."

"She's the same age I was when you initiated me," Nanette said.

"She fraternizes with the children of Marazion. She goes to St. Hilary with them."

"We have to explain to her. She should know her history."

"*You* have to do that," Tante Florence put in.

"I know that, Florence," Nanette snapped.

"*C'est importante.*"

Fleurette broke her habitual silence to whisper, "There is peril in the child."

"Peril! She's thirteen."

"It's time." Fleurette's words were nearly inaudible. She took a step back after she spoke.

Ursule turned to her mother, her hands lifted in question. Nanette put her fists on her hips and glared at her older sisters. "I would have explained to her before! You made me wait, all of you! At Ostara, you told me I had to wait!"

Anne-Marie, the peacemaker, said, "And you did wait, for which we thank you, don't we, everyone? Now, it's midnight. We don't want to miss the hour. Let's be about our business, and we can speak to Ursule afterward."

The quarreling subsided. Louisette scattered a few drops of the salted water onto the altar, and the six women moved to make a circle around it. Each draped a long scarf over her head. When they were all gathered around the stone, Louisette poured a thin stream of the water in a circle, enclosing them. Louisette lighted the new candle that rested beside the crystal. Its clear flame outlined the silhouettes of the women as Ursule watched, wide-eyed, her hands clenched beneath her chin.

The women began to chant in Old French. Ursule understood no more than half the words. Louisette would proclaim something, and the others would answer, and then, in a thready and discordant unison, the women would chant what seemed to be a verse.

It was a hymn of some kind, Ursule thought. She had attended St. Hilary a few times with Meegan's children. She didn't understand much of the service, but she loved the singing, and the way the hymns resounded from the stone walls of the sanctuary. This hymn, too, echoed, but the treble voices with their uncertain pitches produced an effect more weird than beautiful. It made Ursule feel queasy. Her skin began to crawl as the women swayed, eyes closed, hands raised with a fervor the Church of England worshippers never displayed. Ursule had known these women all her life, yet now they seemed as alien as if they had dropped out of the sky.

An hour passed before the ritual wound to its close with a recitation of names, all of them but Grand-mère's unfamiliar to Ursule, beautiful, mysterious names...Liliane, Yvette, Maddalena, Irina. By that time Ursule had sunk down on her folded coat, her back against icy granite, her arms wrapped around herself. As the women turned to face her, she thought it must be over at last, and they could go home. In anticipation she scrambled to her feet and bent to gather up her coat.

When she straightened she found Tante Louisette, her long face drawn and her eyelids heavy, in front of her. Louisette gripped Ursule's wrist with a hand as hard and dry as a chicken's claw. "Come," Louisette growled. "We're ready for you now."

"What?"

Ursule looked past her aunt's shoulder. The other women, her mother included, still stood around the altar. They gazed at her, and not even Nanette was smiling. Louisette tugged, and Ursule stumbled forward across the long-dried circle of water. She came to stand beside her mother, shivering with fatigue and unease in equal parts.

The candle had burned low, and its flame, under the faint currents of air swirling through the cave, danced like some mad ballerina, shimmering this way and that, making the melted wax in its center spit and hiss. Nanette produced another scarf, dyed a deep charcoal color. She draped it across her two palms, and Louisette scattered a few drops of water on it, then lifted it on her own hands and turned to Ursule.

"I thought the craft would die with us, Ursule. Indeed, I think that would have been best. It seems you will stay here, where Grand-mère sent us. You might remain all your life.

"If you are meant to carry on the traditions of the Orchiéres, as your *maman* believes, so be it. It is not for me to question the ways of the Goddess."

She lifted the scarf and let it drift over Ursule's head. A fold of it fell across her face, turning everything to shadow. Ursule wanted to flee, to run back down the dark tor and away from this strangeness.

"Now we will tell you the history, and you must swear never to reveal it."

Confounded, but used to obeying her aunt, Ursule nodded.

"Bon." Louisette twitched the muslin away from Ursule's eyes so she could clearly see the solemn faces around the altar, and the women began a recitation in the French Ursule understood.

Taking turns, they told of passing years and changing times, violent centuries in which the ancient religion gave way before the thundering march of the new one. They spoke of curses, and inquisitions, and persecutions. They spoke of ancestors hounded from one side of Europe to the other, sought out when someone needed magic, reviled when the craft was discovered. They spoke of the worst history of all, the burning times, with screaming women sacrificed on the altar of ignorance. Their voices tumbled over one another, overlapping and urgent.

The history ended with Ursule Orchiére, the greatest of them all, who hid the clan from the torches of its pursuers, and spent the last of her life's strength doing it.

Finally Louisette pointed to the chunk of crystal resting on the altar. "This," she pronounced, "is Grand-mère's scrying stone. It is useless without her. None of us have seen anything in it for a very long time. The gift is dying out because our talents are nothing compared to hers. Still, the stone is a symbol of Grand-mère's strength and devotion. It will always belong to the Orchiéres."

Ursule, so tired she could hardly keep her head up, leaned closer to the crystal to peer into its depths. She wondered if her namesake had pretended to see things. She would do that herself, if it suited her.

But she hadn't known Grand-mère Ursule. She might not have been capable of pretense.

The one thing Ursule did know, with a certainty as clear and strong as the light of a full moon, was that Grand-mère had not been a witch. Nor were these others, these batty old women, witches. She understood they had seen hard times. She felt their need to cling to their history. She respected their wish to honor their tradition.

But she was a modern girl. She was practical. She put no trust in fables. She didn't believe what the priest prattled on about at Mass, bread turning into flesh, wine turning into blood, babies born sinful, murderers being forgiven. She scorned the idea of virgin birth. She took her she-goats to be covered by the neighbor's billy, and she knew how birth came about.

This—this wild tale of witches and scrying and so forth—this was a fairy tale. It was detailed and colorful, dramatic and mysterious. It must be satisfying for her mother, the aunts.

Ursule didn't believe a word of it.

3

One of the uncles died in the spring. The other two followed swiftly after, as if their life spans were linked, or as if they couldn't bear to face the heavy work of summer even one more time. Tante Louisette said, after they buried Claude, "Now we're a house of old women. We must have a care. They will be watching us."

The others nodded and sighed, but Ursule said, "There are other old women in the county. Widows, even spinsters. They're left in peace."

"They're not Romani," Louisette said, and there were more nods of resignation.

Ursule pressed her lips together. She felt no sense of danger. It seemed to her that the people of Marazion behaved toward her as they always had. If a few of them seemed envious, or if the priest at St. Hilary sometimes seemed to be eyeing her, that meant nothing. Her aunts might be superstitious and fearful, but she saw no need to be that way herself.

The year turned steadily, as always. The Sabbat of Lammas arrived to signal the beginning of the harvest season. Ursule climbed the tor with her mother and her aunts, and watched their ceremony in silence. She felt her mother's glances at her throughout the night, and the next morning as well, but Nanette didn't speak until late in the day, as Ursule picked up her boots to carry them out onto the porch. The evening breeze was sharp with the scents of heather and gorse and sea. Ursule paused to savor the autumnal perfume, and to glimpse the gray water tossing beyond the cliff.

"Ursule," Nanette murmured. She cast a glance over her shoulder to be certain the aunts were occupied elsewhere. "Listen to me."

"Oui, Maman?"

"English, please."

"Fine, but they'll know we're keeping secrets if they hear us."

"Just the same."

"What is it, then?"

"I have to warn you, Ursule. I know you don't believe me, but we're your elders, and we know the truth. There's danger for us."

"That's what you wanted to tell me?"

"Isabelle had a dream that you betrayed us."

"I would never betray you. I would never betray any of you! Surely you know that."

"She didn't want me to tell you."

"Well, now you have, and now I've promised."

Nanette crossed to the peg rack, where the thick coats hung like shapeless bodies on a gibbet. She stopped there, turning to her daughter with a worried look. "The stories we told you are true, Ursule. Women like us are persecuted because we're different."

"You don't have to be different. Tell your sisters to learn to speak English. To go into the village and talk to people, the way I do. Instead they huddle out here like sheep on the moor."

"They're afraid."

"Why should they be afraid?"

"Because if anyone suspects the truth about them—about us—" A shadow crossed Nanette's face and she shivered. "That priest, that Father Maddock—"

"He's just a superstitious old man." Ursule shrugged into a coat. "I don't want to hurt anyone's feelings, Maman," she said, as she reached for her boots, "but all I see is an old crystal, and all I hear is a lot of old stories. You observe the Sabbats, and I do it with you, because I suppose one ritual is as good as another, but nothing ever changes. That's the truth."

Nanette's eyes glistened suddenly, and Ursule tapped an impatient toe. "Maman, I promised! What else can I do? Whatever all that is, up on the tor, it's your secret, and I will keep it. Don't worry."

Nanette averted her gaze and pulled on her own coat.

Ursule plunged one foot into its boot. She had to tug at the top to pull the boot on, and she scowled at it, wondering if she could still be growing. She was already taller than her mother. She stamped her other foot into the second boot. "I'll be taller than Louisette if I keep this up."

"No doubt." Nanette sounded like her usual self, which was a relief to her daughter. "Your father was one of the tallest men I ever saw."

Ursule was pulling her knit cap down over her thick hair. She cast her mother a challenging glance. "When are you going to tell me about him?"

Nanette shrugged, avoiding her eyes. "There's nothing to tell. He came, he gave me you, and he left."

"Why did he leave?"

Her mother didn't look up from putting on her own boots. "He didn't belong here."

"Or you drove him away."

Again the Gallic shrug. "I summoned him. It was never my intention to keep him."

Ursule, with her hand already on the latch of the door, stared over her shoulder at her mother. "What do you mean?" she hissed. "You *summoned* him?"

Nanette started toward the door. Ursule held it open for her and watched her pass through. Nanette's face revealed nothing. With the milk bucket swinging from her hand, Ursule followed her down the path to the byre.

She waited until they were inside the byre, where the air smelled of fresh straw and hay and the clean, warm smell of the she-goats. They pressed around her, nosing at her pockets for the bits of carrot and twigs of parsley she carried for them. She put the treats into the trough, and, as the goats put their heads through, closed the stanchions. "Tell me what you meant, Maman," she said, as she pulled her stool close to the first doe. She sponged off the udder with a damp towel, then began to milk. The she-goat gave a contented groan and moved her hind leg a little to allow Ursule better access. Ursule's fingers automatically stripped the doe's teats, and the milk sang a sweet tune as it splashed into her bucket.

Nanette reached for a broom and began to sweep the floor. The dirt was packed so hard by generations of feet that it was nearly as solid as stone. "There's no point in telling you, Ursule," she said, as she swept the broomstraw back and forth. "You won't believe me anyway."

"You're going to tell me you cast a spell?"

Nanette moved the broom faster. "Isabelle dreamed he would come, and I used my power to make her dream come true."

"How?"

"I asked the Goddess, and she heard me."

"I don't see that the Goddess has any more to do with us than the God they call upon at All Saints'." Ursule sat down and began to milk the second doe. "It's pretense. Making things up because you want to believe them."

"If you had seen Grand-mère work, you wouldn't doubt."

Ursule heard the distress in her mother's voice, and she sighed. "Well, then. Perhaps there once was power. But it's gone now."

"We're not as strong as Grand-mère, that's true. You know our small talents, Anne-Marie and her potions, Fleurette's simples, Isabelle's dreams. I had real power, for a while, a power beyond recipes from the grimoire. It didn't last, but before it faded, it brought your father to me."

Ursule looked up from her stool. "Is that what you think?"

"I knew you wouldn't believe me."

Ursule moved more slowly now, settling herself beside the third doe, frowning as she began to milk. She didn't want to look at her mother any longer. She hated the idea of Nanette's chanting a spell, waving her arms around, burning magical candles. It was embarrassing. Ursule could accept that the old aunts placed their faith in such nonsense, but Nanette was her mother. The closest person in the world to her. Part of herself.

Nanette spoke in a low and passionate voice. "I can't be sorry, *ma fille*. I knew one day the old ones would die, as they have begun to do, and I was frightened. I was lonely."

Ursule sighed. Her mother loved her, and she loved her mother in return. She had no wish to hurt her. She took the brimming milk pail out from beneath the doe's udder, and set it carefully on the stone ledge that circled the byre. She opened the stanchions to release the goats, and they trotted cheerfully out into the twilight. "Leave the sweeping," she said. "I'll scrub down the stalls after I put the milk in the cellar."

"I'll take the milk." Nanette reached for the bucket, lifting it carefully so it swung by her side. "The ice is getting low, though."

"It always does by autumn. We'll put all this into the cheese vat."

"Your uncle was right, *ma fille*, may he rest in peace. You're a born farmer."

Nanette stooped to pass under the low lintel of the doorway. When she was outside, she bent to glance back. "I know you don't believe me about the spell, but it's true."

Ursule had picked up the broom again, but she made herself meet her mother's gaze. "No, Maman. I don't believe it."

"It happened, nonetheless."

"You loved him?"

"There was no time for that. I saved my love for you, little one."

"But, Maman—did he know there was a child? Was he kind to you, or did he—"

Nanette waved a hand. "None of that matters, Ursule. It doesn't matter now."

She straightened and set off into the dusk with the milk pail swinging beside her. Ursule gazed after her, broom forgotten in her hand. She couldn't make the pieces fall into place. The life of Orchard Farm was one of crops and seasons and livestock. It didn't lend itself to fantasies. Her aunts, though they were so advanced in years, labored for hours every day, and had few entertainments. Her mother, the storyteller, told tales of real men and women, never of anything mystical. She had taught Ursule to read with a single book of fables, but they both knew they weren't true.

Ursule set the broom aside and went out to the washhouse pump to fill a bucket. As she worked the handle, she glanced up past the kitchen garden to the lighted windows of the farmhouse. Shadows moved this way and that behind the curtains as her aunts prepared the meal, soup and bread and their own cheese. They seemed no different from the other farmwives of the county, except that they so rarely left Orchard Farm.

As she dipped her scrub brush into the cold water, Ursule tried to imagine her mother at eighteen. Pretty, she supposed. She was still pretty, though she was thirty-four now. And the man? Ursule tried to imagine what he must have been like—dark, no doubt, because she herself was as dark as Nanette. Tall, though, so probably not a Cornishman. What kind of man bedded a lonely girl and then abandoned her?

When the billy goat covered the nannies, he butted them away the moment it was done. Had it been like that with her father? Did Nanette care?

Ursule groaned in frustration. She understood no more now than she had before.

She didn't go in to supper until the milking stalls were scrubbed spotless and the goats settled on beds of fresh straw for the night. The ponies, six of them at the moment, blinked sleepily in their paddock, chins resting on one another's withers. Stars glimmered to life in the east, chasing the sun down over the western sea. A warm night breeze stirred up tiny opaque dust devils that spun across the dirt road separating the farm from the moor.

Ursule paused on her way through the garden to look down the road, thinking of where it led. Marazion, of course, where she had been countless times. On to Penzance, and then St Ives, where she had been only once, with a pony to sell. If a traveler kept on, he could go right through the west country, on to the River Tamar that separated Cornwall from England. Her cousins had taken that road, cousins she had never met. They had fled, and left her to deal with the remnants of the clan on her own.

She would hate to leave Cornwall, and Orchard Farm. She reveled in her knowledge of the paths and swales and hillocks of the moor, so certain she could have walked them blindfolded. She loved her goats, and the ponies and their foals. She savored the solitude of the tor and the vista of Mount's Bay.

She could understand, though, her cousins wishing to leave the dour company of the Orchiéres. Louisette scowled, and Anne-Marie fussed. Florence stalked between the stove and the pantry as if she were the very Beast of Bodmin Moor. Isabelle clattered pottery and clanged flatware. Fleurette spoke only if she had to, and then in a hoarse whisper.

Nanette had said she feared being left alone on Orchard Farm. Her daughter, though she wished no one into the grave before her time, looked forward to it.

4

Despite herself, Ursule learned to think of the year in Sabbats, as her aunts did. Samhain, which the Cornish churchgoers called All Hallows' Eve, was a particularly welcome one, marking the end of the labors of the harvest season.

All the women, and especially Ursule, with her strong young back, had labored harder than ever during the summer and fall. It was the only time, as far as Ursule could tell, that anyone missed the uncles. Despite their age, and the stooping of their shoulders, the three men had done a prodigious amount of work. Now all of it fell to the women. They scythed hay, dug potatoes and beets and carrots and garlic, stored preserved foods and cheeses and their home-brewed ale in the cellar. Ursule repaired chinks in the stone walls around the byre and filled the loft with hay and straw against the cold season, when neither ponies nor goats could find much to eat on the moor.

By the eve of Samhain they were all weary to the bone, but the aunts insisted they would make their observation. When Ursule protested, her mother pinched her arm and hissed at her. "You must come, or Louisette will say she was right all along!" Ursule, with a resigned sigh, promised she would.

At supper, before they climbed the tor, Isabelle laid three empty places on the far side of the kitchen table. When Ursule came in from the byre, she cast the empty bowls a curious glance.

The other women were busy at the stove and the stone sink, but Florence took notice. She said, "For the ones who have passed, Ursule. Always set places for them at Samhain, to show we have not forgotten."

"Like the Catholics," Ursule said. Florence gave her a blank look. "All Saints'," Ursule told her. "That's what they celebrate in this season."

Florence shrugged her disinterest. Ursule frowned, but Nanette, coming toward the table carrying the breadboard with a sliced loaf, shook her head. Ursule glanced across the room at Louisette, who was scowling at the pottage as if it had let her down in some way.

It would be, Ursule thought, a long and tiresome night.

Now that the uncles were gone, there was no need to slip away from the house in secret to observe the Sabbats. When the hour arrived, the materials were gathered and packed, coats and boots were found and put on, and a lamp was left burning against their return. The six women and one girl trooped out through the garden and turned up the path to the tor. They were mostly silent, but that was from habit rather than necessity. Anne-Marie had taken to carrying a small lantern to light the way, since there was no one to notice their progress.

On Lammas, the Sabbat of first harvest, the breezes sweeping down from the moor had been mild, but by Samhain the wind had a bite, snapping at coats and scarves. To Ursule the women looked like great crows flapping their way up the hill. She felt the chill the moment she stepped onto the path, and gave serious thought to turning back, leaving her aunts to their nonsense. Only loyalty to her mother kept her moving. Eight nights a year, she told herself. She could make that sacrifice for Nanette's sake.

When she stepped inside the cave and out of the wind, the sudden warmth enveloped her like an embrace, relaxing her chilled muscles and freeing the breath in her cold lungs. Seated cross-legged in a corner, she grew drowsy as the aunts chanted and the candle flames painted specters in shadowed corners. Ursule's eyelids drooped as water was sprinkled, scarves draped and fluttered, reverences made to Grand-mère's crystal. As before, it lay quiescent, showing nothing but the dancing reflections of candlelight.

The ceremony wound to its close. Ursule joined the circle when she was asked, linking hands with her mother on one side and Fleurette on the other. The night seemed far gone to her when they finally gathered their things, but once they were outside, she saw by the stars that the night had not advanced much past one. A half-moon lent brightness to the path, and Anne-Marie carried her lantern unlit as the women filed downhill.

When they arrived back at the farmhouse, everyone but Ursule went straight to bed. She climbed the stairs to her room, but once she was in her nightdress and dressing gown, she decided to go back to the kitchen for a cup of warm milk. The house was quiet except for faint snores here and there. The kitchen was filled with moonlight. Ursule stoked the fire and fetched milk from the pantry. As it warmed, she stood gazing out at the garden and the byre, shining silver beneath the moon. She wondered what it would be like to have Orchard Farm all to herself.

When the milk began to steam, she lifted the small saucepan from the stove and stirred in a teaspoon of the honey they had collected only the month before. She measured it carefully, knowing it had to last the winter. She was just tying the cloth cap back over the jar when Fleurette appeared in the doorway, tugging her nightcap lower against the chill air.

Ursule nodded toward the saucepan. *"Du lait, Tante Fleurette? Avec du miel?"*

Fleurette nodded and brought a second mug to the table. Ursule tipped the saucepan to pour out the sweetened milk. She sat down, cupping her palms around the warm mug, and gazing into the faint cloud of steam rising from it.

When Fleurette spoke, Ursule started.

"Nanette won't tell you," her aunt said in her whispery voice. "But you should know."

Ursule lifted her head to gaze at Fleurette. The slanting moonlight from the window made furrows in her aunt's wrinkled cheeks, and shadowed her eyes so they looked as if they were closed. "What should I know?" she asked softly.

"Spells are not free," Fleurette said, and stopped.

Ursule waited. After a moment Fleurette stirred and spoke again.

"Everything has a cost. Magic, too." Another pause, while tendrils of steam curled up into the silvery light. "Especially magic."

Ursule shifted in her chair. Fleurette's heavy-lidded eyes glittered faintly in the moonlight. "You doubt us."

Ursule blew out a small breath. "I'm sorry, Tante Fleurette. It's true. I do."

"You are mistaken."

"Witchcraft? I don't want to be disrespectful, but it makes no sense." She brought her mug to her lips and drank.

Her aunt's own milk waited untouched on the table before her. She said, pursing her wrinkled lips, "Seventeen. An age at which a girl knows everything."

"Of course I don't. But I don't believe in magic." Ursule did her best to speak kindly. Fleurette lived in the shadow of Florence, her twin, indeed in the shadows of all the clan, as if she had no individual life. This was the longest conversation the two of them had ever had.

Fleurette said, "Your gift with animals."

"That's not magic."

"It's power. The same thing."

This thought intrigued Ursule, and for a moment it was she who sat in silence, contemplating the white shimmer of milk in the gloom and considering the idea.

Fleurette leaned forward so the ribbon on her nightcap trailed in the mug before her. "Your mother still longs for him."

Ursule shivered before her aunt's hooded gaze. She whispered, too, though she didn't know why. "I don't know what you mean."

"I mean, beware what you ask for."

"What are you saying?"

"Nanette summoned him, and she has suffered his absence ever since."

Ursule put her mug down and stared at her aunt across the table. "She has?"

"Of course she has."

"She's never said so."

"Nor will she. But we have all seen her gazing down the road with her eyes full of tears."

"I haven't seen that!"

"She doesn't want you to see. But you need to know."

"Why? Why do I need to know?"

"Because you have the power. You laugh at us—" When Ursule began to protest, her aunt clicked her tongue. "We're not stupid. We know how it is between old people and young people."

"I . . . I really don't laugh at you, Tante Fleurette."

Fleurette lifted her shoulders in the familiar Orchiére shrug. "Remember what I tell you. The exercise of power has a price." She pushed herself up, leaving her milk cooling in its mug, and braced herself on her spotted fists. "There is a cloud around you. I fear for Nanette."

"What? Why?" But Fleurette was done speaking. She turned and walked stiffly out of the kitchen. The hem of her dressing gown brushed faintly against the flagstones.

Ursule said again, "Why?" but her aunt was gone, fading into the darkness, leaving her niece chewing her lip in confusion.

❧

If she had any real talent, Ursule thought, it was the talent for patience. She depended upon it when she was assisting a nanny goat in labor, or assessing the mood of the black honeybees so she could harvest their combs. Exercising that modest and unmagical gift, she awaited the perfect moment to ask her mother for the truth.

Winter was closing in around Orchard Farm, and the moor was soggy and brown. The ocean turned a forbidding iron gray, and the silhouette of St. Michael's Mount faded in and out of view as thunderstorms swept across the water. Ursule and Nanette had put the garden to bed and sold the last of their produce at the Thursday market. The Sabbat of Yule was approaching. A sense of restfulness settled over the farmhouse and the byre, with all inhabitants warm and dry and safe from the storms.

The aunts had begun the winter-long task of mending clothes and sheets and blankets. Louisette and Anne-Marie and Florence were seated around the kitchen table with mounds of fabric and spools of thread. Fleurette was carding wool near the stove.

In the pantry Nanette and Ursule were bundling parsley and eyebright, moneywort and rosemary, and hanging the bundles from hooks to dry. It was pleasant work, breathing the fragrance of their harvest, listening to the percussion of rain against the roof. Ursule handed her mother a piece of twine to tie around several sprigs of rosemary. "Maman," she began.

"*Oui?*" Nanette's gaze was fixed on her task, and Ursule watched her mouth twist as she concentrated on her knot.

Ursule switched to English, in case anyone came in. "I want to ask you something."

Nanette's eyes flicked up to her face, and when she perceived nothing was amiss, she smiled and went back to her task. "Anything, my sweet."

"It's something Fleurette said."

Nanette's eyebrows rose. "Fleurette said something to you?"

"She told me you grieve for the man who was my father."

"Ah." Nanette laid the bundle of rosemary to one side. She braced her elbows on the rough table and rested her chin on her twined hands. "Well, sweetheart. I didn't mean to lie to you, but I couldn't bear for you to pity me. No mother wants that."

"Tell me about him. Tell me what happened. What he was like."

Nanette picked up a loose twig of rosemary and brushed it beneath her nose to sniff its sharp scent. "His name was Michael Kilduff, and he was beautiful, Ursule. So beautiful I could hardly bear it."

❧

Nanette spoke for some time, telling Ursule about her father. She described him, and his wagon, and his powerful body bent over the ponies' hooves. She told of the young Nanette slipping back to the byre when her family had gone to bed, and staying with Michael Kilduff until the stars were fading over the sea.

"I don't understand," Ursule said, when her mother finished her tale. "Surely you knew you might conceive."

"Of course."

"Then why did you . . . Why didn't you send him packing?"

Nanette's lips curved, making her look young. "Ursule, is there no romance in that practical soul of yours? I wasn't thinking about that. I was eighteen, and Michael was sweet, and charming, the loveliest man I ever saw . . ." She lifted one hand and let it fall. "It was the Goddess's doing, Daughter."

With her finger Ursule traced a line through the dust left on the counter by drying leaves. "You stayed with him. You lay with him, a stranger."

"Yes. And next morning, he and his wagon and his gray horse were gone."

"The clan never knew?"

At this Nanette snorted. "They knew well enough when my belly began to swell."

"And what Fleurette said? Was that true?"

"Yes. It was, and it is."

"All this time, Maman? Seventeen years, and you still think of him?"

Nanette looked into her daughter's face with eyes that glowed with love. "It was the price I paid for you. And worth it a thousand times."

Ursule entwined her fingers with her mother's. "But by now— he could be anywhere. He could be married. Or dead. Or..."

"Do you think you won't still love me when I'm dead?" A strange expression, half amusement, half sorrow, flickered in Nanette's eyes. "Love is a certain kind of magic, Ursule. A specific kind of magic. I asked for it, and the Goddess provided it."

"But surely now, after all this time..."

Nanette released Ursule's hand and reached for another handful of rosemary. "I could have asked the Goddess to take back her magic, but I didn't. And yes, I still think of him. Sometimes I long for him. I'm not so old that I wouldn't like having a man by my side."

"There are other men."

Nanette took up the knife and cut a bit of twine. "Not for me. *Pour moi, jamais.*"

Nanette resumed her task, winding the twine around the twigs of rosemary, tying it neatly. Ursule couldn't be certain, but she thought she detected a shine in her mother's eyes, and she marveled at it. After seventeen years, could the memory of Michael Kilduff still bring tears?

Nanette sniffed and laid the bundle of rosemary aside. As she reached for more, she said, "You see why Fleurette wanted you to know."

"I don't, really."

"Magic costs us." Nanette didn't look up from her work as she bound the fresh twigs together. "If you practice the craft, you will pay a price."

Ursule pressed her lips together. The story of Michael Kilduff was fascinating, and she was glad to have heard it. She was sorry her mother longed for someone she hadn't seen in so many years, someone she had known for a single day and night. She could see that eighteen-year-old Nanette had fallen helplessly into love, and had never fallen out of it.

That still didn't make it magic. And she herself, of course, would never give in to such feelings.

5

Ursule was twenty-one when the aunts began to die. Tante Louisette was first.

It made sense, Ursule supposed, as Louisette was the eldest of the Orchiére sisters, but Louisette had always seemed eternal, looming over all of them like one of the granite towers at the crest of the tor, gray and creased, but irrevocably set into the earth. It didn't seem possible she could topple, like some ordinary human being, her long bones crashing to the earth like a felled tree. A stroke, cerebral apoplexy, that took her in a single moment.

Nanette tried to assure her older sisters it had been a mercy, that Louisette would have loathed being an invalid, but they were inconsolable. They seemed to shrink, to desiccate in the aftermath of the death, as if the effects of age had been postponed and now swept over them all at once. Straight spines bent, clear eyes dimmed, veined hands that had remained steady for so long developed tremors. They moved around Orchard Farm like wraiths, fading more and more each day, and they followed Louisette in order, one by one, as if it were all preordained.

Anne-Marie died in her sleep one stormy winter night just a few days before the Sabbat of Yule. Florence found her, still and stiff in her bed, and shrieked as if she had never seen death before. Her cries brought the whole household to the bedroom, where the old women wept together. Ursule hovered in the doorway, wishing she knew some way to comfort them.

Though Nanette gathered the usual herbs and candles and salt for the Yule celebration, Isabelle and the twins refused to climb the tor. Ursule, seeing her mother's distress over this lapse in tradition, offered to carry the pack Nanette had prepared. They conducted the observance alone, just the two of them. The dullness of Grand-mère's crystal, its refusal even to reflect the candle flames, seemed to reflect the mood of grief and loss that gripped the clan.

"I may not have done it right," Nanette mourned, as she packed the things away.

"I don't see how you can tell, Maman. Nothing ever happens anyway."

Her mother turned, the little salt dish in her hand, and gazed at Ursule with a hurt look. "How can you say that?"

"Well—I don't—" Ursule bit her lip. She hadn't meant to remind her mother of her skepticism. She knew the craft gave her comfort.

"What is it?" Nanette demanded.

"It's just that I never feel any different, afterward."

Her mother sniffed. "Well, I do," she said. "You must put your energy into it, after all."

"*Oui, Maman,*" Ursule said. She understood her mother's sorrow was real, though Nanette did her best to behave with her usual good cheer. Despite Louisette's gruffness and Anne-Marie's blandness, Nanette grieved for them even as she strove to fill the empty spaces created by their passing. Ursule, too, though she had so often felt the impatience of youth with old age, felt their absences as if some essential furnishing or farm implement had gone missing.

The losses continued. Isabelle was gone before Imbolc, dead of a fever. They buried her beside her sisters in the expanding grave-yard on a windy slope facing the sea. As they had with the uncles, and with Louisette and Anne-Marie, they marked the graves with blank stones dug out of the tor, the largest ones they could man-age to move. The evening after Isabelle's interment, Fleurette and Florence slumped side by side at the kitchen table in mute despair. Ursule could see, looking into the twins' disconsolate faces, that they knew they were next. She and Nanette hovered over them, pouring tea, coaxing them to eat, touching their shoulders. Ursule would have liked to hold them close to her, the same way she cradled a new, soft-skinned kid, but gestures of affection were rare at Orchard Farm. She couldn't do it.

When Florence began to walk unevenly, bent to one side as if something pained her, Nanette begged her to send for a doctor. Florence refused. The pain grew worse until Ursule, from her attic bedroom, could hear her groaning all through the night. Fleurette concocted a simple of mint and ginger and fennel, which eased Florence somewhat, but couldn't stop the progress of whatever was growing inside her. Like a beast, she said, when Nanette pressed her about it. Like a ravenous creature devouring her from within.

On the eve of the lesser Sabbat of Litha, Florence emitted one awful cry of misery and curled beneath her bedclothes, refusing to come out. She was, it seemed to Ursule, like a wounded animal gone to ground. She never again left her bed until her twin and her youngest sister lifted her body between them to be washed and dressed for burial.

After Florence's passing, Fleurette ceased speaking altogether. Though she suffered no illness that Nanette or Ursule could detect, she shrank into herself, growing smaller and grayer and less substantial every day, a creature of dissipating mist. She sur-vived her twin by only a month. Nanette found her in her bed one morning, small and cold and still.

Nanette and Ursule dug her grave and laid her in it, then stood together, gazing at the array of headstones while the wind whipped at their hair and skirts. Nanette said, "I can't picture myself lying here."

"You will, though," Ursule said. "Not for a very long time, but you will."

"I don't think so. I have a feeling about it. I don't know what this feeling means, but I don't think I am meant to lie here beside my sisters."

"Where else would you be, Maman? This is the proper place. And one day I will lie beside you."

Nanette spun toward her, taking both her daughter's hands in her own chilled grip. "No, Ursule! No! You should leave this place of death and loneliness and..." Her voice broke, and her eyes filled with the tears she had not shed for Fleurette.

Ursule stared at her, openmouthed. The wind dried her tongue and made her stumble as she forgot to brace herself. "Leave?" she cried. "Maman, I don't want to leave. Orchard Farm is my home! My goats, and the ponies...the kitchen garden..."

"But when I'm gone, Ursule," Nanette sobbed. "When I am dead and gone, you will be all alone. The work is too much. The solitude will be unbearable. I can't bear to think of you, living out your years all by yourself on this Goddess-forgotten cliff!"

Ursule gathered her thoughts and freed her hands so she could take her mother by the shoulders. "I will marry someone, Maman," she said. She hadn't thought about it before, but now it seemed the perfect answer. "I will marry, and then I won't be alone."

"But who? Who will you find to marry?"

"*Eh bien*, I don't know yet, but someone. Someone with a strong back and a steady hand. Someone to help me with the work, and to keep me company."

"We never meet anyone! You could never fall in love with one of the Marazion yokels."

"I don't need to fall in love," Ursule said. "It's Orchard Farm I love." Nanette shook her head, but Ursule squeezed her shoulders and smiled at her. "You know this about me, surely?"

"I suppose I do," Nanette said doubtfully.

"Come now," Ursule said, encircling her mother's slender shoulders with her young, strong arm. She turned her toward the farmhouse and urged her forward. "Let's have a cup of tea, Maman, and then we'll turn out Fleurette's room before it's time for milking."

Her mother gave her a darkling glance before she dropped her eyelids as if to hide some thought that had occurred to her. Ursule said, "What is it?" but Nanette shook her head. Ursule pressed her further over the pot of tea, but her mother only shrugged and said nothing.

They spent an hour going through Fleurette's paltry belongings. Her dresses and stockings were so threadbare there was nothing to be saved. Nanette wrapped them into a bundle and said she would cut everything into cleaning rags. Ursule took two of Fleurette's books to her room, and made her mother take a woolen scarf for her own use. There was little else. Fleurette had left no keepsakes. It was strange, Ursule thought, that a person could be present one day and absent the next, and leave so little behind she might have never existed.

They spent a dismal evening, Ursule and Nanette. Shadows flickered like ghosts in the empty chairs around the kitchen table, and Ursule found herself turning to them again and again, her nerves crawling. She and her mother did their best to eat their soup as usual. It was dispiriting to see how much was left in the pot when they were done.

"You should move your things downstairs," Nanette said abruptly.

"Why?"

"There's no need for you to sleep in that little attic room any-more. There are four big bedrooms sitting empty. You could take your pick."

"I'll think about it, Maman." Ursule kissed her mother and climbed the stairs to the room where she had spent all her life.

She stood in the doorway and surveyed it. It was true, it was an awkward sort of room. The roof slanted very low over the window, and since she had grown so tall, she had to bend at the waist to reach her bed. It made sense to move down to one of the other bed-rooms, but they had always belonged to her aunts and her uncles. She couldn't imagine feeling comfortable in one of them, sleeping in a wide bed with four carved posts and a sagging canopy, storing her clothes in a real wardrobe instead of hanging them on pegs. The windows might be nice, though. Two of the rooms faced the moor, and the other two looked out beyond the cliff to the sea.

She yawned as she buttoned up her nightdress and folded her-self into bed. Her quilt had gone soft and cozy from years of use. As she pulled it up to her chin, she smiled into the darkness. She had to admit she was set in her ways, like one of her beloved goats. Goats liked everything to happen in the same way every day, every month, every year. Ursule thought, yawning into the darkness, that she was just like that. She wasn't sure she wanted to share Orchard Farm with anyone, even if it meant having only ghosts for company around her table.

She slept deeply, as she always did, lulled by the whisper of the ocean from the south and the answering hush of the wind from the north. She'd expected to sleep until dawn, when the cock's crow would tell her it was time to rise and set about her chores.

A sound startled her awake, and it wasn't from the henhouse or the byre. A shaft of moonlight slanted through her window to illumine the wooden floor, but morning, she felt certain, was still far off. She sat up, sharpening her ears, wondering.

It came again, the click of a door, the sound of footsteps crossing the kitchen below. Ursule threw back her quilt and hurried out to the head of the staircase.

She reached it just in time to see her mother tiptoe across the cramped hall that ran between the bedrooms. She was wrapped in a heavy coat, with Fleurette's scarf tied around her head. She carried something in her arms, a box or a book. The gray cat minced at her heels, its skinny tail high and straight. Ursule hadn't seen the cat in weeks, and she thought it must surely have died. The creature must be more than twenty years old!

She whispered at first, forgetting there was no one else in the house to disturb. "Maman! What are you doing?"

Nanette glanced up from beneath the hem of the old scarf. Her eyes were hollow and her cheeks pale with fatigue. She said, "I have to sleep."

"Wait!" Ursule's voice rose now, and she hurried down the staircase, her stockinged feet slipping on the bare wood. "Wait, Maman! Why aren't you in bed?"

The look her mother gave her then, lifting her head and gazing fully into her face, brought Ursule to a halt, still three treads from the bottom. Nanette said, "You'll find out in time, Ursule. Or you won't. Until then, you'll just have to wait. For now, I must sleep."

She turned away toward her bedroom, hugging the dark object close to her breast. The cat followed, winding past her ankles to precede her into the room. Ursule shook herself and hurried after her mother, but Nanette closed the door firmly in her face. Ursule cried out in shock when she heard the heavy click of the lock.

She stood for a time where she was, as her feet grew cold and chill prickles broke out on her arms. She lifted a hand to knock, but she thought of Nanette's face, gray with exhaustion, and lowered her hand again. Reluctantly she went back up the stairs, consigning the resolution of the mystery to the morning. She lay wakeful in her bed for a long time, watching the bands of moonlight slip across the slanted ceiling. When the goats began to bleat, she had fallen into a deep, numbing slumber. She struggled awake with difficulty, and pulled on her clothes with her eyes still half-shut. Not until she was already on her way to the byre did she feel fully awake.

Nanette slept late that day. Lammas was approaching, the time of first harvest, and Ursule spent her morning in the kitchen garden, weeding, thinning, propping up vines and stems. She was bent over a row of potatoes, plucking beetles from the leaves, when she caught sight of her mother through the kitchen window. She brushed soil from her hands and skirt and strode up through the garden to the house.

She kicked off her boots on the porch and went into the kitchen in her stockings. Nanette had set the kettle on the stove to boil and pulled a half loaf from the keeper. With the bread knife in her hand, she glanced up.

Ursule had meant to press her about where she had been last night, but a wave of concern forestalled her. "Maman, are you well? You look terrible."

Nanette smiled a little as she wielded the knife, cutting two thick slices of bread. "I'm well enough," she said. "I'll be fine after one good night's sleep."

"Eat breakfast and go back to bed," Ursule urged. "I'll take the goats up to the moor."

"No, no. There's too much work to be done."

"Tell me where you were last night, then."

"Ursule, don't be foolish. Where do you think I was? What do you think I was doing?"

"You didn't go up the tor by yourself!"

"I did." The kettle began to whistle, and Nanette turned away to pour water into the waiting teapot.

"But why? If you wanted to say a crossing rite for Fleurette, I would have gone with you, you know that. To go alone in the dark is foolish! What if you had fallen? Or something had attacked you?"

Nanette laughed, a sound that was both weary and satisfied. "I suppose that's why the Goddess sent him." She pointed one finger at the cat, who had slunk beneath the table and lay glaring up at Ursule, his tail lashing back and forth. "He followed me."

"But why did you go to the temple? What was your purpose?"

Nanette poured out a cup of tea and carried it to the table. Before she sat down she said, "Do you have some fresh milk for the cat, Ursule?"

"I'll fetch some, if you like. But tell me, please."

"*Non, ma fille*. You will laugh, and I can't bear it. Not today." She pulled out her chair and sank into it with a groan. "But you're right. I'm terribly tired. Perhaps I will go back to bed, if you will forgive me."

"*Bien sûr, Maman*. Of course. Yesterday was a sad day. And a long one."

"*Merci, ma fille*."

"Where has the cat been?"

Nanette glanced beneath the table at the cat, lying perfectly still except for his restless tail. The smile returned to her lips. "I don't know. He comes and goes."

Ursule eyed the cat, who watched her through slitted yellow eyes. His tail flicked faster as they gazed at each other. She resisted the temptation to urge him out the door with her foot. Instead she went down into the cold cellar to pour fresh goat's milk into a shallow bowl. She would tolerate the creature for her mother's sake, though she had rather hoped he was gone for good. She set the bowl down, and the cat strolled to it and began to drink.

Nanette's eyes held a spark of amusement when she looked up at her daughter. "You don't like him," she said.

"He doesn't like me."

"Actually, he doesn't seem to like me that much, either. But the Goddess sent him, for Her own reasons, so that's that."

Ursule closed her lips and settled with her teacup, resolving for the hundredth time to allow her mother her illusions. There was precious little left to give Nanette comfort.

6

Morcum Cardew, a farmer with a small property west of Marazion, rode up the lane to Orchard Farm on a handsome Shire stallion just three days after Nanette and Ursule laid Fleurette in her grave. It was midafternoon, and a hot August wind tugged at the thatch of the roof and whipped the ends of Ursule's scarf. She had been pulling carrots, shaking the soil from the plump tubers before tossing them into a basket. She was covered in dirt from her skirt hem to the waist of her apron. Hastily she brushed herself as clean as she could and stepped out through the garden gate to greet the visitor.

He lifted his flat cap to her before he dismounted. "Miss Orchard," he said.

"Good day to you, Mr. Cardew." Ursule knew him from the market. He was not tall, but he was strongly built, broad shouldered and ham fisted. His short beard was half gone to gray, but his hair was still shoe-leather brown. His clothes were clean and mended, though he was widowed. He had lost his wife the year before, dead in childbed, and the infant with her.

Ursule was more interested in the Shire than she was in the man. The horse was surely eighteen hands at the withers. His hooves and nose were black, but his hide was a silvery gray, with dapples so faint they vanished in the sunlight. She stepped forward to caress his muscled neck, and he dropped his nose into her hand.

"He's a beauty, this one, Mr. Cardew," she said. "Good under harness as well as saddle?"

"Gentle as a lamb, is Aramis," the farmer said.

"Aramis. Silver."

"Yes. Even Annie used to ride him, though she said it was like riding a mountain."

"I'm sorry about your Annie."

"Thanks. It's been a year now."

"I know." Ursule stepped back to look the horse over from withers to hocks. "I don't suppose Aramis is for sale."

"Nay, not for sale. But—"

He paused, and Ursule turned, her eyebrows lifted and her hands tucked under her apron. When he didn't finish his thought, she said, "What brings you so far from your home, Mr. Cardew? In need of some goat's cheese, perhaps? We have some cheeses ready."

"No, no cheese today." He took off his cap again and turned it in his hands. His cheeks were red with the wind, or with embarrassment, Ursule couldn't tell which. He turned from her and cast his eyes at the byre and tidy fences of Orchard Farm. "Just you two left to manage your farm now, I heard. You've had a lot of death here."

"Yes." Ursule took her hands out from beneath her apron and tightened her scarf over her blowing hair.

"Hard to get by on your own," he said. He turned his head as if to assess the state of the thatch on the roof, or the paint on the walls of the farmhouse.

"Mr. Cardew," Ursule began.

He turned back to her with a look of resolution on his plain face. He said, in a rush, "I wish you'd call me Morcum, Miss Orchard."

"What?"

"I wish you'd call me by my Christian name." He hesitated, chewing on his lower lip, then blurted, "See, I've come courting."

For one long moment Ursule couldn't think what he meant. She stared at him, at his graying beard, his weathered skin, until the import of his words began to sink in. His eyes were a bright blue in the sunshine, and they held a look of pleading.

"Do you—Mr. Cardew—I mean, Morcum—" Ursule floundered to a stop.

He put out one of his thick hands and took hers. His hand was scrubbed clean, while her fingernails were grimy with garden dirt. "I do mean it, Miss Orchard. Ursula, if you don't mind. I'm a plainspoken man, and I'm older than you, but I know how to farm. I think we could do well together."

"But you don't know me at all!" She tried to pull her hand away, but he held it.

"I do," he said. "I've seen you at the market, and I know what you can do. I'm alone now—a year," he reminded her. He had said that before, and she remembered that was the proper length of time for a man to mourn a wife. "You're alone, too, and if you'll forgive me, not getting younger."

At that Ursule laughed aloud. "I'm not yet twenty-two!" she said.

"Aye. Annie was fifteen when we wed."

Ursule, still smiling, shook her head. "This is a strange call," she said.

His sudden grin surprised her. His teeth were white and even, and the grin made him look ten years younger. "I know it," he said. "Girls like romance and all, like in books. I don't have any of that."

"I'm not interested in romance." She retrieved her hand at last and stood, her fists on her hips, gazing at him. "I can't think what put this idea in your head, Morcum Cardew."

"It's a good idea, Ursula," he said stoutly. "I have two good cows and three does to add to your milkers. I'm strong and healthy, and if I sold my farm, the money could be used to improve yours. We could share the work. We'd be better together than apart."

Ursule, considering this, suddenly felt her mother's gaze on her back. She didn't need to turn to know that Nanette had lifted one edge of the curtain so she could see. She wondered why her mother didn't come out to greet their visitor, or invite him in.

Morcum replaced his cap, clearing his throat as he took a final look around Orchard Farm. "Said my piece," he said, with a faint air of relief. "I'd be pleased if you'd do me the honor of thinking about it."

"It's a bit of a shock," she said.

"Take your time," he said, and turned to his horse. She wondered for a moment if he could mount without a block, the stallion was so big. He was, however, strong, just as he had said. He pulled himself up with only a small grunt, and swung his leg over the saddle. He sat for a moment looking down at her. "I'm not asking anyone else," he said. "It's you I want, Ursula."

He touched his cap one more time, lifted the reins, and was off down the lane, leaving Ursule staring after him in amazement.

✦

"Now will you believe me?" Nanette's eyes flashed with triumph, and she tossed her head so that her hair rose like a cloud of smoke and ash around her head. "The same rite I spoke for myself, I spoke for you."

"Maman, you don't think that's why he came!" Ursule turned from the stove, where she had dropped freshly chopped carrots into a simmering broth.

"*Bien sûr!*"

"No," Ursule said. She wiped her hands on a towel and tossed it over her shoulder as she crossed to the bread keeper. "He merely waited out his year of mourning, then came looking for someone to step into Annie Cardew's shoes."

"There are other unmarried women in Cornwall."

"No doubt," Ursule responded. She wielded the bread knife with energy, peeling off thick slices of the brown loaf. "But those women are not in possession of Orchard Farm."

Nanette sighed. "You're so cynical, Ursule."

Ursule laughed. "I'm not a cynic. I'm a realist. They're different things."

Nanette let the matter drop and went to fill the crock with the butter she had churned that morning.

When the soup was ready, they filled their bowls and took their seats at the long table. They had developed the habit of sitting side by side at one end, avoiding the vacant chairs. The gray cat lay between their feet, snapping up any morsels that fell his way.

They set a simple table, with the breadboard and the butter crock between them, and the salt dish within easy reach. They were hungry after a long day of work in the bracing air, and neither spoke until their soup bowls were half-empty.

As she scooped butter onto a second piece of bread, Nanette said, "Tell me what you think of him."

"Who?"

"Who! Why, Morcum Cardew, of course. Have you forgotten him already?"

Ursule took another spoonful of soup, sighed, and laid her spoon down. With her napkin she wiped a bit of butter from her fingers, avoiding her mother's eyes. "No," she said finally. "I haven't forgotten. I just don't know what to think of him. He seems pleasant enough. He can't pronounce my name properly, but I suppose that doesn't matter."

"It's a gift from the Goddess," Nanette said.

"That may be." Ursule looked up. "I'm not sure I want it, Maman."

From his spot beneath the table, the gray cat suddenly hissed, a long, angry sound like water spilled onto a hot stove. Ursule felt the bat of his long tail against her ankles, and she had to resist the urge to kick him away.

Nanette raised her eyebrows. "Sounds as if the cat has his own opinion."

"You should give the creature a name. He's been here for years."

Nanette shrugged. "I never know if he's going to stay."

"But he's ancient, Maman. What cat lives so long?"

"A special one."

"You mean," Ursule said tartly, "that he was sent by the Goddess?"

"Of course. Like your soon-to-be husband. But remember, my dear daughter—" Nanette smiled as she picked up her spoon. "Not all gifts are permanent."

It was a remark made lightly, but it was one Ursule would ponder as the years rolled on.

⁓⅌⅍~

Ursule and Morcum were wed quietly at St. Mary's Church in Penzance, as Father Maddock in Marazion refused to officiate. Nanette was the only guest. The Cardew family, three taciturn brothers and two sour-faced sisters, declined to attend, saying Morcum was marrying a gypsy, a heathen who would lead him straight to hell. Even the priest, paid well by Morcum, looked askance at Ursule, and pressed her on her beliefs. She shrugged and said she had no difficulty with the church as long as it left her alone. Morcum hid a grin at the priest's scowl. For his part he asked nothing about her private beliefs, and as far as she could tell, he didn't care what they were. Ursule thought it best not to press him on his family's doubts.

The priest performed the ceremony in perfunctory fashion. Ursule had attended Mass often enough to take part, after a fashion. She watched Morcum going through the ecclesiastical motions, and thought how similar it all was to the rites her aunts had practiced. It was something she would never tell him, of course.

It was a practical marriage, with neither frill nor flourish. Morcum had already sold his bit of land and moved his stock to Orchard Farm. For days before the wedding he'd labored in the byre, adding new stalls for the extra goats, strengthening the fence around the pasture where the cows grazed. Aramis, the great, gentle Shire, occupied the same paddock as the ponies. Morcum spent an entire night observing the beasts together to be certain there would be no trouble. In the morning, with satisfaction, he reported that the ponies had taken shelter from the wind behind Aramis's bulk, and that Aramis, as usual, took care where he put his feet and even how he swished his enormous tail.

There was to be no wedding journey, because the expanded stock would be too much for Nanette to manage alone, and none of the Cardews would agree to help. Ursule assured her groom she didn't like to leave her animals in any case, and he said, in his blunt fashion, "Good. My first wedding journey cost the price of a new calf."

Flashes of humor sometimes eased the edge of such frank speech, and he was, just as he had promised, a hard worker. With his big hands and stout shoulders, he could do twice as much work in a day as Ursule could, and there was no job he scorned. She kept the milking for herself, as it was her favorite chore, but it was good to have someone else to spade hard ground or lift a heavy basket of spuds into the jingle. Morcum regarded Aramis as his own, but when he had occasion to be away from the farm, Ursule spoiled the big horse, carrying him chunks of carrot in her apron pockets and snuggling close to his warm flank on a cold day.

Aramis reciprocated in his ponderous way, lipping her cheek and bending his thick neck to cuddle her. She savored such moments. There was no cuddling to be had in her marriage bed.

Ursule had known little physical affection in her life other than the occasional embrace from Nanette. Her aunts, and the old uncles, had been as stiff and distant as the boulders on the tor. The closest physical contact she had ever experienced with a human being was with her new husband, and Morcum was hardly less perfunctory than the billy goat who covered the nannies each year.

Nanette had taken pains to make the best bedroom ready for the new couple. She aired and turned the mattress and spread it with an eiderdown comforter, new goose-down pillows, and sheets of new linen. Before the wedding night, Ursule looked forward to the marriage bed with curiosity. Afterward she was merely bored.

Nanette tried to draw her out, inviting confidences, but Ursule gave a very good imitation of her mother's Gallic shrug and said she didn't see what all the fuss was about.

Whether because of Morcum's workmanlike approach or Ursule's indifference, the marital bed was the only nonproductive aspect of their union. Orchard Farm prospered under their labors. The goats produced so much milk that their cheese production doubled, and they sold their output at both the Thursday and the Saturday markets. Morcum was brilliant in breeding the ponies, and their foals brought top prices. The kitchen garden flourished, and the cold cellar was full of potatoes and corn and beets.

Nanette claimed that Morcum and Ursule managed so much work between them that she felt like the baroness herself, lounging on a chaise all the day and having every need attended to by her servants. Indeed, she began to put on weight, which rounded out her face and her arms. It was gratifying to Ursule to see the lines of care ease in her mother's face.

Ursule, in fact, was content enough. Morcum repaired the thatch and caulked all the windows against the winter winds that battered the farmhouse. When the weather drove him indoors, he always found something to do, replacing cracked floorboards, clearing a clogged flue, shoring up a broken stair. He had no conversation, but Ursule had Nanette for that. They spoke French with each other, out of habit. Morcum took no offense that they could see.

The years passed, three, five, ten, twelve. Wedding anniversaries, even birthdays, went unremarked. Ursule no longer measured the years by Sabbats, but by the farmer's seasons—spring for selling preserves, summer for tilling the crops, fall for breeding and harvesting, winter for carding and sewing and mending. She had not climbed the tor to the temple in years.

She was surprised one morning, going in search of Nanette, to find her mother with a thick, ancient-looking book laid open on her bed.

"*Maman? Qu'est-ce que c'est?*"

Nanette looked up in surprise. Her hands stretched out as if to hide the page. They hovered above the book, fingers splayed, but then withdrew and dropped into her lap. "You know what this is, do you not, Ursule?"

"No. I've never seen that before." Ursule moved closer. The book was even older than she had thought, with fragile pages closely covered in ink that was faded almost past reading. "That's not—Oh! Is that Grand-mère's book?"

"Close the door."

"Morcum is in the byre."

"Just the same. Lock it. I thought I had done that. I must be getting forgetful."

"Maman, you always talk as if you're getting old."

"I am old, Ursule. I'm fifty-two."

"That's not old, it's only..."

Nanette pressed on. "And you're thirty-four. Today, in fact." Ursule's hand flew to her mouth, and Nanette gave a wry smile. "Morcum doesn't notice, does he?"

"Not just Morcum. I didn't notice, either!"

Nanette smoothed the yellowed vellum beneath her hand. "You're such a comfort to me, *ma chère*. I worry that you will have no babe to comfort you when it's your turn to be old."

"I never think of it."

"You should, Ursule. Don't you want a child?"

"There's nothing I can do about it, is there? Sometimes the nannies catch, and sometimes they don't. Some things are out of our control."

"We can at least try," Nanette said, and returned her gaze to the page under her fingers.

Ursule settled gingerly on the bed beside her mother, careful not to jostle the old book. Its pages were wide, and its cover appeared to be made of leather, but so dry it was almost like wood. She leaned over it to see what her mother had been studying. "What does it say? I can't read the French."

"It's Old French. I couldn't understand it if I hadn't studied it before." Nanette pointed to a thready illustration, a vial with several leaves of different shapes poised above it. "This is a potion," she said reverently.

"A potion for what?"

Nanette cast her daughter a wary glance from beneath her silvery eyebrows. "We haven't spoken of this in a long time, Ursule."

"I never think of it anymore."

"It's such a shame you don't believe."

"I don't believe what Morcum does, either, all that about body and blood and salvation."

Nanette's smile returned. "Still, I don't want you to be alone when I'm gone. I want you to have a child for your old age."

"Is that what this potion is for?"

"Yes. You should have a babe to comfort you, as you comfort me. To carry on here at Orchard Farm."

Ursule pointed to the book and said softly, "You don't expect a child of mine to carry on this particular tradition, I hope?"

Nanette's smile faded. "No," she said in a rusty whisper. "No, I used to think so, but now... I expect the craft will die with me."

"But Maman, you're not going to die for a very long time!" Ursule put up her hand to touch her mother's shoulder.

Nanette shook her head. "None of us can know the day. But I feel it coming."

"What does that mean, you feel it coming? How could you?"

"You know the way you feel a storm building over Mount's Bay? How the air seems to vibrate? Your skin tingles, and your hair crackles. It feels something like that."

"I don't believe that, either!"

"*Eh, bien.* It doesn't matter whether I'm right or I'm wrong. Either way, you have Morcum now, and if the Goddess wishes—and if I am strong enough—you will have a babe, too." She let her voice trail off, and laid her hand on the book again.

"Maman, I don't want you going up to the tor alone at night."

"I will be safe," Nanette said.

"You could fall, or..."

"Oh no. The cat will be with me."

"Oh, the blessèd cat!" Ursule expostulated. "He can barely walk himself!" The ancient beast still clung to life, long past any natural life span. Morcum detested it, and threatened often to drown it if it got in his way. "If it matters so much to you, I'll come along."

"No. Morcum mustn't suspect."

"He wouldn't mind, Maman."

"He would!" Nanette stiffened in alarm. "Ursule, you must believe me! Nothing has changed because we've left Brittany. These people still hate us."

"Surely not! Why should they?"

"Because men believe it's their right to tell women how to live. They tell us who to marry, what to wear, when to go out and when to stay. Some men beat their wives, and no one speaks a word about it. But despite all the power they hold over us, they feel powerless against our kind. We resist. We cause things to happen. We interfere with their plans, with what they think is the natural order. That frightens them. Men hate being afraid, so they hate us instead."

"Morcum doesn't hate me."

"He doesn't understand your power."

"I'm not sure I have any."

"Ursule, listen to me! They will pursue us, if they suspect, whether we have the true power or we don't. You haven't seen this, but I have."

"You were only four," Ursule reminded her.

"I remember. I remember the dark, and the cold. The terror."

"Maman—"

"I remember finding Grand-mère." Nanette shivered. "Her eyes were open, staring at the sky, but when I touched her, she was as stiff as the standing stones."

"Oh, Maman." Ursule found her mother's hand and held it. It felt shockingly small and cold in her strong one.

Nanette bent her head. "I started to scream, but they shushed me. The mob was looking for us, and it wasn't safe. I couldn't even cry for Grand-mère."

"I'm so sorry," Ursule whispered.

"Listen to me," Nanette said, passing her hand over her eyes as if she could erase the old memory. "You mustn't trust them, any of them. Not even Morcum."

"Promise me you won't go up to the tor alone."

Nanette cast her a sidelong glance. "Can you slip away without Morcum knowing?"

Ursule squeezed her mother's hand. "I can. I will."

Nanette nodded and closed the book with care. "Very well. Soon, Ursule. We have to go soon. There's no time to waste."

7

Ursule, fearful that her mother would attempt the climb to the temple on her own, made plans with her for the very next night. It wasn't difficult. Morcum worked long days, and when he laid his head on his pillow, he slept soundly until the morning. Ursule waited until he began to snore, then slid out from beneath the comforter in the cold darkness. She had left clothes in Nanette's room, and there she dressed for the cold night.

It reminded her of the days when the uncles were still alive, and the Orchiére sisters prepared in secret, crept out in darkness, and returned in utter silence. Nanette had already gathered her materials, and the two of them went out through the kitchen, closing the door with only a faint creak, then on to the garden gate. They climbed the tor under a gray marine layer that shifted and roiled above them, an ocean of cloud drowning the stars.

They were halfway up the steep slope before Ursule realized her mother was carrying the gray cat in her arms. "Maman, do you mean to carry that nasty creature all the way up and all the way down again?"

Nanette was already breathing hard. She just nodded.

Ursule shifted her bundle and reached for the cat. "I'll carry him, then," she said, "although it seems to me if he can't make the climb on his own he should stay home."

As her fingers touched the rough gray fur, the cat hissed at her, and shrank deeper into Nanette's grasp. "Never mind," Nanette said, her voice thin for lack of breath. "I can manage."

"It's ridiculous," Ursule said, glowering at the cat.

"He knows," Nanette panted, "that you don't like him."

"Not stupid, then," Ursule said tartly.

It was an old argument. The cat had remained with them, nameless, sour-tempered, and aloof. He had learned to stay clear of Morcum's boots, and though Ursule had attempted to befriend him once or twice, the cat would have nothing to do with her. He followed Nanette everywhere, and slept under her bed. He had grown steadily thinner over the years, despite the table scraps Nanette fed him, and his coat remained ragged and coarse. As he got older, one foot began to drag, and he sometimes yowled as if he were in pain. Nanette brewed concoctions to make him comfortable, and wrapped him in blankets against the cold. Morcum suggested that he put the creature out of its misery. It was the single time Ursule saw her mother turn on Morcum, hissing with fury as if she were a cat herself.

Nanette was laboring by the time they reached the top of the tor, but Ursule said nothing more, only stayed close to catch her mother should she stumble. They wound through the dark stone entrance, relieved to be out of the wind. Nanette put the cat down and struck a sulfur match to light the lantern waiting in one of the niches. Its light revealed an accumulation of leaves and twigs and feathers fouling the cave floor, unswept for years. She insisted on cleaning before she began the ceremony, and Ursule helped her, wielding the broom while her mother wiped dust from the pedestal and rubbed grime from Grand-mère's stone. The crystal, with its rounded upper surface and jagged base, looked as timeless as the stalagmite it rested upon.

When the cave—the temple, as Nanette called it—was more or

less clean, Nanette set a thick candle beside the scrying stone and set a flame to the wick. She sprinkled water, burned herbs, and recited the words from the grimoire in a rhythmic singsong, three times three times, following the old ways.

The ritual seemed much as it always had to Ursule, and just as pointless. She yawned, waiting for it to be over so she could return to her bed.

At last, after the chill of the stone walls had begun to make her bones ache, the rite wound down. Nanette's scarf slipped to her shoulders as she bent over the crystal. She laid her hands on it, and she spoke a few more words, not in Old French, but in the French Ursule understood.

Mother Goddess, hear my plea:
Let my daughter blessèd be
With the very gift you gave to me.

The sweet naïveté with which her mother recited the little verse made Ursule's eyes sting with tears. Nanette spoke the rhyme three times three times. When she finished, she stood for a moment, her head bowed over the stone, her palms pressed together before her face.

Sure now that the rite was finished, Ursule moved toward the altar. Before she reached it, the candle's wick guttered in its pool of hot wax and went out.

Nanette pulled the scarf from her shoulders and took a step back.

Ursule, both hands reaching for the stub of the candle, froze.

Something flickered inside the murky crystal, feeble but distinct, like the farthest star in a dark sky. It glowed red, as if an ember had leaped from the candle flame into the depths of the polished stone.

Ursule cried out.

Her mother started and turned to her. "What? What happened?"

Ursule bent to look closer. The light was still there. Nanette's shoulder pressed hers as she, too, gazed into the crystal. The cat pushed between them, twining around their ankles with an insistent hiss.

Stunned, Ursule breathed, "Do you see, Maman?"

Nanette was silent for a long moment. When she spoke, her voice trembled with wonder. "Oh, Ursule. I haven't seen that light in such a very long time."

Ursule straightened, staring at her mother in disbelief. "Did you make that happen? Another candle, or a mirror..."

Nanette gazed back at her daughter, excitement overcoming her fatigue. "Ursule!" she exclaimed. "It speaks to you!"

"What?"

Nanette's voice vibrated now with triumph. "I was right! If only Louisette could see!"

Nanette seized up the scarf she had dropped, and draped it over Ursule's head. "Look again!" she commanded. "Look into Grand-mère's stone! Oh, Ursule! I knew, when you were born—I just *knew*!"

She put her hands on Ursule's chin and turned her face back to the stone. From beneath the hem of the scarf, Ursule peered into it. The light was still there, a glimmering, coruscating spark. It made her feel oddly dizzy, and a vague ache began to spread from her hipbones and up through her spine.

"Now put your hands on the stone. Ask the Goddess!"

"Ask for what?"

"A babe, of course! Ask Her! The crystal is speaking to you. It's Her way!"

Ursule's head spun, but when she put her hands on the stone it steadied, and the light—there was no denying it—the light grew brighter.

"Ask!" Nanette hissed.

But how could she make such a request, she who had always disdained every ritual she observed? Ursule gripped the crystal with her palms, trying to think of what to say and how to say it. Finally she whispered, "A babe. Great Goddess, Mother of Earth, a babe for me."

"Not that way! Let it come to you, let it come through you."

"I don't know how, Maman!"

"You do. It's what Grand-mère did. It's what I used to do. Don't try to think of the words, but when they come to you, speak them. The spoken word holds so much power! You'll see."

Ursule was not convinced, but her mother was gazing at her with shining eyes, her hands linked together under her chin in an age-old gesture of supplication. Ursule wished she had time to think this through. She could at least go through the motions, she decided. She expected nothing, but then, she had never expected to see anything in the old stone.

She moved her hands a little apart and gazed into it once again. The faint, flickering light, like a lamp in the darkness, still shone. It was, she thought, like a light left in a window, to call a traveler home. She felt the rush of energy in her backbone, in her thighs, in her hands. The rush of power. Of magic.

A moment later the words were in her mind. She didn't trust them, or believe in them, but they were there. They issued from her mouth almost without her volition:

Mother Goddess, hear my plea:
Though I all unworthy be
Let there be a babe for me.

She glanced up and saw her mother's face aglow with hope, and with the faith she herself did not possess. Nanette said, joyously, "Again, Ursule! Three times three times!"

Ursule did as she asked, reciting the bit of verse again and again, until she had fulfilled the proper repetitions. Then, silently, she added to her prayer: *To please Maman.*

8

Despite Nanette's hopefulness, and despite Ursule's efforts to entice her husband more frequently to the pleasures of the marriage bed, nothing happened. Yule came and went, though Ursule was careful to call it Christmas, following Morcum's tradition. Then there was Candlemas, and the dark days of Lent, a time when Morcum flatly refused all Ursule's advances. He relented after Easter, but still Ursule did not conceive.

She worried more over her mother than over her lack of pregnancy. Nanette was growing thin again, and the last remaining dark strands of her hair turned to silver. There came a day when a bucket brimful of milk was too heavy for her to lift, and then a day when even an hour of weeding the kitchen garden stole her breath, and she had to sit down in the shade. By Pentecost she had given up even churning butter. She spent her days sewing or reading at the kitchen table. The gray cat lay across her feet as if she might float away if he didn't hold her in place.

Every month she asked Ursule if there was any sign yet, and each time, when Ursule shook her head, Nanette seemed to wither a little bit more. She refused to see a doctor, and refused Ursule's efforts to get her to eat more, or sleep longer. She ceased speaking to Morcum, as if it were all his fault. The blessing, Ursule thought, was that Morcum didn't appear to notice.

"You must go back," Nanette said one morning, when Morcum was off on Aramis to look at a pony he was thinking of buying.

"Go back where, Maman?"

"To the temple. To ask the Goddess again."

"There's no point," Ursule said.

"There is! The crystal responded to you. You must give Her another chance."

"If She's there, I'm afraid She knows I don't believe."

"You have to try, Ursule," Nanette said. "I can no longer climb the tor. It has to be you."

"I don't know the rite, Maman."

"It's in Grand-mère's book. There are written rites and spoken rites. I'll show you."

Ursule didn't want to do it, but Nanette persisted. Her body was failing, but her spirit was strong. She won out in the end. Ursule told herself she was giving in only for her mother's sake as she found herself, one moonlit night in August, climbing the tor with a strong step. It had been a day of blazing sun, and the cool night air was invigorating. With no one to slow her down, she reached the top more swiftly than she ever had.

Following Nanette's instructions, she gave the floor of the cave a cursory sweep, and gingerly dusted off the pedestal and wiped the scrying stone, but carefully, not looking into it. She opened her pack of things and performed each of the tasks in order, lighting the candle, sprinkling the water, burning sprigs of heather and rosemary and sage. Puffs of sweet-smelling smoke circled around her, then rose to dissipate into the shadows as she pulled a scarf over her head and faced the stone. Nanette had found the rite in the grimoire, the spell for conception, and made her repeat the words a dozen times until they were memorized.

They faded from her mind the moment she looked into the dark center of the crystal. It was there again, that beckoning spark. She leaned forward, one hand pressed to her mouth, and it swelled as if a bellows had been applied to a flame. It rose and brightened until the whole interior of the stone glowed. Ursule stared at it, not realizing she was biting her forefinger until it began to ache.

She straightened, and the scarf slipped from her hair to pool about her feet. The words of the ancient rite filled her head, thundering to be released. She spoke them in a voice that quivered with excitement. The cave resounded so that her words cascaded back to her, piling upon one another in a mystic, manic harmony.

Mother Goddess, hear my prayer:
Send to me a child to bear.
Whither it comes I do not care,
So long as it be strong and fair.

Three times three she proclaimed it, urged on by instinct, an instinct as old as motherhood itself. After she stopped, as the echoes faded around her, she still gazed into the stone, mesmerized. Was that a face in the glimmering light? A woman? For an instant she thought someone looked back at her, someone with a halo of grizzled hair and deep black eyes. Holding her breath, she leaned closer, but she couldn't be sure. She searched through the light, but the image faded and disappeared as the stone gradually darkened and the light died away. Still Ursule stood, unable to tear her eyes from the scrying stone. Not until the candle guttered out did she rouse and shake herself.

As she bent to pick up the dropped scarf, to gather her things and make her way out of the cave, she remembered her Tante Louisette's scorn. Louisette might have accused her of inventing the entire scene, of pretending for Nanette's sake, but Ursule knew better now. This was not her imagination. This was not a fantasy. Her spine thrummed with it, the power of magic rushing through her bones from her toes to her skull.

She was as hardheaded a woman as any she knew, and more practical than most. She had seen what she had seen, and felt what she had felt. This was real. It would be foolish to deny it.

The moon was gone, and dawn outlined the horizon to the east as Ursule found the path and made the descent as quickly as she could. Morcum would be awake soon. She had no way to explain where she had been, or what she had been doing. And now—now that this had happened, that she had seen what the crystal could do—she was changed. She had to hide that from Morcum, to appear the same as she had always been.

What did it all mean? she wondered. And what would happen next?

⁓✤⁓

It hardly seemed possible that, after her experience in the temple, life could go on as usual. Everything looked different. The work of Orchard Farm, the calls of her stock, the knowing look on her mother's face, all these things acquired significance beyond the mundane. Only Morcum—stolid, blunt, hardworking Morcum—was unchanged. For the first time in the years of her marriage, Ursule chafed at his predictability, his rigid routines, his indifference.

And so it was that when she met Sebastien, she was vulnerable. She was ready.

She went to the Thursday market in Marazion on her own, driving the jingle with Aramis in the harness. She left Nanette simmering blackberries for jam, and Morcum scything grass in the ponies' pasture.

The market was lively, the green crowded with kiosks and stands hawking fruit and vegetables, cider and bread and smoked meats. Ursule took care to arrive early so she could back the jingle into a good spot, release Aramis from his harness, and tether him where he could crop grass and drink from a bucket she set beneath a tree. She raised the gay blue-and-white canopy Nanette had made, and dropped the back of the jingle for access to her produce. She had a capacious purse beneath her apron in anticipation of a profitable day, and she arranged her wares in appealing piles—vivid red radishes, dark-green bundles of spinach, paler watercress, bunches of orange carrots with their feathery tops tied with twine.

The cleverest housewives came early for the first pick of the farmers' wares. By midmorning Ursule had almost sold out. She stepped to a nearby kiosk, where one of the bakers of Marazion was selling pasties, and bought herself one, hot and fragrant, wrapped in a napkin. When she turned back toward the jingle, she saw a man waiting beside it.

She was sure she had never seen him before, which was odd. Few strangers found their way into the Thursday market. Outsiders, from Penzance or St Ives, mostly came on Saturdays, when the jewelry makers and seamstresses set up their tents.

Ursule eyed the man as she approached. The warm pasty in her hands steamed in the fresh air, and a breeze teased strands of her hair from beneath her cap. She startled herself with a sudden wish that she had worn a newer dress, and a better pair of boots. She had to suppress an urge to take off her apron, which was clean, but stained from packing vegetables.

"Good day to you, sir," she said when she was close enough. She moved forward to set the pasty inside the jingle, and wiped her hands as she turned to face him. "Is there something you'd like?"

He snatched off his flat cap to reveal a shock of fine straight hair the color of straw. Holding the cap to his breast, he bowed slightly. *"Bonjour, mademoiselle."*

Ursule drew breath to correct him, to tell him she was *madame*, but then, her lips parted and her cheeks warming, she let the words die unspoken.

He was a slight man, and no taller than herself. His eyes were a silver gray, a color she had never seen before, with long pale lashes. His cheeks were clean shaven and unlined, and even his neck, where she could see it above his neckcloth, was smooth. The hand that pressed his cap to his chest was fine-fingered. His smile widened under her regard, revealing white, straight teeth. Ursule was lost.

In impeccable French he said, "I was told you make the best goat's cheese in Cornwall. I hoped you might have some to sell."

Ursule could hardly hear his voice above the rush of her hastening pulse. She blinked, trying to recover herself, and said in a rush, "*Oui, monsieur, bien sûr.*" Flustered in a way she had never been in her life, she turned toward the front of the jingle, where she kept a few wrapped cheeses in a lidded basket. She stood on tiptoe to draw one out, and drew a breath to compose herself. She told herself he could not possibly be as handsome as she had first thought. She lifted her chin as she turned back to him, ready to resume the businesslike manner she used with all her customers. "*Le voici, monsieur,*" she said. She held out the cheese and lifted her eyes to his face again.

It was no use. He was almost too handsome, with a delicate nose and a finely cut chin. She collected herself enough to name a price, and he replaced his cap so he could plunge his hand into his pocket for the money. As he placed the coins in her hand, the touch of his skin sent a thrill up her arm.

"How did you know I speak French?"

"A guess. You look French—dark hair, those eyes…"

She feared her cheeks had gone as red as her radishes.

"*Je m'appelle Sebastien,*" he said. He spoke in a normal tone of voice, but he contrived to make the simple introduction as inti-mate as if he had whispered it into her ear.

Or perhaps she imagined that. Pragmatic, practical Ursule was shaken to her toes by the utterly unfamiliar feeling of infatuation. Her hands were busy with cheese and money, but her mind and her heart both raced. She managed to say, "Ursule," but nothing else.

Another customer approached, and she had to turn away to take her payment. When she had counted the money into her purse, she turned back, but Sebastien had disappeared.

She clicked her tongue, embarrassed by the wave of disappoint-ment that swept over her. She reached for her pasty, cooling now in its napkin, and started toward the clump of elm trees edging the green, where she usually sat in the shade to eat her midday meal. As she approached, the beautiful Sebastien reappeared. He held a cup of cider in each hand.

"I guessed you would be thirsty," he said. "And I hoped you wouldn't mind if I kept you company." He nodded to the pasty. "I doubt you've eaten anything today."

"A bit of bread and butter as I drove here," she admitted. "Thank you." She found a place to sit beneath one of the deep-boughed trees, and rested her back against its trunk. She wished she could take off her boots to cool her hot feet, but she was loath to reveal the state of her stockings. She accepted the cup of cider and drained half of it immediately. "I was more thirsty than I knew," she said.

Sebastien gave her his white smile and tossed back his own cider in one long draft. "Best to drink it while it's cold," he said. "Now, Mademoiselle Ursule, you eat your pasty while I do the talking. I'll tell you everything there is to know about me, and when you've done with your meal, you can tell me all about yourself."

Ursule filled her mouth with pastry and meat filling, managing to postpone, once again, correcting him. She chewed, and drank cider, and listened to Sebastien's easy chatter. She couldn't imagine how anyone could be so comfortable with someone he had just met, so sure of the reception he would get. Was that because he was beautiful? Was every woman happy to sit and listen to him talk?

She was confident enough when haggling over the price of cheese or a pony to add to Orchard Farm's herd. But this—this was different.

She supposed, if she herself were beautiful to look at, she might have such confidence in meeting a stranger, talking with him, sharing a drink. She had never given much thought to whether she was fair or plain. She thought more of her goats' appearance than her own, brushing them, washing their muddy feet, tugging burrs from their beards.

Sebastien said, "I'm a traveling musician, Mademoiselle Ursule. A jongleur, who sings and plays the harp wherever audiences gather. I was born in Paris, and made my way here by following a troupe of jugglers and acrobats."

The harp, Ursule thought. With her mouth full, she gazed at his slender fingers, and forgot to chew for several seconds. No wonder his hands were so clean. Just looking at the trimmed nails and the spotless cuffs at his wrists made her heart flutter. Morcum's hands were forever stained with dirt and coal, the nails black rimmed and jagged, because he cut them with a knife.

"And so," he was saying, "I found myself on St. Michael's Mount, singing for the lord's family and teaching the harp to his children. My troupe went on without me, and I've stayed all the summer."

Ursule could picture it. The baron and his family were said to live in fine rooms, furnished with carpets and heavy furniture, with a pianoforte and a clavichord for the young ladies to play upon. She had never seen any of the St. Aubyns, but she could imagine them, richly dressed, elegant in their speech and manners. The baron must have been glad of the chance to have a well-spoken Frenchman tutor his daughters in an unusual instrument.

She made herself swallow the last of her pasty and dabbed at her mouth with the napkin. Sebastien had fallen silent, lying propped on one elbow just at her feet. He twinkled up at her as she folded the napkin. "Your turn," he said. "I want to know all about the *mademoiselle* with the beautiful black curls and enchanting sloe eyes."

Ursule sighed and spread her hands. "There is nothing to tell, in truth, except that it's not *mademoiselle*. It's *madame*. I am Madame Cardew, née Orchiére, of Orchard Farm."

Sebastien clutched at his chest in mock grief. "*Madame!* But no, you are too young and too lovely to be a farmwife!"

Ursule laughed. "I am old and work worn, sir, and you knew already I was a farmwife by the wares in my wagon. That big lad over there—" She pointed to Aramis cropping grass at the far side of the green. "That is my—our—horse, and when the last of my produce is gone, I shall hitch him up again and drive back up the road that runs along the cliff."

"I'll go with you!"

A laugh bubbled from Ursule's throat. "And what should I tell my husband and my mother about my new friend? That he comes to play his harp for us?"

"You could do that." He chuckled and gestured with his thumb. "My harp is in my room at the inn, just there."

"I would love to hear you play, Sebastien. But not at Orchard Farm." Ursule's cheeks burned anew at her own daring. She had to look away, fidgeting at the hem of her apron with nervous fingers.

"Will you wait? I can fetch my harp *toute de suite*."

"I don't know... You won't play here, surely?"

He leaped to his feet in a movement so graceful she had to catch her breath. *"Mais, bien sûr, mademois*—I mean to say *madame!"* He was gone, dashing across the green like an impetuous boy.

No doubt he was a boy, or at the least several years younger than her own thirty-four. Ursule felt a rush of shame at her behavior. She was no naive girl, to be flirting with a traveling minstrel! She was a married woman, with responsibilities. Now that Sebastien had disappeared, taking his glorious smile and beautiful hands with him, she would take herself in hand, like one of the green ponies in need of discipline.

She got up from the ground more slowly than Sebastien had, and smoothed her apron over her skirt. She returned to the wagon to gather up the things she hadn't sold, tucking them into baskets for the return journey. She put up the rear panel and crossed the grass to Aramis.

When she came back, with the big stallion's head nodding above her shoulder, Sebastien had also returned, and was carrying a small harp made of shining dark wood, strung with catgut and bristling with tuning pegs. Ursule stopped so abruptly that Aramis's chest bumped her back.

Sebastien jumped up onto the corner of the wagon frame, with the vegetable baskets at his feet. He settled the harp across his lap. He struck one string, then another, and twisted pegs until he had the sound he wanted. He smiled at Ursule, tucked his chin, and began to play.

The only music Ursule ever heard was the music sometimes sung at Mass. One of Meegan's boys played a whistle, but there had been no music at Orchard Farm, ever. No one sang or hummed. Even the chants in the temple were tuneless. Now Sebastien's fine fingers plucked and strummed, and he began to croon a tune, something simple and sweet, a melody that turned and turned again, harmonizing with the fragile sound of the strings.

The music filled Ursule's ears. She found herself closing her eyes, leaning back against Aramis, listening with all the intensity she could muster. The sheer beauty of it, with the sun slanting across the green and a gentle breeze rising, made tears well beneath her closed eyelids.

And in her head words sounded, as if borne on the slender tide of music:

This one, Ursule. This one will give you a babe.

—⁂—

It wasn't what Nanette had intended, Ursule knew. What her mother had meant was for Morcum to sire a child on his wife in the proper way, a babe they would both love and who would care for them in their old age.

But Nanette had also said the Goddess had her own ways. Ursule understood, before the day was out, that it was true.

Sebastien invited her to come with him to his room at the inn, but Ursule shook her head. She was known in the village. Everyone would see her. Word of her transgression would fly on the wind to Morcum's ears, doubtless even before she reached home.

Sebastien chuckled as he wrapped his harp. "At least let me ride with you along the cliff. I want to see you driving your great gray horse with your curls flying and your eyes shining."

Ursule gazed into his silvery eyes and remembered the words spoken in her mind. Her skin tingled with the wish—no, the need—to touch him. Her belly ached with the desire to press against him, to possess his beauty and his music and his lovely manners.

She knew what he was asking. She knew what she was doing when she fastened Aramis's harness, stepped up onto the bench, and nodded to Sebastien to climb into the back. She felt eyes upon her, but she hoped they would assume she was giving a traveler a lift, something she could explain to Morcum. Sebastien stayed in the back, perched among the empty baskets, until they were well out of sight of the village.

The sun was setting behind them as Aramis pulled the wagon along the road. The water beyond the cliff to their right had gone glassy and smooth. In the waning light it was precisely the shade of Sebastien's eyes. The breeze had sharpened by the time they reached the lay-by. It cooled Aramis's withers and rump as he stood, switching his tail, while Ursule and Sebastien climbed down a little way to a level place Ursule knew.

There was an outcropping of rock that blocked the wind, and a flat surface of fine sand punctuated by clumps of sea grass. Ursule and Sebastien took shelter there. She would be late. Nanette and Morcum would be looking for her from the kitchen windows or the garden gate. But when Sebastien smoothed a place for her to sit, and then to lie down, when he stroked her cheeks with his fine fingers, then touched her breast through her homespun dress, she banished all thoughts of her husband, or her mother, or the chores awaiting her.

Sebastien did not hurry. He kissed her lips and her eyes and her throat. He held her gently, patiently, not lifting her skirts until she began to writhe against him, her desire erasing her shyness. When his body found hers, when he lifted himself so he could press into her, she gasped in wonder as if she were an untouched maiden. Her body melted beneath him, opened to receive him, welcomed every movement and every sensation.

It was nothing like lying with Morcum, that routine sense of a task to be accomplished, disposed of as quickly as might be. Sebastien took his time. He savored her, holding her thighs with his hands, kissing her breast, urging her to an intensity she had never experienced, had never known existed.

The sea sang beneath their shelter. The wind encircled it, blow-

ing from every direction, Cornish fashion. The sand of their bed
was soft and yielding. Ursule cried out, a long, ecstatic cry that
made Aramis whicker from his place above them. Sebastien, too,
gave a cry, deep in his throat, and it was over.

But Sebastien was not Morcum. He was not the billy who
covered his doe, then turned to cropping grass as if nothing of
importance had taken place.

Sebastien held her and murmured sweet things into her hair.
He said her name, again and again. He stroked her belly and
kissed her forehead. As darkness fell around them, he took her
again, with such sweetness she thought she could die of it. They
lay in their bower of sand and stone and sea grass until the stars
began to prick the deep blackness above them.

Ursule shivered, and sat up to draw her clothes back into order.
Sebastien did the same, and gave her his hand to help her stand.
Without speaking, but with many touches and soft glances, they
climbed back up the path to the lay-by. Aramis snorted when he
saw them, and stamped his feet with impatience.

"He wants his box and his oats," Ursule said. The impending
farewell tightened her throat. "Sebastien, I have to go."

"I know you do." He spoke close to her ear, and kissed it.
"Remember me, Ursule."

She could barely speak for the pain beginning to swell in her
chest. She choked, "I could never forget."

He kissed her again, on the forehead this time. "Nor will I. My
love songs will all be for you." He squeezed her hand and looked
once more into her eyes before he spun and trotted back down the
road toward Marazion.

Ursule went to Aramis's head and shed the tears of parting
against his broad neck. She wept for a while, until Aramis dropped
his chin to bump her shoulder, making her laugh through her

tears. "All right, Aramis. I know." She was still sobbing, but smiling, too. She patted the horse's smooth, warm skin and thought of Sebastien's smooth, warm hands with a piercing pang of loss. At last, resignedly, she swallowed the last of her tears and turned toward the wagon to gather up the reins. "All right, Aramis. We'll go home."

9

Morcum, when he heard the wagon rumbling down the lane at last, strode toward the byre to meet them. "Ursula, what happened? You're three hours past your usual time! Your mother is frantic!"

Ursule could see that he was frantic, too, though he would never admit to such a feeling. She tried to feel some sort of shame, but it seemed she had left all such emotions in the little shelter below the cliff. With a deftness that surprised her, she lied. "It was a loose wheel, Morcum. It wasn't safe for Aramis. I stopped to repair it, and then I got worried the other was loose, so I worked on it, too. It was hard in the dark."

"I'm that sorry, Ursula. I should have checked them. You go have your supper. I'll see to Aramis."

At last a twinge of remorse wriggled in Ursule's breast, but it flickered and died almost at once. She was sorry to have frightened her mother, though. When she stepped into the bright kitchen from the cold dark, she faced Nanette with the excuse ready on her lips.

She never spoke it. There was no need. Her mother took one look at her and her hands flew to her mouth. "Oh, Ursule!" she breathed.

"What? What is it?"

"I can see—why, it's written all over your face!"

Ursule put her hands to her hair, as if that would set things to rights. "How could that be, Maman? Nothing should show on my face. Morcum didn't—"

"*Pfft!* Morcum! He sees nothing! What have you done?"

Ursule unwrapped her scarf from her head and pulled it through her fingers. Through dry lips she whispered, "I'm not sure."

Nanette held out her arms, and Ursule, with a shuddering sigh, stepped into them. She embraced her mother and held her tight for a moment, whispering into her cloud of silver hair. "I'm not sure it was my own doing." She felt Nanette tremble in her arms, and she hugged her tighter. "It will be all right. Don't worry."

"Oh, Ursule! You must make sure...You must convince Morcum..."

"I know. I will."

They heard Morcum's heavy tread on the porch and pulled apart. Nanette went to the stove and ladled a bowlful of soup, setting it on the table with a half loaf of bread and a crock of freshly churned butter. Ursule did her best to eat, but she felt tender, fragile, as if she had been injured in some way. She had to force herself to speak to Morcum as usual, to elaborate on the loose wheel, the place where it had happened, how hard it had been to repair. She gave an account of the market, and set the purse on the table so Morcum could count their earnings.

When it was time to retire, Ursule turned toward the bedroom with dragging steps. She felt her mother's gaze on her as distinctly as if Nanette had put both hands on her back and pushed. Weary though she was, and still sore at heart, she tried. She washed herself carefully, and put on a fresh nightdress scented with the lavender sachet she kept in her cupboard. She brushed her hair till it flowed like ribbons of silk around her shoulders. She slipped beneath the covers next to her husband. His back was to her, but she put a hand on his hip, and slid close to him so that her breasts grazed his shoulder blades.

She felt his heavy sigh through her palm. "I'm tired, Ursula," he groaned.

"It's been so long, Morcum," she murmured.

"Yes."

"It's been too long." She pressed herself closer. "I can't remember the last time..."

"No." He yawned. "That's the way things are, lass. You married an old man."

At his words a faint shock ran through her, and she lifted her hand with an abrupt movement. She pulled sharply away to her own side of the bed, and turned on her side to gaze into the darkness. In moments Morcum was snoring with the resonant rumble of a sound sleeper.

Ursule lay awake for a long time, wishing the man lying next to her were Sebastien. Even the thought of him made her stomach contract and her breathing quicken. If only, if only...

But she knew better. Longing for what could never be would not solve her problem.

She had set her course. She could hold Sebastien in her memory, but she did not expect to meet him again. What she must do, somehow, was rouse Morcum to his duty.

It became a task for the two of them, mother and daughter. Nanette presented Ursule with a newly sewn nightdress, made of fine cotton so thin it was nearly transparent. Ursule bathed more often than usual, especially when she had been working in the byre. She washed her hair, and dried it in the autumn sunshine so it curled fetchingly around her face. Nanette climbed down the steep path

to the beach and lugged up a basket of oysters to prompt Morcum
to some marital urge. Ursule took care to smile pleasantly around
her husband, to tease him, to draw him out when they were at
supper or when they had occasion to be together on the moor.

None of it answered. Ursule commanded Morcum's attention
more by brushing Aramis's mane and tail than by brushing her
own hair. He took more notice of new twin kids than he did
of her new nightdress. He fell into his bed like a dead man each
night, and slept the heavy sleep of the tired and just.

"I suppose he has always been like this," Ursule said to her
mother as they wrapped a new batch of cheese and set it to age in
the cold cellar. "I'm the one who's different."

"When will you know, Ursule?"

"I know now," Ursule said shortly. "I can feel it. I sense her."

"Her? Are you sure?"

Ursule folded the last flap of cheesecloth under and straightened. "Oh yes. The Orchiéres do produce a preponderance of
females, but it's not that. I know her already, though my stomach
doesn't yet swell."

"It will soon enough. There's no time to waste."

"I don't know what else I can do."

Nanette pushed the wheel of cheese into its place on the shelf,
deep under the hill, where it would stay cool until it was ready.
She turned, wiping her hands on her apron. "I will make you a
potion," she said.

"Morcum will never drink it."

"Morcum will never know."

Morcum announced he would drive the goats up to the moor for
the last of the summer grass. Ursule prepared a packet of bread
and cheese and beer, and sent him off with a smile. The instant

he was gone, Nanette brought out the grimoire and opened it on the kitchen table. Ursule puzzled out the archaic French as her mother ran back and forth between the pantry and the garden, now beginning to sleep for the winter, but still offering a few fading herbs and a clutch of garlic scapes. She found mistletoe and coltsfoot, lovage roots and lady's mantle and mullein. The potion simmered on the stove all day, reducing to just a few tablespoons of pungent syrup. It was supposed to rest on the altar for a night, but there was no time. Nanette stewed a rabbit with onions and potatoes and carrots. She hid the potion inside a cupboard, and at supper she slipped it—all of it—into Morcum's serving of stew. It amazed Ursule that he didn't rebel at the flavor. Perhaps the beer he had drunk with his packet of sandwiches had dulled his taste, or perhaps the onions in the stew masked it.

He woke Ursule very late that same night, after she had been asleep for hours. She cried out in surprise and alarm as he fell upon her. He used her with less ceremony than a moor stallion mounting one of his mares, violently, quickly. When it was over he fell back, pushing her away with an expression of disgust, as if it had been she who'd savaged him instead of the other way round.

She thought, for a moment, that all would be well. It had been unpleasant, but it was done. It had been accomplished just in time for him to be convinced he was the father of the baby that would come in the spring.

But Morcum was as shocked by his sudden passion as she had been. As she lay back on her pillow, breathing hard and trying to straighten her nightdress, he seized her wrist. "What did you do, Ursula?" he growled. "What have you done to me?"

"Morcum," she protested, trying to tug herself free of his big fist. "I did nothing!"

"What was it?" he demanded, his voice rising. "Something unnatural!"

The fury in his voice, the hate in the gleam of his eyes, half-seen in faint moonlight, chilled Ursule's blood. All her mother's warnings came back to her in a flood, and she struggled away from Morcum with her heart racing. "Where did you get such an idea? Why should a husband not want to lie with his wife?"

"I do want to lie with my wife. Sometimes. Not wake from a sound sleep with an urge to rape her."

"You didn't—it wasn't like that." She put her hand on his arm, but he threw it off.

"They warned me," he said. He shoved back the quilt and stood up. He was naked, his body a dully visible shape in the first light of coming dawn, bulky and beast-like.

The contrast to Sebastien, with his fine bones and slim hips, was unbearable.

Ursule, with a tiny groan, averted her eyes.

Morcum, who she would have sworn was sensitive to nothing, took notice.

"Don't like what you see?" he spit at her.

A wave of revulsion swept her, and left her trembling with anger. "No," she said tightly. "At this moment, Morcum, no."

"All these weeks you've been after me, trying to tempt me with your fancy nightdress and your oysters. You got what you wanted, and now you can't stand the sight of me."

It was true enough. She fussed with her nightdress, then stood up on her side of the bed, keeping her eyes away from him. When she looked at him again, he had pulled on a shirt and trousers, and stood with his hands on his hips and his jaw jutting.

Ursule turned her back, but he came around the bed in two swift steps to grab her with his heavy hands. The delicate night-dress tore along the bodice, but he paid no attention. He shook her hard, the way a terrier shakes a rat. He grated, "They warned me, all those years ago! I should have listened!"

Ursule was strong, a woman used to lifting and digging, but Morcum was stronger. She tried to pull free of his iron grip, but he held on. "Tell me!" he commanded, and shook her again.

"Tell you what, Morcum? Let me go!"

"What did you do to me?"

"Nothing, I've already said!"

"Then your mother! Just as they said!"

Ursule felt the first shivers of real terror, and her voice scraped in her throat. "What are you talking about? I don't know what you're talking about!"

He released her with a little shove, so she stumbled and stepped on the hem of the nightdress, which tore again. They glared at each other. Beyond the window the stars had begun to fade, and the air in their bedroom was ice cold.

Bitterly Morcum said, "My brothers said you were witches, all of you, descended from witches, birthing witches. That's why they wouldn't come to our wedding, though I swore it wasn't true." He leaned toward her, his hot breath sour with fury. "But it is true, isn't it, Ursula? Your mother is a witch, and she poisoned me so I—so I would act like an *animal!*"

Ursule's temper flared at that. "So you would act like a *husband!*" she snapped, then gasped, and covered her mouth with both hands. At the movement her nightdress parted into two pieces, and fell in shreds around her feet.

Morcum, with a hoarse cry of triumph, pointed his thick finger at her. "You admit it!"

"No!" she shrilled. "I do not! It's ridiculous!"

His hand closed into a fist, and he raised it as if he would strike her. She stood, naked and shivering, and closed her eyes. *Let him do it*, she prayed. *Let him hit me, and then he'll feel better. Let all this be over. Oh, Goddess, I didn't mean to say it, I didn't mean to . . .*

If there was anyone to hear her prayer, she would never know.

The blow didn't come, and when she opened her eyes, Morcum was gone.

She ran to the door, still naked, to follow him. She met only Nanette, standing in the hall barefoot, clutching her dressing gown around her. The front door stood open to the freezing dawn. Of Morcum there was no sign at all.

10

I have to stay, Maman," Ursule said, her voice tight with tension. "I can't leave my animals."

"No, Ursule," Nanette whispered. She was throwing things into a valise so ancient it looked as if it might have come over on the boat from Brittany. The gray cat leaped up onto the bed and paced from side to side, his tail twitching. Nanette closed the valise and tied its frayed ribbons. "You must come with me. Morcum won't let the animals come to harm, but you..."

"He would never hurt me, Maman. Not really."

"You think not? I heard him shouting at you!"

"He lost his temper."

"Ursule, listen to me." Nanette leaned on the valise with both hands. Her voice shook. "You haven't seen them coming after us, their faces full of hate and their torches burning. You haven't heard the screams of women being stripped and searched for signs of witchcraft, the shrieks of women burning alive."

"Maman—you haven't seen such things, surely!"

"I have heard the stories all my life," Nanette said, so hoarsely Ursule could barely hear her. "I was a child, but I remember those people, hunting for us, searching for someone to blame, someone to accuse. They hated us—or hated the idea of us."

"Even if that's true—"

"Of course it's true!"

"But this isn't Brittany, it's Cornwall. Farmers and villagers we know. Neighbors!"

"Who never speak to us if they can avoid it."

"They speak to me!"

"You can't trust them." Nanette lifted her valise and turned to the door. "I've had nightmares about burning all my life," she said.

"You never told me that."

"I never thought you needed to know."

"I'll protect you, Maman."

"You can't. I did what I did, and Morcum knows it. They will come after me, and there won't be anything you can do."

Ursule hugged herself against the cold. "But where will you go?"

Nanette turned in the doorway, and Ursule saw that her face was gray with fear. "For now, up the tor. I'll hide in the temple. Come with me!"

"I can't," Ursule cried. "My goats, and the ponies..." She was interrupted by the sound of hooves on the dirt lane, and the ringing of bells on a jingle, deeper than the sound their own jingle made. She covered her mouth with one hand as her heart lurched.

Nanette slumped against the doorframe. "Too late," she moaned. "Oh, Goddess, they've caught me..."

"No, no! Go now," Ursule reached for Nanette and urged her toward the door. "Go down through the garden! Use the paddock gate. I'll... I'll talk to them. Tell them you've gone away. I'll come up to you later."

Nanette, though she trembled so she could hardly stay on her feet, gathered up her bag and turned toward the kitchen door. Just as she reached for the latch, the door exploded inward, jarring off its lower hinge. Morcum, glowering with fury, filled the doorway with his bulk.

Nanette fell back, and her legs crumpled. She sagged to the floor, her valise in her hands, tears of terror streaking her face. The cat pressed itself against her.

Morcum took a mighty swipe with his heavy boot to kick the cat away. It hit the side of the stove with a sickening thud and lay still.

Ursule shouted, "Morcum!" and strode forward.

"Get back," he snarled. He smacked her with his elbow so hard that she, too, fell. His big hands reached down for his mother-in-law and hauled her to her feet. She whimpered with panic, but he paid no attention. Ursule scrambled up, grasping at his arms, screaming threats and imprecations, but he ignored that, too. He pulled Nanette out through the broken door as if she weighed nothing at all.

When Nanette appeared on the porch step, a clamor of voices rose, darkening the crystal morning air as if a thunderstorm had swept down from the moor. Ursule, still clawing at her husband's hard hands, shook with horror.

They were her neighbors, these men, people she had known all her life, but at this moment they were strangers. They were the monsters of nightmare, perhaps a dozen of them, their faces distorted, their voices shrill as cawing crows. Morcum dragged Nanette out to them as he might deliver a sheep for slaughter. They seized her with their brutal hands and bundled her into their waiting cart. Some were on foot, and some rode ponies. One drove the cart, and two more jumped into the back to hold Nanette.

Ursule tried to push past Morcum to get to her mother, but he seized her around the neck with his hairy forearm and squeezed her under his elbow until she couldn't breathe. Nanette ceased struggling. She slumped between her two captors, her head falling forward, her hands hanging nervelessly from her wrists. Ursule, struggling for air, could not even cry out her name.

The whole hideous scene took no more than ninety seconds, and was seared into Ursule's memory forever.

As the cart set off down the lane, Morcum shoved her aside with a grunt. She cried his name, and called her mother's, but neither he nor the other men—nor even Nanette, collapsed between her guards in the back of the cart—responded. In moments the cart, the men following it, and Morcum himself had disappeared. His final gesture to his wife was a shaken fist, and an order to stay where she was.

Ursule hurried back into the house to fetch boots and a coat. The goats had begun to bleat, and the ponies stamped nervously in the paddock, disturbed by the shouts in the lane. Ursule had no choice but to ignore them. She seized the crock where she kept her market-day money and scooped all of it into her pockets before she raced to the byre to throw a halter on Aramis. She cinched a blanket around his broad back and stood on the mounting stool to get up. It hurt her heart to leave her goats crying to be milked, but it hurt far worse to think of her mother fainting, bumping along in a cart with neither cushion nor coat.

Ursule could think of only one person to turn to, and it wouldn't be easy. She would have to beg Father Maddock to intervene.

She put her heels to Aramis's ribs and urged him into his ponderous trot.

❧

St. Hilary Church had never seemed so cold and unwelcoming as it did on that awful morning. Ursule left Aramis tethered on the cobbled street and pushed open the heavy door to the sanctuary. The church was empty, and her footsteps made forlorn echoes against the stone walls and the arched ceiling. She ran to the sacristy, but the door was locked, and pounding her fists on it brought no answer. She had to run outside again, around to the back, where Father Maddock had his rooms. She dashed up the short stair to knock on that door, too, again without result. Just as she turned to go back down the steps, the bell sounded from the campanile with a thunderous gong that made her bones ache.

There was a commotion on the green, a short distance from the church. With thudding heart and trembling hands, Ursule led Aramis in that direction. Just beyond the corner of the inn, where its sign swung over the street, she hesitated. The men who had come to Orchard Farm were clustered on the site where the market would set up. The cart that had borne her mother away was parked under the trees, the pony's reins tossed negligently onto the ground and the pony himself cropping grass. Other townspeople, women, old men, even a few children, had joined the crowd, and at its center Ursule spied Father Maddock in his cassock and collar. He held a Bible in one raised hand, and he was shouting, but the wind whirled his words away.

Ursule didn't need to hear. His intent, and his rage, were all too clear.

A knot of men around the priest turned as one, like a flock of ugly birds, and thrust through the crowd toward the church. Ursule stepped behind the drooping branches of a dead elm tree to watch them make their way to a door she hadn't seen, which led down into the basement. Father Maddock followed them and closed the door behind him with a stern glance at the crowd outside.

An old woman in an apron crowed to a companion, "They'll find out now! They'll see the mark of the witch!"

Ursule stepped out from behind the branches that were hiding her and stared at the woman in shock. "What did you say?" she demanded. "What mark of the witch?"

The old woman cackled, a vicious sound that turned Ursule's

stomach. "Don't you know?" she cried with relish. "All witches have an extra teat! They hide it under their clothes!"

Her companion, slightly younger, with a thick-featured face and a drooping bosom, emitted a scornful laugh. "All us knew it all along, din't we, Pansy? All us knew those old women out to Orchard Farm was witches!"

"Why do you say that?" Ursule demanded, but weakly. Her legs would barely hold her. She gripped the trunk of the dead tree for support.

Both women turned suddenly to face her. Ursule felt like a cornered fox facing a pack of terriers. The older one said, "Don't speak to us, do they?"

The younger one said, "Allus jabberin' away in some strange language, won't speak Cornish, or English. Keepin' up there in that old house and never comin' down!"

"Afraid they'll be found out, like!" said the older one.

The younger woman bent forward at her thick waist to peer at Ursule from beneath the brim of her hat. "Aren't you one of them? You are! You're the one that comes to the market—"

The bang of the basement door interrupted her. The men who had gone in surged back up the stairs, with Father Maddock at their head. But this time they had Nanette with them, Nanette boneless, limp, her head hanging and her feet dragging as they hauled her up the steps.

"A witch!" one of the men yelled in triumph.

The crowd took up the cry. "A witch! A witch!"

Ursule's head whirled so suddenly she thought she would vomit. Her muscles turned to water. She lost her hold on the elm, crumpling to her knees among twigs and dry leaves.

The two women lost interest in her in their haste to follow the mob carrying Nanette away. Ursule struggled to regain her feet.

An unexpected bank of charcoal clouds rolled in from the west, covering Mount's Bay, casting its shade over Marazion. Ursule, groping for something to pull herself up on, found a fine, soft hand beneath hers.

She panted, gripping the hand like a drowning woman, and looked up into the face of her lover.

It was Sebastien, his face drawn, his wonderful eyes clouded with anger.

She moaned, "My mother... I must go after her... Help me!"

"It's too late, Ursule." He drew her to him and put an arm around her shoulders, not as a lover, but as a brother. As a friend.

"Sebastien, help me! You must help me! Maman—"

He held her close to his chest. "*Chut, chut, ma chère.* There's nothing you can do."

The realization struck her like a blow. He wouldn't fight them. No one would fight them. She was utterly alone in this battle.

She pulled herself free of his hands, though he tried to restrain her. The crowd had already disappeared, shouting and jeering, down the road that led to the cliff. Ursule spun in a whirl of skirts and ran back toward where she had tethered Aramis.

It was like running in a nightmare. Her feet were made of lead. Her arms flailed uselessly beside her. She reached the horse in moments, but every one of those moments felt like an hour. Aramis threw up his head, alarmed by her rush and her panting, but though he trembled, he stood still as she crawled up onto his back and turned him toward the cliff. He broke into a trot and then his awkward, rocking canter when she smacked his ribs with her heels and called his name.

She didn't realize she was sobbing until the tears on her cheeks chilled in the cold air. She urged Aramis on, one hand on his reins and the other gripping his mane at the withers so she wouldn't slide off. Her scarf was gone, and her skirt was rucked up around her knees. Her hands ached, and her neck, where Morcum had gripped it, sent blazing pains into her skull.

By the time she caught up with the villagers, the cloud cover had parted. The sun glinted cruelly on the tossing sea below the cliff. It was the most frightening spot on the cliff road, a place Ursule always drove by with great care, a place where people came to throw things over when they didn't want them found. It was said a popish priest had died there once, years before, slipped and fallen to his death on the rocks below.

The shouts of the mob had diminished, but hatred was in every face, in the twisting lips, the reddened faces. Ursule tried to urge Aramis among them, but a lifetime of taking care with his enormous feet held him back. He wouldn't force his way into a throng of people. He resisted her, pacing back and forth at the edge of the crowd, acknowledging her with nods of his head and anxious snorts, but refusing her order.

On the far side of the crowd she saw Morcum, his broad figure swathed in his worn black coat, his hat pushed back, and his face, too, twisted with fury.

Ursule turned Aramis, and tried to ride around the crowd, but the people had spread out, standing on tiptoe, shoving one another, vying for a better vantage point. Ursule desperately cast about for something she could do, someone she could appeal to, but she found no one. She could just see Nanette's head and the tops of her shoulders; she was supported by two men who pulled her, unresisting, toward the edge of the precipice.

Ursule didn't realize she was screaming until Aramis reared, his huge hooves clawing the air, his head thrashing, his hind legs trembling. She clung to his back, her legs sliding, her hand cramping as she gripped his mane. Still she screamed, in wordless, blind panic, as strands of Aramis's coarse mane stung her cheeks.

Faces turned to her, ugly, ravening faces, blind with anger, hungry for violence. Only Aramis's fearsome hooves kept them at a distance.

The men were at the cliff edge now, Nanette helpless in their hands. Ursule felt as if her mind had left her. All her control was shattered. She could only shout, as impotent as her mother, "No! No! Please, no!"

Aramis's forefeet crashed down to the earth just as two burly men, one on either side, reached for Ursule. They surely meant to pull her down into their midst, possibly to share the witch's fate. She felt an urge to give in to them, to resign herself. Better, perhaps, to die with her mother than to live with this memory.

Aramis decided for her. He reared again, a silver monster of a horse, and the men fell back. Aramis spun on his hocks to get away from them, to get away from the mob. Away from Nanette.

The big Shire struck out at a strong gallop, leaving the road, heading north toward the moor. Ursule's legs automatically clamped around his barrel.

She had never ridden Aramis at a gallop, and the speed and power of it shocked her. As if from a great distance, she heard the rhythm of his hooves on the ground, and the noise of the mayhem behind them began to fade.

Except for one, final, devastating sound.

The shriek could have come only from Nanette. It was a sound Ursule had never heard before, and would pray never to hear again. It was a long, winding scream that split the morning and silenced even the hysterical voices of the mob. It was a death cry, rising until it seemed it could go no higher, then dwindling into a mournful, hopeless, ghastly farewell. Nanette Orchiére, sister and lover and mother, Romani and witch, fell to the rocks below.

When the cry ceased, Ursule knew her mother's suffering was over.

Aramis galloped on, his big body growing hot beneath her thighs. He carried her away, running long past the point at which his endurance should have given out. He showed no sign of stopping, charging across the moor as if he knew her life depended on him. When he finally slowed to a walk, his sides heaved, and spittle flew from his lips. His nostrils rattled with each desperate breath.

Ursule didn't try to guide him. She was sobbing with despair and sorrow and shock, and when he finally stumbled to a halt, she slid from his back to land hard on her feet. The two of them stood together, her forehead against his shoulder, his head drooping in exhaustion.

She didn't realize they had returned to Orchard Farm until, at length, she lifted her swollen face. Her poor goats had given up bleating. The ponies were gathered at one end of the paddock, clustered together with their tails to the wind as if they knew something was wrong. The door to the kitchen hung open, slanting from its remaining hinge.

"Wait," Ursule croaked to Aramis. He stood where he was, his head hanging so low she feared he might not recover his strength.

She hurried through the gate and up the path to the kitchen door. She didn't bother trying to close it, but raced into the pantry to find Grand-mère's book. In moments she was on her way out. She seized a half loaf of bread and a wheel of cheese resting on the counter, thrusting everything into an empty flour sack, and trotted back to Aramis.

As she jumped up on the mounting block, the rising wind and slanting sun told her the day was far gone. Ursule slung the flour sack across Aramis's withers, then paused to gaze at her beloved farm, at the house where she had expected to live out her days, at the graveyard where she had meant one day to lie. She would rescue the crystal from its hiding place in the cave, and she and Aramis would depart from Cornwall forever. They would leave Orchard Farm behind. Leave Nanette's shattered body to float in its watery grave. Leave Morcum to stew in his righteous loneliness.

For a second time that terrible day, Ursule was tempted to surrender, to give up her life as her mother had given up hers.

But she had the babe to think of. Her daughter.

The infant chose that very moment to quicken. She wriggled in Ursule's belly with the undeniable sensation of life to come. Fresh tears, of grief and horror and gratitude, burned Ursule's swollen eyes.

She lifted Aramis's reins and turned him toward the tor. For the babe's sake, for the sake of the Orchiére line, they would go on.

THE BOOK OF IRÈNE

1

Irène shook the remnants of chicken scratch from her skirt as she crossed the kitchen garden and let herself out through the slatted gate in the stone wall. She turned up the dirt lane to the cottage, pulling down the brim of her straw hat against the Welsh sun. She was halfway home when a horse's hoofbeats quickened behind her. She stepped out of the lane and onto the weedy verge that ran along the forest's edge.

The Grange's best gig was bowling toward her, the master's thick-waisted daughter at the reins and his prized dapple gray between the shafts. Irène, though it galled her to do it, dropped a curtsy as it passed. Blodwyn Hughes flicked her whip to acknowledge the obeisance, and the gray broke into a canter. Dust rose from the wheels to cloud around Irène as she trudged on. She tugged up the hem of her apron to keep the swirling dirt from her nose and mouth.

Blodwyn was no doubt on her way into Tenby for tea, or perhaps a visit to her dressmaker's shop, in the High Street beyond the city wall. Irène imagined her driving the gig up to the stables, being helped down by a stableboy who would tug his forelock. Blodwyn would unfurl her parasol and stroll past the blue-and-yellow buildings, with the sea glinting green in the distance. The citizens would nod to her, call her Miss Blodwyn, hasten to open doors as she approached.

Fiery resentment of all these things burned in Irène's breast, and when she went into the cottage she slammed the door with unnecessary force, making the cast-iron soup pot rattle against the hob of their open fireplace.

Ursule turned from the sink, her brows rising. "Such violence! What is it this time?"

Irène took off her hat and threw it at the rack. "I hate that girl!"

"Which girl might that be, Daughter?" Ursule's voice was mild, but Irène wasn't fooled. Her mother would brook her bad tempers just so far.

She slapped the dust from her printed cotton skirt. "Blodwyn Hughes."

"Miss Blodwyn."

Irène snorted. "I *know*, Mother. *Miss* Blodwyn. Dumpy, stupid Miss Blodwyn, who's on her way into Tenby for a new dress that won't make her look any better than that hideous thing she's wearing."

"Master Hughes provides us a home, Irène. And work."

"I hate the work."

She saw she might have gone too far. Ursule's voice sharpened, and her eyebrows drew together. "You would hate starving more. Or sleeping rough."

Irène had heard the story often enough. She hated being reminded of it. It wasn't her fault her mother had had to flee Cornwall with nothing but her Shire stallion and a scrying stone! She stamped across the room to the peg rack for a fresh apron. "It's all wasted on her," she muttered. "When was the last time you or I had new dresses?"

"If you want a new dress, I'll ask at the Grange. They'll give us a bolt of fabric."

"Mother! I don't want to make my *own* dress! I want it made for me, properly fitted, with boning and a bustle and lace at the bodice!"

"And what, daughter mine, would you do with such a dress?"

Irène heard the sharpening edge in Ursule's voice, but she was in full spate now, and she couldn't stop herself. "Why shouldn't I wear such a dress? Why should I be trapped in a house with three rooms, wearing hand-me-down boots, mucking out pigpens and chicken coops?"

"Why should you live in the Grange, and be waited on hand and foot? What have you given to the world?"

"What has that fat Blodwyn ever given to the world?"

"She was born into privilege, Irène. That's her good fortune." Ursule's voice was hard as she handed Irène a paring knife and two potatoes. "You have your own good fortune, remember. Your own inheritance."

Irène sneered at her mother. "Oh, the craft! What good is it, if we spend our lives working like animals and living like peasants?" She waved the paring knife around at the cramped cottage, the soot-stained fireplace, the heavy oak table, the mismatched armchairs and assorted oil lamps.

"We're not peasants," Ursule snapped, "though we might well have been, if Master Hughes had not given a lost, pregnant woman a chance to earn her living."

"I don't want to live my life on charity!"

"Charity?" Ursule banged the roast she was trussing onto the counter and whirled to seize her daughter's arm. She was still a strong woman, broad shouldered and muscular, with a man's hands and a man's courage. Her eyes flashed dark fire, and her daughter knew she had now certainly gone too far. "You listen to me, Irène Orchiére. I've earned every bit of our living by good, clean hard work."

"Hardly clean—" Irène began, but Ursule shook her arm so hard that pain lanced through her shoulder and up her neck.

"Clean and honorable!" Ursule cried. "I won't have you saying otherwise!"

Tears stung Irène's eyes, and she rubbed her arm where her mother's fingers had bruised it. "I just meant—shoveling pig manure and raking up chicken mess—"

Ursule exhaled a long, noisy breath. She turned back to the pork roast, prodding it with her fingers. "I know, Irène. Not the life you would have chosen."

"At least if my father—"

Without turning, Ursule threw up a hand. "Please don't start on that again. Sebastien is doing the best he can."

"He's never here!"

Ursule exhaled again. She didn't turn, but her voice was as sharp as the paring knife. "He's here when he can be. The Grange might hire a musician once or twice a year, or there might be a wedding or a funeral in Tenby...It's not enough for him. You know this."

Irène knew she should leave it at that, but it rankled. She never knew when Sebastien would show up, tutor her in French, teach her a few simple chords on his harp, then disappear again, and the harp with him. He could hardly have been more different from her mother, with his soft, clean hands, his spotless clothes, his fine manners. She began to peel the potatoes with quick, angry strokes of the knife, but she made her voice conciliatory. "I wish I could go with him when he travels."

Her mother's tone softened, too, but there was a note of warning in it just the same. "I know, Irène. You can see why it's not possible."

Irène quartered the potatoes and dropped them into the pot waiting on the hob. She pulled back her skirts so she could kneel on the hearth and add wood to the fire. "If Master Hughes is so wonderfully generous, why doesn't he see to it we have a proper cooker?" she said, but under her breath so her mother wouldn't hear.

❧

Irène suspected her mother thought she was lazy, because she complained so much about the farm work, but it wasn't that. It was the mud and offal and filth that offended her. Since she had been a tiny girl, the chickens and their coop had been her job. As she grew older, Ursule had added feeding and caring for the pigs to her daughter's chores. When she objected, Ursule said, "Why do you mind? Pigs are sensitive creatures. Intelligent."

"Then they should clean their own sty," Irène muttered. Her mother had laughed then, but she no longer seemed to find Irène's complaints amusing. By the time Irène had reached her mother's height, Ursule expected her to weed and dig and haul just as much as she herself did, and none of Irène's scowls dissuaded her.

The only task she didn't ask—in fact, would not allow—her daughter to share was the care of the Shire stallion. Aramis was old, and no longer able to pull a plow, but he was still an elegant creature, tall and silver and shining. Irène wouldn't have minded brushing his thick, silky mane or riding him out where the two of them could be seen together. She would have loved to go trotting past the Grange on Aramis, looking down on the gardeners and grooms and dairymaids—and on Miss Blodwyn and Master Hughes.

Ursule insisted on being the only person to handle Aramis. Master Hughes had allowed her to set aside a small pasture for the stallion, with a lean-to where he could escape the weather. She saw to his feed and grooming every day, no matter how long or hard the workday had been.

To justify the expense of Aramis's upkeep, Ursule had agreed to let Master Hughes breed the old stallion to one of his mares, a fine gray Percheron. The mare foaled a strong, handsome colt for the Grange's stables. On the rare days when work could be suspended for a time, Ursule took Irène up to to see the colt, which Miss Blodwyn had named Ynyr. Tom Butler, the horsemaster, said that Miss Blodwyn had taken a fancy to Aramis, and wanted a big horse of her own to ride.

The stables at the Grange were elegantly laid out, with wide loose boxes, raked gravel paths, manicured paddocks, and modern coal-burning stoves to keep the horses warm on cold nights. They were, like the grounds and the great brick block of the manor house, scrupulously clean. Irène, whenever she visited the Grange, grew silent and heavy footed, oppressed by the bitter weight of envy. Even Tom Butler's livery, well-cut jodhpurs and tall leather boots, made her feel dowdy, invisible in her cotton dresses. If Miss Blodwyn appeared in one of her elaborate riding habits, slapping at her leg with a braided leather quirt, nodding to the farmwife and the farmwife's daughter as if she were a queen, Irène's misery intensified. She curtsied, as she must, and kept her eyes down, not out of humility, but to hide her avarice.

She knew well she was more beautiful, more intelligent, even better educated than the master's daughter. Her troubadour father had taught her to speak fluent French. Her mother had taught her to read and do sums, and made her puzzle out recipes in Old French from her ancient grimoire. Irène had many virtues indeed. Humility wasn't one of them.

Nor was patience.

As they walked home from one of their visits to the colt, Ursule said, "He's growing nicely, I think. Such a pretty dappled gray. The stableman tells me he'll try him under harness soon."

"I don't know why you care, Mother," Irène snapped. "He's not yours. You'll never be allowed to drive him."

Ursule answered with uncharacteristic mildness. "I wish you would call me Maman, Irène. And I feel as if Ynyr is mine, in a way. Because Aramis is mine, and Ynyr is a part of Aramis."

"Aramis is just a horse."

"He's not just a horse. He's much more than that. I would have no life without him, nor would you."

"I hate it when you talk like that!"

They were in the lane, with the manor house and its landscaped grounds looming behind them, blocking their view of the setting sun. Stars winked above the expanse of the forest, as if they had emerged from the tips of the dark trees. Their cottage huddled like a cowed puppy, squat and dull, a thin stream of smoke rising above its flat roof.

Ursule stopped and faced her daughter with her hands on her hips. The fading light caught the weathered lines in her face and picked out silver strands in her dark hair. Irène was startled at these signs of age. Ursule had always seemed as eternal as the sea stacks along Castle Beach, and no softer than those looming rocks.

Ursule said, "I know you're unhappy, and I'm sorry. I was also discontented at sixteen."

"But you like being a farmer."

"I do."

"Did you at sixteen?"

Ursule's lips curved. "I've loved working the land since I was a little child. It was the craft I was unhappy about. But I learned— my *maman* and I both did—that the craft will not be denied."

Irène blurted, "We don't even know yet if I'm a witch."

"Shhh!" Ursule's eyes widened and she cast a quick glance behind them. "Someone might hear you."

"They wouldn't believe me! This isn't the Dark Ages!"

"It might as well be. There is always danger for such as us."

"You, perhaps. Not me." She couldn't help a reflexive glance around them, wary despite her denials. "If I'm not going to be—well, that—then I want to be a lady. I *feel* like a lady."

Ursule sighed and looked away from her daughter. "We should go. It's getting dark." She resumed her walk, and Irène matched her pace. Ursule said with a wry smile, "I will say, Irène, you look like a lady, thanks to your father. You are not one, though, and nothing you or I or Sebastien can do will change that."

"Even if I—"

"If you what?"

"I don't know. Something." Irène couldn't bear the thought of spending her life as a farmwife, shoveling and feeding, digging and weeding. She shuddered at the idea of becoming her mother—growing gray, wrinkled, with perpetually dirty fingernails and filthy boots.

"You will have to accept the way things are eventually. Your inheritance is different from that of Miss Blodwyn. That's the way of the world."

"It's not fair!"

"It rarely is."

Irène simmered in silence for the rest of their walk. The cottage was dark and cold when they went in, and Ursule hurried to light an oil lamp while Irène kindled the fire in the hearth. There was a bit of cold ham for their supper, with boiled potatoes and half a loaf of dark bread. Irène looked at it with distaste.

"I suppose Miss Blodwyn is drinking champagne and eating roasted grouse."

"She may be. You're having ham and potatoes." Ursule sat down and used the carving knife to cut the ham into two equal parts. "Be glad you have anything to eat, Irène. Some don't."

Irène took her seat and accepted a plate. She would have liked to refuse, but it had been a long day, and she was too hungry to make the gesture. When she had finished it all, and eaten two slices of bread with fresh butter from the Grange's dairy, she rose to carry the dishes to the stone sink.

"It's Mabon, remember," Ursule said, as she wrapped the remains of the bread.

"Oh, Mother! Must we?"

Her mother didn't bother to answer.

2

Irène had begun to celebrate the Sabbats with Ursule when her monthlies began at thirteen. The only rites they had missed since that time were those that had fallen when Sebastien was with them. "He may or may not understand the truth about what we are," Ursule said. "I don't want to ask him, and if he doesn't already realize, I don't want to tell him. If he knew—if he knows—he could also be at risk."

Irène didn't scoff. They had heard from one of the Grange's cooks, when she came for garden produce, that a witch had been caught near Aberystwyth. Irène had seen her mother turn white beneath her sunburn, and clench her hands under her apron. The cook, Sally, told the story with relish, describing in awful detail how the witch had been stripped, examined by the deacons and the local priest, and denounced on the steps of the church. The witch—if witch she was—had been turned out of her village with nothing but the clothes on her back.

"At least she's alive," Ursule had said bitterly, when Sally had departed with her basket of greens.

"Why would she not be alive?" Irène had asked.

Ursule drew her hands out from beneath her apron and looked at the palms. Her nails had cut into them, and they were spotted with thin lines of blood. "I've told you what happened to my *maman*, Irène."

"But that wasn't Tenby. That was Cornwall! And it was sixteen years ago!"

Her mother fixed her with a sorrowful gaze. "It never ends," she said.

"What doesn't end?"

"The persecution."

"But why should they go after some poor old woman in Aberystwyth?"

Ursule sniffed and rubbed her nose with a grimy hand. "She probably cured someone of a cold, or a wart. Or failed to cure them. Either way, they think she knows things they don't, and that frightens them."

"You would think they'd be grateful for women with knowledge."

"It's rarely true. Men are vain."

"Even when they're wrong?" Irène laughed. "That's stupid!"

"Don't laugh, Irène. We have to be clever. We have to let men think they are stronger, smarter, wiser than women."

"Oh, Maman! Who cares what men think?"

Ursule stood up, ready to return to her work. As she picked up her gloves she said, "Men make decisions for women, Irène, whether we like it or not. A kind man, like Sebastien, is a blessing. A cruel one—or a thoughtless one—is a curse. That's life."

"It's foolish. And not fair!"

"I have no argument with that. Nevertheless, it's the way it is. Men need to believe they're in control."

"Then I hope I have the power, too, the way you do."

Her mother shrugged as she started for the door. "You may inherit it. You may not."

"And if I don't?"

"There would be no more Orchiére witches. We are all that's left."

"When will we know?" Irène demanded.

"Only the Goddess has the answer to that."

Irène didn't care if there were any more Orchiére witches. She cared about the power, though. She wanted it as much as she wanted to be a lady.

Every minor or major Sabbat, so long as Sebastien was absent, Irène followed Ursule down to the root cellar beneath the cottage. They lifted the slanting door with care to prevent the screech of the hinges, and descended into the windowless space that smelled of cold earth and vegetables and drying herbs. They had to feel their way in the dark, because Ursule wouldn't light a candle until they were down the three steps and had pulled the door closed above their heads. There was barely enough room to stand upright.

Each rite began the same way. They covered their heads with long scarves, sprinkled a circle of salted water, and set a new white candle burning on their altar, a three-legged stool scavenged years before from a garden shed. Next to the candle Ursule set the ancient crystal with its jagged granite base. She kept a scarf over it until she was ready to begin, then uncovered it with a flourish. Irène thought the gesture should be accompanied with a swirl of music, the way they did things in the Tenby church.

Irène wasn't sure if it was the candlelight or the crystal that softened Ursule's leathery face. Strands of her hair lifted as if in a light breeze, and sparkled silver in the darkness. Wisps of mist hung in the corners of the root cellar, barely illumined by the flame of the candle. The floor was so dark it was invisible. Ursule chanted praises to the Goddess and acknowledgment of the Sabbat. Irène watched intently, though she had to hug herself against the damp, and her breath fogged in the cold air. When her power came at last, she meant to be ready. She wanted to remember every moment of the ceremony, to repeat it in the proper way when her own turn came.

Ursule always finished with a recitation of their history, the one she had learned from her own mother. She had made Irène memorize it, long ago, so they could chant it together:

On this Sabbat of Mabon, we honor our foremothers: sweet Nanette, great Ursule, the prophetess Liliane, the Lady Yvette, Maddalena of Milano, Irina from the east, and all those whose precious names have been lost. We vow to pass the craft to our daughters so long as our line endures.

When the echoes of their voices died away, they stood in silence for a moment before Ursule concluded with her own particular rite. She extended her hands above the crystal, spreading her strong fingers in supplication:

Mother Goddess, hear my plea:
Show my one true love to me.

Ursule had explained how late she had come to the craft, how many years had passed before she believed. Irène supposed she might have had the same experience were it not for this rite. The crystal never failed to respond to this particular call.

Magic descended around the miserable little cellar, warming the air, glittering here and there on jars and tins and hanging spoons. A light began as a spark deep within the ancient stone, visible only because the root cellar was so dark. It flickered and bloomed into a glow like that of a summer evening, and in its center, as if seen through thick, wavy glass, or as in a dream, was Sebastien. It was a marvel, and Irène longed to be able to make it happen herself.

She bent over the stone to gaze at her father. He was asleep, his head nestled on a pillow, a blanket pulled up to his clean-shaven chin, his eyelids closed to hide his wonderful silver-gray eyes. He was still handsome. The lines in his face were somehow lighter, less marked, than those in her mother's. If there was gray, it didn't show in his fair hair. In the dimness of wherever it was he was sleeping, starlight gleamed on his clear profile and his closed eyelids. "Maman, do you know where he is?"

"No." Ursule withdrew her hands to tuck them into her sleeves. "I think he was going north, perhaps to Scotland. He wanted to go where his songs would be new."

Irène's chest ached with the urge to go away herself, anyplace that wasn't Tenby and a tawdry farmhouse with its unending chores. She thought of lovely dresses, fine foods, a house with windows and stairs and servants. She thought of Ynyr, the beautiful colt claimed by ugly Blodwyn, and could have wept with longing.

3

Sebastien managed to return to the Grange the day before his daughter's seventeenth birthday. He came trudging up the lane from the Tenby railway station, his harp slung over one shoulder, his rucksack over the other.

Ursule and Irène had spent the morning slicing potatoes into chunks, careful that each had an eye. After a hasty lunch they had begun the planting process, working up the plowed rows on their knees, setting the chunks under the loose soil. They were both muddy from ankle to knee, their hands grimy and their nails black with dirt. They wore broad-brimmed straw hats, but Irène felt the beginning of sunburn on her neck, above the collar of her faded work dress, and soil had gotten into her boots to chafe her toes. She was in as foul a mood as she could remember when her mother suddenly jumped to her feet, hissing, "He's here!"

Irène sat back on her heels. "Who's here?"

Ursule cried joyfully, "Sebastien!"

"How do you know?" Irène asked, but her mother was already on her way to the gate in the stone wall. It was a foolish question in any case. Ursule often, she suspected, consulted the stone alone in the root cellar, following Sebastien's progress, searching for hints of where he might be. She often knew he would arrive before the sound of his footsteps reached their ears.

She stood up and scraped the worst of the mud from her boots before following her mother. Three hens clucked at her ankles, and she shooed them away before she slipped through the gate. Ursule, who hadn't bothered to so much as take off her disreputable hat, had thrown her arms around Sebastien, knocking her hat off into the mud of the lane and smudging his coat with garden dirt.

Irène shut the gate against the chickens and paused to watch her parents embrace. The contrast between them had always surprised her, but now it filled her with suspicion.

Sebastien wasn't tall, but he was slender and fine featured, youthful even in middle age, with an unlined face and fine pale hair falling to his shoulders. Ursule was...Ursule. Her shoulders were broad, muscular from a lifetime of manual labor. Her skin was weathered, and darkened by the sun. Her hair was still thick and curly, but salted with gray, and her dark eyes had developed a squint from working outdoors. Her hands, twined now with Sebastien's, had long, strong fingers, swollen knuckles, and nails she could never get clean. Irène supposed her mother might have been pretty in her youth, but now...How could such a person hold a man like Sebastien? Was this the way she used her power? Was it possible to use magic for such a thing?

Irène looked down at her own hands and experienced a clutch of panic. They were smoother than her mother's, and her knuckles had not begun to thicken, but they were Ursule's hands, the fingers long, the palm broad, the veins already showing in the wrists. She pressed her palms to her cheeks, wondering if her skin, too, had begun to brown, and if the first betraying threads of gray were woven into her own hair.

"Irène!" Sebastien called, and held out his free arm to her. "Ma fille!" She pulled off her hat and did her best to shake the garden soil from the ends of her hair as she crossed the lane to meet her father, but she carried her doubts with her.

That night, after Ursule and Sebastien had retired, and the cottage was dark and quiet, Irène set a fresh candle in a candleholder and dropped a box of sulfur matches into the pocket of her coat. She slipped out the door on stockinged feet, silent as a cat, and made her way around to the root cellar. She lifted the slanting door slowly, slowly, to avoid the squeak of the hinges. Only when she was safely down the stairs, the door pulled shut above her head, did she strike a match and set the flame to the candlewick. It flickered in the cobwebbed corners and made her shadow shudder against the walls as if a specter were watching her.

She didn't uncover the stone, but crouched beside the stool it rested on, and pulled out the wrapped book that lay among the three legs. She set the grimoire on the work counter, and in the light from the candle she folded back the burlap that protected it and opened the age-darkened leather cover.

Under Ursule's strict eye she had spent hours huddled at the kitchen table with the grimoire. The book had no particular order or organization, just a collection of recipes for charms, simples, potions, and spells. She had read through every page many times. She remembered the title of the spell she was looking for because it had been so devilishly hard to translate:

A Philter to Persuade the Reluctant Lover

She also remembered it because it was the one recipe Ursule had wanted her to skip. Her mother had snatched the book away before she could touch the page. When she asked why, her mother said, "This may be the most dangerous spell in all of the grimoire."

"But why? It's only a love potion, is it not?"

"Irène, love is the most perilous emotion there is. When you force it—when you use it as a weapon—terrible things can happen. You cannot create real love with a potion or a spell."

"Let me read it, at least. Let me see how—"

"Non! Absolument pas!" As Ursule switched to French, her voice hardened. "You are playing with things you don't understand, Daughter."

"I still don't see—"

Ursule had startled her by pulling her hand away from the page and slamming the book closed without her usual care for its fragile pages. "Don't argue!"

Ursule supervised every session with the grimoire, and she saw to it that it never lay open to the forbidden page. Irène wondered, now, if this was the reason. Perhaps Ursule had lied to her. Perhaps her mother had worked a spell on her father, binding him to her not through love, but through magic.

If it was true, it was a demonstration of stunning power, and Irène wanted it for herself.

In the unsteady light of the candle she found the page and bent over it to decipher the straggling handwriting. It was all but impossible for her to read. She could make out the required herbs, coltsfoot, lovage root, lady's mantle, mullein, mistletoe. The instructions made no sense to her, a jumble of antique words too hard to see in the darkness. She needed more light. And a dictionary.

She lifted her hands from the page and turned them over. There was grime on her palms, black and sticky, the dust of decades. As she looked at it, the first stirrings of her power began to ache in her belly. She pressed her hand to her middle, wondering at the sensation, and at the same moment she knew, with bone-deep certainty, that her mother had never used this page. Someone had, or Ursule would not be convinced of its danger, but it had not been Ursule herself.

Irène closed the book with care and replaced its burlap covering. She slid it beneath the stool, blew out her candle, and felt her way back to the stairs. Once she was out of the root cellar and safely hidden in her room again, she stripped off her clothes and pulled on her nightdress with hands that shook with excitement. It was far past midnight, but she lay wakeful on her bed, curled around the ache in her belly, wondering when the rest of her power would reveal itself.

Never in all the long line of Orchiére witches, she thought, had a girl wanted more to be a witch. A real witch, like the great Ursule or the prophetess Liliane. A powerful witch, who could bend people to her will. A subtle witch, who could rise above her lowly roots to become a lady.

She hugged her knees and savored her pain. It was coming. She sensed it. The power was coming.

She could hardly wait.

4

"You should treat your *maman* with respect," Sebastien said. "She nearly died saving you."

"Oh, Papa, I've heard the story a thousand times! Please don't tell it again."

"Then don't make me remind you."

Irène grimaced and pushed away her bowl of mutton stew, appetite forgotten. She hated being criticized by her father. He was the one person in the world whose opinion mattered to her.

"You should go after her. Apologize."

Apologizing was another thing she hated. None of this seemed fair, not on this day. "I only said I wished we had something nicer than mutton stew today."

"Then perhaps you should have cooked it yourself."

"It's my birthday!"

"Yes. Seventeen. No longer a child."

"You're taking her side, aren't you? That's what you always do!"

Sebastien was silent for a time, crumbling a piece of brown bread between his elegant fingers and gazing into the fireplace, where yellow flames danced, mellowing the drabness of the cottage and its dark old furniture. When he spoke, his voice throbbed with sorrow. "It's not a question of sides, you know," he said, speaking French with her as he always did when they were alone.

"Your mother has been faithful to you from before your birth, and almost all on her own. I'm hardly a father to you—"

She drew breath to object to this, but he put his finger to his lips, and she subsided. "A good father would be here always. Could provide you your own harp to practice on. Would see that your husband is a good, hardworking, honest man, better than he himself has ever been."

"Papa! A husband?"

"You're of an age. It could happen at any time."

"I know no one I would want to marry."

"This is a fine village. I've seen more than one strapping young fellow plying his trade or plowing his fields."

"In *Tenbury*? I would never marry one of these yokels!"

He looked up at her, his silvery eyes like aged pewter in the firelight. "Why, then, Daughter, whom do you think you should marry?"

She meant not to answer, but the words erupted from her with the force of a volcano's flow. "I will marry a lord. I'm going to be a lady." As she spoke, the ache returned to her belly, a confirmation of her own prediction.

Sebastien didn't laugh at this, though they both knew it was an outrageous thing to say. He considered it for another space of silence. At last he said, "So long as you don't forget your *maman*, and what you owe to her."

Irène thought of how ill her mother would fit into a fine house. "She prefers the company of the beasts to mine, Papa. I think you know this."

"You're wrong about that, *ma fille*."

"How would you know? You're never here! You know nothing about my life!"

He gave her a long, mournful glance and made no effort to

argue. On the table between them lay her birthday gifts, a secondhand book on herbs from her mother, a pair of lace gloves from her father, pretty things she could never wear on the farm. She eyed them and gritted her teeth in frustration.

⁓✺⁓

Sebastien was off the next morning, striding away with his harp over his shoulder and his rucksack on his back. He lifted his hat at the turn to say farewell, and his long hair fluttered in the breeze and glinted gold in the sunshine. Irène and Ursule watched him go, Irène with her hands clasped before her, Ursule already tying on her canvas apron.

When he was gone, Ursule said briskly, "Better get on with those spuds, I suppose."

Irène shuddered with distaste. She was tired, full of impatience. She had hardly slept the night before, tossing from side to side on her pillow, gazing out her window at a full moon that called to her and made her heart burn with wanting.

Wakeful, she had risen at midnight to kneel beside the sash and gaze down at the stone wall around the garden, made silver gilt by moonlight. The distant bulk of the Grange was outlined by stars, imposing and elegant, remote as any castle. It symbolized everything she dreamed of, and as she yearned toward it, the ache returned to her belly. The pain was intensifying, as if her body was giving birth to her power. She sensed the crystal calling to her from the dank and dark of the root cellar.

Did Ursule hear it? Or was she so mired in the constant creeping dirt, the humiliation of mucking out stalls and fussing over filthy animals, that the magic had abandoned her?

Irène went back to her bed, but still she lay sleepless, worrying that the drudgery of the farm would destroy her growing power.

Now, as she thought of all this in the bright morning light, the ache in her belly expanded into her chest, and she couldn't help pressing her hands over her heart.

Her mother said, "Are you ill?"

"Monthlies," Irène groaned.

It wasn't true, though it felt much the same. It was her magic, coming upon her in full spate, like a river threatening to overflow its banks.

"Are you feverish?" Ursule put out a hand to test her daughter's forehead.

Irène, with a shudder of revulsion, drew away from the hand with its black-rimmed nails and calloused fingers. Ursule snatched it back. "What troubles you now?" she demanded.

"Your hand is dirty, Mother."

"You're too fine and clean to be touched by your mother, then?"

"I didn't mean—"

"Oh, you did. Of course you did. Your meaning was perfectly clear." Ursule's eyes shone suddenly. Irène had never seen her mother shed tears. "You think because you're seventeen, and pretty as a summer sky, that you will never be faded and gray as I am now. You think—"

"I *think*," Irène burst out, "that you could do something about all that if you tried! What good is your power, your craft, if you waste it in a barnyard?"

"*Chut!*" Ursule hissed, switching languages. This time she thrust her palm over her daughter's mouth before Irène could pull away. "If you must speak about the craft where people might hear, at least do not speak in English!"

Irène, in an act of rebellion such as she had never dared before, jerked herself free. Glaring at her mother, she deliberately spit into the dirt at her feet.

A dark fire blazed up in Ursule's eyes. She drew back her arm, opened her hand, and slapped Irène's cheek so hard it sounded like the crack of a farrier's hammer. She was as strong as any man from years of digging and hauling and lifting. The blow hurt.

Irène, nearly blind with pain and the rush of magic in her blood, covered her burning cheek with her hand and screamed, "I hate you! Hate you! You *disgust* me!"

The fire in her mother's eyes died away in the instant, drowned in very real tears. They brimmed against her eyelids and spilled, one at a time, down her cheeks. Irène sucked in her breath at the sight of them. Ursule spun away, canvas apron fluttering at her ankles, and marched to the garden gate. She was through it, gone, before Irène could gather her thoughts.

She stood where she was in the lane, trembling with shock even as she seethed with rage. What had just happened? She felt like a pot on the boil, juddering and rattling this way and that. When she could take it no longer—and when Ursule did not come back to apologize—she picked up her skirts and ran toward the forest to seek the solitude and comfort of the trees.

The forest that encircled the Grange was old, yew and elm and rowan trees with great spaces between them. Cast-off leaves softened the ground, and great mushrooms grew among the massive roots. Irène ran until the flame of her fury burned down, then stumbled to a walk. When she reached the unnamed thread of water that wound through the woods to the River Ritec, she knelt on the bank and bent to splash water on her burning face.

She caught sight of herself and gasped in horror. Even in the uncertain mirror of the brook, her left cheek bore the clear imprint of Ursule's hand. She glared at her reflection for long minutes, and her anger flared anew. What had she done to deserve such an attack? She had spoken the truth! Her mother had wasted her life, wasted her gift! She wasn't so powerful a witch as her namesake, perhaps, but she was strong enough. She could scry, which Irène knew many in their line could not. She could make a simple to ease a mare in foal or a cow with mastitis. Sometimes when the soup was too salty or the bread failed to rise, she would flick her fingers, mutter a few words, and remedy the fault.

When Irène asked for those spells, Ursule invariably said, "Wait. Wait till your power comes in."

And now, Irène was certain, it had arrived. She felt it in her belly and in her blood, and in the throb of wanting that thrummed in her chest, but she no longer wanted to make simples. She would never waste this power digging potatoes and shoveling manure. There must be a way. She would demand it of the Goddess.

She sank back into the duff, heedless of the stains of leaf and dirt that would mark her skirt. All she owned were work dresses in any case, and they were never clean. She circled her knees with her arms and rested her forehead there, thinking hard. She was seventeen, slender, bright eyed, smooth skinned. She would never be more beautiful than she was at this moment. There was no time to waste.

Her mother would be no help. Irène suspected her mother was jealous of her because she was still pretty, still young, with her life ahead of her instead of nearly over.

A rustle on the opposite side of the brook startled Irène. She raised her head.

A rowan tree, bent nearly sideways by age and the weight of its splaying branches, leaned into the little stream of water. On its trunk, peering through a tremulous curtain of leaves, perched a magnificent fox, redder than any Irène had ever seen, with a snowy breast and sharp black muzzle. Its slanting yellow eyes gleamed through the forest shade, and its peaked ears turned toward her as if it was waiting for her to do something. To say something.

Or to think of something.

Suddenly the recipe appeared in her mind's eye, as clearly as if the grimoire were open before her, and now she remembered how it began:

Take three leaves and two flowers of coltsfoot, along with an inch of the root; add three inches of lovage root, well dried; flowers of lady's mantle; three spikes of mullein; and a twig of mistletoe, crushed.

But whom would she use the potion on?

The fox barked at her, one sharp, short sound.

Without expecting to, Irène laughed. "What?" she said aloud.

The fox's mouth opened, showing its white teeth, and its tongue lolled, laughing with her.

A sense of recognition tingled in Irène's bones and throbbed in her forehead. Her laughter died. She came to her feet, facing the creature. It scrambled down from the tree trunk, its lithe body weaving through the branches as easily as a stream of water might. It stood on the opposite bank. Its tail arced above its back, a plume of red and black. Its unblinking gaze fixed itself on her.

Irène whispered, "Are you here for me?"

Again the fox's mouth opened in its grin, and its tail waved once, twice, before it leaped the little brook as easily as if it could fly. Irène stood very still as the fox stepped toward her on narrow black feet as dainty as a dancer's. It—he, she could see now—pressed his cold black nose against the back of her hand, and, when she turned it, nosed her palm.

She thrilled at the touch, though the touch of so many other beasts disgusted her. He was different, this fox. It was not just that he was beautiful, and graceful. It was more, much more. Her soul knew him. Her power flared in his presence.

He took a step back, his eyes never leaving hers, then whirled and leaped back over the brook to disappear into the forest on the other side. The last thing she saw was that lush red-and-black tail, switching back and forth as he faded into the dimness of the woods.

Irène brought her palm to her nose and sniffed the toasty smell of him. She knew what he was, and she knew what it meant. Her mother had Aramis. Her grandmother, Ursule had told her, had had an ugly gray cat. And she—now, surely, a witch in full possession of her power—had a glorious vulpine creature like no other. She had her fox. She would see him again.

She leaned over the brook to look into the water again. The red echo of her mother's palm had faded from her cheek. She straightened her hair and brushed leaves and soil from the back of her dress. She was shaking out the hem of it when she caught a flash of red among the brambles at her feet. She had almost missed it.

She bent and tugged. As she straightened she saw that her fox had left her a tiny swatch of his fur, perhaps a dozen red-and-black hairs, long and coarse and tangled together. Irène curled them around her finger, then tucked them inside her bodice, next to her heart. With a longing glance at the woods where the fox had disappeared, she started toward home.

But she would not, she swore to herself, be planting potatoes on this day. Or ever again.

5

Irène stopped doing farmwork. She stopped doing housework. She ceased all of it. The first few days her mother kept her distance, neither asking nor telling her what chores needed doing. Irène thought she might even apologize, eventually.

That didn't happen. They didn't speak for three days, while Ursule, with a resigned look, took on Irène's chores in addition to her own. Irène understood. Animals had to be cared for, vegetables had to be weeded and harvested. It was too bad, but hard things required hard decisions.

Those first days, Ursule also came into the cottage at night and cooked their supper, as was her habit. When the meal was finished, Irène carried the dishes and the pot to the sink, but after pumping water to soak the pot, she left everything as it was.

On the fourth day Ursule set out their breakfast of cider and bread and butter, but she didn't sit down. She stood opposite Irène, hands on hips, and said, "So, Daughter. Do you ever plan to work again?"

Irène felt at a disadvantage, looking up at her mother from her chair. She pushed it back and stood up before she answered. "I do not, Mother."

"Are you going to tell me why?"

Irène held out her hands, which were already softer and whiter since she had stopped digging in the garden and scrubbing pans. "A lady doesn't have a laborer's hands."

"In the name of the Goddess, Irène, how do you expect to become a lady?"

"I don't know yet."

Ursule's eyes narrowed. "Do you also expect me to wait upon you as if I were your servant? Do your chores, clean your room, fix your meals?"

Irène shrugged. "I don't expect it. That will be your own choice."

"You're not a child anymore, Irène."

"Exactly what Father said."

"Your father was right."

It wasn't easy, staring into her mother's face that way, but Irène had decided. She was committed. She tightened her jaw, hardened her heart, and held firm.

Ursule asked, "Are you no longer my daughter, then?"

The answer to this question came to Irène's lips without forethought. "I am the daughter of all our line, Maman. Of the mothers and grandmothers and great-grandmothers who have gone before. I may, in fact, be the last."

Ursule said, with deep bitterness, "Perhaps that would be best."

"Do you think so?"

"At this moment I do," her mother said tiredly.

"I can't live your life, Maman."

"No, I can see that."

"You think I'm being selfish."

"Yes. Shockingly selfish. But I suppose a child conceived selfishly is destined to be selfish herself."

"I'm not responsible for my conception."

Ursule picked up her mug of cider from the table, and turned away to drink it at the sink. When she had drained it, she said, her eyes on the summer day beyond the window, "It's true, Irène. You were not responsible for your conception. Nevertheless, you owe me—and your father—your life."

Irène said, without a trace of irony, "And I thank you. Now please let me live it."

⁂

Ursule went on with the work of the farm, but she no longer set breakfast and dinner on the table. Irène felt a grudging admiration for her mother's compromise, but she felt no compunction. She had no more choice in this matter than Ursule did. When she felt hungry, which wasn't often, she sliced herself a piece of bread, or dished up cold stew from the pot. When Ursule came in from her long day of work, Irène went to her room and closed the door so as not to watch her mother eating cold meat and raw vegetables from the garden.

A week later Ursule broke the silence between them. "Could I at least," she said, "prevail upon you to go into Tenby? We need flour and salt. Along the way you could deliver a basket of eggs to the Grange, and tell them we will need food for the hens."

Irène nodded, hiding the burst of enthusiasm the scheme gave her. She had read the herb book straight through, twice. She had mended clothes that needed it, and brushed her long hair until her scalp burned. She would not work, at least not in any way that harmed her hands, but she was unaccustomed to idleness, and she found she didn't like it. "I will do that, Maman," she said. "Let me get my hat."

Although they were incongruous with her dress, she wore the lace gloves Sebastien had given her. She wore her good hat, kept for the church services Ursule insisted they attend for appearances' sake. She wiped dust from her best shoes, and clipped a couple of threads coming loose from their seams. She looked as much like a lady as she could at this moment. Under her bodice, tucked inside her camisole, was the curl of fox hair, tied with a bit of thread.

She accepted the basket of eggs and a small purse of cash from her mother. In her slightly incongruous outfit, she set off down the lane under a hot summer sun.

The gravel path to the kitchen door of the Grange led past the grassy paddock where Aramis's colt was kept. Ynyr wasn't in it, but as Irène approached, a ruckus arose inside the stables. She tried to ignore it, hurrying up the steps to the kitchen and knocking firmly. Sally, the cook, greeted her with a smile and the offer of a cup of tea. Irène pleaded the need to hurry, ignoring Sally's surprised glance at her lace gloves as she handed over the basket, and went back down the path.

The noises from the stable intensified, a loud whinny, the banging of hooves on wood, and a feminine shriek that could have been one of fury, or might have been one of pain. Curious despite herself, Irène turned aside and went to peek through the open door.

Tom Butler, red faced and sweating, was hauling on a longe line, cursing under his breath in fluent but nearly inaudible Welsh. The line was snapped into Ynyr's halter, and the big colt was alternately rearing and striking out with his hind feet. Blodwyn Hughes stood to one side, her whip in her hand. Just as Irène looked in, she brought it down with a crack on the dappled gray hindquarters, screaming imprecations.

It was none of Irène's business, though her mother would be furious at this treatment of Aramis's offspring. She was about to draw back, out of sight, when the colt caught sight of her. Sweat blotted out the silver dapples on his neck and flanks, and he trembled from head to tail, but he stopped kicking. He threw his head high, and his dark eyes fixed themselves on Irène with an intensity that made her shiver.

The cramp in her belly was becoming familiar. She pressed her hand to her chest, and felt the talisman of fox hair hidden there. Ynyr exhaled a long, noisy breath that made his nostrils quiver.

They gazed at each other, and an uncanny moment passed in utter stillness.

Tom and Blodwyn turned as one to see what had attracted the colt's attention. "What do you think you're doing?" Blodwyn demanded.

Irène took satisfaction in noting that Blodwyn's voice was as thick and coarse as her body, though her accent was pure aristocracy. She answered, in as haughty a tone as she could manage, "I? You're the one beating a two-year-old colt with a whip."

Tom loosened the longe line, and stood panting. "Irène," he began, "you shouldn't speak that way to Miss Blodwyn—"

Emboldened by the magic of Ynyr's attention, Irène lifted her chin. "*Miss* Blodwyn should stop whipping the colt." She could have left it at that. But while she knew little about horses, she knew an opportunity when she saw one.

Blodwyn stood agape as Irène walked toward the horse with a calm, steady step. He was almost as tall as Aramis. Her head reached only the peak of his withers. As she came near, he dropped his head to press his muzzle into her gloved palm. "There now," she said, casting a sly look at Blodwyn from beneath her eyelids. She noted with satisfaction that her own eyelashes were twice as thick as the other girl's. "This is how you deal with a sensitive animal."

"Sensitive!" Blodwyn exploded. At the sound of her voice, Ynyr took a step back, tossing his head, his eyes showing their whites. His hocks struck the stall gate behind him, and he began to tremble again.

Irène was no horsewoman, but at this moment Ynyr was not a horse. He was much, much more.

She turned to the horsemaster and took the longe line in her own lace-gloved hand. Limply he gave it up, avoiding his mistress's eyes. Without looking at Blodwyn, obeying her instinct,

Irène led the colt out of the stable and around to the paddock gate. Side by side they went through, and walked the fence line for a few moments. Her soft shoes sank into the grass. Ynyr stepped close beside her, his wide hooves careful of her small feet. His trembling eased the moment he was away from the stables. She kept a hand on his neck, though her glove would be stained. Only when he had begun to cool down did she coax him to lower his head so she could unclip the line. She stepped back then, and watched him trot away from her, circling the paddock once, twice, dipping his elegant head in her direction.

Irène took care to lock the gate as she left the paddock. Blodwyn stood just in the doorway to the stables, flicking her whip and scowling. "How dare you?" she snapped. "I'll be telling Papa about this, I can promise you!"

"It's clear you can't handle a Shire," Irène said. She herself had never done it, either, but she had no intention of sharing that knowledge with Blodwyn. "Will you tell him that? Perhaps your papa could find you a pony. Something you could manage. An easier disposition."

She didn't look back as she walked away, but she heard Blodwyn sputtering complaints to Tom. Irène hurried, wanting to get away before either of them could delay her. She wasn't quite sure herself what had just happened, but seeing Blodwyn's cheeks burn with embarrassment had given her intense pleasure. As she strode out to the road, she saw the flicker of a red-and-black tail in the shadow of the woods. She glanced in that direction, smiling. He was there, aiding her magic, nourishing her power. He followed her, flashing in and out of the trees, until she had to turn onto the road to Tenby.

6

Mabon came around again in its due course, and by the time it arrived Irène's hands were even softer and cleaner than her father's. Her skin had regained its childish pallor, and her hair, from being brushed often, was a mass of shining black curls. She had eaten so little over the summer that her waist was more slender than ever.

Ursule had grown thinner, too, but with her the condition had less appeal. The tendons on her neck and hands stood out, and her cheeks were hollow. Once or twice Irène felt an unwelcome stab of sympathy for her mother, but she gritted her teeth against it.

They descended to the root cellar an hour before midnight, the only thing they had done together since Irène's birthday. Ursule set out the herbs, and Irène sprinkled salted water. Ursule lit the candle and uncovered the stone.

All was as usual with their celebration, except that Irène's belly writhed with pain as Ursule chanted. At the end, when Ursule spread her hands over the stone and spoke her special plea, Irène stood close, leaning over the crystal to see. Sebastien was there, half-hidden in a cloud of smoke, his harp on his lap, with people around him. "Playing," Ursule sighed. "I wish I could hear him."

Irène's white hands lifted as of their own accord, and gently pushed Ursule's weathered ones aside. She hadn't made a deliberate decision to do it, but as she spread her fingers over the crystal, in the same way her mother always did, the pain in her middle spread and thinned until her whole body felt achy and hot. She closed her eyes, feeling heat running through her blood, expanding from her bones, radiating from her fingertips.

When the sound began, a thin, ghostly echo of the music Sebastien must be making, Ursule gasped, and staggered so that her scarf slipped from her head and drifted to the cold floor.

Irène opened her eyes to see her mother half-bent, her hands still extended as if she had forgotten to lower them, her lips parted in wonder. They listened, the two of them, straining their ears to find the thread of song. When it ended, and Irène pulled back her hands, the image in the crystal shimmered for a moment, as if someone had put a finger into a reflective pool, then disappeared.

Ursule lifted hooded eyes to her daughter. "Your power," she said in a hoarse voice.

Irène stood erect, her body afire with it. "Yes!"

"When?"

"My birthday."

"You didn't tell me."

"No."

"But why?"

"I didn't think you would be happy about it, Maman."

"Not be happy! Part of my duty, part of my reason for being, is to pass on the craft! I had thought, perhaps . . ."

"You thought I didn't inherit," Irène said, and smiled. "But I did. And I think my time has come."

Ursule said, with what Irène mistook at first for humility, "It appears that it has." She stepped back from the crystal and bent to retrieve her fallen scarf. When she had replaced it on her head, she nodded toward the stone. "Shall we find out?"

When they emerged from the root cellar, the night was very far gone. The stars had already begun to fade in the east, and the wind bore the chill of autumn. They were at the doorstep when Irène saw the fox's yellow eyes gleaming at her from the edge of the wood, on the opposite side of the lane. She drew a little breath, catching Ursule's attention.

"What is it?"

Irène didn't answer, but she pointed.

"What's that?"

"It's a fox. A magnificent red-and-black fox."

Ursule exhaled a long, slow breath. "So. Your spirit familiar has appeared as well."

"Yes."

When her mother gripped her shoulder with her hard hand, Irène didn't pull away or object. It was a gesture of respect, because a spell had come to her and she had spoken it, though neither of them was sure what it meant. Ursule spoke in a low voice, close to her ear. The fox's ears pricked higher at the sound of her voice. "You will be stronger than I, Daughter. Take care with the craft."

"I mean to use it."

"I know. But remember what my own *maman* taught me: if you practice the craft, you will pay a price."

"It will be worth it."

"By the Goddess, I hope so."

They parted then, Ursule to her labors, Irène to her idleness. She paused in the kitchen to make a cup of tea, then carried it into her bedroom. She set the teacup on the rickety stand that served as her bedside table, picked up her hairbrush, and sat on the edge of her narrow bed. As she began to brush, she pondered the words of the spell that had come to her. Come *through* her, really. She wondered if other witches had that same experience, or if hers was unique.

Mother Goddess, hark to me:
Farmer's wife I will not be.
Free me from this harsh estate.
Guide me to my better fate.

Ursule, standing beside her, had seen the flicker of light in the crystal, inchoate but unmistakable. She had reminded her, in a whisper, "Three times three times," and Irène had repeated the spell, counting the repetitions on her fingers. The dark cellar, she thought, was a poor temple. One day she would create a better one, and her rites would have the majesty and ceremony they deserved.

For today, she could only wonder how her spell would be made to work.

She was sure it would. She felt it. And though she had abandoned her mother to the endless work of the farm, she would not feel guilty. She was fighting a war, a war for her life. In any war, sacrifices were unavoidable.

She heard the clank of the garden gate in the stone wall, and left her bedroom to go to the kitchen window. Ursule, gray hair straggling beneath her straw hat, started down the lane toward the Grange, a basket of squashes and potatoes over her arm. Irène watched her, noticing her uneven hem, the canvas apron stiff with garden dirt, her plodding step in her heavy boots.

A moment later she realized this was the time she had been waiting for. If Ursule was off to the Grange kitchen with her produce, she would be gone at least two hours. Sally always gave her a cup of tea and a couple of biscuits in exchange for a nice chat.

There was time to get down to the cellar, study the recipe, and collect the ingredients.

She grabbed an apron on her way out the door, to keep her best dress clean. She hurried, shoving up the slanting door, scrambling down the steps. She decided it would be faster to carry the grimoire up to the kitchen, where the light was good, and write out the translation of the Old French. Surely Ursule could not object now? She had proven herself. It was her right.

Because she had puzzled out the instructions once before, it took her only fifteen minutes to write out the recipe in contemporary French:

Take three leaves and two flowers of coltsfoot, along with an inch of the root; add three inches of lovage root, well dried; flowers of lady's mantle; three spikes of mullein; and a twig of mistletoe, crushed. Mix with water that has been boiled and cooled, and let rest on the altar until the morning star rises.

Irène left the grimoire where it was while she ran to the pantry to see what herbs were available. She found everything she needed except mistletoe, but she had seen a great misty-green cloud of it hanging in the crook of a double-trunked elm. She seized her hat and the sharpest knife in the kitchen drawer, and hurried out.

She thought the fox might appear to guide her on this errand, but there was no sign of him. It didn't matter. She knew where the mistletoe hung. It was only five minutes' walk into the forest, and a matter of moments to slice two thick stems. She dropped them into her apron and was back in the kitchen before a quarter of an hour had elapsed. Within the hour she had sliced and chopped and crushed and measured, and set her mixture to steep in an amber glass jar. She corked the jar and carried it to the altar in the root cellar. Before she left it, she let her fingers linger on the glass for a moment. It seemed to vibrate under her fingertips, as if something were alive in the liquid. She whispered the last lines of her spell:

Free me from this harsh estate.
Guide me to my better fate.

The jar shook with such power that it rattled against the wooden surface.

She smiled with satisfaction and went back to the kitchen for the grimoire. Her mother interrupted her, appearing in the doorway with her now-empty basket in her hand. She stared at the book in Irène's hands. "What are you doing with that?"

Irène hesitated, the truth trembling on her lips, the safer lie coming more slowly to her mind. She glanced down at her ink-stained fingers. "I—I thought to work on the translations. Because the pages are fading so badly."

"They will fade worse in this light," Ursule said, turning toward the pantry. "Put it back in the cellar, if you're finished."

Irène hurried to obey, marveling at how simple it was to tell someone what she wanted to hear. Why speak the truth when many people would prefer the falsehood? Life would be easier for all concerned, surely.

Sebastien would not agree. But Sebastien, as usual, was not there.

When Tom Butler appeared at the cottage the next morning, only Ursule was surprised. Irène had heard her fox bark in the night, and felt the energy of her potion from the root cellar. Her spell was at work. When the first star of morning rose, she crept down to the cellar to retrieve the jar, and hid it in her bedroom.

Now, she had only to open the door to the horsemaster and wait to hear how it was all to proceed.

"Miss Blodwyn finds the Shire colt too headstrong for her taste," the horsemaster said, avoiding Irène's eyes and addressing her mother.

Ursule said, "What does she expect us to do about it, Tom?"

Irène stepped aside and gestured Tom into the cottage. He pulled off his cap and ostentatiously wiped his boots on the rag rug inside the door, even though his boots were cleaner than the ones Ursule had been about to put on. "You won't be happy about this, Ursula," he said. "Master Hughes has decided to sell him."

"Sell!" Ursule exclaimed. "Tom, when I agreed to breed Aramis, Master Hughes promised the foal would stay at the Grange!"

"I know," Tom said. "But now Miss Blodwyn..." He spread his hands and turned a pleading glance to Irène. "I'm sorry about what I said. You were right. Miss Blodwyn will never be able to handle Ynyr, and now she's afraid of him."

"You should take her whip away," Irène said crisply. "He was more frightened than she was."

"I still don't know what you want us to do," Ursule said. She was tying her canvas apron over her work dress. "The colt needs training. Can't you persuade your master to allow you to do it?"

"He has buyers here."

"Today?"

Tom nodded. "Afraid so. Miss Blodwyn told him about Irène—"

Ursule frowned. "What about Irène?"

Irène carefully controlled her expression, afraid triumph gleamed in her eyes. "Blodwyn was whipping the colt, Mother. Had him in a frenzy. I calmed him down."

"It was like magic," Tom said, making Ursule turn a startled look on her daughter.

"It was common sense," Irène said. "I gather Master Hughes wants me to come?"

"He does." Tom twisted his cap between his hands. "It would be a great favor to me, too. Ynyr's a fine colt, but he has a rebellious spirit."

"Wait," Ursule said. "Can't we do something about this, Tom? What if I kept the colt here, with his sire? We could—"

He shook his head. "I'm that sorry, Ursula. I tried. I couldn't persuade Master Hughes to it."

"Who are the buyers?" Irène asked.

When he answered, the ache began in her belly, and a private exultation swelled in her breast. Tom said, "It's two men from a place called Morgan Hall. A Lord Llewelyn and his horsemaster."

"Do you think the horsemaster is good?"

"Seems so. But Master Hughes wants to show the colt at his best, get a good price."

Irène said, "Give me five minutes to change, Tom."

"Irène—" Ursule began, but Irène hurried into her bedroom before her mother could think of some objection.

She had washed and pressed a serge skirt, and spent some of her empty hours embroidering a shirtwaist. Wearing them together, she could claim a sort of Gibson Girl effect, and with luck Blodwyn's critical eye would be absent from the stables. The men might not see that her clothes were homemade. She meant for them to admire her tiny waist, her high bosom, and the richness of her hair, which she took a moment to pile on her head in sweeping waves.

She gave herself a final critical glance before secreting the corked jar of her potion in the pocket of her coat, which she draped over her arm as artfully as she could, and hoped she would not need to wear.

When she and Tom Butler reached the stables, they found

Master Hughes, a thickset, russet-headed man, standing outside the stables with two other men, one tall and dark, the shorter man with blond hair going gray and a bristling mustache. Master Hughes and the older man were smoking cigars, while the younger man stood a little apart, hipshot, his riding cap cocked against the slanting autumn sunshine.

As Irène and Tom approached, the older men ground their cigars into the gravel. The younger one straightened and removed his cap, revealing sleepy-looking dark eyes and a shock of black hair to rival Irène's own.

Master Hughes said, "Irene! Good." He turned to his companion to say, "Milord, this is the young woman Tom was telling us about."

Irène said, "Lord Llewelyn, I assume." She dropped an infinitesimal curtsy. "I am Irene Orchard." She spoke in an aristocrat's accent not even she had known she could produce. Master Hughes didn't notice. Tom certainly did. She felt his sidelong glance of surprise as clearly as if he had touched her arm, and she felt the quizzical glance of the other horsemaster. She gave Lord Llewelyn a glacial smile.

He said, "Miss Orchard," and inclined his head to her.

No one bothered to introduce the younger man, nor did anyone speak to Tom.

They all went into the stables, and Tom indicated Ynyr's stall with a gesture of his head. Irène, still with her coat folded over her arm, stepped up to the stall door. She slid back the bolt and opened the door wide.

The colt was crosstied, two thick ropes extending from his halter to iron rings set into the walls of the stall. The ropes stopped him from throwing up his head, but at the sight of Irène and the men behind her, he yanked against them, his ears laid flat and his tail switching. His neck uncomfortably extended, he stamped and kicked, unable to rear. The reek of his anxious sweat nearly overpowered the scents of hay and straw and oiled leather.

Irène could see why Lord Llewelyn wanted the horse. The two-year-old was a beauty, more magnificent even than Aramis, and only a half hand shy of Aramis's great height. The dapples on his white coat made him look as if he had been dusted with silver. His mane and tail were thick and silky, and his wide hooves a shining, uniform gray.

Llewelyn moved into the empty stall next to Ynyr's. He braced his elbows on the separating wall and watched as the colt snorted and kicked out with one enormous hind foot, striking the wall behind him with a jarring bang. Llewelyn jerked back with a wordless exclamation, and Tom moved forward as if to pull Irène out of harm's way. She threw up her free hand to stop him, aware of the picture she must make, a slender dark girl silhouetted by the silver bulk of a nervous stallion.

Irène's performance with Ynyr the last time had been as much a surprise to her as to everyone else, but she couldn't afford doubts now. As she stepped closer to him she pressed a hand to her bodice. Beneath her embroidered shirtwaist she wore her best camisole, and beneath the camisole, nestled against her bare breast, was the curl of the fox's hair in its little snare of silk thread. She carried it now in a dented tin locket she had found in the pantry. She had added a bit of rosemary and a sprig of lavender to make an amulet.

She heard Hughes mutter to Tom, "You're sure about this?"

"Hope so, sir. She worked magic with him before."

Tom was speaking metaphorically, but magic was exactly what she needed now.

Another step brought her nose to nose with the big horse. He pulled back, snorting and pawing, sending spurts of crushed straw over her skirt. She flattened her palm over her amulet, pressing it hard against her skin, and breathed, "Ynyr. Ynyr. You know me. Remember? You know me."

He emitted a long, nostril-ruffling breath and stood still.

Irène gingerly lifted her hand, fearful that when she released the amulet, Ynyr would explode again. Instead he stretched his neck toward her, sniffing at her shirtwaist as if he knew what lay beneath. "Good boy," she whispered. "You remember." With cautious fingers she pulled the knot on one of the ropes that held him.

Tom murmured, "Have a care," but she persisted. She let the rope drop, and Ynyr still didn't move. She ran her hand down his powerful neck under his mane. His skin shivered at her touch, but he stood steady. His breathing slowed, and grew deeper. She untied the remaining rope from its ring, looked once into his eyes, then turned her back to him to lead him out of the stall.

He followed, his head nodding above her shoulder, his steps measured.

Master Hughes said, a little too loudly, "You see, my lord? I told you he's a lamb. Gentle giant, this one."

"Let's see about that." Lord Llewelyn stepped forward. He smelled of cigar smoke and bay rum, and he threw out his hand as if to seize the lead rope.

Ynyr squealed and leaped backward, jerking the rope from Irène's hand.

Llewelyn swore, and so did Hughes. Tom groaned, but Llewelyn's horsemaster only stood to one side, one black eyebrow arched, watching in silence.

Irène snatched up the rope from the straw-covered floor. She said, "Master Hughes, he was never like this until your daughter whipped him."

Tom began, "Irène—" but his master interrupted him.

"Sometimes a horse needs whipping."

Llewelyn's horsemaster, Jago, spoke for the first time. "Nay, sir," he said. "Good horses do better without the use of the whip." He turned his sleepy dark eyes on Irène and asked, "Do you need help with him, lass?"

Irked at being called lass, when Lord Llewelyn had called her miss, Irène allowed her lip to curl. "Of course not," she said haughtily.

Llewelyn cleared his throat. "If we can't manage him on a lead, we have no way of getting him to Morgan Hall. It's two days' ride."

Hughes shuffled his feet, which Irène read as a sign of anxiety over losing his sale.

"Give me a moment, milord," she said. The patrician sound of her voice pleased her. "Miss Blodwyn abused this colt. All he needs is to be confident there will be no more whips."

Hughes would resent that, but she guessed Llewelyn's money was more important to him than the aspersion she had cast on his daughter.

Under the cover of the folds of her coat, still draped over her arm, she slipped her hand into the pocket. As she walked back into the stall, she loosened the cork on the amber glass jar. Ynyr quivered at her approach, but allowed her to come close. She slipped two fingers into the potion, replaced the cork, and extended her wet fingers to Ynyr's muzzle. She whispered, "Be still," and rubbed her potion onto his lips. His broad tongue appeared, incongruously pink against his gray muzzle as he licked his lips. She let her hand slide across his wide cheek and up to scratch behind his ear.

Under her breath, she murmured,

Guide me to my better fate.

Ynyr breathed a deep, horsey sigh and dropped his head so she could rub the spot beneath his forelock. "The colt will be fine," Irène said. "If you will all step aside, please."

The men, as much under her spell as the horse, moved out of her way as she led the Shire out of the stall, down the alley of the stables, and into the cool sunshine. In respectful silence the men followed. Irène, as she tied Ynyr's lead rope to the post, cast them a glance from beneath her eyelashes. Tom looked relieved. Master Hughes was frowning, bemused, but clearly eager to take his payment and send milord on his way. The sleepy eyes of Jago, the horsemaster, gleamed with interest.

Lord Llewelyn stood with his arms folded across his vest, pride of possession already showing in his satisfied expression. He cleared his throat before he said, "Well, Hughes, I think we have a bargain. We should share a stirrup cup, don't you think? Perhaps Miss Orchard will join us."

Irène said, "What a kind thought, milord. Allow me to go to the kitchen and"—she caught herself just in time—"and give the order."

She felt Master Hughes's and Tom's stunned glances burning her back as she walked away, but she lifted her head and held her skirt back with one hand as she had seen Blodwyn do. A lady, she reminded herself. She was a lady.

She whispered again, as she walked:

Free me from this harsh estate.
Guide me to my better fate.

If either Hughes or Tom gave her away, she thought, she would turn them into toads.

7

It was fascinating to watch the effect of the philter. Irène couldn't think why her mother had never employed it. This, surely, would have kept Sebastien at home.

She hadn't dared to actually give the Grange cook an order. Sally knew perfectly well who and what she was. Irène smiled at her, explained the situation in an undertone, and begged to be allowed to carry the stirrup cup out to the men. "Five tumblers," she said. "Lord Llewelyn has invited me to share. I know it's not usual, but I wouldn't want to refuse his kindness."

Sally chuckled. "Has an eye for a pretty girl, I suspect, though he's hardly a young man. I'll have it for you in a moment, and I'll call the downstairs maid to help you carry the tray."

"Thanks, but don't trouble her. I can manage on my own," Irène said. The fewer eyes on her the better.

She carried the heavy tray with no difficulty back over the lawn to the stables, stopping only for the briefest moment to put the tray down, slip the amber glass jar out of her coat pocket, and pour its contents into one of the tumblers. She kept a careful eye on the one she had altered, and offered it to His Lordship first, as was proper. Hughes was ebullient now that an agreement had been reached, money exchanged, the bargain sealed. He snatched up his tumbler with enthusiasm. Llewelyn was more restrained, but he drank as heartily as the others. Irène's tumbler held only a thimbleful, and she sipped it delicately, bestowing on Llewelyn a gracious smile, as if she were the hostess at a tea in the Grange parlor.

Lord Llewelyn lifted his tumbler to his lips again and again. Irène felt an aura bloom around her, a glow, as if she stood in a shaft of moonlight, cool and bright and mysterious. It was a light only she and Llewelyn could see.

His eyes returned to her again and again. As the potion took effect, his lips beneath his mustache grew red and swollen and his breathing quickened and grew shallow. When the stirrup cup had been consumed, Irène left the tray and the tumblers on the grass, and watched with Master Hughes and Tom as Lord Llewelyn mounted his mare and Jago swung himself up on a sturdy gelding, with Ynyr's rope in his hand.

Llewelyn gazed at Irène as he made his farewells, though his words were addressed to Hughes. She barely heard what he said, or what anyone said, but she sensed Llewelyn's reluctance to depart from her. She allowed her own face to mirror it, ever so slightly.

The sun was low on the western horizon as the two men rode away with the Shire in tow. No one spoke until they rounded the turn from the drive into the road. When they were out of sight, Master Hughes whirled to face Irène. "Who do you think you are, putting on airs with His Lordship that way?" he snapped. "Insulting my daughter, giving orders to my cook—"

"Managing your colt," she interrupted. She treated him to her iciest stare. "Saving your sale, in fact."

"You know better than to speak to your betters that way! Acting as if you—as if you—"

"As if I were a lady?" Irène spoke in a silky voice, exaggerating the nasal pronunciation of an aristocrat, and lifting her chin to show that she knew precisely what she was doing.

Hughes began to sputter. "You're a farm girl!"

"And did you inform His Lordship of that?"

"No, I couldn't do that, not in the face of—since you—but you should know your proper place! Ursula should have taught you better!"

"Perhaps, sir," Irène said smoothly, "you should look to your own house before you criticize mine."

Hughes's face reddened, and angry sweat beaded his forehead. "Only for your mother's sake," he hissed, "will I let these insults pass. She has been hardworking and faithful, and I respect her for it. Now get back to your work. I don't want to see you at the Grange again."

"That," Irène said with confidence as she shrugged into her coat, "is something you won't have to worry about."

⁓ঌৎ

She didn't have to wait long for the next act in her drama. Sally was at the door of the cottage early the next morning, clearly in a state of excitement. Ursule had just collected her gloves and her basket, and was on the point of starting out to dig potatoes. Irène had dressed again in her embroidered shirtwaist and serge skirt, in the expectation of some development. She had heard the fox yipping in the night, conveying his assurance that her magic was at work.

Sally said, "Ursula! Irene is wanted at the Grange!"

Ursule frowned and dropped her work gloves into the basket. "What's she done?"

"I don't know, but that lord who bought the horse—you know, the horse Miss Blodwyn didn't like—that Lord Llewelyn is back! He traveled as far as Carmarthen, but left his horsemaster there and returned early this morning. He wants to see Irene!"

Irène had not bothered to tell her mother that Master Hughes had forbidden her to come to the Grange again, and she didn't bother now. Obviously Lord Llewelyn's commands overrode all others. She smoothed her skirt and said, "I'll just get my gloves and hat, Sally."

Her mother followed her into the bedroom, and as she stood before her tiny mirror, pinning her hat into place, Ursule said, "Tell me what's happening."

Irène looked at her mother's tired reflection. "My life is happening, Mother."

"What does that mean?"

Irène picked up her lace gloves and smoothed them on. "It means my chance has come."

"Because of this Llewelyn?"

Irène, aware of Sally listening from the kitchen, switched to French. "Maman, I'm going to tell you, because you taught me, and it's only fair. I made the philter."

"What philter?"

"The potion, from the grimoire. You didn't want me to do it, and I'm sorry, but it obviously worked, or Lord Llewelyn would not have come back for me."

Ursule paled and staggered a step back to sit on the edge of Irène's bed. "You didn't," she whispered. "Tell me you didn't, Daughter."

Irène put her back to the mirror and faced her mother with her hands on her hips. "I did," she said. "I can't think why you haven't done it yourself."

"It's not real, Irène. It's . . . It's artificial. It's dangerous. I should have torn out the page!"

"I'm glad you didn't."

"It's not like scrying, you know. Or making simples for pain or sickness. This sort of magic—it forces people. Manipulates them!"

"If I have the power, why should I not use it, Maman? Why do you try to stand in my way?

"You can't make someone love you, no matter how powerful you are."

"I don't need him to love me."

"What do you need, then?"

"I've told you. I don't want to live the life you have. Is that so hard to understand?"

"But, Irène...think about what he'll want with you. A farm girl!"

"Maman, I'm no longer a farm girl." Irène held up her hands, as white and soft as those of Miss Blodwyn. "You see? All I needed was a chance, and this is it."

"You will pay a terrible price, I fear."

Irène faced the mirror again and adjusted the collar of her shirtwaist. "There is always a price, isn't there?" she said coolly. "You have paid a steep one yourself. Endless work. Loneliness. Poverty." Irène started for the door.

Ursule said softly, "I've had true love in my life. I don't regret a moment."

"No?" Irène glanced over her shoulder at her mother, slumped on the edge of the bed in a posture of defeat. "Well, then. You're willing to settle for less than I am."

With a grunt Ursule pushed herself up. "I don't think of myself as having settled. I think of myself as having survived."

Impatiently Irène said, "I have to go, Maman. Can't you wish me good luck?"

"I do wish you good luck. That's why I hope you'll be back here in an hour. Perhaps you'll be a bit wiser than when you left."

Sally cast Irène a dozen curious glances as they walked to the Grange, but Irène focused on what was to come. Though she couldn't repeat her spell with Sally beside her, she recited it in her mind, over and over. When they reached the curving gravel path that led to the Grange, Sally said, "I'll be leaving you here."

Irène stopped walking. "Where are you going?"

"The kitchen. I was told you are to go to the main entrance."

She turned right, to cross the lawn to the kitchen door. Irène said, "Wait, Sally. What did Master Hughes say? What has he told Lord Llewelyn about me?"

Sally paused. "It's nothing to do with me, Irene. You're my friend's child, and I won't speak against you, but I think you're walking into trouble."

"Why would you say that?"

"Because I know how men are. If he's decided he wants you, he'll use you, then cast you aside when you grow your first gray hair." She went off across the lawn, shaking her head as she walked. Irène drew a breath to calm her racing heart, and walked with a sedate pace up to the big front door of the Grange.

It was a door she had never entered, but she refused to be daunted by the grandeur of the foyer, or troubled by the disdain with which the butler greeted her. She unpinned her hat, and when he didn't take it, she laid it on a sideboard. He pointed the way to the parlor, but she shook her head. Pressing her hand over the amulet hidden beneath her bodice, she said, "Announce me, please." Her imperiousness matched his disdain. For an instant she thought he might refuse. She pretended not to notice, but waited, chin in the air, for him to comply with her request.

Finally he said, "What name shall I say?"

"Irene Orchard. *Miss* Irene Orchard."

The amulet seemed to vibrate against her skin as the butler led the way, opened the door, and did precisely as she had asked.

Irène waited until he had finished speaking her name to move into the doorway. She paused there, aware of the picture she made. Her shirtwaist was a creamy white, and her skirt a pale green. The hall behind her was lined with dark portraits and darker mirrors, dramatizing her silhouette. Her hair was piled in black, shining waves, and her complexion was as pale as milk. She tucked her chin and lifted her eyelids slowly, to show her thick eyelashes and the dark brown of her eyes.

As she had the day before, she curtsied. She gauged the level of it with precision, one hand gracefully holding the edge of her skirt, the other touching her shirtwaist, with the amulet beneath it. "Your Lordship," she said. "Master Hughes."

Llewelyn stood up, and Master Hughes followed his example a moment later. "Miss Orchard," Llewelyn said, and inclined his head to her.

Hughes said stiffly, "Irene. His Lordship has a proposal for you. I felt you would welcome hearing it."

"Of course, Master Hughes. Thank you."

"Won't you sit down?" Llewelyn said, indicating a damask chair near the sofa where he had been sitting.

Irène settled herself in the chair and tilted her head, waiting. Beneath the slight weight of the tin amulet, her heart fluttered in anticipation.

As she gazed at Llewelyn, she couldn't help thinking it was a shame he didn't look more like his horsemaster. That one—Jago, she recalled, not a common name—was lean and dark, with narrow lips and slanting dark eyes. His Lordship, unfortunately, was running slightly to fat, and the brush of his yellow mustache was in need of trimming. His eyes were a milky blue, though they glittered, now that he had consumed her philter, with what she assumed was desire.

However, his clothes were beautifully made, and his boots shone as if he had someone to polish them every time he put them on. Even more important, he had a title. His wife would be Lady Morgan. Or Lady Llewelyn. Titles were complicated things. Perhaps, if she pleased him, she could be styled Lady Irene. She liked the sound of it.

"I am told you are fatherless, Miss Orchard," Llewelyn said. He had resumed his own seat, but he sat stiffly, his spine rigid, his chin tucked. "Otherwise I would address him, as would be proper." He spoke without hurry, but she sensed the need that drove him, that underlay his measured approach.

"It's true, Your Lordship," she said calmly, without the slightest tingle of guilt. Sebastien wasn't with them enough to count as a father. He had said so himself. "I'm obliged to make my own way in the world."

"Of course, your mother—" Hughes began.

Irène shot him a look, and his mouth snapped shut. "I am nearly eighteen," she said. "She and I agree that I should make my own decisions."

Llewelyn cleared his throat. Irène recognized it as a reflexive habit. Over time, listening to that sound might be annoying, but now she welcomed it as a sign that His Lordship meant to take control of the conversation.

"In view of your status as an unwed but fatherless young woman," he said, "I took the liberty of applying to Master Hughes on the subject of your marriage. He is, I perceive, the only male close to you."

Irène put her hand to her throat and felt the amulet quiver against her breast. She breathed, "Marriage?"

Llewelyn gave his dry cough again. "I have startled you, Miss Orchard. I apologize."

Irène said, "I'm not quite sure what you're telling me, Lord Llewelyn. If you could speak plainly, I would be grateful."

"Of course. I know this is not only sudden, but unusual." His cheeks colored above his beard, and he gave her a slight, apologetic smile. "I'm aware you have no dowry, and limited education, but you have made an impression upon me. You are a young lady of poise and wit, as well as a most pleasing appearance."

Irène let her gaze drop down and to the side, to show her cheekbones to their best effect.

"Indeed, you have made me think it may not be necessary to allow my cousin to inherit my title and my land."

Irène lowered her hand to her lap and linked her fingers. She bent a clear gaze on Llewelyn and said, "Forgive me for being blunt, milord, but am I to understand you are proposing marriage—to me?"

Llewelyn cleared his throat again. Truly, it was a habit he would have to break. He put his hands on his knees to push himself up, then held out his hand to her. She stood, too. Slowly, as if she were uncertain about the gesture, she gave him her lace-gloved hand.

Llewelyn said, "Master Hughes has given me permission to address you, Miss Orchard. Yes, I am proposing marriage. I am considerably older than you are, but I have property, and rather a good title. I've never married. I work in government, and have an excellent staff at Morgan Hall. You would be their mistress."

Irène willed herself to blush, and felt warmth creep into her cheeks.

"If you need time to think…"

She remembered her mother's warning. Time to think was a luxury she couldn't risk. She bowed her head for a moment, as if considering this, but lifted it in only seconds. "Milord, you honor me. I'm known to be a decisive person, so I will decline your offer of time to consider. You're offering me a lovely opportunity, and I will accept, with gratitude, and in the hope you will find me worthy."

She heard Master Hughes's skeptical grunt, but Lord Llewelyn smiled and squeezed her hand, patted it, then bent to give her a bristly kiss on her cheek. She smiled up at him—not too far up, as he wasn't tall—and managed to squeeze a tear into her eye, which made him pat her hand again and murmur comforting words about a bright future, a happy life.

There was a little fuss about speaking with her mother, which she managed to prevent, and a bit more fuss about hiring a gig to transport her to Morgan Hall, and about finding a lady's maid to act as chaperone. As they were arranging these details, with a skeptical-looking Hughes presiding, Blodwyn Hughes came into the parlor and stood in the doorway, fists on her hips and a look of pure resentment on her face.

Llewelyn said, "Dear Miss Blodwyn! You may congratulate me! Your father has acted for me in the matter of my marriage to your friend Miss Orchard."

Hughes said, "Yes, Blodwyn. You should wish them happy."

Blodwyn's face turned a most unprepossessing red, and Irène took a step closer to her prospective husband. Fortunately, in this encounter Blodwyn was without her whip. Her eyes narrowed, but she managed to say, "My word! Irene Orchard? This is sudden, isn't it?"

Lord Llewelyn cleared his throat and declared, "Yes, it is. But at my age—" Everyone laughed politely, and that was that.

Within the hour Llewelyn had made arrangements to borrow one of the Grange's gigs, with harness for his horse. Sally called one of the upstairs maids, who agreed to serve as lady's maid for the journey and be escorted home once Irène had engaged one of her own. Irène begged another hour to pack her belongings and bid her mother good-bye, and, with the maid at her heels, set off for the cottage against a backdrop of falling leaves and building clouds.

As she walked she saw the fox weaving among the trees, laughing at her with his black nose lifted and his tongue lolling. Secretly she smiled at him, and touched the amulet in tribute. He flicked his tail in a scarlet-and-black salute before he disappeared into the woods. Her body thrumming with excitement, she walked steadily forward.

8

Irène left the maid standing in the kitchen as she went into her bedroom to collect a few bits of lingerie, her hairbrushes, and one dress that was, if not fashionable, at least clean. The first thing she would do when she reached Morgan Hall would be to send for a dressmaker.

She didn't own a valise, but there was a carpetbag in the back of her mother's wardrobe, one left behind at some point by Sebastien. She called her mother's name, but received no answer. She went into Ursule's room for the carpetbag. When she had packed her things into it, it was no more than half-full. She glanced around the cottage, but there was nothing else she wanted to take.

Except the crystal. And the grimoire.

They were her inheritance, were they not? She was the last of the Orchiére line, inheritor of the power. She could be the last to practice the craft, to wield the magic of the stone.

She said to the maid, "Wait here. I'll be back in a moment." She snatched up a basket as she hurried out the front door of the cottage and around to the slanting door of the root cellar. She lifted it quickly, ignoring the screech of its hinges, and went down the stone steps.

The stone still rested on the three-legged stool, concealed in its linen wrappings. Irène lifted it, wrappings and all, and stowed it in the basket. She was on the point of bending to take the gri-moire from beneath the stool when she heard her mother's voice.

"Irène! Irène? Where are you?"

In real haste now, lest her mother disagree with her judgment about the stone, Irène scrambled up the steps and lowered the door to the root cellar. With the basket casually over her arm, she met Ursule at the garden gate.

"You came back," Ursule said in French. "Did your spell fail?"

Irène answered in the same language. "No, Maman. It was a success."

The spark of hope that had flickered in Ursule's eyes died away. She said, in a resigned voice, "Tell me, then."

"Lord Llewelyn has proposed marriage. I was looking for you, to say good-bye."

Ursule's jaw tightened. "You're going to accept him."

"I have accepted him."

"You know nothing about him, Daughter. Could you not take some time, think it over?"

"I don't know if I have time."

Ursule nodded, but her mouth was tight with disapproval. Or sorrow. Irène couldn't tell which. "You're right, Irène. It won't last long."

"We'll see, I suppose. But if it doesn't, I will already be Lady Llewelyn. Or Lady Irene."

"You're giving up your French name."

"You and Sebastien are the only ones who use it."

"And now no one will."

Irène, even focused as she was on what had transpired on this day, and what was to come, saw the sadness in her mother's eyes. "Can you not be happy for me, Maman?" she asked.

"If I thought you were going to be happy, I would be, too. But

I think your heart will break, sooner or later. I can't bear to think of it."

"To stay here, to live like this—that would break my heart."

"Well, then, Daughter. This is farewell between us."

"Say good-bye to Sebastien for me."

Ursule shrugged. "If I see him, I will."

Irène said, "I have to go, Maman. The maid is waiting. My—my fiancé is waiting."

"Bonne chance, ma fille."

"Merci. Au revoir."

Ursule responded in a choked voice, *"Adieu."*

Irène, with the basket in her hand, opened the cottage door. When she glanced back she saw that Ursule was on her way to Aramis's pasture. She would take her comfort from him.

Irène collected the carpetbag and the maid, and together they started back to the Grange as the sun slipped past its zenith and began to sink into the west. The fox appeared the moment they started down the lane, and ghosted after them, an intermittent streak of red and black amid the dark green of the woods. They hurried on, eager to be off on their journey before darkness fell. The fox followed until they reached the Grange, and turned up the drive.

THE BOOK OF MORWEN

1

1910

The September heat made the River Thaw sluggish. Sun-crisped grasses and rows of tired cornstalks drooped on either side of the water. A red kite circled high above the Vale of Glamorgan, its gaudy wings brilliant against the hard blue sky. Ynyr's dappled gray hide sparkled in the sunshine as if his big shoulders and sweat-damp hindquarters were encrusted with jewels. Morwen, in a rush of affection, leaned forward to encircle his wide neck with her arms. He snorted with his usual good humor, and she laughed, full of joy in the hot day, the shine of the slow-moving river, the inviting bulk of the ruined castle ahead of them.

Ynyr's only tack was a leather halter and an attached rope. Morwen left the rope slack across his withers. He knew where she wanted to go. He always did. His wide back was as familiar to her as her chair in the parlor at Morgan Hall, and his swinging gait, as he paced up the river path, was as gentle as the rocking of her nanny's chair. Her hat lay on her back, the string loose around her neck, and she lifted her face to feel the sun on her cheeks. She would develop freckles, but she didn't care. Should Lady Irene notice the offending spots, she would have forgotten them by the time she went up to dress for dinner.

Morwen wiggled her ankles against Ynyr's barrel, noticing how much farther her feet reached now than they had six months before. She was nearly sixteen, surely done growing. She was as tall as her mother, and half a head taller than her father. She felt Papa's baffled gaze sometimes, measuring her height and coloring against his own. Father and daughter looked nothing alike. Morwen's eyes and hair were dark as midnight, while Lord Llewelyn's eyes were a vague blue, and his wispy hair had been yellow before it faded to gray.

Morwen asked her nanny once, in the days when she still took supper in the nursery, why her papa was so much older than her mama. Nanny had said, "Oh, that's not unusual, Miss Morwen. Lots of papas are older than mamas. Lord Llewelyn had already come into his title when he married Lady Irene."

"Why would she marry someone so old?" Morwen had asked, blunt in her innocence.

"Well," Nanny answered, giving a tiny sniff. "No doubt Lady Irene was honored by his offer. A very good marriage for a girl from an impoverished family—to become a baroness, to live in Morgan Hall..."

"Mama didn't have a title?"

Nanny pursed her lips. "No, Miss Morwen, she did not, but she does now. Enough questions! Eat your supper, and we'll go for a walk before bed."

"Won't I see Mama and Papa?"

"Not tonight. They're out for the evening."

Now that she was older, Morwen understood that her mama had not only possessed no title, but no father, and no dowry. Morwen and her parents lived a different life from the other gentry of the Vale. The Morgans were an old family in St. Hilary, but Lord Llewelyn and his lady attended few of the dinners and garden parties held in other great houses. Morgan Hall was the place where the parish held its fetes and picnics, so Morwen knew most of the laborers' children, and those of the doctor, the schoolteacher, and the rector. She had few acquaintances of her own social class, a circumstance that caused her governess to despair of her ever learning the art of social conversation. There was evidently nothing to be done. Lady Irene's awkward background made her unwelcome among the aristocracy.

Morwen didn't care. She preferred roaming the fields with Ynyr to playing croquet in a lacy white dress, would rather spend her afternoons mucking out a stall than be confined to parlors to sip tea and make small talk. It was a rare day when she didn't manage to slip away from her governess and dash to the stables.

Ynyr always knew when she was coming, stamping his feet and whinnying with impatience until he caught sight of her.

The governess, Mademoiselle Girard, complained to Lady Irene of her charge's intransigence, but it availed her little. Lady Irene more often than not had forgotten all about Mademoiselle's objections by the time she saw her daughter again. Fortunately for Morwen, Mademoiselle was in awe of Lord Llewelyn, his history, his wealth, his important government role. In his presence she was speechless. She never made her complaints known to His Lordship.

Morwen tilted her head back to scan the broken walls of Old Beaupre Castle. She had grown up with this crumbling structure on the horizon, as much a part of the landscape as the river, the fields, and the square tower and ancient tombstones of the fourteenth-century church, but she had visited the castle only once, on an educational outing with Mademoiselle.

She had demurely ridden her pony, following Mademoiselle on a slow, fat mare, with Jago, the horsemaster, bringing up the rear on his gelding. Mademoiselle had organized the trip to illustrate a lecture about Gothic arches and Grecian columns.

There was no mystery about the castle. It had been abandoned long before in favor of a more modern building. Still, Morwen had been thinking of it lately, drawn to the distant silhouette she could see from her bedroom window. Last night she had been there in a dream, hearing her name called by someone she didn't know and couldn't see. In the dream she drifted through empty rooms and struggled up blind staircases, searching in vain for the source of the voice.

The medieval part of the castle had been built in 1300, which hardly seemed possible. How could there have been people who lived their entire lives six centuries before she was born? Mademoiselle said that even the porch was three hundred years old. She refused to allow Morwen to set foot beyond it. One of the walls could collapse on her, and then what would Lord Llewelyn say?

Of course Mademoiselle didn't know about today's visit. She would have been appalled to see Morwen riding Ynyr, and bareback to boot. Morwen pretended she didn't notice the farm laborers' awe as they stared at the slender girl astride the enormous Shire.

Jago understood the accord between Morwen and Ynyr. When the horse began to stamp and whicker in his stall, Jago often came out to meet Morwen in the stable yard, grinning with the knowledge that the stallion had sensed her approach.

Ynyr climbed the grassy hill to the ruin and crossed the last bit of empty field, picking his way among gopher holes and curls of bramble. When they reached the crumbling wall that circled the castle, Morwen sat for a moment, enjoying the quiet. At Morgan Hall there was an unending coming and going, maids and butler and cook and governess dashing up and down stairs, in and out of rooms. It was all but impossible to be alone there, but here, on the hill above the river, was delicious solitude. There was no one to watch her except a few plump red cows grazing in the meadow.

Morwen put one leg over Ynyr's withers and slid to the ground. She unclipped the rope from his halter and let it fall. He bent his head to graze as she brushed horsehair from the back of her riding skirt.

As she stepped into the shade of the ruined walls, she walked on grass. Unglazed windows gaped onto the Vale. The walls were naked stone, and the three floors had long ago crumbled to dust. In truth, there was little left but a skeleton of what had once been a noble family's home. It now stood exposed to the elements, less sheltered than the simplest pigsty. Only the tower at one corner had any protection from the elements. The tower was the only mystery about Old Beaupre. No one knew what its purpose might have been.

Morwen trailed her fingertips against the moss-stained walls as she wandered inward. She followed the ancient outlines of a corridor until she came upon an inner courtyard, where she supposed the family had once gathered. A sudden coolness made her shiver, or perhaps it was the memory of her dream. She wandered on, following the fragments of wall, trying to picture the way the castle had once looked.

In a second courtyard the remains of a fountain lay in shards on the patchy grass. A staircase led upward, its broad treads set with river stone. The stairs led only to the open air, but there was a north-facing window near the top. Morwen thought it might afford a view of Morgan Hall.

If there had ever been a banister, it was gone now. Many of the steps were broken. As she mounted the stairs, her arms and legs tingled with awareness of the drop to her left. When she reached the window she clung to the sill for safety, feeling the chill of stone against her palms as she stood on tiptoe to peer out.

The square outlines of Morgan Hall showed clearly in the distance, framed by fields of yellow and green, its chimney pots sending tendrils of smoke into the clear sky. The roofline of the stables showed just behind, and thatched cottages dotted the farmland around it. As Morwen watched, the Vulcan tonneau pulled up in the circular drive. She squinted, trying to make out Jago at the wheel. Lord Llewelyn climbed out, a plump dark figure with satchel in hand. No doubt he had just come in from Cardiff on the train.

Morwen watched as Jago backed and turned the motorcar. He would be perspiring with the effort of managing the tonneau. He hated the thing, as she knew from the outings they made to the shops in Cowbridge.

Jago was far more comfortable with animals than motors, but Lord Llewelyn refused to hire a separate driver. Morwen and Jago exchanged private smiles whenever the subject of the tonneau arose. Of all the people at Morgan Hall, Jago was the single person Morwen trusted. It was Jago who had taught her to ride her pony, when she was just four years old.

She had been six the first time she rode Ynyr. Jago wouldn't have allowed it, so she waited until he was off driving Lord Llewelyn. She opened Ynyr's stall, and the big horse obligingly lowered his head so she could attach a rope to his halter. The mounting block wasn't high enough, so she climbed up on the fence around the paddock. Again Ynyr obliged, moving close enough for her to jump on. When she thudded his ribs with her small feet, he started off, and Jago had found them circling the paddock at a ponderous walk. He scolded them both, but Morwen had seen the gleam of pride in his eyes.

She was relaxing her stretched toes to lower herself from the window when movement flickered at the edge of her vision. She turned her head, keeping her grip on the windowsill, and saw a narrow window set into the wall of the tower. It seemed to her sun-dazzled eyes that someone—or something—had walked past it. She freed one hand to shade her eyes and looked again, thinking it must have been a trick of the sunlight, a reflection from a bit of quartz in one of the building stones or a shadow from a moving cloud. It came again, a wisp of gray, a flutter of black.

Morwen sucked in a breath. Was that an animal? It would have to be a big one. It couldn't be a person lurking in that dark, vacant tower.

Far below her Ynyr whickered, then whinnied. A muffled thumping followed, his hoofbeats sounding on the grassy interior of the ruin. Cautiously, wary of the abyss beneath her, Morwen made her way down the broken staircase. Ynyr's hoofbeats came closer, and she heard his anxious snort as he searched for her.

She reached the last stair just as the horse edged his way through the doorway, ducking his head to pass through, scraping his hindquarters on the lintel. "Ynyr!" she cried. "You shouldn't be in here!"

For answer he bumped her chest with his nose. She took his broad cheeks in her two hands and planted a kiss just below his forelock. "You great silly. I'm perfectly fine!"

He snorted again and tossed his head, blowing spittle over her face. She wiped it off as she guided him in an awkward turn. He had to duck and scrape his way back through the doorway and out into the first courtyard. Morwen had come into the castle through a side door, but with the horse beside her, she turned toward a gaping space that must once have held a double door. Ynyr fit easily through it, and side by side they walked through the shadowed porch, passing beneath the Tudor archway. The sudden brilliance of the sun brought stinging tears to Morwen's eyes, and she blinked them away as she bent to pick up the halter rope from the grass.

Her eyes were still dazzled as she stepped toward Ynyr to clip the rope into its ring. Her left hand lay on his wide shoulder, and her right reached toward his chin as he dropped his head to accommodate her.

He startled her by shying away, throwing his head up beyond her reach. Her hand, stretched out with the snap in her fingers, groped through empty air. "Ynyr! What's the matter?" He was staring past her, eyes wide and ears laid flat. She spun to see what had frightened him.

A strange figure stood in the shadow of the porch. She wasn't sure if it was male or female, so shrouded was it, covered head to toe in layers of dark fabric. The person might once have been tall, but now was bent, shoulders hunched around a widow's hump, neck jutting forward. The face was hidden behind a voluminous hood that looked to Morwen like something out of a fairy tale. For one disorienting moment she thought a ghost had wandered out of the ruin of Old Beaupre.

The smell of the creature dispelled that notion. This person reeked of much-worn clothes and unbathed flesh. The hand that rose to fold back the hood was dark with dirt, the nails black and ragged and all too real.

Morwen took a step back to stay close to Ynyr. She wasn't really afraid, not with the Shire beside her, but having ridden out with neither maid nor chaperone meant she was vulnerable. If this was a beggar, she had no money to give. If it wasn't a beggar, then...

The hood fell away, revealing a face that must be female, though so seamed and gaunt it was hard to be certain. A cloud of curly hair surrounded it, hair so white it glittered in the sunshine. The eyes were midnight dark, but sharp, beneath thick silver eyebrows. When the woman opened her mouth, her teeth also looked sharp, and as white as her hair.

"You must be Lady Irene's babe," she said.

"I'm not a babe," Morwen said, stung. "I'm fifteen."

"Oh yes, I know that. Fifteen. Morwen." The old woman

grinned suddenly, deepening the creases in her cheeks. "Miss Morwen, they call you." Though she looked ancient, her voice was surprisingly clear, even sweet, with a slight accent Morwen didn't recognize.

The woman took a step closer so she could peer up into Morwen's face. Morwen shrank back against Ynyr. "What do you want?" she asked, ashamed of the quaver in her voice. She straightened, encouraged by Ynyr's bulk behind her. With a decisive movement, she reached up to clip the rope onto his halter. "We have to go!" she said over her shoulder.

"I won't keep you. I wanted to see you." The old woman stood where she was, her ragged layers shifting in the breeze, the sunshine bright on her silver hair.

Morwen, about to lead Ynyr to one of the broken walls to mount, looked back. "What do you mean?"

The old woman grinned again, and though the lines in her face were so deep, the smile brightened her face with the memory of youth. "I wanted to lay my eyes on you, Miss Morwen. One time before I die."

A strange feeling crept over Morwen as she stared at the unwashed crone with her shining black eyes and white smile. It was a sense of recognition. Or premonition. It confounded her and made her head ache. She stammered, "I don't... That doesn't..." but couldn't think how to go on.

"She has never mentioned me, then," the crone said. Her smile faded, and her eyelids lowered. "You have no idea about your *grand-mère*."

"*Ma grand-mère, elle est morte*," Morwen said, then wondered why she had responded in French.

It was the one thing—the only thing—her lady mother took an interest in. She was determined that Morwen should speak unaccented, perfect French. Lord Llewelyn approved because he thought it would aid her chances of an advantageous marriage. Lady Irene had never explained her own motivation, but she engaged a French governess, and she frequently tested Morwen's fluency. It was often their only conversation.

The old woman switched to French as smoothly as Morwen might take a breath. Her eyelids lifted again, and her gaze turned steely. "What makes you think she's dead, Miss Morwen? Who told you that?"

"My mother." Morwen felt transfixed by the crone's eyes, pinned like a butterfly on a board of cork. "M-my nanny."

"Yes? Which?" The crone chuckled. "Which was it? Your mother or your nanny?"

This challenge, given as if this stranger had a right to the answer, was too much. Morwen turned away from the crone in her noisome draperies and hurried Ynyr toward the wall. She found a place high enough, stepped up, then swung her leg over Ynyr's back. She gave the rope a small shake. "Let's go, Ynyr! Go now."

For the second time that day the horse surprised her. Instead of starting down the hill he took two steps backward, his head bobbing, his ears twitching. When she protested, a hand on his neck and her heels digging into his ribs, he shook his head from side to side, as if a fly had bitten his nose. "Ynyr, what is it?"

He turned in place, careful not to dislodge her, but deliberately. In two long strides he carried her back to the old woman, who stood with her hands buried in her sleeves. Ynyr bent his head to the ground at her feet and was still. Through a throat gone dry, Morwen croaked, "What is it you want?"

"I told you," the crone said. "Your horse understands. Indeed, I know this horse."

"You couldn't know Ynyr."

"But I do. And he recognizes me as well."

Morwen couldn't deny it. Ynyr stood with his head bowed and his ears drooping. When she tugged on his mane, he lifted one hind foot and rested it on the point of the hoof, standing hipshot to demonstrate that he had no intention of moving.

"What have you done to him?" Morwen heard the note of pleading in her voice. Why should this woman frighten her? And why would Ynyr—great Ynyr—

The woman withdrew one of her hands from her sleeve and laid it on Ynyr's forehead. It was a surprisingly large hand, with strong-looking fingers. She bent and murmured something into the horse's ear. When she straightened and moved a little away, he lifted his head to look directly at her, a thing he sometimes did with Morwen, and which always made Jago shake his head and mutter about unnatural behavior.

The crone smiled at Ynyr and opened her fingers in his direction. The horse, with a swish of his tail, backed and turned, and started briskly off down the hill. Morwen had to seize his mane with both hands to keep from sliding from his back. When she had regained her seat, she twisted to look back at the strange old woman in the shade of the castle porch, but she had disappeared.

2

Morwen still felt unsettled when she and Ynyr reached the Morgan Hall stables. Jago came out to meet them, giving Morwen his hand as she slid down. He eyed her as he took the halter rope. "Good ride, you?"

Morwen didn't want to tell him about the old woman, or even that she had been in the castle. He wouldn't betray her confidence, but he would worry. She mustered a wan smile. "Lovely," she said. "Perfect day."

"Oh aye?" Jago led Ynyr to the water trough, where the big horse dipped his muzzle and drank thirstily. "Looking a little peaked, you. Tired, mebbe?"

Morwen followed him to the trough and stood with her hip against the weathered wooden vat. She lingered, not wanting to leave Ynyr, enjoying the sound of Jago's lilting Welsh accent. She cocked her head, trying to guess how old Jago might be. Her mama was forty, which Morwen had figured out on her own, because Lady Irene refused to celebrate her birthdays. Her papa, of course, was really old, at least sixty. Jago seemed to be somewhere in between.

Jago was terribly handsome. He had long, lean legs and straight dark hair that fell over his forehead like a horse's forelock. His eyes were narrow, tilting down at the corners as if he were perpetually sleepy. He gestured toward the hall with his head. "I think Mamselle is looking for you."

"Mademoiselle is always looking for me, Jago."

"Lucky girl."

"Oh yes. Lucky me." She straightened and reached to give the horse a final pat on his massive hindquarter. His skin rippled at her touch, and she gave a wistful sigh. "I'd rather stay here with you," she said. "I could sweep the tack room."

"Do me out of a job, you," Jago said, and gave her one of his rare smiles. The corners of his sleepy eyes lifted when he smiled.

She smiled back, a real smile this time. In Jago's steady company, the old woman with her layers of rags and mysterious remarks seemed far away. She had nothing to do with Morgan Hall, after all. Morwen resolved not to go back to the ruin, ever.

"Off now, my girl," Jago said. "Lessons, I believe."

"I suppose. I'll see you tomorrow."

He inclined his head to her, and when Ynyr had finished drinking, led him into the shade of the stable for his rubdown. Morwen turned toward the big Georgian house that was her home.

Jago was right, of course. Mademoiselle Girard would be waiting in the schoolroom, an art book open on her desk, or a passage from some old Greek philosopher for Morwen to puzzle out. There would be reproaches, the scolding over Morwen's going out without a hat, going unescorted, riding bareback, or whatever infraction had caught her attention.

Morwen kept a good pace over the green lawn, but she paused in the side garden, where the sorrel tree's feathery leaves had turned a brilliant scarlet. A great white hydrangea made a backdrop for clumps of lobelia and lilyturf. She bent to brush the blossoms with her fingers. The gardener saw her and tipped his cap, and she waved to him before she started inside.

She would like to live out of doors, she thought. Perhaps to be a gypsy, one of those dark, intriguing folks who wandered the country in caravans, telling fortunes and hawking jewelry and cloth. She had seen such caravans twice. There had been children in them, children who tumbled about on the grass or ran laughing alongside the motor, free as foxes on the open land. It seemed a life far preferable to her enclosed one. She was sure they never had to sit through Sunday services, or make pointless conversation in someone's parlor.

Her mother knew none of these thoughts, because she never spoke them. Lady Irene had said once, in her hearing, that she was "a surprisingly biddable girl." Morwen had stifled a laugh. She could have told her mother—if she had cared to hear it—that she acted biddable because it was easier. Lady Irene would be surprised by her daughter's true spirit, which was a good reason for Morwen to keep it to herself.

She trudged in through the open French windows of the morning room and started through the foyer toward the main staircase. At the sound of her step on the polished floor, Chesley, his black suit protected by a long white apron, put his head out from the dining room. "Ah, Miss Morwen," he said. His voice was as thin as he was, and she always thought it sounded gray somehow, like his hair.

"Yes, Chesley," she said, wishing she could have escaped up the stairs without having to see anyone.

"Her Ladyship is asking for you."

Morwen had one foot on the lowest tread, but she paused. "Mama?"

"Yes, miss."

"Where is she?"

"In her boudoir, I believe."

"But, Chesley…why does she want me?"

Chesley blinked, slowly, as if he were an owl, and not a very bright one. "Not for me to say, miss," he said, and withdrew into the dining room.

Morwen hesitated, one hand on the newel post, one foot on the stair. The setting sun made the narrow leaded glass windows beside the front door glisten, and the wood of the newel post was warm beneath her hand. She looked up the stairs, into the cooler shadows of the second floor, doing battle with an urge to run back to the stables.

It was something Jago always said that made her straighten her riding skirt, smooth her wind-ruffled hair with her fingers, and start up the staircase with strong steps. He meant it to apply to work in the stables or in the schoolroom, but it applied equally to dealing with Lady Irene, though Jago would never dare to say so. It was a proverb, one his mam used to say: "Labor postponed is labor increased." Facing her mother invariably meant work, a test of some kind, or a scolding. Her mother might overlook a fresh crop of freckles, but if she had something on her mind important enough to want to see her daughter outside of teatime or dinner, it was bound not to be pleasant.

Morwen knocked on the door of Lady Irene's boudoir, a nice, firm knock. Her mother's voice, low and smoky, answered at once. *"Entrez."*

So it was to be French. Morwen let herself in. When she had closed the door behind her, she said, careful of her accent, *"Bonjour, Maman."*

Lady Irene could have quibbled with this, insisting she say *bonsoir*, but it seemed that was not the point of this interview. She pointed to the upholstered chair opposite her own brocade settee. "Sit down, Morwen."

Morwen kept a wary eye on her mother as she obeyed, but there was no hint of her mood in her cool gaze. The inner door from the boudoir was firmly closed, as always. Morwen—and everyone else except Lady Irene's personal maid—was allowed only in the sitting room. Morwen had never seen her mother's bedroom.

They looked much alike, the two of them. Both were tall, slender, with thick dark hair and eyes to match. Morwen's nose was longer, and Irene's eyes a shade darker, but the resemblance always caused comment when they were seen together.

Suddenly, oddly, Morwen thought of the crone in Old Beaupre Castle. Her face seemed to overlie Lady Irene's, as if a shadow had fallen over the younger woman's features. The slender nose, the thick eyebrows, the full lips—

The phenomenon faded when Morwen caught a surprised breath.

Irene arched an eyebrow. "Something surprises you in my appearance?"

Morwen sank back in the chair and shook her head. "No," she said.

Her mother didn't press the issue. Lady Irene had no real interest in anything that didn't directly affect her. Morwen had figured this out by the time she was ten, and by the time she was twelve she understood that everyone else in Morgan Hall—the servants, her father, even Jago—had known it for years.

"Chesley said you wanted to see me."

Irene laid aside the book she had been reading. Her face still revealed nothing of her intent. "Where did you go this afternoon?"

"I took Ynyr out for a ride."

Irene pursed her mouth, just for an instant, and again the image of the crone at the ruin seemed to superimpose itself over her face. When she spoke, it faded. "I *know* you went for a ride, Morwen. I want to know where."

"Along the river. Not far."

Irene leaned forward, and her voice hardened. Her eyes did, too, and in that moment she wasn't pretty. She looked mean. "I'm going to ask you one more time, and I want an answer. Where did you go?"

Morwen, for an instant, considered lying to her mother. Why would Irene care, after all, that she had explored the ruined castle? In the usual run of things, she was content to let Mademoiselle manage such matters. She looked into her mother's eyes and recognized the storm of temper building behind them. Irene's tempers were fierce, though rare. When she was angry she could be stunningly cruel—to maids, to her husband, to her daughter. Rank made no difference, and the edge of her tongue was sword sharp and swift. It would probably be easier, in the end, to tell the truth.

Morwen shrugged. "I went to the castle."

"Why?"

"When Mademoiselle took me, she wouldn't let me go in. I wanted to see what's inside."

Irene's expression didn't change, but Morwen knew better than to be deceived by that. She could look one moment as if she were carved from ice, and the next erupt into screaming fury. She said coolly, "Who did you see there?" When Morwen hesitated, her voice dropped. "Morwen. Tell me who you saw."

Morwen's belly turned cold. The resemblance in her mother's rigid features to the grimy, creased ones of the woman in Old Beaupre Castle shocked her. She wished she could unsee it, drive the impression from her mind. She remembered now the odd feeling of recognition she had experienced when she first saw the crone's face, and shuddered.

"What was that?" Irene snapped.

"What?" Morwen breathed, shrinking back into her chair.

"You shivered. You're hiding something from me!" Lady Irene leaped from the settee and seized Morwen's arm. "I won't have it!"

Morwen looked down at her mother's long white hand and thought of the dirty one resting on Ynyr's dappled forehead. A conviction began to grow in her, and with it a rebellious spirit. She spoke in English, hardly believing the words were issuing from her own mouth. "Mother. Take your hand off me."

Such a thing had never happened before, and the shock of it was effective. Lady Irene actually gasped, and though Morwen suspected she didn't mean to do it, she lifted her hand.

Swiftly, with the agility of youth, Morwen edged out of her chair and out of her mother's reach. Irene's face flushed scarlet, and then, in an instant, paled to a deadly white. She stood glaring at her daughter with her hand still outstretched. Her voice was as brittle as a watch crystal, dropped so low Morwen almost couldn't hear. "How *dare* you?"

Morwen trembled with the realization of what she'd done, and the consequences there were likely to be, but she also trembled with a sense of power. It was a bit like riding Ynyr at his ponderous, ground-eating gallop, looking down on the earth and on the upturned faces that gaped at her passing. She felt taller, and stronger, and freer than she had ever felt in her short life. "I've done nothing wrong, Mother. Why should you be angry?"

"You're hiding something." It was a hiss, snakelike, dangerous.

"Why do you say that? I told you where I went." Morwen's back pressed against the boudoir door, but she kept her chin up.

Her mother drew a breath through pinched nostrils. "I know how deceitful girls can be." She turned away and stalked to her dressing table. She swept her long skirt aside and sat on the frilly stool before the mirror. In the glass she met her daughter's eyes. "Don't go there again, Morwen. I'll have Ynyr sent away if you do."

It was the worst punishment she could have invented. It wasn't clear to Morwen what the punishment was for, but she didn't dare ask. "I won't."

Lady Irene blew out her breath and turned to the mirror, picking up a hairbrush as she did so. Her color returned, and her expression settled into one of perfect calm. "Tell Chesley I won't be down for tea," she said. "He can send up a tray."

Morwen said, "Yes, Maman," and made her escape before her mother's unpredictable temper could flare again.

Much later, after the stiff, silent dinner was over, dinner dress exchanged for a nightgown, hair brushed out by her maid, and lights turned off in Morgan Hall, Morwen lay gazing out at the blanket of stars glistening above the Vale of Glamorgan, and wondering what her mother had suspected.

Irene often knew things she shouldn't. The maids and Mademoiselle whispered that Lady Irene had eyes in the back of her head. It never benefited anyone to lie to her, neither Lord Llewelyn nor the staff nor her daughter. She had an uncanny knack for discerning the truth.

Today, though, Morwen considered her to have been particularly unfair. Irene herself often disappeared for hours at a time, and neither her maid nor Chesley could say where she had gone or when she would return. Morwen, as a rule, was glad for her mother to absent herself, but tonight, as the stars wheeled above the Vale and the big house slept around her, Morwen lay wakeful and uneasy.

She kicked off her blankets and padded to the window in her bare feet. Lately she often felt itchy and restless. Her bosom was beginning to swell, and her monthlies had begun a few months ago, making her belly ache and her skin feel too tight for her body. Now she knelt in the window seat, savoring the coolness that seeped through the glass. She gazed out at the gardens and the long, low roof of the stables. Starlight made silvery shadows beneath the trees and the shrubs. The graveled drive glittered with it, and the empty paddocks were painted in shades of gray. Morwen idled away half an hour peering up into the star field, trying to remember which of the constellations was which. Yawning, she had just started to unfold herself from the window seat when something moved against the shining backdrop of the drive where it curved past the stables and up toward the house.

Morwen pressed herself closer to the glass to see better, and caught a startled breath.

A slim figure swept past the towering laurels that edged the gravel, moving swiftly, keeping to the shadows where she could, hurrying toward the house.

Morwen realized with a jolt that it was her mother.

She jumped up and seized her dressing gown from the chair where Rosemary had draped it. She was out the door before she managed to get both arms through its sleeves, and she nearly tripped on its trailing hem as she hurried down the hall toward her mother's rooms.

She stood outside her mother's boudoir, arms folded against the chill, and listened for the opening of the front door.

It didn't come. There should have been at least a click. There was nothing.

Morwen frowned, wondering if her mother had turned off toward the stables, or to the gardens. But the night was half-gone. Surely she meant to seek her bed.

She started when she heard a sound from inside the boudoir, the closing of a door, the clatter of the wardrobe being opened. How could Irene have reached her bedroom without Morwen seeing her?

Puzzled, Morwen lifted her hand. She hesitated, and then, in an act of courage, knocked on her mother's door.

It opened in an instant. Irene stood frozen in the doorway, glaring at her daughter. Then, throwing her head high, she spun, making the long, shapeless coat she wore whirl out around her, revealing her nightdress beneath it.

"Maman! Where have you been? What were you—"

Irene threw up a silencing hand and shrugged out of the dingy old coat, letting it fall to the floor. A tapestry bag had been slung over her shoulder, and this she dropped onto her settee.

Morwen exclaimed, "Maman!"

Her mother sank onto the settee beside the bag and hissed, "Be quiet! And close the door. You'll wake the house!"

Morwen stepped into the boudoir and pulled the door shut behind her. "Why are you dressed like that?"

Irene's eyes narrowed so that her pupils were all but invisible. She whispered fiercely, "Why is it any of your business?"

Morwen's newfound temper, and the burgeoning heat in her body that made her want to jump out of her skin, flared anew. She demanded, "Why is it your business where *I* go, but not mine where *you* go?"

"I'm your mother," Irene said coldly.

"*Du temps en temps*," Morwen snapped. From time to time. She liked the sense that her words had found their mark. She felt a bit like one of the foals, set free in the pasture for the first time.

The two of them stared at each other, Morwen with her pulse pounding in her throat and wrists, Irene with her skin going paler and paler until Morwen thought she might disappear.

At last, with a twist of her lips, Irene said, "Very well. I will tell you, Morwen. I meant to protect you, but apparently you think you know better than I."

It was dark in the room. Irene leaned forward to take a long match from a box on her dressing table. She set the flame to a candle on the inlaid table between the settee and the upholstered chair. She pointed at the chair, and Morwen, rapt with curiosity, sank into it.

With the flickering candle making shadows dance across the flocked wallpaper, Lady Irene opened the tapestry bag and pulled out something bulky, wrapped in a piece of white linen. She laid the object on the table and began to unfold the cloth.

As the fabric fell away, Morwen caught a startled breath. The thing was lovely, a rounded crystal rising from a base of gray stone, the whole perhaps two handspans wide. The crystal reflected the candle's flame, glowing as if it were alive. Without thinking, Morwen reached out her hand to touch it.

Irene slapped her hand away. "Don't!" she commanded.

"Whyever not?" Morwen cried. She cradled her hand against her chest. Although the slap hadn't really hurt, it offended her. "What's the matter with you, Maman?"

"You have no idea what this is, Morwen," Irene said coldly. "But I suppose I'm going to have to tell you." She refolded the linen, covering the glowing crystal, before she leaned back and folded her arms. She fixed her daughter with a hard gaze. "I hope you're not tired," she said. "This will take some time."

"I wasn't born above stairs," Irene began. "Indeed, the house I was born in had no stairs at all." Morwen blinked at her in surprise, and Irene's lip curled. "Of course you wouldn't understand that. You've had everything you could possibly want, since the moment you were born. And before."

Morwen frowned, and Irene flicked one languid hand, brushing the thought away. "Never mind. That isn't part of the story—only the result of it." She pulled a blanket from the back of the settee and spread it over her lap, then turned her face to the starlit night beyond her window. "The only part of your heritage you've kept is the French language. I saw to that, at least." She curled her legs up beneath the blanket. "But I should begin at the beginning."

She began her recitation. Morwen listened, her lips apart and her eyes stretching wider and wider as the story unfolded.

Irene spoke of family roots in rural France. She told of a narrow escape from persecution, a clan fleeing the French shore in a rickety boat, braving cold seas and bad weather to make a new home on the southern coast of Cornwall. She spoke of mysterious rites, and suspicion, and accusation, and, last, an escape.

"Her name was Ursule," she said. "Though outside of her family, most called her Ursula. She was only a farmer, but she was a good one. Good with animals, with a strong back and big hands like a man's. She fled Cornwall with nothing but the clothes on her back, and the Shire stallion she rode."

Morwen had not stirred throughout the long tale, but now she lifted her head. "A Shire? Like Ynyr?"

"Exactly like Ynyr, as it happens. Just listen, Morwen."

Morwen dropped her chin again, and Irene adjusted the blanket over herself. "She was pregnant," she said. "With me."

Morwen couldn't help a little gasp.

"That's right," Irene said. "I was born to a farmwife. She had no husband. No relations. She called me *Irène*."

"That's beautiful."

"*Peut-être*. Hard for the Welsh to pronounce."

"Where did you grow up?"

"Far enough away that no one here knew me."

"But why, Maman? And what happened to Ursule?"

"She's gone."

"I wish I had known her."

"Why? You wouldn't have had a thing to say to her. She spent her days tending cows and mucking out stables."

"She was my *grand-mère*. Your *maman*. Aren't you sorry she's gone?"

Coolly, "We didn't get on."

"You and I don't get on, either, do we?"

Morwen expected anger at that, but she received only a narrow, mirthless smile. "We're more alike than you think."

"In what way?"

Irene moved restlessly, and the blanket slid to the floor. She let it lie, and her gaze drifted again to the window, where the stars were beginning to fade into dawn. "Don't you ever wonder why Ynyr knows your thoughts, Morwen?"

Morwen stammered, "Wh-what do you mean? How do you know that?"

Irene didn't move her head, but her eyes shifted to Morwen's face. "I know everything."

"Jago must have told you."

"He didn't need to."

"Ynyr is smart."

"So was his sire."

"Did you know his sire?"

Irene's smile widened, though there was nothing amused about her expression. "Ynyr's sire was called Aramis. It was Aramis who carried Ursule out of Cornwall."

"Then how—Where did—"

"He was her only possession. Aramis, and this crystal. She used them both."

"The crystal?" Morwen lifted her hands, helplessly, and let them drop. "Maman, please. I can't understand what you're telling me!"

Irene's cold smile faded. "Do I have to start again at the beginning?"

"No! Just tell me what it all means!"

Irene rose from the settee and moved to the window. Her silk nightdress floated around her as lightly as if it were made of the morning fog just beginning to rise. She put her palms on the sash and stared out into the mist for a moment before she turned an impassive face to her daughter. "Witches, Morwen."

Morwen had to moisten her lips before she could speak again. "Wh-what, Maman?"

"Witches. That's what I've been telling you. Is it so hard to understand? They were witches. They fled Brittany, then Cornwall, to escape the witch hunters. Ursule was a witch. *I'm* a witch. In the crystal I see things, like where my daughter goes when she thinks no one is watching."

Morwen jumped to her feet, the blood pounding in her head.

An icy smile grew on her mother's face. "You are, too, as it turns out. I hoped you wouldn't be. Life would have been simpler. I don't trust you, and this is dangerous knowledge."

Morwen croaked, "I don't know what you mean."

"It's not like you to be slow, Morwen! Why do you think Ynyr has always known your thoughts? You're a witch. A *witch*. Like your *maman*. Like your *grand-mère*. Like all the women in the Orchiére line, evidently, unfortunate though that is."

Morwen couldn't breathe. She couldn't speak. A heartbeat later she couldn't see the bitter triumph on her mother's face. A cloud of star-studded darkness enveloped her, and she crumpled to the floor in a dead faint.

3

For days after Irene showed her daughter the crystal, Morwen was ill. Someone had helped her to her bed that night, but she didn't know who. By the next morning she was fevered and sick. The doctor was called and diagnosed influenza, but Morwen didn't believe that. It was confusion and shock that had made her ill.

She tried to convince herself her mother had made up the story of witchcraft to punish her. Or perhaps, even worse, Irene was not in her right mind. If that was the case, what should she do? She couldn't go to Papa, surely, but... what her mother told her couldn't be true! It couldn't. She had never heard of such a thing, and as she tried to wrap her mind around it, she felt worse than ever. She couldn't sleep, she couldn't eat, she could barely speak.

There was no one she could turn to for guidance. She didn't trust Mademoiselle, and she knew her maid reported everything to Lady Irene. Jago was her only confidant, and Irene's warnings made her afraid to mention it to him. She had never felt so alone in her life.

For three days she lay in her bed, burning with fever, struggling to understand. Her father came to see her once. He stood in the doorway to ask if she had everything she needed. Her maid came in and out, carrying trays of food she couldn't eat, offering her broth that she drank but couldn't keep down. Her mother sent a note, but kept her distance from the sickroom.

When word came from Jago that Ynyr wasn't eating, either, she knew she couldn't let the situation go on. She still didn't know what to think, or what to believe, but lying in her bed wasn't helping.

She waited until the maid had left her with a bowl of soup and a tumbler of water. She put them on her side table, swung her legs over the side of the bed, and stood up.

It wasn't easy. Her head swam and her knees trembled, but the thought of Ynyr drove her to the window. She opened it and sat beside it for a few minutes, drawing deep breaths of fresh summer air. After a time she began to feel a bit stronger. She drank all the water in her glass, and managed half of Cook's good chicken soup. She waited a little longer, to be certain she wasn't going to be sick again, and then rang for her maid.

Dressed, and with a shawl around her shoulders despite the bright sunshine, she left the house through the servants' entrance and hurried to the stables. To her relief she heard Ynyr's whicker as she drew closer, and Jago came out to meet her.

"Feeling better, you?" he said. "Yon great horse has been off his feed for days."

"Is he all right?"

"He will be now."

Jago led the way to Ynyr's stall, and Morwen went in to put her arms around the big horse's neck. She stayed to see that he ate a measure of oats and drank a good bit of water. She didn't feel up to a ride, but the two of them went out into the paddock to bask in the sunshine. Jago stayed close by, but they didn't talk except to plan how Ynyr might gain back the weight he'd lost.

That night Lady Irene sent for her daughter very late, when the rest of the house was asleep. Morwen was already in bed, but she jumped up willingly, and with a dressing gown wrapped around her went eagerly down the corridor. Perhaps, she thought, her mother would confess it had all been fiction. Perhaps she would even apologize, though she had never done so before. Perhaps her daughter's illness had changed her mind.

None of that happened. Instead Lady Irene, with an air of ceremony, brought the crystal from wherever it was she kept it hidden, and set it on the inlaid table. She unwrapped it and folded the linen beneath it. She drew a tiny flask from her pocket and sprinkled a circle of water droplets on the floor. She had exchanged the taper for a fat new candle of white wax, and she laid out sprigs of green and brown herbs around it.

Morwen said, "Mother, what—" but Lady Irene threw up one long white hand for silence. She extended both her palms above the stone, and sat in silence for what seemed to Morwen a very long time.

Morwen wriggled with impatience. She looked at the clock. She stared at the ceiling. She gazed out the window, where clouds shifted over a crescent moon. She scowled into the writhing candle flame, and was on the verge of uttering some impatient sound when a change inside the stone caught her attention.

Morwen leaned forward. She supposed she had caught a reflection of the candle flame, or of the moonlight falling through the window. Irene spread her hands, her fingers framing the crystal, and Morwen shot to her feet, horrified.

Inside the stone, where the crystal grew out of rough granite, an image appeared.

Morwen had peered into a Kinetoscope once, on a trip to Cardiff. This figure was like the ones in that device. It looked real, but distant, and unaware of being observed.

"Maman! What's happening?"

"What do you think, Morwen?"

"It looks as if you're . . . as if you can *see* people in that thing."

"It's not a thing. It's the Orchiére crystal. And yes, I can see people. Evidently you can, too."

"That's Jago!"

"Yes," Irene said coolly. "It is."

"But it's—Isn't this like *spying?*"

"It isn't *like* spying, Morwen. It *is* spying. I prefer the traditional term, *scrying*, but I don't care what you call it. It's useful."

Morwen looked down into her mother's eyes. They were nearly black in the shadowed room. "This is how you knew I'd been to the castle."

"Knowing things makes you powerful, Morwen. You will learn that as a female, there are few enough sources of power."

"But Maman, why do you need power? Surely Papa . . ."

The angry glitter in Irene's eyes silenced her. Morwen backed away from the crystal, loath to intrude upon Jago in such a way. She sank into her chair and covered her eyes.

"Be grateful, Morwen," Lady Irene said. "Not everyone could see that, but you have the gift, for better or worse. Your gift is what brought you Ynyr. You might as well be glad."

"Ynyr loves me."

"That may be. It's not the point. Ynyr is your familiar spirit."

Morwen dropped her hands. "My what?"

Irene made an irritated gesture. "The church will tell you it's a bad thing, but they lie."

"Father Pugh doesn't lie!"

"*Pffft.* Everyone lies." Irene snuffed out the candlewick between her thumb and forefinger and began to cover the crystal. "Ynyr is your familiar, the companion of your heart. We all have a familiar, if we're lucky."

"Did Ursule?"

"Ursule was close to all animals, but especially the horse that had belonged to her husband. Her mother's familiar was a cat."

"And...Maman, do you have a...a familiar spirit?"

Her mother laid the last fold of linen over the stone and stood, lifting the bundle in her two hands. "I did."

"But now?"

"Now I don't." Irene turned away, the wrapped stone in her hands.

"Maman, wait! What was it? Why don't you have it anymore?"

Her mother paused halfway to her bedroom, her face turned to the moonlit park beyond the window. "My familiar was a fox," she murmured, as if she were speaking to herself. "A beautiful red fox, who found me at my old home and followed me here to the Vale. To my new life. For that, he was shot and killed."

Morwen clapped both hands to her mouth. Through her fingers she breathed, "Oh no! Oh no, Maman, who—"

All at once she knew. She understood, and it was almost too much to bear.

Lord Llewelyn always boasted to visitors about the fox-fur rug that lay among the chairs in the parlor. He bragged about the difficulty of his shot, its accuracy, the skill of the taxidermist, the cost of the preservation. Morwen had trod on that fox rug a hundred times, and each time must have felt, to her mother, as if she were treading on her very heart.

"Oh, Maman," she whispered. "I'm so sorry." Irene didn't respond. Tentatively Morwen asked, "But what happened?"

Irene still gazed out into the park, her clear profile limned in moonlight. "He came when I found my gift," she said, very low. "I knew right away what he was, and when the time came to...to leave my home, he followed. He found a den in the park. He used to wait right there." She pointed, her long arm outstretched, the silk of her peignoir shimmering. "Right there where the wood begins."

"Papa...did he know?"

Irene's face, as she turned back to her daughter, was as flinty as the gravel in the drive. "I don't know. Llewelyn watches me. I've observed him, in the crystal, going through my wardrobe, looking in my diary."

Morwen blurted, "Why did you marry him?"

"To be Lady Irene, of course. I was sick to death of farm life."

"There was no love between you?"

"Love is an illusion, Morwen. It doesn't last. It can't be trusted."

"And now you hate Papa."

"Why should you think that? I am indifferent to him." Irene gave a shallow sigh, a tiny, impatient sound. "Go to bed now. I will teach you what you need to know, because it's what we do. I will teach you the names of our ancestresses. You'll learn how to summon, and how to observe through the crystal. I will teach you the Sabbats, and the rites as they were passed down to me. But remember—"

Morwen had crossed the room to the door, and her hand was on the lock, but she paused. "Remember what?"

"You must never tell anyone," Irene said tightly. "Not Jago. Not Father Pugh."

"Surely, Maman, Father Pugh—"

"Especially him, Morwen." Irene's lip curled with disdain. "Don't be deceived by that timid manner. His Scriptures tell him to destroy us. He would find the courage somehow."

"But Jago—"

"Morwen. Not *anyone*. For a witch to be exposed means risking death."

"It's the twentieth century!"

"Barely. For some, it might as well be the seventeenth."

Morwen shook her head. "I don't understand."

Irene clicked her tongue. "Morwen, you're old enough to

understand something about men! They like women to look beautiful, to have good manners, to bear their sons. They don't expect them—they don't want them—to have minds of their own. Women must never argue, never cause scenes, never—never *feel.*"

"But Papa—"

"Your papa is no different. Don't be deceived because he indulges you. When he wants something from you, he won't ask your opinion on it. He will take it."

"What does that have to do with being a witch?"

For a moment Irene was still, her eyes gleaming pools of darkness. She smiled, but without mirth. "You're not listening, Morwen. I'm telling you why men hate our kind. Do you think I am the woman I just described? Are you?"

"No," Morwen whispered, her heart sinking.

"Then you see. Your father, like most men, is terrified of a woman who doesn't fit his ideal of womanhood, because he doesn't know how to control her. You need to remember that any frightened man is a dangerous one." Her cold smile faded, and she turned back to the window. Over her shoulder she said, "I will tell you the truth, though, Morwen. I rather like a man to be afraid of me. It's my reward for keeping the craft alive."

***

Lord Llewelyn, only a week later, decreed that Morwen's sixteenth birthday should be the occasion for a ball. Lady Irene accepted his wishes without demur. She would naturally leave all arrangements to Chesley, to Cook, and to Mademoiselle. Mademoiselle informed Morwen that there would be dress fittings and hairdressers and sessions with a dancing master.

Morwen protested. "Papa, we never have balls, or even parties, except for the church fete. Why do we have to do this?"

Her father looked up from his *Times* and scowled over the steel rims of his spectacles. "What?"

"This ball, Papa." Morwen stood beside the fireplace, her arms folded and her fingers tapping impatiently on her elbows. "It's *my* birthday. I don't want a ball."

"What you want is no matter. I know what's best for you. It's time you came out."

"Out of what?" she asked, and was rewarded with a glint of annoyance in her father's milky blue eyes.

"Girls of good family are properly brought out into society," he said, and snapped up his newspaper again, blocking her view of him.

"Society? There is no society here, and I don't care anyway."

"You will care if you fail to make a good marriage," Lord Llewelyn said, speaking to the inside of his newspaper.

"Marriage!" Morwen turned to her mother for help, but Lady Irene was tracing the fox-fur rug with her foot, showing no sign of having heard the conversation.

The rug, with its rich red pelt and head forever frozen by the taxidermist in Cowbridge, made Morwen shudder. She didn't understand how her mother could bear seeing it there on the floor, something to walk across, to step on, as if it had never been a living, breathing, feeling creature. If someone shot Ynyr, she would have murder in her heart for the killer, even if it had been her father who wielded the gun.

Morwen stalked away from the parlor, taking care not to step on the rug. She left her father immersed in the *Times*, contentedly ignorant of the flame of rebellion he had kindled in his daughter.

She marched upstairs and saw that her mother's door stood ajar in anticipation of Lady Irene's coming up to dress for dinner.

In the throes of her anger, Morwen conceived a daring idea. Though she hesitated, wary of her mother's temper, she couldn't banish it. It was dangerous, but she felt an overwhelming urge to try the crystal for herself. To try it *by* herself.

She glanced down the corridor, but no one was about to see her. The maids would be in the kitchen, assembling china and silver under Chesley's critical eye. Mademoiselle would be having tea in her own room. Papa was still in the parlor, Irene sitting dutifully at his side.

Morwen slipped into the boudoir and closed the door behind herself. With a sense of daring, she turned the key in the lock.

She didn't know where her mother hid the crystal, but it had to be somewhere in her bedroom, a place Morwen had never seen. Until this moment she hadn't cared, but now she crept forward on tiptoe and tried the cut-glass knob. It clicked, releasing the door. With a cautious finger, Morwen pushed on it.

The door swung soundlessly on well-oiled hinges, revealing a room in semidarkness, curtains drawn, windows closed. Morwen stepped inside and looked about in wonder.

Morgan Hall was adorned with Oriental carpets and heavy draperies, an abundance of bric-a-brac, statuary, and what seemed a hundred ugly family portraits festooning the stairwell, the foyer, the dining room, even the morning room. It was a well-appointed manor house. What it was not, and Morwen understood this, was tasteful. It was a Georgian house with a Victorian interior and Edwardian aspirations, all jumbled together by Lord Llewelyn and his forebears in the apparent conviction that overdecoration proves worth.

Lady Irene Morgan's private bedroom demonstrated a profoundly different aesthetic. Morwen clasped her hands beneath her chin and turned in a slow circle, absorbing every detail.

The walls were not papered, but painted a delicate ivory. The polished wood floor was bare except for a single rug, finely woven in a pattern of pastel flowers, so pretty Morwen didn't dare put her foot on it. The bed was white wood, a French design, Morwen thought, its delicate carvings outlined in gold. The coverlet was a pale green with white fleurs-de-lis. An enormous mirror filled the wall behind the bed. The wardrobe was the same creamy color as the walls, and a single painting hung on the wall opposite.

Morwen forgot her mission—indeed, forgot about the passage of time—as she stood gazing at the painting. The art books her governess employed featured page after page of Greek sculptures and Renaissance religious figures. Morwen had never seen a painting like this one. A girl in a scarlet robe held a glowing crystal ball in her two hands. On the table beside her lay an enormous book with some sort of wand across it, and next to the book a skull. The woman in the painting could have been Lady Irene herself, slender, dark haired. But she could never have sat for such a painting! Lord Llewelyn would never have allowed her—

The roar of the Vulcan's motor startled Morwen, and reminded her of her purpose. Hastily she cast about for someplace her mother might hide the crystal. She bent to look under the bedstead, but there was nothing there except a pair of bedroom slippers, set side by side. She opened the wardrobe. A cloud of *parfum de rose* wafted from the gowns and cloaks and peignoirs hanging there. She pushed aside the long skirts of these garments and pulled open the drawer to peer among the slippers and boots, but there was no linen-wrapped bundle.

She persisted in her search, though she felt the minutes spinning by. She wondered if Irene had taken the stone with her, carried it to the place where she did her "scrying."

A moment later she knew that was not the case. She felt its presence. It was here, and calling to her as surely as if it could speak her name.

The same way, it occurred to her now, she had been called to the ruined castle, where an old woman said, "I wanted to see you."

All of this spun through her mind in a heartbeat. She backed up until she stood in the very center of her mother's beautiful bed-room, her toes just touching the pretty rug. She closed her eyes and turned her palms upward. She listened, not with her ears, but with her heart.

She couldn't have explained how the information came to her. It was a sensation. A throb, deep in her chest. It intensified until it became a near pain, piercing her breastbone from front to back. She turned to her left and it sharpened. When she turned the other way, still with her eyes closed, it eased. She turned again and it became a tug, as if a thread were attached to her rib cage, and someone—or something—was pulling on it.

She opened her eyes and allowed the thread to draw her toward the window. The window seat was deep, long enough for a woman to stretch her length, and piled with cushions in green and white and beige plush. Morwen removed the pillows and explored the wooden base of the window seat with her fingers. When her fingertips reached the edge, she lifted, and the base rose smoothly to expose a spacious cupboard. A hiding place.

It had probably been meant to hold blankets, or extra pillows. Now it held a linen-wrapped object that Morwen recognized by its shape. She had found the crystal.

At that moment a step sounded in the corridor, followed by a brief knock on the door of the boudoir. There was no time to think. Morwen caught up the crystal, keeping its linen covering securely around it. She replaced the top of the window seat and piled the cushions where they had been, then hurried across the boudoir on her tiptoes. Gingerly, doing her best to make no sound, she unlocked the door, then dashed back into the bedchamber.

There was nowhere for her to go. Someone was at the door, and would report to her lady mother that Morwen had defied her by going into her bedroom. She spun, looking for someplace to hide, but of course there was only one. It was the holy of holies, her mother's private, specially installed, famously expensive bathroom.

It was another forbidden room, put in when Morwen was small. She remembered her father's grumbling over the procession of plumbers and carpenters and tilers trooping up and down the servants' staircase, then his scolding as the invoices arrived. When it was finished, Morwen and her nanny hurried to Lady Irene's rooms, expecting a tour of the marvel. They were refused, without explanation or apology.

The nanny had said nothing, but Morwen saw the raised-eyebrow glance she exchanged with the head housemaid. Only Lady Irene and her personal lady's maid, they soon learned, were allowed to enter the bathroom or, by the next year, the renovated bedchamber. Her Ladyship's maid was a tiny, silent woman who regarded herself as the top of the staff in importance. Morwen heard her nanny, and the housemaids, too, teasing her to tell them what the bathroom was like. They received nothing for their pains but a dismissive sniff.

Now Morwen discovered its glories for herself, and it was astonishing. There were gleaming marble tiles inlaid with mosaics. White was the predominant color, with splashes here and there of azure and scarlet and emerald. The fixtures were white as snow, and the bathtub, standing on four enormous claw feet, immense. The taps gleamed silver, and on an array of silver hooks set into the wall hung a dressing gown, an embroidered sponge bag, and an assortment of brushes and cloths.

Beyond the commode, hidden by an appliquéd curtain hanging from a curved rod, was an odd little door, narrow, painted white, with a low lintel. Morwen pushed aside the curtain to open it. It was dark beyond, but she ducked below the lintel and went through.

Morgan Hall was not old enough to have a priest hole, but the space beyond the door made Morwen think of one. There was a cramped landing with no light, and an even more cramped staircase leading downward. Morwen puzzled over this for a few moments, trying to think where the exit of this secret stairway might be. While she pondered, she heard the door of the boudoir open and close, and the voice of Mademoiselle calling, "My lady? Miss Morwen?"

Mademoiselle would never dare to enter the bedchamber, or my lady's private bath, either, but Morwen was trapped just the same. Cautiously she closed the little door behind her. The light disappeared. She stood for a moment in darkness, hoping her eyes would adjust, but it didn't help, and she began to fear she would meet her mother coming up the stairs.

It was obvious this was how Lady Irene absented herself from Morgan Hall. Morwen sniffed, but there was no smell of dust or dankness. The staircase was used, and used often. Irene no doubt carried a candle, or a lamp.

Morwen had neither. She did have the crystal, though she had never intended to steal it. There was nothing she could do about it now. She held it tight under her right arm and stretched out her left until it met the wall of the staircase. One cautious step at a time, she began to grope her way down the stairs.

She explored each tread with her toes before putting her weight on it and trying the next. A sliver of light appeared at the bottom, and she moved a bit faster, keeping her eye on it. As she neared the light, she caught the spicy smell of wintersweet, which told her precisely where she was. Unlike the main staircase, which broke at a wide landing between the first and second floors, this one led straight down.

The gardener kept the planting of wintersweet against the southern wall, tucked behind an ell, out of sight of the drive or the front entrance. It caught the sun there, he said, and though it was a dull plant when it wasn't in flower, it was useful for perfuming soap. Morwen loved the yellow, waxy blossoms that bloomed when everything else in the garden had gone dormant for the winter. Sometimes she plucked a few to carry to her room.

At the bottom of the stairs was a plain door with an old-fashioned latch and no window. The light came from around its edges, where the wall must have shifted and left the door hanging unevenly in its frame. Morwen lifted the latch and put her head out.

The slanting sunlight of early evening dazzled her eyes, and she blinked away tears. The gardens lay to her right, with the stables beyond. To her left was the wide expanse of the river, glistening lazily in the late sunshine. She stepped outside, closing the door behind her. She had to duck beneath the sprawling branches of wintersweet, and when she glanced back, the door was invisible.

She hurried through the garden toward the stables. She had no clear plan other than to avoid a chance encounter with Mademoiselle, or worse, her mother. Her feet carried her instinctively to the one place she was always welcome.

She was still a hundred yards from the stable when she heard Ynyr's questioning whicker. She broke into a trot, careful to steady the crystal under her arm.

Jago came out to meet her, a piece of harness in one hand and an awl in the other. His hands were rarely empty, and sometimes she suspected he spent his evenings working, too, repairing tack or mending feed sacks. "In a hurry, you," he said.

She slowed to a walk. "I have to get back to change for dinner," she said.

"No time to ride? Yon great horse won't like that." His eyes crinkled at her, eyes as dark as her own. Tall though she had grown, Jago was a head taller, with legs even longer than hers.

"Maybe I'll take a quick trot down to the river."

"Saddle?"

She laughed as she walked past him into the cool dimness of the stable. It was a jest between them, Jago suggesting the saddle and Morwen refusing. Even the halter and rope were more than she needed, but they kept people from asking questions.

Ynyr was waiting, his head over the half door of his loose box. Morwen unlatched the door, and he stepped out, careful where he set his big, feathered feet. She took his halter from the wall hook and slipped it over his head, then stepped up onto the mounting block.

Jago pointed to her bundle. "What's that? Shall I keep it for you?"

"No, thank you," she said. "It's . . . It's sort of a secret."

He touched his forelock with one finger. "Yes, Miss Morwen," he said solemnly. She stuck out her tongue at him, and left him chuckling as she rode out into the golden twilight.

There was a place beside the River Thaw where she sometimes passed a lazy afternoon when she could escape from Mademoiselle. It was a nest of sorts, or a bower, shielded by a stand of three weeping willows so old that their roots extended down the bank into the river itself. Their golden-leaved branches hung right down to the earth, like the ribs of a broken umbrella. Ynyr turned toward this place, and at a steady walk carried her to it in no more than a quarter of an hour. She slid from his back and ducked beneath the drooping branches, leaving him to browse in the shade.

She knelt on the damp earth between the leaning tree trunks to unwrap the crystal.

In the shadows of the yellow boughs, the old stone shone with a light like the setting sun, gold and bronze and rust. Morwen could have been content simply to gaze at it, to let it soothe the sensation in her chest. She marveled at the way the crystal had drawn her, and at how much easier she felt with it resting before her. She caressed its rounded surface. The stone should have been cool beneath her fingers, but it felt strangely warm. She almost expected it to move, to breathe, or to wriggle under her touch.

Instead it flickered to life.

She gasped and fell back on her heels. Her mother had said she had the gift, but this evidence of her own power stunned her. Could it be true? It had been hard enough to believe that her mother, the remote Lady Irene Morgan, was a witch, but she...

She had not yet caught her breath when the light within the scrying stone coalesced into an image.

It was the crone from Old Beaupre Castle. Her seamed face and aureole of silver hair were unmistakable, as were the black eyes that glittered from the shadows as she leaned forward. She gazed out of the scrying stone as if it were a window in some fantastic door. Her lips moved, and she lifted one of her dirty hands and crooked a finger.

Morwen heard nothing with her ears, but the word the old woman spoke sounded in her mind as clearly and as loudly as if a gong had been struck. *"Venez!"* Come!

The image faded as quickly as it had appeared. With trembling fingers Morwen awkwardly covered the crystal, as if by hiding it she could deny what she had seen, and ignore the command that had thrilled through her head.

It did no good. She couldn't unsee the old woman's face any more than she could deny the summons. Though she stayed where she was, kneeling before the shrouded stone, the impulse to obey the call was too strong. She didn't dare carry the crystal up to the castle. She tucked the wrappings tighter around it, then lodged it as securely as she could in a crumbling space between two of the tree roots that rose knee high out of the ground. She ducked out from beneath the willow branches and found Ynyr waiting beside the boulder she used as a mounting block. His head was lifted, and his ears pricked toward the ruined castle.

"You heard it, too," Morwen sighed.

He blew gently and shook his head from side to side.

"All right. We'll go. But I have no idea what any of it means."

Ynyr shifted his feet, which also felt like a command. Morwen stepped up on the boulder and swung her leg over his back. He was off almost before she settled herself. She only just managed to seize the halter rope before it trailed to the ground beneath his feet.

She would be late for dinner. Her father would be irritated. Her mother would be furious. Jago would be worried, which was the worst, but there was nothing she could do about it. Ynyr knew as well as she did that she had to go.

She took a handful of his mane and tightened her legs around his barrel. Feeling her secure in her seat, Ynyr moved into his swinging trot, eating up the path by the river. It seemed no time before he turned up toward the castle, sitting brooding and broken atop its hill. Ynyr slowed to a walk, and Morwen did her best to breathe evenly, to steady her nerves for whatever new mystery awaited her.

4

The shadows stretched long by the time Ynyr reached the broken wall surrounding the castle. He stepped around bits of rock and fallen masonry, picking his way into the outer courtyard. Near the pillared porch he stopped. Morwen, her pulse fluttering in her throat, slid down from his back and stepped forward.

The lowering sun didn't reach inside the walls. Morwen wrapped her arms around herself for warmth, and squinted into the darkness.

The dim figure, shrouded as before, resolved from the shadows bit by bit. Morwen smelled her before she saw her. The crone lurched into the light and peered up at Morwen from beneath her hood. She lifted a hand in greeting, but before she could speak, a voice interrupted.

Morwen's heart jolted when she heard it, and she spun around, even as Ynyr snorted and took two steps backward.

"What are you doing?" Lady Irene's voice was harsh with anger, and something like fear. Morwen struggled for a response that would forestall the storm of temper about to break.

The crone answered in her clear voice. "What do you think I'm doing, *Irène*? I'm going to speak to *ma petite fille*."

Irene snapped, "Who told you Morwen was your grand-daughter?"

Morwen gaped at her mother. She hadn't denied it. The old woman moved farther out into the fading light, and put back her hood to show her mass of silver hair.

"I needed no one to tell me," the crone said. She smiled, showing her sharp white teeth. "You misunderstand, Irène. Even though I no longer have the crystal"—her smile faded, and her black eyes flashed like reflected lightning—"the craft has not entirely abandoned me. I see things in puddles and ponds, in tea leaves, in spilled flour. The crystal was far stronger, but—"

Irene interrupted her, directing a furious glance at Morwen. "What did you do with it?" she hissed. "You went into my room, which I've forbidden you to do, and you stole it!"

Again Morwen had no chance to answer. The crone laughed, a sound like the cawing of a crow. "She stole it? This slip of a girl stole the crystal from you, Irène?"

Morwen faltered, "I didn't steal—I didn't mean to take—" but neither woman paid the slightest attention to her.

They were facing each other now, the hunched silver-haired woman and the dark erect one. The anger between them was as palpable as a lightning bolt, and Morwen thought their furious energy must burn her.

The old woman shifted into French. "Ah, Irène, my daughter. Such irony. You stole the stone from me. Now your daughter has stolen it from you. Are you anything without it?"

"Of course I am, Maman." Morwen gasped at Irene's use of the word, but still neither Irene nor the old woman took notice of her. Irene said, "You seem to know so much! You know I'm called Lady Irene, that I live in a proper house, with a maid and servants and a noble husband."

The crone tossed her head, and her white mane rippled. "Does he love you, Irène, that lord of yours? Does your power extend that far?"

"He married me, and gave me my title. That was all I needed."

"Ah." The old woman grinned again, white teeth gleaming through the gathering dusk. "And there is the matter of your daughter. He gave you your daughter, I assume."

At this, Lady Irene was silent. The crone cackled, and shook her shock of hair so it coruscated in the fading light. "Who, then, Irène?" the old woman crowed. "Who gave you this fine girl?"

"Maman," Morwen said, so sharply both women turned, remembering her presence at last. "What does she mean? Who is she?"

Irene met Morwen's gaze with an icy one. "This is your grandmother, Morwen. Your *grand-mère* Ursule." She added, with a curl of her lip, "The farmer."

Morwen looked past her to the old woman. "Is it true?" she breathed. "Are you my *grand-mère*, truly?"

The crone made an effort to straighten her spine, to meet Morwen's eyes directly. Her lined face softened, and her voice gentled. *"Oui. Bien sûr, ma petite fille."*

Morwen eyed Irene without sympathy. "You stole the crystal from your own mother." It was an accusation, and her voice was as laced with contempt as her mother's had been.

Irene's eyes kindled. "Who are you to judge me, Morwen? You've had the best of everything! You have no idea—"

"The best of everything?" Morwen said, her voice rising. "Why couldn't I know my own grandmother? She might have actually *liked* me!" Her last phrase came out as a shriek, and caused Ynyr to stamp anxiously.

Ursule said, "Such a wonderful horse."

"Yes." Morwen pressed a hand to her chest to calm her pounding heart.

The old woman, whom Morwen could no longer think of as a crone, or as anything other than her grandmother, murmured,

"Let us go and calm him, Morwen." Morwen followed her and noticed that although she still smelled as if she needed bathing, the smell was no longer offensive, but intimate. It felt familiar, like the smells of the stables, scents Morwen loved.

It was dark now, with the first stars pricking the velvet black of the sky. Ynyr glowed silver in the gloom, and his ears twitched forward and back.

They approached him, and, as before, he dropped his head so Ursule could stroke his cheeks and whisper in his ear. Morwen, shaken by her mother's revelation, pressed herself against his shoulder, her eyes closed. She felt the brush of his whiskery chin across her hair, and opened her eyes to see that Ursule had stepped back, and was watching the two of them with something like respect.

"The gift is strong in you," Ursule said. "I'm glad. It doesn't always happen this way."

Morwen put her back to Ynyr, still leaning into his warmth. "I don't know what to say to you."

"No, of course you don't, my dear." Ursule folded her hands into the voluminous sleeves of her cloak. "I'm sure you never speak with farmers."

"That's not it. I speak to Jago all the time."

Ursule's white eyebrows rose. "Jago? Who is this?"

"Jago is my favorite person in the world," Morwen said. "Our horsemaster. I suppose he's not a farmer, not properly, but he lets me clean the byre, and brush Ynyr myself, and—" She shrugged a little.

"Ah." Ursule was smiling again. "You have something of me in you, then."

Irene stood with her fists on her hips and her eyes narrowed. "Don't listen to her, Morwen."

Ursule answered without looking at her. "I haven't said anything you could object to, Irène. Only the truth."

"You know, Maman, I can't help the way I am."

"Can you not?"

"You said once that I was born selfish because I was conceived selfishly."

"Ah. *C'est vrais.* I had no idea how deep such selfishness could run."

Irene's lips twisted. "Come, Morwen. We need to be home. It's already dark."

"We can't leave Grand-mère here, Maman! She should come to Morgan Hall. We have plenty of room."

Irene's control shivered apart at that. "Morgan Hall—no! It's not possible!" she shrilled.

"Why not?"

"Just think, Morwen! Your father...the servants..."

Ursule spoke directly to Morwen. "My dear, I would wager my life that my lord Llewelyn doesn't fully understand who he married. His ignorance was essential to Irène's plan."

"What plan?" Morwen was asking Ursule, though her mother stood so close.

"Her plan to escape from me, and my life of work. To use her pretty face to advantage, make a fine marriage, live in a great house. To be a lady, not a farmwife."

"But Papa—" Tears of confusion and shock flooded Morwen's eyes, and she turned to press her forehead against Ynyr's silken hide. When she felt a hand on her back, a warm, hard hand, she knew it was not her mother's. It was Ursule's. Her grandmother's. It was a touch of reassurance.

Ursule, living rough in an abandoned tower, was offering comfort. While Irene—

"Come, Morwen," Irene said, in a voice like two rocks scraped together. "We'll be late."

Morwen twisted her head to glare at her mother. "I'm not coming," she said.

"You are. And now."

"No! I'm staying with—with my grandmother!"

Irene's lips curled in a mirthless smile. "Oh yes? Do you want to sleep on straw? Eat pottage for breakfast and lunch and dinner? Wear the same dress day in and day out?"

"I don't care about those things!"

"You would, in a very short time."

"Morwen," Ursule said. "Go home with your mother. She's right about that, at least. This is no place for you."

"I won't leave you here!" Morwen cried, astonished at her sudden feeling of connection with an old woman she had met but twice.

"Thank you, my dear, but I wouldn't know how to behave in your grand house," Ursule said. "I'm happier with the beasts."

"But I want to *talk* to you!" Morwen wailed. Her mind seethed with questions, and she felt bruised by her mother's cruelty.

"Come back tomorrow," Ursule said soothingly. She stroked Morwen's arm with her dirty claw, a touch more affectionate than any Irene had ever offered her daughter. "I will be here. I'll wait for you."

"She won't be coming," Irene said, and with her back ramrod straight stalked out of the porch and down the path.

Morwen led Ynyr to a broken wall and used it to hop on to his back. She held the rope in her hand, reining him in for a moment. "I will come, Grand-mère. I swear it."

"She will try to stop you." Ursule sighed, and her spine bent again, as if she had spent the last of her energy.

"She can't."

Ursule gave her a weary smile, and lifted one hand in farewell. Morwen returned the gesture as Ynyr stepped forward.

"I wish I could stay," Morwen said.

Ursule shook her head. "There is no bed for you here. Go home, and have a good sleep. It's what I wish for you."

Ynyr started toward the river, where the starlit sparkle of the water silhouetted Irene's slender form. Morwen turned in her seat for a last look at Ursule, but the old woman had already faded into the shadows.

It didn't matter. She would be back the next morning no matter what her mother said.

⁓✥⁓

Ursule was right, of course. Irene had no intention of allowing Morwen to return to the ruined castle. After a painful dinner, during which the only sounds were the clink of flatware and the clatter of china, Irene paused in the hall as they left Lord Llewelyn to his pipe and his port.

"Morwen, come to my boudoir. Now, before you change."

Morwen was tempted to refuse, but thought better of it. Perhaps, if she was tactful, she could persuade her mother to help Ursule. A cottage, perhaps, or a place in one of the tenants' households. She nodded and turned to follow Irene up the wide staircase.

Irene didn't speak until they were inside her boudoir, and the door shut behind them. Without preamble, she snapped, "Where is it?"

Morwen didn't need to ask what she meant. "I'll bring it back," she said. "But I had to find it, Maman."

"What do you mean, you *had* to?"

"I mean," Morwen said, "that it called to me."

"How could it call to you?"

Morwen shrugged. "I don't know, but it did. That's how I knew Ursule wanted me." With emphasis she added, "My grandmother."

"She has always been strong," Irene admitted. "I used to think she could force anyone to do anything."

"Including you?"

"Not once I came into my own power."

"She taught you, then. The way you're teaching me."

Her mother turned away without responding, and sank onto her settee with an irritated sigh. Morwen took the upholstered chair and folded her hands in her lap.

Irene glanced up at her, then away, to the dark night beyond the window. "In our line," she said, "we have no choice about that. We have to instruct our daughters. It's a compulsion, irresistible as breathing. It's one of the prices we pay for being what we are." She let her head drop back against the brocade, and her eyes closed. "I don't want you to see her again, Morwen."

"Why not?"

"Because there's nothing to be gained from it."

"I want to know her."

"I forbid it," Irene said.

"You can't stop me, Maman."

"Of course I can."

There were things Irene could do. She could lock Morwen in her room, or drag her off to Cardiff. She could order Jago not to allow Ynyr out of the stables.

But Morwen had a weapon of her own now. "If you try to stop me," she said, "you will never see the crystal again."

Irene's eyes opened wide, and she shot upright. "What! How *dare* you?" Her voice rose and thinned. Morwen thought she sounded like a squalling cat. "You will bring it back this very moment!"

"I will bring it back, certainly," Morwen said. She rose and smoothed her dinner dress. "But tomorrow. After I've seen Grand-mère Ursule."

Her mother rose, too, but her shoulders shook with fury. "You thankless chit!" she hissed. "I've given you everything, and now this?"

Morwen paused, her hand on the doorknob. "It is strange, isn't it?" she said, in the most pleasant tone she could manage. "I wonder if that's how Grand-mère felt."

Irene's mouth opened, closed, and opened again, but it seemed she could find no words.

"Stop that, Maman. You look like a fish." Morwen turned the knob, opened the door, and left without glancing back.

Once she was in the corridor, and a few steps along the way to her own room, her bravado failed her. She stopped and leaned against the wall, her heart thudding.

Nothing would ever be the same between her mother and her. It had never been a loving connection, but now it would be openly antagonistic. Papa would side with his wife, of course, as would Mademoiselle. Perhaps even Jago. Everyone in this house owed their living to Lord Llewelyn and Lady Irene. Morwen had no one.

Except her grandmother.

5

Morwen woke well before the sun rose over the autumnal fields, eager to get out of the house before her mother was awake. She dressed in her oldest riding skirt and remembered to take a jacket against the chill that had begun to crisp the grass. She was hungry. Dinner had been so unpleasant the night before that she had eaten almost nothing. She didn't want to ring, in case she woke Mademoiselle, nor to wait for breakfast to be set out in the morning room. Instead she crept down the servants' staircase, which she wasn't supposed to use, and found one of the maids trudging up the stairs with a coal scuttle. She begged her to fetch a slice of bread and butter, and the maid, with a sigh, set down her burden and turned back down the stairs to the kitchen.

Bread in hand, Morwen slipped out the side door into the garden and hurried toward the stables. The sun was peeping over the hills to the east, and the rows of beans and peas, stripped now of their bounty, gleamed as if brushed with gold. A lamp was alight in the tack room, and as she drew close she heard Ynyr's greeting. She paused to pull up a carrot from the soil, and scrubbed the dirt from it as she moved on.

In a way, she hated knowing that there was a name for her relationship to the Shire. To think that he was filling some preordained role in her life as a witch seemed to diminish his affection, as if his being designated a spirit familiar meant Ynyr's devotion was less than voluntary.

He whickered again, and Jago appeared in the window, his dark head silhouetted by lamplight. Morwen hurried her steps, eager to go into that safe, warm space, to be in the presence of two beings who loved her, who had always loved her.

"Up early, you," Jago said when she stepped into the straw-strewn aisle. He had come to the door of the tack room, and was wiping his hands on a rag that smelled strongly of saddle soap. He smiled, his sleepy eyelids curving upward. "Tea?"

"Yes, please, Jago." She returned his smile with a generous one of her own. "I'll just say hello to Ynyr."

"He's waiting."

She went down the aisle to Ynyr's box and fed him the carrot, feathery top and all. He munched while she combed his forelock with her fingers, murmuring endearments. When the treat was finished, she planted a kiss on his wide forehead. "I'll be back soon."

The tea was ready in the tack room, prepared on the little coal-burning stove, and a cup laid ready for her on the workbench. She wriggled her way onto one of the high stools and picked up the cup. "Thanks for this, Jago."

"Always welcome," he said.

She didn't feel the least bit put off by his laconic manner. She never had. Though they didn't touch—that would have been shocking, the young lady and the horsemaster—the bond between them was nearly as strong as the one she had with Ynyr. As Jago went on with the task she had interrupted, she watched his lean face, dark eyes intent on his work, a lock of black hair falling over his forehead.

She said, "You're so handsome, Jago. Why have you never married?"

He looked up at her. "Odd question."

"No, it's not. Everyone seems to get married, eventually."

"Never met anyone I cared to marry."

She thought about this as she sipped her tea. After a time she said, "I don't care to marry, either."

"May not have a choice, you."

This made her sigh. "So I'm told. Papa wants me to meet someone at my birthday ball. Mama says I have to do it."

"Hard being a young lady."

"Sometimes." An easy silence stretched between them, filled only by the sound of Jago's punch as he made holes in the leather strap before him. Morwen finished her tea and slid from the stool. "I'm going to take Ynyr out now. The sun's up."

"Any place in particular?"

"Yes. Old Beaupre Castle."

Jago laid down his leather punch. A small frown drew his eyebrows together. "Gone twice already, you."

She stopped in the doorway, staring back at him. "How did you know that, Jago?"

For answer he pointed above his head, to where the hayloft stretched the length of the stables. She knew that loft. As a little girl she'd loved to play there, and Jago had pretended he didn't know. One end was open so hay could be forked out into a waiting wagon, and from there a person could see for miles downriver and across the fields.

"You watched me."

"Always, Miss Morwen."

"And you told my mother?"

His face tightened, and a muscle rippled down his long jaw. "No," he said in a toneless voice. "Not for me to tell the Lady Irene nought. Nor would I."

Morwen had the horrible feeling she had just hurt his feelings. She said hastily, "Oh, Jago, of course not! I'm sorry. I spoke without thinking."

His face relaxed, but he kept his eyes averted. "It's all right, miss."

She took a step back into the tack room and spread her hands. "It's just that she asked me about it, the first time, and the next time she followed me, as if she knew."

The muscle flexed again, like a fish wriggling upstream. "She's like that," Jago said. "She knows things."

"The maids say she has eyes in the back of her head."

"Close enough."

He still wouldn't look at her, but she saw a flush creep up his neck, and an uneasy feeling stole over her. She said, her voice catching, "Jago?"

He blew out a breath. "Never mind, you. I don't say things about your mama."

Morwen knew better than to press him about something he didn't want to discuss. Still feeling uneasy, she went out into the stables to release Ynyr from his box.

The big horse was unusually restive. She had trouble persuading him to hold still so she could clip the rope onto his halter. He stood beside the mounting block for her, but he shifted his feet and flicked his tail with impatience. She had barely found her seat before he was off, breaking into his swinging trot as he started toward the path along the river.

"Ynyr!" she said. "You should warm up a little first." He paid no attention, but moved even faster. She knew in her bones that Ursule was calling him, as she had called Morwen. The realization distracted her from her worry about Jago.

An autumn mist lay over the hills along the river, and thickened over the broken ramparts of the castle. Ynyr took the slope with strong, effortless strides, carrying Morwen upward, out of the thin sunshine and into the drifting fog. She was glad of her jacket, and of the thick socks she wore under her riding boots. When they reached the outer courtyard, she slid from Ynyr's back and unclipped the halter rope. He watched her with his head high as she approached the porch, wading through wisps of wet mist that curled around her ankles. The grass and stones were slippery with it, and the tops of the castle walls were obscured. She had to tread carefully, and didn't look up into the porch until she was only a few steps away.

Her grandmother was waiting for her.

"Are you going to give the crystal back to Irène?"

Morwen and Ursule sat together on the broken wall surrounding the outer courtyard. Ynyr grazed nearby, his ears flicking this way and that as he listened to their voices. The mist had burned off, and the autumn sunshine warmed the old stones and glistened gently on the river below the hill.

"I said I would."

"Ah. You gave your word." Ursule shrugged. "Then of course you must."

Morwen nodded. *"Madame—"*

"You can call me Grand-mère, Morwen."

"I would like that. I was going to say, I'm sorry I couldn't bring you anything. Any food, or tea, or..."

"I have food. And tea. You don't need to worry about me."

Ynyr lifted his head and snorted in their direction. Ursule chuckled. "My Aramis used to do that, when he wanted to tell me something."

"Ynyr's reminding me I have something to ask you."

"You may ask me anything, my dear. I'm long past the age of keeping secrets."

Morwen said, choosing her words with care, "What I'm wondering about is...well...you asked Maman about me. You asked who had given me to her. She didn't answer, and I don't know what you meant."

"Ah. Yes. That must confuse you." Ursule tipped her head back, lifting her face into the sunshine. "I wonder how much Irène has told you, *ma petite*? About your ancestresses?"

"A bit. I didn't know how much of it was true."

For an instant Ursule's lip curled with disdain, and Morwen saw again the resemblance between mother and daughter. The moment passed, and Ursule breathed out through pursed lips. "I will answer you, *ma petite*, but it's a long story. I want to start by telling you—" She hesitated, and the look of great age settled over her face again. "I want you to know that I loved my own mother very much. I betrayed her, though I never meant to. I didn't believe what she told me, either, but she was right."

Ursule's eyes glistened. Morwen prompted, "What did she tell you, Grand-mère?"

"She told me, if they knew what she was, they would kill her." Ursule turned her head to look full into Morwen's face. "It's true, *ma petite*. If they know—if they discover what we are—they will try to kill us."

Morwen shuddered at the thought.

Ursule put out her hard, dry hand and patted Morwen's where it rested on the warm stone. "It will be all right. We know how to hide."

"Maman doesn't—I mean—she keeps the crystal right in her bedroom!"

"Well. Irène knows what she's doing, I expect. She always has." Ursule withdrew her hand and pushed away a strand of hair that straggled across her eyes. "And now, *ma petite*, I will answer your question."

It was a long answer, told while Morwen's legs chafed against the rough stone wall, and her back ached from sitting on its uneven surface. She didn't dare move for fear she would interrupt Ursule's fascinating, terrifying, compelling account of their shared history. Irene had recounted some of it, but her version had been a dry listing of names and places and events. Now Morwen listened in awe to the tale of a desperate woman casting a spell to protect her clan, holding it through the night until her strength gave out. She shed tears over the solitary grave among the menhirs of Brittany.

The story of the clan's journey to Cornwall, of the magical discovery of the farmhouse their *grand-mère* had prophesied, and of the establishment of Orchard Farm, left her breathless with admiration. Ursule said the clan believed the gift had died with old Ursule, until her own mother summoned a man by magic, a man who left her with a daughter to raise alone. "It's our constant fear the craft will die out," she said. "The power is passed down from mother to daughter, but I had five aunts with almost none. Only my *maman* had the gift, and she wasn't sure for a long time if she would be the last."

She told her own story, too. She described a practical but childless marriage, a life of farming and husbandry. She admitted her skepticism of the craft, wiped away when the crystal woke for her. Morwen wept again when she heard how her great-grandmother Nanette was exposed, and gritted her teeth in anger over Morcum's part in it.

Though she knew Ursule's flight had been successful, still she held her breath at the descriptions of her escape on Aramis, sire of Ynyr. She sighed over the devotion of Sebastien, her grandfather, who had followed Ursule into Wales and visited as often as his travels allowed.

"Irène resented him," Ursule said, with sad resignation. "She thought he should stay at home and be a proper father. But he was no farmer, my Sebastien. His hands were as soft as your own, *ma petite*. He played the harp, and had the sweetest voice I've ever heard in this world. Your *maman* thought he should take her with him, and teach her to play and sing. She didn't know what his life was like, traveling from town to town, never sure where he would lay his head or who would pay to hear his music.

"But he came back, often and often. Whenever he could." Her eyes shone at the memory. "Sometimes he would slip in through my bedroom window late at night, and I would wake to feel his kiss on my hair, or his hand on my shoulder. I wish you had known him."

"What happened to him, Grand-mère?"

"I've never known. One day he went off, saying he was going to play with a troupe in London town. He never returned. I think…" She sighed and turned her gaze to the sun-spangled river. "I think he died, *ma petite*. If he'd lived, he would have come back to me."

"Couldn't you have used the crystal to discover what had happened?"

"No. Irène was gone by then, off to become a lady. Took the stone with her. I can see a good deal, but not far enough to follow my Sebastien."

"I'm sorry for that."

Ursule shrugged and spread her hands. "I worked on a manor farm, you know, near Tenby. It was a hard life, but a good one. I was happy enough, but Irène was not. She had her heart set on being a lady, and when she had inherited the power, she used it to make her wish come true."

"I'll give the stone back to you."

"Oh no, don't do that. It doesn't matter now, *ma petite*. I no longer have use for it. It's time for me to join my mother."

"Grand-mère, your mother is dead!"

"She left this world, it's true. She'll be waiting for me in the next."

"No! Not when I've just found you! I mean, of course, you found *me*, but..."

"Morwen, this is the way life is. It is both too long and much too brief, sometimes sweet, often bitter. Try not to feel bad about it. Remember that we women of the craft have more power over it than most. And remember that there is power in words. Power in ritual."

"I don't know any rituals."

"You will learn. Or you will not, according to the Mother Goddess's will." She touched Morwen's arm with a gentle hand. "I'm tired, dear heart. I've held on past my time. I can feel the thinning of the veil..." She took a long, rasping breath and whispered, "Samhain is almost here, the harvest Sabbat, the turning of the great wheel of seasons. It's a good time."

"I don't want you to go," Morwen said.

"I won't be far away," her grandmother assured her. "Just look into the stone, *ma petite*. I'll be there."

﹋

The sun was high above the Vale by the time Ynyr carried Morwen back to Morgan Hall. The day felt like a farewell to summer, the river a glittering blue under a faded sky, the fields gold and rust beneath slanting sunshine. Morwen's head thrummed with all she had heard, stories of love and lust, of sorrows and triumphs, her great-grandmother's awful death, her mother's betrayal. The crystal, which she had retrieved from the willow grove, felt heavy and lifeless under her arm.

She still didn't know whether Papa was really her papa. Only her mother, Ursule said, knew that, and she would no doubt carry the knowledge with her to the grave. Morwen knew almost nothing of how things stood between wives and husbands. She wasn't sure she wanted to know.

Jago appeared as she and Ynyr arrived at the stables. "Miss Morwen. Wanted in the hall, you."

Morwen had been hoping to spend some time grooming Ynyr and cleaning his box. She slid from his back and landed on the packed earth of the stable yard with an irritated thump. Usually this demonstration brought a smile to Jago's lips, but not today. She eyed him doubtfully. "Jago? Who asked for me?"

"I couldn't say, miss," he said evasively. His eyes passed over her and went straight to Ynyr. "Chesley sent your maid. I'll take the horse. You'd best go up."

Reluctantly Morwen handed over Ynyr's halter rope. As she turned away, Ynyr startled her with a long, loud whinny. She whirled back to him but saw Jago tugging on his halter rope, persuading him into the shadows of the stable. Ynyr whinnied again, his head up, his lip curling in the stallion's challenge. He had never done such a thing before. It filled Morwen with anxiety.

In a cloud of uneasy confusion she walked with dragging steps up through the garden and around to the entrance of Morgan Hall. She held the wrapped crystal close.

Chesley opened the doors at her approach and stood back as she entered, his gaze somewhere above her head. "His Lordship is waiting for you in the parlor," he intoned.

"Thank you, Chesley."

"His Lordship directs you to dress. There are guests for tea."

"Who is it?"

Chesley sniffed. "His Lordship will introduce you, Miss Morwen. Do you want your maid?"

"No. I can manage. I'll go along after I've changed."

"I will inform His Lordship," Chesley said, and closed the door without having once met her eyes.

Morwen trudged up the staircase, weighed down by doubts and confusion. Grand-mère had spoken of power, but Morwen felt anything but powerful. She felt as if she were living in a prison—a comfortable one, but still a prison, where she couldn't make her own decisions, where she had to do as she was told, without regard for her feelings. She wished she could run back to the castle or hide in the stables with Jago and Ynyr. The last thing she wanted to do, while her head still whirled with Grand-mère's stories, was meet strangers at a formal tea.

"Morwen!" It was a loud hiss, meant to carry but not be heard below stairs. Irene was waiting on the landing.

Morwen faced her mother. "Yes, Maman," she said.

"Do you have it?"

Morwen held up the linen-wrapped bundle.

Irene exclaimed and snatched the stone from Morwen's hands. She scratched her wrist with her sharp fingernails, but didn't notice Morwen's wince. Irene whirled and all but ran toward her own apartment. Morwen stood gazing after her, thinking that her mother was a terrible disappointment. That she was ashamed to be her daughter.

When she was in her own room, taking a brush to her tangled hair, she caught sight of her face in the mirror and laid down her hairbrush. She looked just like her mother at that moment. Her lips were compressed, her eyes gleaming with anger. Deliberately she passed her hands slowly over her face. When she dropped them again, the alien look had disappeared. She leaned closer to the glass to gaze into her own eyes.

"If I have to look like someone," she said to her image, "let it be Ursule. Not Maman." She willed it so, and she thought, after a

few moments, that she had succeeded. Perhaps she was not without some power after all.

She nodded to her reflection and rose from the dressing table to
find a fresh frock.

⁂

"Morwen, at last." Papa stood up at her entrance, a thing he never
did when the family was alone. He came to meet her, holding out
his hand for her gloved one. He tucked hers under his arm and
turned her toward the man standing beside one of the straight-
backed chairs. "This is Lord William Selwyn, Morwen." He
added, as an afterthought, "And his son Dafydd. Lord William,
my daughter, Morwen."

The older gentleman, and his son, who looked as if he must be
about Morwen's age, bowed. Lord William was a thickset man
with brown hair beginning to gray at the temples. He smiled,
making his drooping brown mustache quiver. It looked, Morwen
thought, like a squirrel's tail.

"Well, Llewelyn," Lord William said heartily. "She is everything you said. A lovely girl. And so tall!"

Dafydd, still slender, but with the same thick brown hair as his
father, stared at his well-polished boots. Morwen wondered if he
was shy, or if he—like her—didn't want to be here.

Lady Irene was seated beside the table, the skirts of her best tea
dress draped neatly around her crossed ankles. She didn't speak,
either, nor did she look up at her daughter.

"Lord William will be our special guest at your coming-out
ball," Papa said. He guided Morwen to a seat and gestured to the
men to take chairs as well. Everyone sat, and Chesley appeared,
holding the door to allow the housemaid to pass through with the
tea tray.

As Irene poured the tea and served the cups, Papa and Lord

William chatted. Morwen and Dafydd sat at opposite sides of the table and listened to their parents discuss them as if they were livestock to be traded.

"Morwen speaks fluent French," Papa said.

"Does she indeed," Lord William responded, again bestowing that squirrel-tail smile on her. "Excellent. I understand she is also an accomplished horsewoman. Dafydd has a fine seat as well. Loves the fox hunt, don't you, Dafydd?"

Dafydd said, "Yes, Father."

Irene said, "Won't you have a sandwich, Dafydd?" He took one and set it on his plate, but didn't taste it. Morwen did the same. She pushed at the sandwich, letting her thoughts stray back to Ursule. She longed to be alone, to think about what the stories meant, to ponder her mother's deception. She wanted to see Ynyr, and understand what was bothering him.

The men droned on, the perfect illustration of why Morwen hated formal teas. Politics bored her. The launching of a new ship, *Lusitania*, held no interest unless she would be allowed to sail on it. The quarreling of kings and dukes in Europe surely didn't matter here in Wales.

Morwen felt the twinge that meant someone was watching her. She peeked up from beneath her eyebrows to find Dafydd Selwyn was looking directly at her. His expression didn't change, but he lowered one eyelid, slowly, in a deliberate wink.

Morwen stifled a giggle just as Lord William seemed to suddenly remember her presence. He said, with unconvincing jollity, "Miss Morwen, I have something serious to discuss with your papa. Perhaps you wouldn't mind showing Dafydd your stables?"

Lady Irene said nothing. Lord Llewelyn, however, nodded agreement with this suggestion, and bestowed an affectionate and completely unfamiliar smile on his daughter.

She seized the chance to escape, jumping to her feet. She almost

dashed straight out of the room, but remembered her training enough to curtsy to Lord William, then again to her father.
"Thank you, sir," she said in her most maidenly tone.

She didn't need to look at Dafydd to know he was biting back
his own laugh. In moments they had left the men to their conversation and were running down through the garden like children
freed from the schoolroom. They were still some distance from
the stables when Ynyr whinnied, the full-throated call of a big
stallion.

Dafydd skidded to a stop. "What was *that*?" he said.

Other than formal phrases, they were the first words he had
spoken. Morwen slowed, too, so she could walk beside him. He
had a pleasant face, and she liked the look of humor around his
mouth and eyes. She said, "That's Ynyr. My horse."

His eyes widened. "You don't ride a—a pony?"

Morwen laughed. "I'm far too tall for a pony! Wait until you
see my Ynyr. He's as big as two ponies piled together!"

"You're exaggerating."

"Come on and see!" Morwen dashed ahead, leading the way
into the straw-scented aisle between the loose boxes. Ynyr was
waiting, his head extended over the half gate, his ears pricked forward. When he saw Morwen, he nickered and pressed against the
gate, making the wood creak.

Jago appeared, a bridle in one hand, an awl in the other. When
he saw that Morwen wasn't alone, he dipped his head to Dafydd
and faded back into the tack room.

Dafydd's eyes were all for Ynyr. "But," he said wonderingly,
"that can't be your horse! He's—he's a Shire, isn't he?"

"Yes." Morwen, feeling smug, crossed to Ynyr, and as he lowered his head to her, laid her cheek against his broad forehead. "I
ride him everywhere," she said.

"I don't see how you could find a saddle to fit him!"

Morwen turned, keeping her back to the stall gate, letting Ynyr nuzzle her hair. "I don't use a saddle," she said.

"You ride *astride*?"

Morwen shrugged. "Women do, you know," she said. "Side-saddles are ridiculous. And dangerous," she added, giving him a warning look.

She thought he might say something scornful. Outraged articles appeared now and then in the newspapers about women who refused to ride sidesaddle. But Dafydd laughed. "Of course they're dangerous!" he said. "If all women would refuse them, the whole silly concept would vanish within a year. I never expected, though, that Lord Llewelyn's daughter would be a rebel! He's so . . . so—"

He colored suddenly. Again Morwen shrugged. "I know," she said. "Papa is extremely conventional."

"My father is, too," Dafydd said. He took a step forward, and gingerly put out a hand to touch Ynyr's silver mane. "I hope you won't mind that."

Morwen shot him a curious glance. "Why should I care?"

"Why should you care?" Dafydd, with his hand on Ynyr's neck, gave her an odd look. "Surely you—I mean—Miss Morgan, you *do* know why we're here, don't you?"

Morwen's heart missed a beat. Ynyr snorted. He stamped a hind foot and threw up his head, causing Dafydd to jump back. Morwen said, "Ynyr! What's the matter?"

Ynyr's reaction meant something. It always did. Suspicion dawned, and grew swiftly. She thought she might understand now why Sir William and his son had come, and why she had been commanded to dress with care.

Jago appeared in the door to the tack room. "Miss Morwen," he said. "All right, you?"

Tightly she answered, "Yes. Thank you, Jago."

Dafydd said awkwardly, "I'm terribly sorry, Miss Morgan. I thought you knew."

"It was my father's task to warn me."

"You haven't consented, then."

"Consented to marry you?" She glared at him. "I haven't been asked. This is hardly the way to—"

"Oh no, Miss Morgan!" Dafydd said. His face reddened. "Oh, damn! I'm so sorry. I—Oh, damn and blast. You see, it's not me."

"What do you mean?" He looked utterly miserable, and terribly young. A warning chill began in her belly.

Dafydd said, "Miss Morgan. It's my father who wants a wife. Your father and mine—they came to an agreement."

The chill spread into Morwen's chest and threatened to freeze her thoughts. She stammered, "Your father? That—that old man?"

Dafydd looked on the verge of tears. "I wish it weren't true."

Morwen's knees trembled, and she took one stumbling step. Jago said, "Morwen! All right, you?"

Dafydd was closer. He took a quick step forward to put his hand under her arm. She leaned against it and drew a shuddering breath. He said, "I can't believe no one told you."

"Nor can I," she said. She straightened, and freed herself from his hand.

"I don't know what to say, Miss Morgan. Since my mother died, my father has been looking for someone to marry, and Lord Llewelyn said, as you were about to come out..."

"As if I were a horse for sale. Or a cow!" she said bitterly.

"I know. It's the way they do things."

"I won't agree to it."

"Obviously, my father's too old for you. He wanted me to let you know I didn't mind that you're so young. Now that I've met you, though..."

Morwen's knees no longer trembled, and the cold feeling had been replaced by an angry fire. "Now that you've met me—what?"

"Well," Dafydd said, looking past her to Ynyr. The Shire stood with his head high, glaring at the boy as if it were all his fault. "Well, now I do mind. That you're so young, I mean, to be married off to someone so old. It's not fair."

"And it's not going to happen." Morwen held out a hand to Jago. "Ynyr's tack, please, Jago. I'm going out."

Jago disappeared into the tack room and reappeared with Ynyr's halter. He crossed the aisle and held it up. Ynyr ducked his head and slipped his nose neatly inside the straps.

Dafydd said, "Is that all? No bridle, or bit?"

"We don't need it," Morwen told him.

Jago asked, "Change clothes, you?"

Morwen shook her head. "Papa will stop me. There's someone I need to see."

Dafydd said, "I'll come with you, Miss Morgan, if you have a horse I can borrow."

Jago raised his eyebrows, but Morwen shook her head again. "I thank you, Dafydd. It's kind of you, but your father would be furious. *My* father will be furious, when he finds out he can't—" Her voice grew harsh. "He can't *sell* me, as if I were one of his racehorses!"

"Nor can my father buy you," Dafydd said. "Shall I tell them that?"

Morwen was clipping the rope beneath Ynyr's chin, but she paused and looked back at her new and unlikely champion. "Do you dare? There's going to be a frightful scene."

"Yes, there is." He grinned, revealing an endearing dimple in one cheek. She noticed how thick his eyelashes were, how clear his blue eyes. "It should make a fine entertainment."

She tried to smile in answer. "Indeed, Dafydd, you make me wish I could take you with me, but I can't." She opened the half gate to the loose box and led Ynyr out. Dafydd's eyes widened at the full sight of the big horse, but he overcame his awe to come around to Ynyr's left and make a stirrup of his hands. Morwen put her slippered foot into his palms and jumped up to Ynyr's back. Her skirts rode up around her knees, exposing her white-stockinged legs. Dafydd, with touching gallantry, averted his gaze.

"Off to the castle, you?" said Jago.

"Yes. Now, don't fuss, Jago. I might be there for some time."

"Have a care."

"I will. Good-bye, Dafydd. I don't know if I'll see you again."

Dafydd bowed to her, and she urged Ynyr out of the stables and down toward the river at a full gallop.

6

By the time Morwen and Ynyr climbed up from the river, shadows stretched down to meet them, elongated echoes of the jagged castle walls. Morwen, in her white tea gown, shivered with the sudden chill of premonition. For the comfort of his presence, she coaxed Ynyr to follow her in through the porch, where his hooves echoed on fragmented stone.

Morwen called, "Ursule? Grand-mère?" There was no answer.

There was little light except for the last glimmers of sunshine on the highest points of the walls. Reluctantly Morwen turned toward the tower. Only Ynyr's bulk behind her gave her the courage to make her way there, to peek in through the empty doorway, and to call again, "Grand-mère? Are you there?"

The lintel was too low for Ynyr to pass beneath it. Morwen patted him, as much to calm herself as for his sake, then stepped through the doorway into the dimness of the tower.

She hadn't been inside before, since Ursule had contrived to meet her in the porch. It was too dark to see details, but it was clear her grandmother had been living here for a time. Against the circular wall she made out the shape of a brazier on a tripod, and a little pile of things, a pot, a bowl, what looked as if it might be a coal scuttle. On the opposite side, a bundle slumped against the stone wall. Morwen thought it might be blankets, perhaps a pillow, things for Ursule to sleep on. She crept toward it, fighting an urge to flee back to Ynyr. Her heart hammered beneath her breastbone, and she whispered, "Grand-mère?"

Her eyes, adjusting to the gloom, made out what did indeed look like a pallet of blankets, mounded slightly in the middle. A thin pillow rested at one end, and on it there seemed to be something lying. An animal, perhaps? A white cat, glowing subtly in the darkness? It didn't move as she drew closer.

She put out her hand to touch it, then snatched it back with a cry.

It was Ursule's silver hair, spilled in a shining cascade over the dingy cushion.

Morwen fell to her knees beside the blanketed form of her dead grandmother. "Oh no," she breathed. "Oh, poor, poor Grandmère, to die here, all alone in the cold. Oh no..."

She had known Ursule Orchiére such a short time, too short a time, but the pain of loss pierced her heart as if she had known her all her life. She knelt on the icy stones and wept a torrent of tears that burned her cheeks and fell on the white lace of her gown.

When Ynyr nickered a warning, she gulped back her tears and looked up. Evening had closed in around the castle, but it was still darker within than without. She clearly saw the silhouette of her mother in the doorway, outlined by the paler gloom of the sky. Irene, too, still wore her tea gown, but she had a woolen coat over it, and a scarf around her throat. She said, "Morwen! Whatever do you think you're doing?"

"She's dead, Maman," Morwen said, in a voice rusty with weeping. "She died, all alone." A fresh sob shook her, and she wailed, "All alone!"

Irene was at her side in a moment. She bent and put a hand beneath the ragged blanket that covered her mother's body. With a sigh she straightened, and stood with her hands clasped before her. "You're right," she said. "She's gone."

Morwen struggled to her feet, her knees numb from contact with the cold stones. "You left her here to die!" she cried. "You left your *mother* here, to die in the dark, with no one to comfort her, no one to help her!"

"Don't be a fool," Irene said tightly. "She didn't have to die here. She has a home."

"Where? Where is her home?"

"The farm where I grew up."

"But how far is it? How was she to get there?" Morwen was shouting now, leaning toward her mother, so close that her spittle, glistening in the low light, struck Irene's pale face.

Irene pulled away from her. "How do you think she got *here?*" she said, but in a distracted way. She was frowning, looking down at the lifeless bundle of blankets. "Have you been in here before? Do you know where her things are?"

Morwen pressed her shaking hands to her face and groaned with impotent fury. "Things!" she grated. "Maman, she didn't have any *things*. She had nothing!"

"She has Grand-mère's book. She wouldn't leave it behind."

"Book? What do you mean, a book? She didn't even have a proper bed!"

"I mean the grimoire, Morwen." Irene was lifting the ragged blankets around Ursule's body, feeling beneath them with her hands.

"Grimoire? What is that?"

"I haven't explained it to you yet." Irene straightened and crossed to the brazier to scatter Ursule's few utensils. Over her shoulder she said, "It's a book of spells. And potions, and other things."

Morwen dropped her hands from her face and hugged herself against the dank cold of the tower. "I don't know what you're talking about."

Irene put her hands on her hips, gazing at her daughter with irritation. "It's invaluable. Trust me, she would never have left it behind. We have to find it."

"I don't care about a book," Morwen said. "I'm going to fetch Jago, so we can see that Ursule has a proper burial."

"Not until we find it."

"I told you, Maman, I don't care, and I'm not going to help—"

Irene uttered an exclamation that echoed from the stone walls. "Here it is!" she cried. In her hands she held a thick, misshapen volume with a heavy, old-fashioned cover of cracked leather. She lifted it up to show Morwen. "This is the rest of my birthright," she said triumphantly. "Now I have it all."

Morwen felt the curl of her lip, her mother's customary expression of disdain, but she couldn't help it. "You didn't care for her at all, did you?" she said. "The woman who bore you, who raised you, who—"

"Don't be a fool." Irene snatched up a bit of cloth and began to fold the old book into it. "What good would it do her now for me to wail and tear my hair? She wouldn't expect it."

Bitingly Morwen asked, "What would you do if it were me lying there?"

Her mother paused, the book in her arms, and turned a cold glance on her daughter. "Why speculate?" she said. "It's not you."

"Would you just leave her there to—to molder?"

"Molder?" Irene barked a laugh. "Where do you get such words?"

"Would you?" Morwen repeated, ignoring the barb.

"I didn't ask her to come here," Irene said, turning toward the door. "You had better go apologize to your father for vanishing without so much as a word of farewell to his guests."

"His guests?" Morwen followed her mother and stood in the doorway. Irene stepped around Ynyr, who threw up his head and snorted as she passed him. "Do you know what his intention was?"

Irene cast her a brief glance over her shoulder. The stars had come out, and her pale face gleamed in their faint light. "Of course," she said.

"And you said nothing?"

"What could I say? These are men's decisions."

"Sir William is old enough to be my father. My grandfather!"

"What difference does that make?"

"It's disgusting!"

"You will be Lady Selwyn. The mistress of Sweetbriar."

"I will not."

Irene paced on through the courtyard to the entrance of the porch. There she hesitated and turned back. "The choice of your husband is not yours to make, nor is it mine. This is the way for women of our class. You'll be happier when you accept that."

"What good is our power, then?"

A chilly smile crossed Irene's face, and she emitted the ghost of a laugh. "Our power makes it bearable," she said softly. "We let them think they're in control, but we take what we want, when they would refuse us." The smile faded. "You'll see," she said, turning away, starting through the porch. "You'll learn, just as I did."

Morwen barely heard these last words, uttered when her mother was already in the outer courtyard. Ynyr bumped her with his nose as if to ask why they weren't also on their way. Morwen encircled his head with her arm. "Ynyr," she murmured. "I need Jago, but I don't dare return to Morgan Hall. Will you fetch him for me?"

⁂

"Gave me a fright, you," said Jago. He threw his leg over Ynyr's withers and slid down to the ground, where Morwen, shivering in earnest now, waited for him. "Here. I brought you one of my coats, and some boots. Knew you left with nothing but your fancy dress, there." She had drawn one of Ursule's ancient blankets around her shoulders, but her slippers were too thin to block the chill of the hard ground.

"Th-thank you," she stammered, through chattering teeth.

"When Ynyr came back without you..." Jago shook his head. "Lucky for me your note didn't fall off his halter, or I'd have the constable searching for you right now, and His Lordship wouldn't like that. Now, what's this about?"

It was easier to lead Jago into the tower and show him than to try to explain. He had an oil lamp with him, and he held it high when they were inside the dank tower room. In an instant he grasped the situation. "This is your reason for riding up here so often."

"Yes." Morwen went to crouch beside Ursule's small, still form. She touched the cascade of silver hair, which shone in the lamplight as if there were still life in it. "She's my grandmother," Morwen said brokenly. "I've only just found her, and now I've lost her again!"

"Miss Morwen—your grandmother?" Jago frowned and held the lamp higher. "Why do you think that?"

"She told me. And Maman said so, too."

"Was she here? Lady Irene?"

"Yes."

"But not today! Not since—" Jago nodded toward the pitiful little form on the pallet.

"Yes, today," Morwen said mournfully.

"She left you here with a corpse?" Jago's voice dropped ominously, and a note came into it that Morwen had heard only twice. Once was when a stablehand had whipped a colt until it bled. The other was when a careless rider had startled her pony

so she was thrown; though she hadn't been hurt, Jago had threatened to whip the other rider.

In the flickering lamplight, Jago's face hardened. His dark
eyes narrowed to slits. "Your mother left you here with a dead
woman."

There was no need to answer. The evidence lay, still and sad, at
their feet.

In that same harsh voice, Jago said, "What do you want to do,
Miss Morwen?"

"I want to take my *grand-mère* to Father Pugh. He'll see she's
properly buried."

"Then that we shall do."

"You're so good, Jago," she said impulsively. "You're like—like
a father to me!"

It was as if she had thrown her arms around him, or kissed his
cheek. Despite the uncertainty of the light, she saw his cheeks blaze.
His lips parted as if he would answer her, but he shook his head and
turned abruptly away. Intuition pierced her breastbone. "Jago?"

He was almost to the doorway. His steps faltered, then steadied. He set the lamp down inside the wall and went out. She heard
Ynyr's hooves on the stones of the porch, and then, with softer
thuds, in the grassy inner courtyard. Jago reappeared in the tower.
"It won't seem respectful," he said. "But it's best to put—to put
the body—to let Ynyr carry her."

"Jago." Morwen crossed to him, her hands out. She gripped his
arm and didn't let go until he dropped his gaze to hers. "It's you,
isn't it?" she whispered. "It's not Papa. It's you."

"Morwen, I can't—I wouldn't presume—"

"I would be glad of it." She squeezed his arm with both hands,
willing him to confirm what her gift was telling her. He had
never, in her memory, called her by her Christian name alone. It
was always "Miss Morwen."

But now she knew, though she didn't quite understand how it could be. "Did you love her?" she asked. "Did she love you?"

"I can't speak of this," he said. He removed her hands from his arm, but gently, and he patted them before he let them go. "She'll send me away."

"I'm leaving anyway," Morwen said. "I must. They want me to marry that—that old man—Dafydd's father. I won't."

"But she knows where you are. She'll send them after you."

The truth of this made Morwen shiver, and she pulled his coat tighter around her. "I can't leave my grandmother here in the cold," she said.

"Then we'd best hurry."

It was not wasted on Morwen that Jago had not admitted to being her father, nor had he answered her questions. He worked beside her in silence. The two of them tenderly wrapped Ursule in her blankets, then carried her out to the courtyard. At the smell of death, Ynyr pulled back at first, but Morwen put her mouth close to his ear and whispered to him. "Please, Ynyr. Do this for me. It won't be for long." He settled down, though his tail switched restlessly and he laid his ears back at the first touch of his burden. She patted his shoulder, thanking him. He bent his head and touched her hand with his whiskery muzzle.

Jago said, "Will you ride behind?"

"No. I'll walk."

"Long walk."

"I know."

"Follow me, then." Jago led the way, turning away from the usual path down the hill to the river. He took the route that would skirt the hill on the southern side of the castle, leading them away from Morgan Hall and directly to St. Hilary.

For some time they walked in silence, Jago ahead, Morwen and Ynyr coming after. Jago held the lamp high whenever there were obstacles, stones or roots in the path or thorns to catch at Ynyr's sides or Morwen's skirts. Morwen was grateful for the boots Jago had brought her. Her slippers would have been torn to shreds before they had gone half a mile.

As they made their way, she thought hard. She would need money, and clothes. She would have to slip into Morgan Hall unseen, then hurry back to the stables for Ynyr. And she needed somewhere to go. Someplace where her parents would never find her.

"Jago," she called softly.

"Yes."

"Do you know anyone in London?"

It was well past midnight when they reached the church. They had to wait on the step for some minutes before Father Pugh, in a plaid wool dressing gown, answered Morwen's knock. His mousy hair was rumpled, as if he hadn't taken time to comb it, and his eyes were swollen with sleep. His housekeeper appeared behind him, also in her dressing gown, and with a cap over her gray hair. The priest, holding an oil lamp high, mustered a smile of greeting when he recognized the daughter of Lord Llewelyn, but it dissolved when he caught sight of Jago behind her, and Ynyr with a strange burden draped across his withers. "Why, Miss Morwen—"

"Father Pugh, forgive this intrusion. A woman has died, and there's no one to see to her."

"That is—it's a body? On the horse?" The priest had a narrow face, and a small mouth that often trembled as if he were about to weep. Morwen had always felt rather sorry for him.

"She is—she was—" Morwen felt a warning from Jago, though he made no sound. "She was someone who was kind to me. I hoped you could see to a proper burial."

Father Pugh's lips had already begun to quiver. "Ah, well, Miss Morwen, this is not the—that is, most unusual—perhaps not quite the done thing? But if the woman was one of your family's retainers, perhaps—that is, I would have thought milord would—"

Morwen thought of her grandmother's body, lying across Ynyr as if it were no more meaningful than a sack of oats, and tears sprang to her eyes. She tried to speak, but only a sob came out.

"Oh, tsk, tsk, tsk," Father Pugh said instantly. He stood back, holding the door to the rectory wide. "I didn't see that you were upset, my dear. I'm so sorry. I wouldn't want your father to think...Oh, tsk, tsk, tsk. Come in, and Mrs. Welland will make you a cup of tea. Your man and I will handle the—that is, we'll the remains..."

"You see, miss?" Jago said, without a trace of guile in his voice. "Didn't I say? Just as I told you, Father Pugh will know what to do with old Mairie here. Go and have that cuppa, you. Father and I will manage between us."

Soon Morwen was seated on a plush settee in the rectory parlor, with a cup of tea in her hands and her feet warming at a hastily lit coal fire, and not long after that she and Jago were on their way back to Morgan Hall, Morwen on Ynyr's back and Jago walking alongside.

Morwen was so weary she could barely think. "It felt so wrong to leave her there, Jago. How do we know—"

Jago must have been tired, too, but he showed no sign of it. He said, "Father Pugh is a timid man, but a kind one. Your gran will receive a Christian burial."

Morwen was certain her *grand-mère* Ursule had not been Christian, but it hardly mattered now. The pink and lavender streaks of first light were developing in the east, and she had to hurry to complete her preparations before the household woke. She said, "I'll be back for Ynyr within the hour."

"Take care, you. Remember, she knows things."

So do I. But she didn't speak the thought, and she wouldn't know how to explain it to Jago even if there were time. She gave him back his jacket and boots, picked up the tattered skirts of her tea gown, and ran.

She abandoned her ruined slippers beneath the rosemary bush at the back door, where Cook kept a key hidden in case she found herself locked out. Barefoot, Morwen dashed up the servants' staircase and crept cautiously along the corridor to her own bedroom.

It seemed a lifetime since she had seen it last. She had left it, wearing her nicest day frock, to meet her father's guests for tea. She returned to it with her world turned upside down and all her plans as tattered as her once-pristine dress.

The room was tidy, her nightdress laid out on her bed, a dress and smallclothes hanging ready on the wardrobe. Morwen stripped off her soiled clothes and left them in a heap on the cold hearth. She ignored the dress, instead choosing her warmest riding habit, with a divided skirt and a thick, long-skirted coat. As she dressed she scanned the room, deciding what she would take and how quickly she could pack her traveling case.

Fifteen minutes later, noises began below stairs, the sounds of the servants starting their daily tasks. Morwen drew a deep breath and opened her bedroom door. She took a cautious look into the corridor before she slipped out, and pulled the door shut. With her case in one hand and her riding boots in the other, she made her way in stealth toward the servants' staircase.

She was too late. Even as she opened the door, she heard the stumping tread of the housemaid starting up.

Morwen whirled and started back the other way, thinking she could go out through the front door, simply walk down into the foyer and straight outside. She reached the staircase, but before she could put a foot on the top tread she heard Chesley in the morning room. More time must have passed than she realized. If Chesley saw her, she would never make her escape.

She turned again, to hasten along the corridor to Irene's boudoir. There was nothing else for it. If her mother was asleep, perhaps she could tiptoe through her bedroom, into her beautiful bathroom, and down her secret staircase.

She hesitated, her hand on the doorknob, but the ringing of a bell from her father's bedroom made her start with alarm. If he caught her—if any of them stopped her now—her freedom would be forever at an end.

She set her teeth, turned the knob, and went in.

The boudoir was dim, the early sunlight not yet penetrating its heavily curtained window. Morwen locked the boudoir door behind her, and cautiously, gingerly, eased her mother's bedroom door open.

She managed to keep the latch from clicking, but it was as if she had walked straight into the morning sun. The curtains were drawn back, and the enormous mirror and creamy walls blazed with light. For long seconds she stood blinking against the brilliance.

She heard her mother's voice before she could make out her form. "They won't bury her in the churchyard, you know," Irene said. "Your efforts are wasted, yours and Jago's."

Morwen blinked again and began to perceive her mother standing in the very center of the room, on her pretty green-patterned rug. She wore a white peignoir, and her thick dark hair was caught up with white ribbon. She seemed to materialize out of the light, and the effect was unnerving. The crystal lay at her feet in a pool of crumpled linen, its smooth top afire with sunshine.

Morwen pointed at it. She couldn't stop her voice from shaking. "You spied on us."

"Scried. You really should use the proper verb, Morwen."

Morwen took a step forward. "I'm leaving, Maman."

Irene didn't move. "You're not going anywhere. I've seen to it."

"What does that mean?"

"I sent him away."

"Who?"

"The damned horse, of course."

Morwen gasped. "You can't do that! Ynyr is mine!"

"I know what's best for you, Morwen." Irene bent to fold the linen around the crystal.

"Maman, how could you? You lost your own familiar, and you would take mine away?"

"We'll find you another spirit familiar, one that's more— appropriate."

Morwen said, in a voice tight with bitterness, "I have a lot left to learn, but I know familiars choose us, not the other way around."

Irene said, "Well, then, you'll do without. Just as I have done." She straightened with the stone in her arms and turned, her peignoir swirling around her, toward the window seat.

Fury emptied Morwen's mind of all but the need to find Ynyr. It fired her muscles and freed her mind from doubt. Silent and determined, she sprang forward. In one efficient movement she snatched the wrapped crystal from her mother's arms. She dashed into the bathroom and ripped aside the curtain that disguised the secret staircase. Irene, immobilized by shock, cried out. The sound meant nothing to Morwen. She was through the little door and halfway down the dark stairs before she realized she had abandoned her traveling case, her coat, and her money.

She couldn't think of any of that now. She didn't slow her frantic pace. All that mattered was Ynyr. All she cared about was reaching the stables before someone took him away.

Such things took time, she assured herself, as she clattered down the final steps and unlatched the door with shaking fingers. It wasn't as simple as just ordering Ynyr removed, or sold, or whatever Irene had tried to do. Someone would have to come for him, tack him up, lead him away, or put him in traces. The sun had not been up an hour, and though farmers began their labors early, surely it couldn't yet have been accomplished...

She ran down through the garden, her breaths coming as sobs and the stone growing heavy in her arms. She reached the stables and raced into the center aisle.

She was met with silence. There was no welcoming nicker from Ynyr, no impatient stamping, no greeting from Jago as he emerged from the tack room.

With the crystal clutched to her chest, she called, "Jago? Are you there?"

He didn't answer. The door to the tack room was closed, as was the door to the loft.

At the sound of her voice, two other horses put their heads outside their stalls and regarded her with curiosity. She heard the bleating of sheep in their pasture, and cows lowing in the milking shed, but no whinny or whicker. She ran down the aisle, peering over the gates and through the bars of every stall. In a panic she raced to the far end of the stables and out into the empty paddock. She shaded her eyes with her hand, straining her eyes to see down the road, over the fields, searching for any glimpse of Ynyr's silver coat shining in the morning sun.

There was nothing. She trembled from her head to her toes, and squeezed the crystal against her so hard she could feel the edges of its rough base through the folds of linen. She didn't know precisely why she had taken it, but—

"I told you," came her mother's cold voice behind her. "He's gone." Morwen whirled to face her. "So is Jago. I sent them both away."

"Jago! But why? I don't see how——"

Irene took a step toward her. The corners of her mouth were pinched tight, and her eyes were narrow as a cat's. "I'm not a fool, Morwen. I've been wielding the power for a long time. I saw you and Jago come in, and I gave my orders."

"But surely—Papa——"

"Your father and I had already agreed, after your behavior yesterday, that the horse should go." Irene shrugged. "It's done, Morwen. One day, when the grimoire comes to you, you can look up the spell I used to effect all this. In the meantime I'll take the crystal back, and you can go unpack that silly case. I don't know what you thought you were going to do—run away, a girl on her own?"

"Grand-mère Ursule ran away on her own."

"She wasn't a girl. And look where it got her!"

"What do you mean? She was happy!"

"Being a farmer?" Irene spit the words. "Digging in the dirt, cleaning pigsties?"

"I wouldn't mind," Morwen said. "I prefer animals to silly people in silly clothes, doing nothing all day!"

"You wouldn't," Irene said. "You have no idea what it's like."

"I don't want to live the way you do, Maman."

"You're too young to know what you want." Irene took another step toward her. "I'm through talking, Morwen. You'll understand one day. Now give me the crystal." Her hands, sharp nailed, long fingered, reached for the stone.

Morwen looked at her reaching hands, and a powerful revulsion rose in her. Her heart seemed to swell to a great size. It beat more and more strongly, so that a wave of heat built in her chest—or perhaps the heat was in the crystal. She couldn't distinguish between the two. The energy of her anger over Ynyr focused in the stone, gathering itself like a storm cloud above the Vale. She had no control over it, any more than she would over a lightning storm. When it manifested in a bolt of energy, it burst out with the force of a blow.

Or the devastating kick of a Shire stallion.

Irene froze. Her face went white and her reaching hands flailed. Her throat worked as she struggled to draw a breath. She swayed like a sapling before a stiff wind, and her knees gave way. She crumpled to the ground, the white material of her peignoir fluttering around her like the broken wings of a dying swan.

Morwen gaped, shocked by what she had caused to happen. When a host of black stars blurred her vision, she found she wasn't breathing, either. The need for air conquered the explosive power within her, and with a harsh rasp, she sucked in a deep, relieving breath.

Irene's breath returned when Morwen's did. Her chest heaved, and her head hung low as she struggled to recover herself. When her color began to return, she braced herself on the ground with both hands and glared up at her daughter, baring her teeth like a predatory animal. She hissed, "I should have smothered you the moment you were born!"

Morwen spun away from her and began to run.

7

The bower of willow branches was cool and damp now, as autumn rains had begun to swell the river. Morwen huddled in its green shadow, shivering and thirsty. She had neither eaten nor slept for more than a day, and she felt the loss of Ynyr as if someone had carved out a piece of her heart and tossed it into the River Thaw.

She longed for Jago, and she worried for him. It was a terrible thing, Mademoiselle said, for a servant to be turned off without a reference. It meant he could never find another position. Whatever became of him would be her fault.

For that matter, what was to become of her? She didn't dare show her face in St. Hilary. She had no clothes, no money, and no one to turn to.

She had nothing, in fact. Except...

The crystal. Her birthright.

It lay near her knee, covered in muddy linen. She wasn't sorry she had taken it from her mother. Irene had shown no pity for her daughter, nor her mother, nor Ynyr. Morwen had no intention of returning the stone. Irene had her grimoire. She could make do.

Irene had used the crystal to scry on Jago, and other human beings. Morwen prayed, as she tried to unwrap the stone with unsteady fingers, that it could also be used to find a horse.

She knew very little about her power, really. She had never had access to the grimoire, and now supposed she never would. She had only her instinct.

She spread the soiled linen wrappings across the damp earth and passed her hands over the rounded top of the crystal. It glowed with greenish light, reflecting the trailing branches of the willow trees, but there was no spark within, no movement, no vision in its crystalline depths. It was just a stone, beautiful, shining, lifeless.

Morwen slumped forward, her shoulders weighed down by fatigue and loneliness and an overwhelming sense of defeat. She longed to hear Ynyr cropping grass outside her hiding place. She longed to know where Jago had gone, so she could go after him. She thought of Ursule, cold and abandoned in the tower of Old Beaupre Castle.

"I think I know how you felt, Grand-mère," she whispered. "There was no one left to you. I wish—oh, how I wish you were here now, with me!"

As if in answer, a light kindled deep inside the crystal. Morwen gazed at it with disbelieving eyes. Was she imagining it? She rubbed her tired eyes and looked again. It was still there, a tiny flame like the wick of a burning candle. It swelled and steadied as she watched it, and colors flickered here and there, like fireflies in the dusk. She leaned closer.

The voice sounded inside her head, gentle and familiar, blending with the murmur of the river. "*Ma petite fille*," it said. "Don't try. It will come. Don't try."

Tears filled Morwen's eyes. "Grand-mère! Tell me what to do!"

There was no reply.

Don't try, Morwen thought. Don't try. Even if she had dreamed she heard Ursule's voice, it was good advice.

She ran her fingers over the crystal again. The light was still there, though the stone was cold to the touch. Morwen bowed her head above it, thinking of her ancestresses, the line of Orchiéres who had preceded her, the women of the craft. It seemed unbearably cruel that each of them should have suffered moments like this, times of betrayal and abandonment and despair. She felt the connection with them in her heart, in her soul. The swell of energy in her breast that had proved so devastating against her mother rose again, but it was different this time, a sense of outreach, of searching, of asking.

She murmured to the stone, "Can you show me my Ynyr?"

The flittering lights in the crystal stilled and coalesced. Ynyr, her beautiful silver stallion, stood with his head high, his mane lifting in a breeze, and his ears cocked toward her as if he knew she was there. Behind him rose the arched windows of St. Hilary Church, where she and Jago had left Ursule with Father Pugh.

And beside him, eyes narrowing as he tried to see what Ynyr sensed, was Jago himself.

She should have known. Irene had rid herself of both of them with a single stroke. She had been certain she could control Morwen if Ynyr was gone, and sending Jago off with the horse solved both her problems.

Morwen's fatigue lifted from her like a mist dissipating in the morning sun. She cried to the image in the crystal, "I see you, Ynyr! I'm coming! Jago, wait for me!"

Jago still peered forward, unaware of her, but Ynyr—marvelous, magical Ynyr—nodded his head, and though she couldn't hear his snort, she could see his feet stamping, and his long tail switching back and forth. Jago pulled on his rope, trying to make him move, but Ynyr tossed his head in refusal. Jago tugged again, scowling. Though she could hear nothing, Morwen thought she saw his lips move in a curse, or perhaps a plea.

Swiftly she caressed the stone and murmured her thanks. She covered it again and gathered it into her arms as she stood up. It was a long walk back to St. Hilary, and she must hurry. Ynyr understood her call, but Jago did not. She had to reach them before he forced Ynyr to move even farther away from her.

❧

The sun was high by the time Morwen spotted the gray stone spire of St. Hilary Church rising against the cloud-flecked sky. Sweat rolled down her ribs beneath her heavy jacket, but her weary brain couldn't think how to remove it without laying down the crystal, and she dared not do that. Her legs cried out for respite, and her sleepless eyes were dry and scratchy, but she pressed on, squinting from beneath the brim of her hat, searching for a glimpse of a dapple-gray horse or Jago's slim dark figure. Another twenty minutes passed, the tension growing in her back and shoulders. At last she reached the little graveyard with its array of ancient headstones, and circled the stone wall to the back of the church.

Relief weakened her knees.

She could see Jago had been trying, and failing, to persuade the Shire to walk on. He had gotten Ynyr as far as the shade offered by a stand of gnarled elms at the edge of the village square. There, it seemed, Ynyr had planted his feet and refused to move. Jago slumped on the ground, his back braced against a trunk and his head bent in an attitude of exhaustion. Ynyr's head, too, sagged toward the ground, and his ears drooped in dispirited fashion.

Morwen tried to call out to them, but her voice cracked in her dry throat. She staggered forward, nearly at the end of her strength.

Ynyr sensed her approach. His head flew up, and his nostrils fluttered as he drew a deep breath to whinny.

"No, Ynyr," Morwen cried. Her voice was thin, almost inaudible, but Ynyr understood. He made no sound, but jerked the rope from Jago's limp hand and trotted toward her, the halter rope trailing between his forelegs. He stopped when he reached her, dropping his muzzle to her shoulder. With a sob she pressed close to him, holding the crystal in one arm and encircling his neck with the other. For a moment they stood that way, Ynyr trembling as much as Morwen.

"Miss Morwen," Jago said. His voice, too, broke with fatigue.

Morwen twisted so she could see him without leaving the comfort of Ynyr's bulk. "Oh, Jago," she said miserably. "We have to get away, and soon! My mother—"

"She ordered me to take Ynyr to the horse market at Cardiff. I wanted to refuse, but she has her ways. I couldn't do it. You're meant to stay here."

"I'm going to London. I'm never going back to Morgan Hall."

"She'll come after you, lass," Jago said tiredly. "No one can stand up to her."

"I can," Morwen said. She took Ynyr's rope and looped it over her shoulder.

"I fear not, Miss Morwen. It's something I know better than most."

"But why, Jago?" Morwen heard the quaver in her voice, but she was half-crazed with tiredness, and she couldn't help it. "Did you not—I mean—if it's you who fathered me, in truth—did you not care for her?"

Jago, too, was too weary to be careful in his words. He spit upon the ground beneath the elm trees, and said with deep bitterness, "Care for her? No, lass. I'm sorry to say it, but I have hated her from the day she came to Morgan Hall."

"Then why, Jago? Why did you—you and she—"

He looked away from her, out beyond the slanting gravestones and the lichened stones of the church wall. "They're coming," he said.

Morwen whirled and saw a cloud of dust on the road, a cloud only the motorcar could raise. "Hurry!" she cried. "Ynyr will carry us."

"He's that tired, Morwen. I don't know—"

"We all are, but we have to get away!" She led Ynyr to a jagged stump in the center of the little grove, and gestured to Jago to follow. "Hurry, hurry!"

Even then Jago hesitated, as the growing sound of the tonneau reached their ears. At last he stepped up on the stump, but his expression was as bleak as if he were stepping up onto a gallows. Morwen swung herself up onto Ynyr's broad back and reached down to help Jago do the same. When they were both settled, and she had the crystal cradled neatly between her belly and Ynyr's withers, she said, "Now, Ynyr! Swiftly!"

The horse sprang forward into his strong, swinging trot. Jago gasped and seized Morwen's waist. She had clamped her long legs firmly around Ynyr's barrel, and her right hand held a fist of his mane. Her left balanced the stone and held the end of the rope, which swung in a loose loop below his neck. As he always did, Ynyr knew the direction she wanted. He struck out smoothly toward the track that led from St. Hilary to the point where the river curved to the southeast. The track was too narrow and rough for the motorcar.

"Just till we're out of their reach," she told Jago over her shoulder. "Then we'll rest."

"If they catch us, they'll hang me," he said.

"And burn me," she answered.

When he made no response, she suspected he knew what she

was, and knew what her mother was. She snugged the crystal close against her body, and felt the assurance of Ursule from beyond the grave. "They won't find us, Jago."

"Sure of that, you?"

"Yes." She felt the tingle of energy from the stone, vibrating through its linen wrappings, and she closed her eyes in a rush of gratitude toward her ancestress. "Yes. I'm quite, quite sure."

8

When Morwen and Ynyr and Jago reached London, and found their first grimy flat above a fish shop, Morwen took care to hide the crystal where no one could find it. In those first tumultuous weeks, while Jago scrambled to find work and Morwen struggled to look after Ynyr in the noisy and noisome streets of the city, the two of them were constantly looking over their shoulders, fearful of being discovered. It was a time of uncertainty and revelation, of despair over finding enough to eat, and the hope of being free of Lady Irene's power.

Morwen knew, now, how her mother had used Jago. She had brewed a potion, a concoction of coltsfoot and lovage roots, lady's mantle and mullein and mistletoe, innocent enough in themselves, dangerously potent when combined by a witch in full command of her powers. Jago had a prodigious memory for words, and he recalled Lady Irene triumphantly reciting it to him.

"Couldn't resist it," he confessed. "She put it in my cider, and I drank it before I understood. After that, it was like—like being hungrier than you've ever been in your life, starving. And the food is right there, tempting you, even forced upon you. I hated myself afterward, but it was too late. It was done."

Morwen reached out to touch his arm, and felt the responding quiver of his muscles that told her he still wasn't easy with her treating him as an equal. As a father.

"I'm sorry," she said.

He turned his dark eyes on her, and she saw pride and sadness and fear in them. "I'm not," he said. "She forced me to give her the babe she wanted, that's true. But I could never be sorry you're in this world, Morwen."

She had, at least, persuaded him to stop calling her Miss Morwen, mostly in order to avoid drawing attention. When asked, they said they were father and daughter, come from Wales in search of work. They explained Ynyr as the last of their farm stock, and they had to dodge several offers to buy him.

That first flat, reeking of fish from the shop below, they paid for with the meager cash Jago had carried away in his pockets. The landlord, who was stout and rather stupid, but painfully honest, allowed Morwen to stable Ynyr in the yard. She paid for this privilege by driving to the Docklands each morning with an empty cart, returning with it full of fish. Jago objected at first to Morwen's rising before dawn to drive out among a throng of rowdy fishmongers, but she tossed her head, dismissing his fears. "I can handle them."

"Not the daughter of the manor anymore, you," was Jago's response.

"I have Ynyr to protect me."

Jago scowled, but there was little he could say. They had few choices. In the actual event, Morwen found the Docklands fascinating, with fishermen and fishwives hawking the day's catch. She worried about Ynyr slipping on the slimy cobblestones, but the sheer size of him meant her cart was treated with respect. When Jago found a job driving a Humber taxicab, and they moved to a better part of town, leaving the fish cart behind, Morwen missed her trips along the Thames, though she could not be sorry to leave the stench of fish.

Life was far easier in Islington, with its sturdy houses and wider streets, than it had been in the East End. They found a roomy flat above the Chapel Market, with windows on three sides, and a small parlor between the kitchen and the two bedrooms. Ynyr was stabled at the end of the road, with several carriage horses and a few mounts kept for ladies and gentlemen to ride. Jago and another taxicab driver considered starting their own firm, with a little fleet of vehicles, employing out-of-work horsemen. Morwen consulted the crystal over this, and it showed her an image of a thriving business, with a garage and a staff of drivers and mechanics.

The crystal's prophecy came true swiftly, and Morwen settled in over the next months to learn to cook, to clean, and to manage a house on her own, all things she had never learned under Mademoiselle's tutelage. It was a different life from anything she had ever expected, but it was not unpleasant. She mourned Ursule, so briefly known, but she was occupied morning and night with housewifery, and in the afternoons with riding Ynyr in Regent's Park among the palfreys and high-steppers. Many months passed, and she left the crystal in its hiding place, untouched, living as any other young woman of modest station might live.

She often sat with Jago in their parlor in the evenings. As Jago drowsed, his hands across his lean belly, Morwen read the *Evening News*. One night, when she happened across a piece about Welsh politics, she was startled to realize that a year had passed since her escape from Morgan Hall, a startlingly brief time for her life to have been so thoroughly transformed. Lord Llewelyn's name appeared in the article, though it gave no personal information. Morwen let the paper fall into her lap and stared into the flames of the coal fire, thinking about him, and about her mother.

Lady Irene, she had decided, for all her beauty and power, was a woman without love. She cared for no one except herself. She had not loved her own mother, nor had she loved her husband.

She had, in her odd way, tried to do her duty by her daughter, explaining the mystery of her birthright, but that, too, had been done without affection. It must be a lonely life.

As the coal in the grate turned to ash and disintegrated, Morwen pondered, and wondered if she could have managed things better. Her father—or the man who thought he was her father—must have been hurt, or at least humiliated, by her disappearance. Irene had lost the thing most precious to her in the world, the Orchiére crystal. There was, Morwen thought, a great deal of pain in the world. She wished she hadn't had to inflict more of it.

She was still thinking of this the next day. She and Ynyr indulged in a longer ride than usual, enjoying an unusually warm October day. A brief rain the night before had cleared the coal dust from the air, and they were both exhilarated by the clouds of golden leaves and the sparkle of sunshine on the canal. When the angle of the sunlight told Morwen it was time to turn back toward Islington, she stopped at the fountain to let Ynyr dip his muzzle into the water.

She dismounted, ignoring the curious glances, and wondering if the city people would ever get used to the sight of a girl riding a draft horse instead of being properly mounted, and bareback instead of in a ladylike sidesaddle. At first the stares of Londoners had made her cheeks burn and her neck prickle. She was tempted, often, to snap at them, to point out that her much-mended riding habit should make it clear she wasn't a lady. She wanted to tell them to mind their own business, but she held her tongue. The last thing she and Jago needed was to draw attention to themselves.

While Ynyr drank she leaned her forehead against his neck and murmured her thoughts, still upon her mother.

"She couldn't change the way she was, could she, Ynyr? I could forgive her not loving me, even forgive her for what she did to

Jago. But she tried to send you away—when she knows what it is to lose your spirit familiar—and that I will never forgive."

Ynyr, muzzle dripping, lifted his head and blew, spattering drops of water across her skirt. Laughing, she patted him and brushed at the spots. "So you agree," she said. "In that case, I'll stop worrying about it!"

Again he blew, and bent his neck deeply so he could butt her gently with his broad head. She seized his forelock and tugged it. "I would have done anything," she whispered, fiercely now. "Anything! Rather than lose you."

The big horse held very still as she embraced his neck, and she felt the beating of his great heart near her own as if the two of them inhabited one body.

"Still riding that giant, I see!" came a laughing voice behind her.

Tension closed Morwen's throat. In all these long months, she had encountered no one in London who could recognize her. But now . . .

Slowly, warily, she turned toward the speaker, narrowing her eyes and preparing to deny the acquaintance. When she realized who it was, she caught a breath. "Dafydd Selwyn! However did you come to be here?"

Dafydd said cheerily, "I might ask you the same, Miss Morgan. Such a turnup you left behind! Both our fathers were furious, and not a soul had a clue where you went. Everyone went on about it for months."

She remembered, as she watched his laughing face, how much she had liked him at their brief meeting. He had grown taller, and his chest and shoulders had filled out. His legs showed ridges of muscle beneath his jodhpurs. He lifted his charmingly battered trilby, grinning as he slid down from his chestnut gelding.

Ynyr turned his head to regard Dafydd with calm eyes. He blew once through his nostrils and nodded, jingling the buckle on his halter. Morwen said gravely, "It appears the giant likes you, Master Selwyn."

"I count myself fortunate, then." Dafydd patted Ynyr's shoulder and loosened the rein so his own horse could drink. "We have stories to tell each other, I think, Miss Morgan."

"You won't betray me to my father?"

"Not if you won't betray me to mine." Dafydd's gay expression sobered. "We have fallen out, I fear, although not as dramatically as you and your parents did."

"If you were close, then I'm sorry."

Dafydd sighed and ran a hand through his thick brown hair. He wore it shorter than she remembered, and he sported a slender mustache. "We were not close," he said, "but I am his heir, and it's awkward to be estranged."

"Did he remarry?"

"He did. An amiable widow, twice your age. Far more suitable."

"You like her, then."

"She's tolerable. More so than Sir William has ever been!"

"You came to London to live? By yourself?"

"Well, with my staff. I inherited a house from my mother."

Morwen, averting her eyes, stroked the chestnut's neck. After a moment's hesitation she asked, "Do you have news of my parents?"

"No good news, I'm afraid. Do you want to hear it?"

She hesitated again before she said, "Yes. I—I think I should."

"We should talk over a cup of tea or something. Not out here in Regent's Park, with the whole world watching."

She took a startled look around. "Is there someone who could see us? Who would carry the tale all the way back to Wales?"

"Oh no, I don't think so. It's just that—well. I don't want to upset you."

Morwen emitted a bitter laugh. "Upset me! Dafydd, after the year I've had, I'm not sure you can say anything that will upset me!"

"It's your mother."

At this, Morwen's laugh died away. "What is it?" she whispered.

Dafydd spoke with reluctance. "The rumor is that Lord Llewelyn accused his wife of something. Some people say it was infidelity. Others say it was something worse. Something evil. But it's all rumor, Miss Morgan. Servants' gossip."

"Tell me what happened."

"Well." He tapped his thigh with his quirt. "It was months after you disappeared, I believe. It seems—that is, what they say is—there was a terrible row, and after it the Lady Irene disappeared. Vanished. The servants say she departed Morgan Hall in the middle of the night, alone, leaving all her belongings behind."

"But where? And how?"

"If anyone knows, they haven't said. Lord Llewelyn forbade anyone to look for her. There's a rumor that he—" He paused and cleared his throat.

"What?" Morwen whispered.

"It's just a wild rumor. Some say Lord Llewelyn killed his wife, but I won't believe that. I know him, and he wouldn't..."

Words, spoken long ago in Irene's hard voice, sounded from Morwen's memory: *For a witch to be exposed means risking death*. But surely Papa couldn't have—he wouldn't...

Would he? If he discovered somehow that he was not his daughter's father, would he care enough to harm his wife? Morwen shuddered to think of it. She would have said, until this moment, that she didn't care what happened to her mother, but now—with this terrible possibility—she found herself sick with worry.

She said, "Dafydd, you must excuse me. I have to go."

"Miss Morgan, I don't believe that story! You must know that."

"No, I don't, either, but—I must go home...There's some-thing I have to do." She jumped up onto the edge of the fountain, then onto Ynyr's back.

"But, Miss Morgan—Morwen—can't we—"

She lifted the halter rope and said hastily, "Come again tomor-row! I'll come back, but now I must..."

Ynyr, anticipating, whirled and began his ground-devouring trot. She didn't finish her sentence, but she looked back over her shoulder to see Dafydd, his trilby in his hands, squinting against the sunshine. She lifted a hand in hasty farewell, but she doubted he could see her.

With trembling fingers Morwen drew the covering from Grand-mère's crystal. The covering was new, a piece of embroidered silk found in a shop in Piccadilly. She hadn't touched it—or the stone—in months. She had tried to forget it was there, hidden behind a board she had loosened in her bedroom wall. Now it lay, glowing faintly in its nest of silk, on the tea table in the cramped parlor.

Morwen shivered, though the room was warm with autumn sunshine. She had left Ynyr in his stable, but she could feel him, stamping and whinnying, sharing her anxiety.

On her hurried ride back to Islington, she had searched for a scrap of affection in her heart. She didn't find it. What she found, what Ursule had tried to explain, was loyalty, fealty to the line of women from which she sprang. Irene, with all her faults and weaknesses, was still her mother. Morwen had to know what had happened to her. If she was dead, she would mourn her. If she was in need, she would help her. She was an Orchiére.

She drew the curtain over the parlor window before she brought a new white candle from her small larder and set it in a saucer on the tea table. She wet one finger and dipped it into the salt dish, then dissolved the grains in a beaker of water. She sprinkled a circle of saltwater drops around the table, aware as she did so that she knew how to do these things only because Irene, albeit unwillingly, had taught her.

With her preparations made, she knelt on the carpet and drew her fingers across the smooth surface of the crystal. The darkness within it receded swiftly, reassuring her that the craft was still strong in her, perhaps stronger than it had been, as if it had matured and deepened on its own. With confidence she gazed into the shadowy depths of the stone. "Show me Maman," she murmured. "Irène Orchiére. By the power of my ancestresses, by the privilege of my birthright, I ask to see her. To—to *scry* her."

Sparks of light spun and grew immediately, as if some energy had only been awaiting her command. The interior of the crystal bloomed with light, and in its center, in the space of a few breaths, the sparks began to coalesce.

It was a blur at first, seen through a veil of mist, but the mist soon shredded and disappeared. The image resolved into a small but fully recognizable figure, and Morwen experienced a wrench of sorrow.

Irene crouched, cloaked and bedraggled, on the same pallet of old blankets Ursule had used. It hardly seemed possible that her hair should have grayed so quickly, or that her shoulders should be so bent. Around her ranged the paltry things Ursule had used to sustain herself, a crude stove, a smoky lamp, a chamber pot.

Irene had taken her mother's place in the tower of Old Beaupre Castle. She had lost everything her treachery had gained for her, and more. All that was left to her—the object that rested in clear view on the crumpled pallet of blankets—was the grimoire.

Morwen fell back on her heels, and the image dimmed and faded into darkness. Heavy-hearted, she stared into the smoky depths of the crystal. She felt no tenderness for her mother, but could she leave her in such a condition?

When Jago returned from his day's work, she told him everything—about Dafydd, about her mother, even about using the crystal. Jago sat in his easy chair, a piece of whittling wood in one hand and a knife in the other. He gazed at her from beneath drawn brows, and his eyelids drooped with sympathy.

"Jago, I don't know what I can do. If Papa threw her out, he would surely not welcome seeing me."

"No. Can't return, you."

"But I can't just abandon her."

A long, tense silence hung in the parlor. Jago sat staring at the piece of wood in his lap. Morwen's head ached, as if the vision of her mother in the broken tower had taken hold of her brain with a physical grip. Darkness fell beyond the window, and the sounds and smells of Islington swirled upward into the night. At last, when Morwen thought her head might burst, Jago stirred and set down his knife and chunk of wood.

"I'll go," he said.

Morwen started. "What?"

Stiffly he got to his feet and stood with his hands hanging at his sides, gazing down at her. "I'll go to her," he said. "I'm the one who can. No one has any complaint against me. Not any longer."

"But—but you *hate* her!"

"I did once. It seems I no longer do."

Morwen could have argued, protested it was too far, too hard, that he had other things to manage. All of that was true, but at the same time she knew he was right.

They had never embraced, though they had acknowledged their true relationship. Now, however, filled with gratitude, Morwen stepped forward. The habits of a lifetime made Jago flinch back, but she paid no attention. She was nearly as tall as he was, and she put her arms around his shoulders, holding him to her. When she pressed her cheek to his, she felt the melting of his heart, so close to her own.

"You will be careful," she whispered. "And come back to me."

"Aye, lass," he said. "There's no need to worry, in any case. You can watch me in yon scrying stone."

⁓✦⁓

Morwen did watch. She kept the crystal beside her bed, and peered into it morning and night while he was away. She knew when he reached Wales, driving one of his own taxicabs. She knew when he climbed the hill to the castle. She watched Irene hide her face in shame when he stepped into the broken tower. When he made his way at last back to Islington, she already knew he had returned her mother to the cottage where she had grown up. Elegant, aristocratic Lady Irene Morgan was now working for the Grange as a milkmaid.

Morwen was surprised, though, when Jago carried in a bulky package, wrapped in brown paper and tied up with string. He pressed it into her hands. "Jago, what is this?"

"She said you would know."

"Oh," Morwen breathed. She took the parcel, feeling its weight, sensing the texture of it through the paper. "Oh, I do, Jago. Though I can hardly believe she gave it up."

"Said she never wants to see it again. That it was her undoing."

"That's what happened, then. Papa found it. He knows."

"Afraid so. He threw her out."

"What about other people? Did he tell anyone else? Father Pugh?"

The faint curl of Jago's lips faded. "Lass, if the priest knew what she was, there would be no saving her."

"But you saved her."

"Did my best."

She said softly, "Thank you."

He turned his head, as if in embarrassment, and said, "Did it for you, Daughter."

"I will always be grateful."

They never spoke of it again.

9

Many months passed before Morwen dared to undo the strings on the package Jago had carried from Wales. She hid the crystal away and laid the grimoire alongside it. She and Jago were making a life in London, a new, productive life like the ones other people made. Normal people. She had no more need of magic.

She saw Dafydd Selwyn often in Regent's Park, where they walked their horses side by side, and talked about travel, and books, and exhibits at the V&A. They didn't speak of her parents, or of his father. Dafydd was all the society Morwen had, beyond Jago's silent company. On the days they were to meet, her step was lighter, her mood brighter. She would have been desperately lonely without their afternoons together.

Still, on the day before the eve of Lammas, just after her eighteenth birthday, Morwen felt unusually restless and out of sorts. She longed for something, but it was hard to know what. Other women, perhaps. Someone she could speak to about the things she felt, the things she dreamed of, things that were hard to name but real nonetheless.

A sense of isolation weighed on her. She bid Jago a rather curt good night and went into her bedroom. She changed into her nightgown and braided her hair for the night, but still felt restive.

She stared into the mirror above her dressing table and saw, with a shiver, her mother's face looking back.

A compulsion seized her. She told herself she wanted to see her mother again, to know that she was safe, that she was well, but of course that wasn't it. It was the crystal tempting her. She recognized the invitation, that tug on her breastbone as if someone had tied a silken cord around her chest and was pulling on it.

She fought the impulse for a time, standing beside her window to look down on Chapel Market. The lights went out one by one, leaving the street in darkness.

At last, with a muttered exclamation, she gave in. She crossed to the wardrobe where she had hidden the stone, with the grimoire beside it. She drew them both out.

She had no unburned candle at hand, and to fetch one she needed to slip out to the kitchen, where she kept new candles in the pantry. Cautiously, not wanting to wake Jago, she crept on her bare feet across the little parlor and into the kitchen. She made her way back as quietly as she could. Jago's bedroom door was closed, and no light showed beneath it. Carefully she drew her own door shut. When she turned the lock, the click of the tumblers seemed to reverberate in the stillness of the flat, and made her nerves jump.

She set the candle into a holder and sprinkled salt water around the little pedestal table that held the crystal and the grimoire. She unfolded the embroidered silk to expose the darkly shining stone. When she knelt beside the table and set a match to the candle, lights blazed up instantly inside the crystal. Her heart leaped in response, and she leaned close to peer into it, whispering, "Maman?"

It was not Irene who appeared out of the swirling pool of sparks. It was Dafydd.

He wore a morning coat and gloves, and his thick hair was smoothly brushed and dressed. There were people with him, also in formal day dress, but Morwen couldn't make them out in detail—except for one.

It was a girl, slim and fair and very pretty. She was leaning on Dafydd's arm, laughing up into his face. He was smiling, too, and as Morwen watched he patted her white-gloved hand where it rested on his sleeve.

Morwen's heart suddenly pained her so that she pressed her hands to it, and she closed her eyes against the sight of Dafydd—charming, handsome, fair Dafydd—with another girl. A suitable girl, no doubt, with a family and a dowry and a name to be proud of. Morwen hadn't fully realized until this moment that she thought of him as *her* Dafydd. Her special friend, even her sweetheart. If this was what love felt like—this pain, and this fear—she wished she had never discovered it.

She sat back on her heels and dropped her hands. "Why?" she whispered into the candlelit room. "Why show me this? If Dafydd has met someone, there's nothing I can do!"

But even as she said it, she knew it wasn't true. She was no ordinary girl. She was her mother's daughter, and she was a witch. There would be something in the grimoire, a remedy hidden beneath its cracked leather. Her mother had created a potion that Jago had been unable to resist. Her daughter could do the same. The instructions were somewhere in the notes of an ancestress, waiting only to be found, and followed.

For a time she did battle with her conscience. The potion had not made Jago love her mother, after all, but—her own motivations were not at all like her mother's. She would be acting out of love, not ambition! If she used the potion only to encourage what was already between them...

Her fingers were busy with the string even as these thoughts tumbled through her mind. Her hands were smoothing back the stiff brown paper, opening the ancient leather cover, touching, oh so gently, the stained and browning pages. In some places the ink had faded so much that whatever had been written there was lost forever. In others it had run and blurred so that she had to light a lamp to read the words. All of it, as Irene had warned her, was written in Old French. It would take her hours, perhaps days, to decipher.

Then, as she gingerly turned the pages, she saw words in her mother's modern hand, written in good Egyptian black ink, carefully blotted and dried. Irene had done the work for her, had translated the recipe from Old French into the modern language. The ingredients were clearly listed, and the steps laid out.

Take three leaves and two flowers of coltsfoot, along with an inch of the root; add three inches of lovage root, well dried; flowers of lady's mantle; three spikes of mullein; and a twig of mistletoe, crushed. Mix with water that has been boiled and cooled, and let rest on the altar until the morning star rises.

Make an offering of sage to the Mother of All, and speak your intention three times three times. The syrup can be mixed with wine or cider, and should be drunk in one draft.

The list of ingredients was long. The greengrocer would have sage, but not such things as mullein or lady's mantle. Coltsfoot grew everywhere in the countryside, but would it grow in the ditches of London?

Her mind and her heart warred with one another, but her

heart, at this moment in her young life, dominated. She would do it. She had to do it.

She had sacrificed so much. Surely she could at least keep Dafydd Selwyn for herself. What was the good of being a descendant of the Ochiéres—of being a witch—if she couldn't use her power? It was her right.

❧

Morwen slept little that night, and was off on her search even before the Chapel Market vendors lifted their awnings. She set out through a chilly autumn mist, a basket over her arm and her housekeeping money in the pochette that dangled from her waist. She tried an apothecary's shop first, and was rewarded by discovering a small amount of dried lovage root, clearly labeled on a wooden shelf.

She carried the little jar to the counter. "Your young 'un has the colic, I expect?" the apothecary asked her, in a voice warm with sympathy.

Morwen was almost startled into denying it, but realized he assumed she had a baby at home. "Yes," she said hastily, as she counted out coins. "But this should help."

"You come back if it doesn't," he said. "We can try something else."

She thanked him and went on with her mission. After walking down several streets into a neighborhood she didn't recognize, she came across a dark little shop with bundles of herbs and jars of syrups and ointments in the window. This turned out to be a Chinese herbalist, and though she had some trouble making herself understood, she managed to find both lady's mantle and mullein. The woman who sold them to her spoke so little English that when it was time to pay, Morwen simply held out coins on her palm and allowed the herbalist to choose the ones she wanted.

The price was surprisingly low, and Morwen silently blessed the woman's honesty.

She lacked only mistletoe, but she knew where that could be found. She hurried back to the flat to deposit her basket on the kitchen sideboard. She found a pair of shears and thrust them into her pochette before she strode down the street to the stables, where she could hear Ynyr nickering to her before she reached the door.

The stableboy, a jug-eared lad of perhaps twelve, met her in the aisle between the stalls. "That big horse allus knows when you's comin', don't he, miss? Why's that?"

Morwen grinned at him and fished a coin out of her pochette to press into his hand. "That's the smartest horse in the world, Georgie," she said. "But don't tell anyone!" He laughed and tossed the coin in the air before he thrust it into the pocket of his canvas trousers.

A ragged column of poplar trees grew at the far edge of Regent's Park, and high among their branches bloomed great clouds of mistletoe. The mist had cleared by the time Morwen and Ynyr reached the park. They had to dodge crowds of walkers and riders to reach the trees. Morwen urged Ynyr as close to one of the trunks as he could get. Steadying herself with one hand on a branch, she put her feet on his back, one on either side of his sturdy spine, and cautiously pulled herself upright, holding the shears in her free hand.

Moments later, ignoring the curious and even scandalized glances that pursued her, she was happily on her way back to Islington, a generous clump of mistletoe in her fist.

She spent the day in preparation. She found an unburned candle, she boiled water, and chopped and crushed her ingredients according to the transcribed recipe. She set the soup pot simmering for Jago's dinner, dashed down to the baker's for a fresh loaf, and then, though she herself simmered with impatience, she paced the floor and waited for night to come.

Doubts assailed her. What would Ursule think if she knew what Morwen planned? How would she herself feel, knowing she had tricked him?

Worst of all, what if Dafydd found out? The memory of Jago's look of revulsion when he spoke of Irene filled her with dread.

On the other hand, she asked herself, what is love but magic, after all? She pictured Dafydd as she had last seen him, riding alongside her in Regent's Park. She thought of the way his hair fell over his forehead, how his eyes sparkled, how his dimple flashed when he laughed. She remembered the spicy smell of bay rum that always surrounded him, and the feel of his sun-warmed cheek when he pressed it to hers in farewell, and her belly contracted with longing.

Dafydd Selwyn was worth any risk. Worth the use of magic. She was so terribly lonely! And she would, she swore to herself, do everything in her power to make him happy.

By the time Jago arrived home, she was jumpy as a cat. He looked at her strangely once or twice as she served his meal, and as she did the washing up afterward.

He didn't say anything, but she felt his attention all the evening, as if his hand were on her shoulder. She pretended to read while he worked on the loose stitching of a boot, and then, as early as she dared, she bid him good night and escaped to her bedroom.

She changed out of her dress and into a nightgown, with a robe over it against the evening chill, and she extinguished her lamp, though she knew there would be no sleep for her. After a time she heard the thump of Jago's boots across the parlor, followed by the click of his bedroom door closing. The noises from the street below dwindled into silence. Beyond her window a fresh mist rose, obscuring the stars and even the buildings on the opposite side of the street. Morwen arranged and rearranged her candle, the crystal, her dish of herbs, the small pottery jug of water.

The fog blotted out the stars, but she could hear the bells from St. Mary the Virgin. One o'clock came, and two. Three o'clock, then four. She was sure by then the morning star was beginning its rise, though she couldn't see it through the heavy mist.

Trembling with excitement, Morwen lit the candle. She sprinkled water in a generous circle. She took the twist of sage stems from their protective paper and set a match to them. Careful to stay within her circle, she walked around the table, once, twice, three times. The sage smoked gently, filling the air of her bedroom with its spicy scent. She laid it in a saucer to burn itself out, and took up the potion in her two hands.

Holding the little jug above the crystal, she felt the magic of her ancestresses sing in her blood and vibrate through her bones. It was an old spell, and a strong one. The very idea of it made her feel reckless with power.

Mother Goddess, hear my prayer
All your power bring to bear
For me only, none to share
Dafydd Selwyn cause to care.

Three times three times she spoke the words. Tendrils of sage smoke curled around her, reflecting the flicker of the candle flame. Between her hands she felt energy increase. The water in the jug swirled in glistening eddies. The crystal began to shine with coruscating light, yellow and gold and red, as if it were afire.

Morwen closed her eyes, exulting in the witch's power, her body and brain throbbing with the strength of her magic.

At that moment, as she stood wreathed in smoke and candlelight, the door banged open.

Morwen's eyes flew open, and she beheld Jago's pale face. He glared at her, his eyes narrowed, his jaw tight.

He growled, "What's this?"

Her mouth opened, but no words of explanation would come. Suddenly, devastatingly, she saw herself through his eyes. She saw herself in a loose robe with the crystal blazing beside her, the candle wildly flickering, smoke hovering around her. Just as devastating was the conviction, belated but overwhelming, that she was committing a terrible act, a crime against the person she loved, and against the person she herself wished to be. All the doubts she had felt at the beginning returned in a rush, and left her trembling with shame.

Slowly she lowered the jug. The energy dissipated around her, dimming the crystal, drowning the candle flame in a pool of melted wax. The sage smoke drifted toward the ceiling, where it hung in lifeless shreds.

Morwen whispered, "It's—it was—for Dafydd."

Jago's grim expression was terrible to see. Morwen's eyes suddenly welled with tears. They blinded her, dripping down her cheeks to fall onto her hands, which still held the pottery jug and its dangerous contents.

Jago's strong arm came around her shoulders. His hand guided hers to set down the jug before he led her across the room, through the door, and into the parlor. She was sobbing now, her chest aching. She wrapped her arms around herself, crying so hard she didn't hear Jago stir up the fire, or go to his own room and return.

He had brought a blanket, which he draped around her. He crouched beside her chair, not speaking, waiting for her spate of tears to abate. It took a long time for her to cry herself out. She huddled beneath the blanket, sniffling and shuddering like a child. When her tears ceased at last, she had to gather what was left of her courage to lift her head and look into his eyes.

He spoke gruffly. "Wouldn't want him that way, you."

"No," she choked. "No, I—I see that now. I didn't—I just—"

"Great temptation."

"That's no excuse."

"No." With a tired grunt he got to his feet. He patted her shoulder, once, before crossing to his own chair and settling into it. He let his head fall back and his eyes close. "The thing is," he said, in such a low voice that Morwen had to lean forward to hear him. "I admired her. Wanted her, even, though she was so far above me, older, of course. Married to boot."

"You mean Maman?"

"She was beautiful. Mysterious. Had a sort of power around her, aside from—" His hand lifted and fell on the arm of his chair.

Morwen listened, watching him, still shivering with the aftermath of crying.

"After she magicked me, all that changed. I didn't want her anymore. A man doesn't like to feel he has no power of his own."

Morwen waited a bit more, in case Jago would reveal anything else. When he didn't speak again, she rose and crossed to his chair to kneel beside it. She took his hand between hers and saw how similar their hands were, with long fingers and broad palms. "Go back to bed, Jago," she said softly. She gently stroked the back of his hand, though she felt his fingers quiver with embarrassment at the familiarity. "I'll get rid of the potion. I promise."

Without opening his eyes, he said, "You love him, young Dafydd?"

"Yes. Very much."

"If it's meant to be, Morwen . . ."

"I know."

She couldn't understand why she hadn't seen it before. Perhaps a fit of madness had come over her, brought on by the crystal. She should have resisted, whatever the source. She should have had more respect for herself.

Morwen sighed and got up from her knees. She planted a single kiss on Jago's forehead, though she knew he wouldn't like it, then trudged back to her room. She poured the potion out her window, careful that it fell into the shrubbery. She covered the crystal without looking in it again, and put it away with the grimoire. When everything was restored to its customary order, she stood by the window for a long time, watching the outlines of the city emerge from the fog.

Her heart yearned for Dafydd, but her mind had cleared.

She would go to Ynyr, as soon as it was light enough. She would ride, and ride, and take comfort in his massive, gentle presence. She would stay away from Regent's Park. If Dafydd wanted her, he would find her. And if he didn't—there was Ynyr. And Jago. And perhaps some other use for her power.

She stood by her window, lonely but relieved, until the full sun of Lammas rose over the city to banish the mysteries of the night.

THE BOOK OF VERONICA

1

Young ladies in white dresses crowded the throne room. Their feathers nodded above their too-warm faces as chaperones and palace officials shepherded them into the proper places. Veronica Selwyn was grateful her own dress was silk, and nearly weightless. She couldn't think how Queen Elizabeth could bear being trapped in her vast gold chair, weighed down by brocade and pearls and her elaborate crown. The face of the new king, sitting next to her, was scarlet, and the hair showing beneath his crown was dark with sweat. Everyone said he was shy, this youthful man who had never expected to be king, but Elizabeth, next to him, was all charm and confidence. If the heat bothered her, she gave no sign. She smiled and nodded to each debutante in turn, behaving as if she had all the time in the world.

Veronica did not share her patience. She would have much preferred to be at Sweetbriar, dressed in her riding clothes, counting livestock or conferring with the farm managers. The train of her dress tangled every time she turned and made her want to tear the thing off. She wore three feathers in her hair, as prescribed, and they itched. She also carried a fan, something she had never done before and vowed she would never do again. An inherited pearl necklace, an adornment that had sent her dressmaker into rhapsodies, wound four times around her throat, with enough length still for one loop to hang to her waist.

The lord chamberlain clanked his silver mace against the floor as he made his introductions. Three clanks for each name. The girls, backs straight and eyes cast down, each took their turn to curtsy to the royals. Veronica had been spared the lessons with Mrs. Vacani, who taught the knee-behind-the-knee curtsy all the girls employed, and which they studied for weeks before the event.

"I think you can manage a curtsy, darling," Papa had said in a wry tone. They had been in the Sweetbriar stables, their favorite place in the world, surrounded by horses and ponies and assorted dogs. "Just tuck one knee behind the other, and down you go."

"Do I have to be presented, Papa?" she had asked. "It's archaic!"

"It is that, Veronica. But I'm mending fences."

"You mean Grandfather Selwyn wants me to do it."

"That's it, I'm afraid. You're making the sacrifice so I can have some peace." He poked her with a gentle finger.

She laughed and sidestepped out of his reach. "For you, Papa, anything. Even the throne room!"

"Thank you, dear heart." He shifted his cane so he could press his hand over his heart and bow to her. "I'm in your debt."

"It really is stupid, though. I mean, with the war coming..."

"There may not be a war."

"Phillip thinks there will."

"Phillip is a bright young man. I hope he's wrong."

Veronica hoped so, too. She couldn't bear the idea of her brother, quiet, artistic Thomas, going off to fight. Phillip was another matter. He found the idea of war exciting. He didn't understand how much her papa suffered still from the wounds he'd received at Belleau Wood. To Phillip, Dafydd was a romantic figure, leaning on his ebony cane, his back soldier straight and his head held high. Phillip thought giving a leg for your country covered you in glory. He had no idea of the pain that darkened her father's nights, or how many times the doctor had to be called in the small hours, when the agony grew unbearable. No one should have to suffer—

The thump of the mace jarred Veronica from her reverie. One, two, three it clanged against the floor, and the lord chamberlain, sounding even more bored than Veronica felt, intoned, "The Honourable Veronica Selwyn." It was her turn.

She managed well enough. She didn't trip on her long skirt, and the train floated obediently behind her, as it was meant to do. She tucked one knee behind the other, her hands hanging straight, and curtsied, first to Queen Elizabeth and then to King George. Elizabeth smiled pleasantly and nodded, as she had done with every other girl. George—poor George, who they say dreaded speaking or even appearing in public—gazed at some point above Veronica's head. As she rose she saw a drop of perspiration roll down his forehead and along his nose, and she felt a stab of sympathy. It must tickle like the very devil.

She was just stepping to the side, as she had been instructed, when a stiff man with a blond mustache stepped forward. The lord chamberlain pronounced a long string of German names, of which Veronica caught only "von Ribbentrop." She was much better in French. His Majesty George VI got to his feet to greet the dignitary in person.

Von Ribbentrop stiffened and clicked his heels together. Then, in an appalling gesture, he threw up his right arm in a stiff-armed salute. His hand came so close to striking the king in the chest that His Majesty instinctively rocked back on his heels.

The assembly sucked in a horrified collective breath, followed by several seconds of frozen silence. Disbelieving faces turned toward von Ribbentrop, and the lord chamberlain made a small, involuntary movement, lifting his ceremonial mace as if he might wield it to force the German away from the king.

Veronica couldn't see precisely what happened next. One moment she was gazing with horror, like everyone else, at the man who had given offense to King George. The next the scene around her blurred, suddenly enveloped in smoke. The room— the walls, the hangings, the rich carpet—disappeared behind red and yellow flames. Her brain felt as if it were swelling inside her skull, and she had the vertiginous sense of rising above herself, looking down on a bizarre view of her own feathered head, her white dress, the sparkling crowns of the royals.

Her view shifted, and she found herself inexplicably gazing down on the roof as Buckingham Palace began to burn. The city beyond was also afire, great gouts of smoke obscuring the river and the docks of the East End. Walls collapsed and blocked the streets. Roofs shattered and broken windows gaped. Her ears rang with the sounds of explosions and bells and sirens punctuated by the screams of injured and frightened people.

She couldn't bear to see it. With an effort of will she forced herself back into the throne room, but the scene was no better. At least half the people there now sprawled on the marble floor, clearly dead. Blood puddled around them, staining the girls' gowns, the fawn trousers of the men, ruining the beautiful carpet. Smoke hung in the room like a fog. In the middle of the chaos, the German—von Ribbentrop—stood erect and proud, his plumed hat under his left arm, his right arm raised toward the king like the blade of a sword. His fair hair shone red in the light of the flames. Veronica struggled to breathe.

A heartbeat later the vision vanished as if it had never been. She found herself on her feet, automatically sidling away from the royals. It was obvious no real time had passed. The German was bowing to the king, his arm now dropped to his side. King

George, his face stiff but composed, spoke to him. The queen hadn't moved a muscle, but her famous violet eyes were nearly black with fury.

Veronica stumbled back to her place, trembling, and sank down hard into her chair, her legs weak with shock. Her stomach quivered, and her gorge rose almost too swiftly for her to control it. For one terrible second she thought she might be sick, right here in front of the debutantes, their chaperones, and Their Majesties.

She closed her eyes and made herself picture Sweetbriar. She imagined driving up the tree-shaded drive to the house, strolling out to the cool, shadowed stables, or reading in the arbor in the south garden. She thought of Honeychurch, waiting faithfully outside the throne room, and Papa in his study at home.

Her stomach settled. Her composure returned. She opened her eyes as the last girl was presented, curtsied, and did the complicated sidestep that brought her back to her seat. Veronica exhaled with relief and lifted her head.

The queen was watching her.

That couldn't be. Surely Elizabeth was looking at something else, someone behind her, or next to her...

But no. Elizabeth Windsor, said to be gentle and kindly and motherly, met Veronica's startled eyes with a gaze of cool blue steel, as if she knew exactly what Veronica had seen. With deliberation Elizabeth nodded, once.

Veronica, mystified, inclined her head in courteous response. She wished she understood what had just happened.

2

"Veronica, could you take this out to the Home Farm this afternoon?" Papa pointed to a thick envelope lying on the sideboard in the morning room. "It's not heavy. You could ride."

"What is it?"

"Just some papers for Jago, from the sale of his business. I promised I'd send them."

Veronica pushed away from the table. "I would be happy to, Papa. I don't have anything on my schedule this morning."

Her father smiled at her, but there were white lines around his mouth, and his eyelids drooped. His once-thick hair had grown thin, and now, in the sunlight, she saw that it was silver all through. She moved around the table to him, and crouched beside his chair. "You look like you had a bad night, Papa."

"I'm all right," he said, as he always did. "But I'd rather not have to take the car out."

"It's fine. I haven't seen Jago in days, and Mouse could use a gallop."

"Thank you. Give Jago my greetings, and explain why I didn't come myself, will you?"

"Of course, Papa." She dropped a kiss on his head. "Do you want Honeychurch to call Dr. Jacobsen?"

"No. No, thank you. There's no point. He's done all he can."

"Oh, Papa." Veronica paused, her hand still on her father's shoulder. "Are you sure? Maybe in London, a specialist…"

He reached up to pat her hand. "No more specialists, dear heart. It's just what I have to live with. It's probably the weather. I think it's going to rain later on."

She kissed him again and went off to change into her jodhpurs, but she frowned into her dressing table mirror as she buttoned her shirt. Her father's pain was getting worse. He had refused to try a new prosthesis, and the old one hurt him. With her brother away at school, it was left to her to help with the tasks of running the estate.

As she trotted down the stairs, she thought it was better that way in any case. She was far more suited to country life than Thomas.

✦

The Home Farm was barely a farm anymore, now that Jago had grown old. The barn was empty, and the stables held only a single horse. The fields were rented out to other farmers. Jago lived alone in the old stone house with its huge kitchen and shabby, comfortable parlor.

As Veronica trotted Mouse, her gray Arab gelding, up the dirt-and-gravel road, Jago emerged from the front door. He came down the steps and along the weedy flagstone path to wait for her at the gate. A dog, a disreputable-looking terrier bitch with one floppy ear and a wiry black-and-brown coat, trotted at his heels.

As Veronica dismounted, Jago said, "A sight for sore eyes, you." The dog laughed up at her, ragged tail waving. "Oona's glad to see you, too, it seems."

She looped the reins over her wrist and went to kiss Jago's cheek and tug Oona's ears. "You look well," she said. She set the package on the fence post.

"Fighting fit," he said. "Yon Mouse is looking fit, too."

"I was worried he might still be favoring that left foreleg, but I didn't feel it, at the trot or at the gallop."

"I think it's healed." Jago came through the gate and bent to run his hand down Mouse's finely cut foreleg. He rubbed the shin and the pastern and lifted the hoof to flex the ankle. When he set the foot down again, he patted Mouse's smooth shoulder. "You'll do, lad," he said. To Veronica he said, "Come with us into the stables? Ynyr knows you're here."

"He always does, doesn't he?" She chuckled as they walked toward the stables, where the ancient Shire stallion, the horse that had belonged to her mother, lived comfortably in a box stall, with access to the paddock whenever he liked. "I do worry he's lonely, Jago."

"I go out to see him every day, Miss Veronica."

"Are you lonely? I should have asked that."

"No, no, miss. You're here," he said. "And Thomas comes to see me at hols." A long whinny sounded from the barn, and he nodded in that direction. "He started that an hour ago."

"I hadn't even left the stables an hour ago!"

"That's Ynyr. Always been a funny kind of beast."

Veronica and her brother, as children, had often visited Jago at the Home Farm, especially when the weather was bad. They would gallop over on their ponies and hurry in to the warmth of the hearth fire to sprawl on the worn rug and drink cocoa brewed on the old-fashioned hob. Their mother, Morwen, had died when Veronica was born. Jago had said enough for Veronica to understand that her mother and the Shire had enjoyed a special bond.

"You're like her," Jago said. "Same way of speaking. Ynyr knows it."

Veronica led Mouse inside the barn, where Ynyr stamped impatiently. Jago took Mouse to unsaddle him and bring him oats and water. Veronica walked down the aisle to Ynyr's stall, digging in her jodhpur pocket for the bit of apple she'd brought. His teeth weren't as strong as they once had been, so she had asked Cook to slice it thin. He nibbled the slices delicately from her palm, his big head nodding appreciation as he chewed. She stroked his neck and threaded her fingers through his silvery mane as Jago came up behind her.

"We should have bred him while we could," she said.

"Aye, perhaps, Miss Veronica. He's too old now."

"I know. But I wish I had a colt out of him."

"Miss Morwen was a sight, sitting up on that broad back."

"No saddle, you said."

"Never needed one. They looked like one creature, the two of them."

"I suppose I'm not the rider Mama was."

"You are, though. Maybe better. You can ride any horse comes your way."

She stroked the Shire's wide cheek. "If so, that's because you taught me." Ynyr nibbled at her hair, and she scratched the backs of his ears. "There's something I want to tell you, Jago. To ask you about, really. I don't want to bother Papa, because he's not feeling well."

"Come into the house," Jago said. "I'll make a pot of tea."

Veronica gave Ynyr another pat, then followed Jago out of the barn and up through the bit of garden to the kitchen door, the terrier trotting at her heels. Raindrops began to spatter the tiled roof of the old stone house as they settled at the plank table with tea and a saucer of biscuits. The sound of the rain was familiar, comforting. Jago took up a knife and a small piece of wood and began to whittle.

"What's that going to be?" Veronica asked.

He held it up. "Bear, I think. Thomas says he can't find the one I made him before."

"I have a whole menagerie. Tiger, giraffe, cow…everything."

"I thought you would have outgrown my little toys."

"Never." Veronica sipped her tea for a moment, thinking how to begin. Jago, as always, waited in patient silence. She said, "I don't know how you were always so good with us. Since you don't have your own children."

"You and your brother are like my children. No disrespect to Lord Dafydd."

"He's not Lord Dafydd yet, not until Grandpapa goes."

"Coming soon, from what I hear."

"I suppose that's to be expected."

"Then you'll be Lady Veronica."

She made a face. "Isn't that ridiculous?"

"Some girls would like it." She let that go without comment. He knew she wouldn't care about a title.

An easy silence stretched between them, broken only by the patter of the rain. She watched his deft hands as the bear began to emerge from the wood, ears, blunt little nose, paws crossed on its breast.

At last she found the words she needed to say to him. "Something strange happened to me last year, when I was presented."

"Oh, aye?"

"I tried to put it out of my mind, all this time. I told myself it was just the heat, or my imagination, or something, but—now it's happened again."

He didn't look up from his carving, but she knew he was paying attention. He had always had the gift of listening, she thought, whether it was to Thomas sorrowing over some dead bird he had found in the copse, or to her describing taking a horse over a jump, elaborating the dangers and exaggerating her speed.

The terrier had been lying under Jago's chair. Now she wriggled out and sat beside Veronica, staring at her with round, bright eyes.

Veronica absently stroked the dog's head. "At the presentation, I had this awful vision. At least I think it was a vision. It *felt* like a vision. Everything was burning, the palace, the city. People were dying. It terrified me." She left out the part about the queen. It was too hard to explain. "That was more than a year ago. I decided it was all the war talk that made me imagine it, but then, yesterday..."

Veronica's hand began to tremble, and she set down her teacup. It rattled in the saucer until she released it. She wound her hands together in her lap.

She wasn't fearful, as a rule. She wasn't sensitive, like Thomas. When Phillip fell off his pony and cut his arm, Thomas couldn't look at the wound. It was she who had been the calm one, stanching the blood, pressing the cut closed until the doctor came.

When Mouse pulled the tendon in his foreleg, she had stayed right beside him in the road until it grew so dark she could barely see. She was shivering with cold by the time the searchers found her, but she hadn't been afraid of anything except Mouse trying to move, and making his injury worse.

But what had happened the day before was so much like the experience on her presentation day that all the nausea and panic had come rushing back. It was because, she thought, she didn't understand it. How could she?

"I was dressing for dinner. The maid brought the post up, and there was a letter from Thomas. I had time, so I picked it up to open the envelope, and then..." She shuddered and closed her eyes. "Oh, Jago, it was awful."

"Best to talk it out, you," he said. His knife kept moving, shaving away precise little bits of wood and letting them fall onto the table.

She took a quivering breath as she opened her eyes. She fixed her gaze on the little wooden bear, thinking that speaking it aloud made it all too real. "This time it wasn't the palace, and London. It was Thomas! It was as if I could see him, though I don't know where he was. He was running, and he was wearing one of those hats—the metal kind the soldiers wear, the ones that look like upended pots. He was running, and there was noise all around, gunfire, I think, and men shouting, and then—Thomas—" She pressed her fingers to her lips.

Thomas was the sort of young man who, in another day and time, and without Sweetbriar to inherit, might have gone into the church. He was easygoing, soft-spoken, bookish. He didn't care much for horses, except to ride off somewhere with a packet of books, to read in peace. He hated sports, and played only the ones he had to when he was at school. No one laughed at him for any of that. Everyone loved Thomas.

"He fell," she said inadequately. It was a terrible description of what she had seen. In truth, he had jerked into the air as if someone or something had thrown him, and then he had gone limp and fallen to the earth the way a sack of oats might fall, heavy and lifeless. "He looked…" She pressed her palm over her trembling mouth.

Jago set his carving aside. He reached across the table and laid his big hand on her head as she cried. She wept for a few moments, and then, when she managed to choke back her tears, he handed her an enormous blue handkerchief.

She blew her nose and wiped her cheeks. "Sorry," she said.

"No need."

"It can't be war," she blurted. "It can't be! Chamberlain says Hitler is a gentleman, and we will have peace in our time."

"What does Lord Dafydd have to say?"

She folded the handkerchief before her on the table, creasing it and recreasing it. "Papa says Chamberlain is a fool. So does Phillip."

"Ah." Jago reached for the little bear again and took up his knife. "Phillip is still young."

"He's so smart, though, Jago. I've always thought so."

"Handsome feller, too. Fond of him, you?"

"Oh yes. I've known him since I was small."

"Best way to go about it," he said.

"Go about what?"

"Oh now, Miss Veronica, you're not such a babe as all that." Her cheeks warmed, and for a moment she and Jago grinned at each other. Both the Paxtons and the Selwyns had assumed for years that one day she and Phillip would join the two families, but Veronica didn't think about it much. Phillip had been her playmate, and now was her dearest friend. It was enough for the moment.

After the moment passed she returned to the reason for her visit. "Jago, I don't understand why this is happening to me. I've always had strange dreams, but I was sure they were just that—dreams. I'm not the least bit hysterical, like some girls at school…"

"No."

"And I can't worry Papa with such nonsense, not when he's feeling so ill."

Jago carved a whorl on one side of the bear's head, and it became a pert little ear. "Not nonsense. But don't bother your papa with it."

"But what if it happens again? What if I'm going mad?"

Jago carved another ear, then set his knife down with deliberation. "Not going mad," he said. His voice was low, but assured. He set the bear between them, an uncanny little figure that, on another day, she would have exclaimed over. "I have something to give you," he added, and pushed back from the table. "Wait there."

He was gone only a moment. When he returned he carried a Fortnum & Mason hamper, one of the heavy, old-style ones, made of wicker gone dark with age. It clunked when he set it on the table. He fiddled with the leather-and-metal fastening, then lifted the top to reveal folds of white silk. Veronica reached for the material, but Jago stopped her with an uplifted hand. "I need to explain first."

She felt sadness emanate from him like the chill of a fog bank. A crooked furrow appeared between his brows, strangely reminiscent of the one she often saw in her own mirror. "So like your mama, you," he said. "She thought you might be."

"What do you mean? Papa says she never saw me, never held me . . ." It had always grieved her, knowing her mother had been gone from the moment she drew her first breath.

"She never held you." He passed his hand over the crumpled silk, but without removing it. He sat down, and his gaze drifted to the window, where the autumn leaves glinted gold and bronze in the thin sunshine. "But she saw you. She saw you before you were born."

"That's not possible."

"It was possible for her. As it seems it is with you. I promised, if it came about this way—the way she thought it might—that I would explain to you. I promised to tell you the story."

"But I don't—"

He held up one work-worn hand. "I'm not much of a talker. It will help me if you don't ask me anything until I'm done."

Feeling uneasy, Veronica leaned back in her chair. She steepled her fingers before her mouth, to remind herself not to interrupt, as Jago began to speak at length. As he did, her discomfort grew. By the end, when he stood to fold back the coverings in the Fortnum & Mason hamper, she was staring at him in disbelief. Her eyes felt dry, as if she had forgotten to blink. Her mouth was dry, too, and she realized it had been hanging open for some minutes.

During the recitation Oona the dog inched closer and closer to Veronica, until her whiskery muzzle pressed against her knee.

Veronica came slowly to her feet, half-convinced there would be nothing at all in the hamper. Oona moved aside just enough for her to lean over the table, but she stayed close, her rough coat catching on the wool of Veronica's jodhpurs.

"She put it away when Lord Dafydd went off to war," Jago said, laying aside each fold of silk with deliberate care. "He came home grievous wounded, as you know, and she sat by him in hospital for weeks on end. They married the very day he came out. After their wedding, and all the years after, she never touched the stone, or her grandmother's old book. Then, when you were expected...She knew, you see."

"She knew?"

"She was warned not to have another child, but she said—" Jago paused for a moment, and closed his eyes as if the memory still pained him. "She said she needed a daughter. A lass to inherit the craft. To carry on the Orchiére line."

He paused, his hand on the last layer of old silk. He spoke with the kind of infinite sadness that never abates. "Morwen had great power, Miss Veronica. Real power. She set it aside for love." As he said the words, he pulled back the last of the fabric. "And she asked me, if it turned out you also had the power, to see you received your birthright."

It was there, just as he had described it. The crystal in its bed of granite glowed gently in the filtered light. Beneath it lay the grimoire in its ancient leather binding.

"Jago, what am I supposed to do with it?"

"I can't tell you that. Your mama said some can use it, some can't. Same with the book."

"How do I know if I have the power?"

"Can't answer that, either. I guess you'll just have to try."

Veronica wrapped her arms around herself, chilled by the import of Jago's story, and the thought of what might lie ahead for her. Oona, watching, thumped her tail on the floor.

~❧~

Strangeness followed strangeness after her visit with Jago. She rode away with the Fortnum & Mason hamper balanced on her saddle. Oona, the terrier, trotted at Mouse's heels. Veronica ordered her to go home several times, and even turned Mouse to guide the dog back to the Home Farm, but Oona refused to stay there. When Veronica reached Sweetbriar, the dog followed her in from the stables, staying close beside her as she lugged the old hamper up the stairs to her bedroom.

The rain had eased during the ride home, but now, as Veronica went into her bedroom with Oona close behind, it resumed with a roar of thunder and a torrent of raindrops that rattled her bedroom window. The housemaid had laid a fire, and Veronica set a match to it to banish the chill. As the yellow flames leaped around the little pile of dried cedar, she faced her bed. The hamper lay there, looking ominous in the dimness, its old, shiny wicker reflecting the firelight.

She was torn between an aversion to opening it and a compulsion to see the stone once again, to prove to herself it was really there, that Jago's story was—at least when it came to the old crystal—a true one. She had always trusted him, and she didn't want to stop now. But what he had told her seemed as unreal as the visions she had experienced. Another clap of thunder shook the house as she stood, irresolute, staring at the mystery Jago had delivered over to her.

Oona, as if she understood Veronica's ambivalence, gathered her small body and leaped up onto the bed, muddying the beige coverlet with her paws. She nosed the hamper, then sat down next to it, her tongue hanging out, her sparkling black gaze fixed on Veronica.

"You think I should look at it, don't you?" Veronica approached the bed, and Oona jumped to her feet. The dog's scruffy tail waved steadily as Veronica released the leather straps and lifted the lid. She folded back the slippery layers of fabric, braced both hands on the sides of the hamper, and bent to look inside.

What she saw made her dizzy. Her stomach clenched. Lights glimmered and spun within the cloudy stone. She hadn't touched it, yet images began to peer out of the maelstrom, the more vivid because of the dimness of the room. There was a succession of half-seen faces, dark eyed, dusky skinned, all of them—every single one—female. Her hands grew slippery with sweat on the wicker, and she swallowed, wondering at the sensations in her body.

What did it all mean? How would she make sense of this, all by herself?

With a groan she slammed the lid of the hamper down. Oona backed away and leaped down from the bed. Veronica retreated to the fireplace, shivering.

It was real. It was all true. Though it went against everything she had always believed, everything her church taught, that her father put his faith in—

She, Veronica Selwyn, daughter of the English aristocracy, was descended from a line of witches.

She had no idea what to do about it.

3

About Hitler, Papa was correct, as he so often was. Phillip was, too. Chamberlain was disgraced, Churchill returned to Number 10, and England winced over the reports of Kristallnacht and the invasion of Poland. In September of 1939, just over two years after Veronica was presented at court, the war began.

The staff of Sweetbriar melted away. To a man, everyone who worked for Lord Dafydd Selwyn joined up before the conscription law was passed. Most went into the infantry, but one went into the Royal Artillery and another into the 27th Armoured Brigade. The youngest cook left without notice, and they learned she had joined the Auxiliary Territorial Service. An elderly gardener joined the Local Defence Volunteers, later to be called the Home Guard.

Phillip Paxton, like other young men of his class, went into the RAF as a commissioned officer, and Veronica went to the station to see him off for pilot's training. He had always been good-looking, but in his uniform and officer's cap he was heartbreakingly handsome. They hadn't spoken of love between them. It had always seemed there was plenty of time for that, time for them to grow, to be independent, and ultimately to follow their families' wishes.

But the English air was electric with romance, charged with the sense of peril and adventure and vitality. Every young person, and many not so young, felt romantic.

Phillip did, too, and his urgency infected Veronica. Five minutes before his train departed, he took her left hand, deftly pulled off her calfskin glove, and slipped something heavy onto her finger. She looked down to see a ring of heavy white gold, with an old-fashioned square sapphire in a surround of diamonds.

"Oh! Phillip! Your mother's ring!"

He caught her to him in a crushing embrace, knocking her hat askew. "I would have waited, Veronica," he said in a husky voice. "I meant to wait until your twenty-first birthday, but now..."

All around them were men in uniform, weeping girls clutching handkerchiefs, mothers and fathers and siblings there to see their soldiers off to war. The train's whistle pierced the hubbub, and Phillip released Veronica to look into her face for her answer.

There was no time to think, to consider. Veronica had never questioned their future together, but it had always seemed very far off. Phillip was a fine young man, from an outstanding family. He was honest and loyal and brave, but...

Was she in love? She didn't know. She would have decided, in time. She might even have decided true friendship was more important than romance.

But there was a war on. Time was a lost luxury.

"Will you?" Phillip asked, grinning.

"Of course I will!" she cried. He bent to kiss her, and she closed her eyes, hoping for a rush of emotion, that delirium girls were supposed to feel when they became engaged. His lips were smooth and cool, his arms around her strong, the buttons on his uniform pressing into her bosom in a delightfully masculine way. She loved him, of course. She had always loved him.

She wasn't *in* love. But at this moment, as they tore themselves apart and he jumped onto the already-moving train, it didn't seem to matter. They were part of something greater than the two of them. They were actors in this national drama.

He clung to the handrail and saluted her, grinning. She saluted back, smiling through her own tears, laughing at the hoots and whistles from the soldiers hanging from the windows. They doffed their caps as their girls and their mothers called farewells and fluttered their handkerchiefs. Everyone blew kisses, men and women alike. No one allowed their tears to spoil the moment.

Veronica stood on the platform for a long time after the train had chugged away. She held her glove in her hand, because it wouldn't fit over the bulk of Phillip's ring. She knew Chesley was waiting for her in the car, but she still remained, trying to understand what had just happened. Hoping that, in time, she would feel what she was supposed to feel.

Veronica tried to ignore the crystal, hiding in its hamper in her wardrobe. Certainly she had masses of things to distract her from the possibility of witchcraft.

The staff was alarmingly short at Sweetbriar. Since Cook had lost her assistant, Veronica gave up her daily rides in order to help with the shopping as well as planning menus that were restricted by shortages. She worried about Mouse getting exercised, but a weekly outing was all she could manage.

She had never before cleaned a bathroom or dusted furniture, but now, with only one housemaid left to them, she added those things to her chores. She even made an attempt to keep the shrubberies around the front lawn weeded, but that job was monumental. Lord Dafydd advised her to give it up, and with her hands full and her energy taxed to its full extent, she agreed. The weeds grew enthusiastically around the junipers and cotoneasters, and as she hurried to and fro on errands for her father, she did her best to shut her eyes to them.

If there was ever an extra minute, she spent it worrying about house repairs that couldn't be postponed. She had never been particularly social, but there had customarily been at least one engagement each week, a tea or a cocktail party. Since the war began, most such invitations had ceased, and those that did arrive she was obliged to decline. At night she fell into bed as early as she could, exhausted.

"You're working too hard," her father said one morning as they finished breakfast.

She rose and kissed his cheek. "Let's hope the war doesn't last long, and everything can go back to normal."

"Of course," he said, but without conviction. "Where are you off to today?"

"Butcher," she said. "And Cottage Farm. I think they have some eggs for us. We're going to need them."

"Not more than our share, though, Veronica."

"Of course not, Papa."

"They'll have to ration eggs, I'm afraid. And cheese, and a lot of other things."

"As if petrol and meat aren't bad enough. Bacon. Sugar!"

He was getting to his feet, leaning hard on his cane. She didn't offer to help, because she knew how much he hated that. "I miss sweets," he admitted. "Maybe you could ask at Cottage Farm for some honey. They keep hives, don't they?"

"They did. I don't know if there's anyone to mind them."

"Are you going to have Chesley drive you?"

"No. We have to conserve petrol." She pointed at her jodhpurs. "I'll take Mouse. He needs a gallop, and I won't have enough to carry that it will be a problem."

"It's cold, though. February."

"I know. I'll bundle up."

They had fallen into a routine, comfortable enough despite the straitened circumstances. Lord Dafydd had offered Sweetbriar as a potential hospital, though the War Office had not yet taken up his offer. Veronica couldn't imagine their beautiful house filled with hospital beds and medical equipment, much less injured soldiers, but she supposed it was inevitable. She was resigned to it.

She wasn't accustomed, though, to constant worry. She feared for Phillip, of course, imagining him in his aircraft, preparing to do battle with vicious German fighters. She feared even more for her brother. She couldn't imagine anyone less suited to be in the infantry than Thomas. She saw her father's frequent glances at Thomas's photograph in its pride of place in the morning room, and she knew he was worried, too. It wasn't just that Thomas was his only son, his heir, the hope for the Selwyn name to carry on. Thomas was a shining star in their family, the smartest, sweetest, kindest young man they knew. He was gentle with servants and with friends, and honest to a fault. He was generous with his time and his energy. He never seemed to have any money, because he gave it all away.

Veronica idolized her older brother. Her father, she understood without the slightest resentment, doted on him.

At night she was haunted by the vision she had suffered before the war began. She tried to let her exhaustion carry her off to sleep, but too often the image of Thomas falling to the ground, limp and lifeless, rose over and over again into her weary mind. At last that image drove her to bring out the Fortnum & Mason hamper.

She decided, as that cold and dismal February wound down, to explore the grimoire. Leaving the stone in its wrappings, she opened the book on her bed and struggled to decipher its fading, spotted script.

She didn't get far. Her French wasn't strong, and the language in the book was old-fashioned. She could identify recipes for potions and simples, which she supposed could be useful, if they worked. There were instructions for spells, too, with specific guidelines for herbs to be used and candles to be burned. None of it seemed any more real to her than the ancient and rather silly text on alchemy she had found in Lord Dafydd's library.

Was there, as Jago had implied, real power in the grimoire? Specifically, was there something she could do to protect Thomas? Every Sunday they offered prayers for him, of course, kneeling in the village church. Was this any different?

"The thing is," she told Oona, who sat gazing up at her as she turned the fragile pages of the old book, "that I'm supposed to be a witch, but I don't know how."

The dog blinked at her, and lay down with her head on her paws.

"Not your problem, is it?" Veronica closed the book with care and laid it back in the hamper. "I think I need a different book."

The Sweetbriar library was extensive, with volumes collected by Lord Dafydd, by his father Lord William, and a precious few added by Morwen during her lifetime. Those were arranged in their own special section in a glass-fronted cabinet. Veronica had looked them over before, out of curiosity and a vague longing for the mother she had never known. Now she opened the cabinet and took each book out, searching for anything Morwen might have left behind for her to find.

She opened the books, shook them, scanned their titles and chapter headings. She looked on the frontispieces and examined the flyleafs, but there was not so much as a note in Morwen's hand. Jago was right. She had given it all up when she married Dafydd. She had lived a conventional life. A safe one.

The sound of the front door opening meant her father had returned from his meeting. Veronica got up from the floor, where she had been sitting. She knew she needed to go to the kitchen, to make sure dinner was underway and Cook had everything she needed, but something made her pause in the act of closing the cabinet doors.

A phrase sounded in her head. The words came so clearly she jumped, and glanced around in the expectation that someone had come into the room with her. There was no one. Her father had already made his painful way up the staircase. Chesley would be garaging the car. She was alone.

In the drawer. Those were the words she had heard.

"What drawer?" she muttered. "Which one?"

There was no repetition of the phrase, but the sense of having heard it was so distinct she began to search, though she felt a bit sheepish about it. There was a desk in the library, of course, but it was Lord Dafydd's. Its drawers held his pens, bottles of ink, blotting papers, and stationery, everything neatly organized in compartments. There was a sideboard, where occasionally tea might be set out, but its drawers were full of napkins, coasters, and trays, with a small collection of butter knives and teaspoons.

Veronica stood in the very center of the room, trying to discern another drawer, something she hadn't noticed in all the years of using this library. Some instinct made her close her eyes and reach out with her empty hands. She felt a tug, as if someone had taken her hand and was leading her.

She hadn't moved, but when she opened her eyes, her gaze fell directly onto a narrow slat of wood at the bottom of the glass-fronted cabinet. There was no drawer pull, no knob to reveal it, but she could see it was there. She wondered why she hadn't noticed it before. In a flash she was crouching beside the cabinet again. She put her fingers underneath and pulled.

A shallow drawer slid out at the command of her fingers. It was no more than four inches front to back, and surely only one inch deep, barely worthy of the word *drawer*. On first glance it seemed to be empty, but then she spotted a card that looked as if it had been left behind by accident, caught on a splinter at one side.

Veronica lifted it out and read, in old-fashioned copperplate script:

Atlantis Bookshop
Museum Street
London

The card was thick, the name, which she had never heard before, heavily embossed.

She heard her father's cane clicking on the floor and hastily closed the drawer and jumped to her feet. She tucked the card into the pocket of her tweed skirt and went to see about dinner.

Veronica had no excuse for going down to London just then. Phillip wouldn't have leave for some time, and there was no extra money for shopping or dining out or staying in a hotel. She had to settle for writing to the bookshop.

She worded her request as cautiously as she could. She asked for books on sorcery, inspired by the French word. In response the bookseller sent her three old volumes: Sir Walter Scott's *Letters on Demonology and Witchcraft*; Orcutt's *The Spell*, which turned out to be a novel; and *Goetia*, an unsettling collection of essays about calling up spirits. She read them all, struggling to divine what was invention and what might be useful.

On a cold March night, when she had digested the books as best she could, she judged it was time to bring out the crystal once again. She decided to follow a pattern in *Goetia*. She used her dressing table stool as a makeshift altar and sprinkled salted water around it. She brought an unburned candle up from the butler's pantry and lighted it. She set the crystal on the stool, knelt inside the circle of water, and waited. Oona sat outside the circle, watching, her mouth closed and her tail stretched straight out behind her. Veronica felt a bit foolish over the whole thing, and was glad there was no one but the dog to observe her.

For at least twenty minutes nothing happened. Not even the lights she had seen the first time appeared, much less the whirl of strange faces. She supposed she was doing something wrong, but she didn't know what to change. Or maybe she had no power after all. The whole thing seemed foolish, in any case, as fantastic as a fairy tale.

Her knees began to ache with the chill, and her toes to cramp from the uncomfortable position. She began to think of giving it up, but when she shifted her position, Oona jumped to her feet and stood with her ears and tail drooping. She whined until Veronica, startled, settled back on her heels. "What is it?" she whispered. Oona stopped whining, but watched her, as if afraid she might change her mind. The dog, too, settled back to the floor.

Seconds later a face began to emerge from the smoky depths of the stone.

Veronica's heart lurched. It was the face of a woman, much aged, with a mass of white hair and wrinkled eyelids hooding eyes as dark and glittering as Oona's. She gazed out of the stone as if she knew who was looking back, and lifted one age-spotted hand in greeting.

Veronica stared, openmouthed. The woman crooked one arthritic finger in invitation, and her mouth stretched into a sharp-toothed smile.

Veronica froze, unable to respond, unable even to think. She remembered the sensation in her stomach as she first looked into the stone. It returned now, swelled until it was almost unbearable, and then, bit by bit, subsided. The face in the stone faded as if someone had turned out a light. Veronica inhaled a sudden, much-needed breath. Her candle guttered out in a pool of wax, telling her that more time had passed than she realized. The water drops had dried long before.

Oona lay flat on her side, her eyes closed.

Veronica sat back on her heels and looked around her dressing room. What could be more ordinary than this room, with its mirrored bureau, lacy dressing table, cabbage rose wallpaper? How could there be lights in a stone, or a mysterious woman beckoning to her? What did that woman want?

Veronica seized up the silk and folded it over the crystal. She hastily stowed the crystal and grimoire back in the hamper, and hid the whole behind the dresses in her wardrobe.

She didn't understand what was happening. If there was magic in her, how was she supposed to use it? What good was it if she couldn't do something to protect Thomas, or to support Phillip? She was as fearful as ever, no less worried than she had been.

She couldn't help wishing that the stone and its mysteries had never come into her possession.

4

Veronica turned and turned her engagement ring as she gazed up at the bulk of Sweetbriar from her post on the south lawn. Stars outlined the silhouette of the house. Blackout curtains covered every window, like shrouds over the faces of the dead. The house seemed dead, in a way. Its life as a home was at an end. The dining room, the parlor, the morning room, even the great hall had all been turned over to wounded officers and their doctors and nurses.

She twisted the ring again, knowing she should break the habit. She didn't wear it often these days. It felt heavy and constricting, and she found herself removing it whenever she had a reason. Working in Sweetbriar's makeshift hospital gave her very good reason. She worked a great deal with her hands, changing bandages, emptying bedpans, writing letters for the men, but she wasn't doing any of that this evening. She had made herself take it from the small cut-glass tray on her dressing table and slide it onto her finger.

An air of grim resignation pervaded the house. Everyone felt it, from Lord Dafydd to Jago and Honeychurch to Cook and the one remaining housemaid. Even Oona looked unhappy, her stiff tail drooping as she followed Veronica around the house and the grounds.

Except for Honeychurch, now nearing seventy, there was only

a skeleton staff left. Jago had returned to fill in where he could, moving from the Home Farm to the apartment above the garage. Ynyr had come as well, to drowse away his days in the main stables. All the other horses were gone, sold off or moved to country farms for their safety.

Veronica thought Oona might go back to Jago, now that he was so close, but the dog wouldn't budge. Veronica tried to apologize to Jago about stealing his dog, but he shook his head, smiling. "Yours now," he said. "Made her own choice."

No bombs had fallen near Sweetbriar, but the threat of the *blitzkrieg* loomed over all of England. On this night, as on so many others, residents and patients and nurses stood or sat on the lawn to watch the fireworks created by the Luftwaffe's bombs. Clear skies and starlight worked in the enemy's favor. London—and the residents of the surrounding countryside—could do nothing but hold their breath and pray the ack-ack guns would deter the worst of it.

The stars illuminated the bombers, too. Several officers, in stoic tones, named the airplanes for their comrades who could no longer see them. "Heinkel. Messerschmidt. Junkers. Fokker." The blinded ones, leaning on a nurse's shoulder or sitting in a wheelchair, nodded, and sometimes growled curses.

Most of the soldiers were British and Canadian, but there were one American, two Australians, and a Frenchman, a casualty of the Dunkirk evacuation. Valéry Chirac, the French soldier, probably should not have been allowed out of his bed, but the physician in charge shrugged and said it hardly mattered now.

No one expected him to survive. He was one of too many patients for whom the nurses could do little but offer comfort. Both his legs had been broken when one of the valiant little fishing boats trying to save soldiers like him crashed into another craft. He had spent hours standing in seawater up to his shoulders before suffering a miserable crossing to England. By the time he reached Sweetbriar, he had double pneumonia, casts on both legs, and a suppurating gash in his scalp that had required his head to be shaven. He might once have been a strapping young man, but illness and pain had thinned him until his collarbones jutted and his ribs showed beneath his scratched and scarred skin.

Veronica, moving between wheelchairs with blankets and shawls, saw Valéry tip his head up into the starlight, though his eyes were closed. He had wrapped his long arms around himself as if he were cold, so she crossed the grass to drape a knitted shawl around his shoulders. It was, incongruously, pink, knitted by one of the church ladies in the village. As she tucked it behind the soldier's wasted shoulders, his eyes opened. They were red with illness, but dark and deep, reflecting the stars and the distant bursts of the bombs. He whispered, "*Merci.*"

"*De rien.*" No one was sure how much English he spoke, or if he spoke any. He had been unconscious for a long time, and the nurses had learned nothing about him. Veronica's schoolgirl French wasn't up to real conversations, but so far it hadn't mattered. She pressed the back of her hand to his forehead. He was burning with fever.

She said, in halting French, "You should be in your bed."

He licked his dry lips and shook his head. "I want to watch," he answered, in the same language.

Veronica gazed down at him, her heart aching with pity. He must once have been handsome, she thought, with a long, straight nose and narrow lips. His hands, plucking restively at the pink shawl, were fine boned and long fingered. She said, softly, "Monsieur Chirac. Can I bring you something? Tea? Brandy?"

"Brandy," he whispered. His eyes closed, as if the lids were too heavy to hold up. "I would love a bit of brandy."

Veronica knew there was no brandy in the hospital stores, but

Lord Dafydd kept a bottle in his private study, one of the few rooms that had not been invaded by doctors or nurses. She ran up the stairs, poured some into a teacup, and carried it carefully back, braced on a saucer.

The soldier didn't move when she crouched beside him, but when she held the cup to his lips, his eyelids fluttered, and he took a sip. "*Bon,*" he whispered.

"Drink it all," she advised.

He did, and it seemed to give him strength. When he had drained the teacup, he drew a noisy breath that rattled in his agonized lungs, but his eyes were open and he even lifted his head for a moment and tried to smile at her.

A fresh burst of explosions filled the air over London, the concussions coming a few seconds afterward, made faint by the distance. Veronica said haltingly, searching for the verbs, "I was afraid of those, but no more."

He used a French word she didn't recognize. His eyes closed again, and white marks appeared around his mouth. "Some things," he said, surprising her by speaking English, "we cannot get used to."

The effort of speaking seemed to drain his fragile energy, so she didn't pursue it. Nurses were beginning to collect their patients, wheeling chairs back inside, urging those on chairs or on the grass to go in. She said, in English this time, "I'm going to take you inside, *monsieur.*"

He didn't answer, but he lifted one trembling hand in assent.

❧

There was little left of routine at Sweetbriar, but Veronica still sat down for breakfast with her father each day, as much for his sake as for her own. He was reading the *Times* and she was making a list of pressing chores when Honeychurch came in with a note on a tray. Lord Dafydd reached for it, but Honeychurch said, "It's for Lady Veronica, sir."

She took it, thanking Honeychurch, and read it quickly. "It's from the matron, Papa. There is a patient—do you remember, the French soldier brought from Dunkirk? He's asked for me to write a letter, since I have some French."

"Do you have enough French?"

"I guess I'll find out. Will you excuse me? I'll take this list to the requisition officer as long as I'm going to the hall." She jumped up and kissed her father's cheek, saying, "Don't overdo it today, promise me." He patted her hand in answer.

Veronica pattered up the stairs for her French dictionary before going to the hall. Oona, resting on her bed, looked up hopefully when she came in. Veronica stroked her head. "Sorry, girl. You really can't be in the hospital." The dog sighed and laid her head on her paws.

Veronica was glad she had the dictionary with her when she began the soldier's letter. She suspected his English would have been far better than her French, had he been well. He was terribly weak, slipping in and out of consciousness as she sat beside his bed, leaning close to hear his whispered words. He was trying to write a farewell letter to his mother.

The words were heartbreaking, but she steeled herself. He would not be the first soldier to die here at the Sweetbriar hospital. She wrote what he said, filling in blanks here and there when he fell silent, willing her tears of sympathy away.

When they reached the end, she read it back to him, and he whispered, "*Oui. Merci.*"

"You need to tell me where to send it," she said.

"Drancy," he said. "I think she's in Drancy."

"Is that a city? A village?"

His eyes opened and looked directly into hers. "A camp. Drancy is a work camp."

She didn't need to look up the words. They were all too obvious, *camp de travail*. Valéry Chirac's mother was in a concentration camp.

Shocked and miserable, she couldn't think of the sentence she needed in French. "I'll send it through the Red Cross," she said in English. "It may not reach her."

He responded in the same language, though his eyes had closed. "Please try."

She touched his arm in assent, said, "Rest now," and rose.

His hand, hot with fever, found hers. "They took them all," he whispered.

She bent over him again. "Sorry? All?"

"All. My mother. My aunt. My students."

Veronica sank back onto her chair. "You're a teacher, *monsieur?*"

"*Oui. Musique.*"

She turned her hand to gently hold his. She noticed again the long, tapering fingers. A musician's fingers. "I'm so sorry, Valéry," she murmured. "Surely they didn't take all of your students."

"*Les Juifs.*" The Jews. "*Les petits Juifs.*"

"Oh no." Her own worries, the endless chores awaiting her, her fears for Thomas and for Phillip, seemed as nothing before these losses. Some were still trying to pretend the Germans were protecting those they arrested and interned, but Lord Dafydd said the authorities knew the truth. They were killing them, or allowing them to die of hunger and cold and illness, even the children. She would send the letter, but it was no wonder the will to live was failing in this man.

He was asleep again. She sat on for a moment, holding his nerveless hand in hers, wishing she could share her own vitality with him. He was one among many who would be lost. She knew that. She wished, just the same, that she could save this one. For his mother, for his students. Even, selfishly, for herself, because it seemed so pointless to waste another young life.

It was a day for moping, she found. She dragged herself through her list of tasks, including a long discussion over the telephone with a regimental quartermaster who was questioning their latest supply requisition. She managed to get outside for an hour, with Oona bounding gleefully around her ankles, to ride Mouse for a bit and see that Ynyr was eating well enough, and that the stables were in decent order. At least there was still a supply of hay, brought in the previous summer, but stores of oats were getting low. Through the fog of sorrow and fatigue, she couldn't think of a remedy for that just now. She decided to put that problem off for a better day.

As she had for months now, Veronica fell into bed that night half-asleep already, but with a dozen worries plaguing her tired brain. Oona snuggled close to her, whiskery chin over her ankles, and she forced herself to breathe slowly, to blank her mind, until she could sleep. In the distance she heard the crackle of ack-ack.

She had been asleep for perhaps three or four hours when she startled awake and found herself sitting straight up in her bed. Oona was awake, too, standing at the foot of the bed with her tail straight out. She turned her head and fixed Veronica with an intense stare.

Veronica listened but didn't hear anything. The blackout curtain was in place, and the room lay in almost complete darkness. Only the faint glow of the moon shone past the edges of the curtain. What had waked her? She wasn't sure, but an overwhelming feeling of anxiety drove her from the bed. She hesitated before opening the door, deciding it would be wise to slip into the blouse and skirt she had been wearing all day. She stuck her feet into a pair of flat slippers and, with Oona close behind, went out into the corridor.

Sweetbriar was never silent these days. There was always a muted hum of activity from the hall, where the rows of hospital beds were arranged. It seemed to her there was something else going on tonight, a slight fuss of people coming and going, trying to be quiet. She didn't work there in the night, since she had so much to do in the daylight hours. She was on the point of going back into her bedroom, but Oona had gone to the head of the staircase and was facing down the stairs, whining.

"Oona, quiet!" Veronica hissed, but the dog paid no attention. Sighing, supposing she had to go out, Veronica gave in. The moment her foot touched the first tread, Oona was skipping downstairs, where she waited at the bottom. Veronica turned toward the kitchen and the back door, but the dog headed straight for the front of the house. "Oona!" Veronica whispered again, to no avail. She had no choice but to follow.

She meant to stop the dog before she made it into the hall, but Oona stayed three steps ahead of her. Veronica trotted after her, weaving among the beds of the sleeping men, casting apologetic glances to the nurses working here and there. Oona didn't stop until she reached the bed of Valéry Chirac. She sat beside it, her head tilted to one side, her eyes fixed expectantly on Veronica.

This, Veronica could see, was the source of the commotion she had heard. Two nurses and a doctor were murmuring orders to one another. It was terrible to watch. Valéry, worn down by his ordeal and the pain of his fractured bones, had no resistance to the infection that had settled into his lungs. He was struggling for breath, his lips and nostrils mottled blue as he gasped and thrashed. One nurse held his arm, and the doctor bent over him to administer an injection. The other nurse stood beside the bed, her hands clasped, tears trickling down her cheeks.

The injection seemed to ease Valéry a bit, at least enough to stop his thrashing. His breathing was still labored, bubbling alarmingly in his lungs. The doctor straightened and backed away, shaking his head. Veronica took his place, pulling up a stool to sit on, laying one hand on the patient's arm. It was as cold and clammy as if he were already dead. She said softly, "I'm here, Valéry. I'll sit with you." There was no response.

"Nothing to be done," the doctor said gruffly. Veronica glanced up at him. He wasn't much older than his patient, and his face was drawn with weariness. "Keep him comfortable if you can. Pray for him."

He turned away and went to the far end of the room, where another soldier was groaning in pain. One of the nurses followed him, while the one in tears brought a chair to sit opposite Veronica. For a time they sat that way, waiting in silent misery as their patient's suffering dragged on and on. The nurse's tears dried, and she let her head fall forward onto her breast. Veronica could see she had fallen asleep. She thought she might do the same, inching her stool a little closer so she could lean against the bed.

It was Oona, once again, who interfered. The dog had scrambled under the bed, out of everyone's way. Now she crept to Veronica's foot and scratched at it with one paw.

Veronica glanced down. She had forgotten Oona was there.

Oona looked back at her, one ear up and one ear down, button eyes bright in the dimness.

Under her breath Veronica said, "What now?" and the dog scooted out from under the bed. She moved to the end of the bed and glanced back with an expectant air. Veronica muttered, "All right, Oona. I'm coming." She pushed herself up. The nurse opposite slept on, and Valéry, at least for the moment, did, too. It was likely he would die before she made it back to his bedside, but it was also clear he didn't know she was there.

She followed Oona, thinking now she would be going out onto the lawn, but the dog led her up the stairs and into her bedroom. Oona padded to the walnut wardrobe and glared fixedly at it, that expressive tail like an arrow behind her. "I don't know what you expect me to do," Veronica murmured.

Oona looked back at her, then again at the wardrobe, her tail vibrating. "You think I should bring out the stone, don't you?" Veronica sighed. "I don't know why. I have no idea how to use it."

The dog's hackles lifted, and she began to growl, a deep, menacing sound Veronica hadn't known she could make.

"Hush!" Veronica said. "You'll wake the house." Oona's growl went on, rising and falling, a sound too big for her small body. Veronica blew out a tired breath and surrendered. "Very well. I suppose at least I can try. Hush now, I'll do it. Hush, please."

Oona's growl fell to a grumble, then died away.

Remembering Jago's warning that she must never be caught, Veronica locked the door before she went to open the wardrobe. She knelt to reach far into the back, past dresses and coats and suits, to pull out the old Fortnum & Mason hamper.

It still frightened her to open the lid and fold back the wrappings. She had no idea what would happen, or if anything would. Breathing with exaggerated evenness to screw up her courage, she lifted the crystal out of the hamper and set it on her table. She had kept the vial of salt water in the hamper, and she sprinkled drops in a circle. She had no white candle, but she had a slender beeswax taper tucked into the drawer of her dressing table in case of a power cut. This she set into a holder and put a match to. In a saucer she also set fire to a twist of dried herbs, ones she had managed to decipher from the book she now knew was called a grimoire: *romarin*, rosemary; *sauge*, sage; *écorce de bouleau*, birch bark.

She didn't know if they were the right ones, but they were what she had. They filled the room with pungent smoke, making her eyes water and her nose sting.

Beyond the blackout curtains the moon had set, and dawn was still an hour away. The room was murky, lit only by the dancing flame of the taper. Veronica sank to her knees beside the table, as she had before, and extended her hands to the smooth top of the crystal. She felt as if she were feeling her way through an unknown landscape, blundering in the dark with nothing to guide her.

She stiffened and snatched her hands back. A light had begun to glimmer inside the stone the moment she touched it. Others joined it, whirling, touching, breaking apart like fireflies on a summer night. For a moment she gazed into the stone, confounded, with no idea of how to proceed. Oona whined.

At a loss, Veronica whispered, "Help me. Please. I don't know the words to say, or what I'm supposed to do. I need help."

Gooseflesh prickled her arms as a face emerged, a different one this time, younger, prettier. It coalesced from the shifting lights like a reflection steadying itself in the ripples of a pond. The woman seemed familiar, with dark curls over her forehead and eyes of midnight. She gazed at Veronica for a moment, her eyes searching, struggling to focus as if she, too, were peering through a cloud. A sense of longing radiated from her, distinct as a wisp of perfume.

Veronica pressed her hand to her breast. She recognized this face. This woman's portrait—the portrait of the mother she had never known—hung in the great hall.

She said, wonderingly, "Mama?"

She heard Morwen's answering voice, not through her ears, but *between* them.

Mother Goddess, hear my prayer:
No sorrow for my child to bear.

Take pity on one so young and fair.
Heal the man who is in her care.

Veronica said, "Oh!" and the words came again, the odd, old-fashioned rhyme. Veronica repeated them aloud, stumbling at first. Morwen, the spirit in the crystal, spoke them with her. Together they repeated the words, the simple, straightforward spell, over and over. Veronica lost count of how many times they said them. None of it felt real. She would not have been surprised to find herself starting awake in her bed, shedding the remnants of a bizarre dream.

It was not a dream. Her aching knees told her she was awake. Her burning eyes reminded her time was spinning past. By the time Morwen's face began to fade back among the whirling lights, the candle had burned to a nub. Nothing remained of the herbs but a mound of ash, and even their smoke had dispersed. The room felt empty, as if it had been crowded with people who all departed at once. Oona lay flat on her side. Veronica shivered with cold and fatigue, and with the memory of an ache deep in her body.

Stiffly she rose, covered the crystal, and restored it to its hamper. When it was safely hidden away in the wardrobe, she walked downstairs, trepidation warring with hope in her heart.

When she reached Valéry Chirac's bedside, she thought it must be finished at last. He lay utterly still. The rattle that had marked his breathing for hours had ceased. His face looked as if it were carved out of marble, the features clarified and exaggerated by illness. The sleeping nurse slumped in her chair, her head falling back, her mouth open.

Veronica touched Valéry's hand, and found it cool and dry. She pressed her palm to his forehead, and that was cool, too. His lips and nostrils, indeed, his entire face, was a healthy pink, and his breathing, she realized now, was not silent but light and steady, free of the rales that had so frightened them all. Veronica pulled a chair close to his bed, and for a long time, until the sun crept over the horizon and the makeshift ward began to stir, she sat gazing at the sleeping soldier, silently offering thanks for the craft that had saved him.

⁓⅊⁓

When Valéry opened his eyes after the long night, Veronica was still there. He whispered, *"Merci, mademoiselle. Merci beaucoup."*

"De rien." She smoothed his blankets and reached behind his head to plump his pillow.

He said, still in French, "I thought I would die."

She was too weary to judge her response. She blurted, "I thought so, too."

The young soldier said, his eyes drooping, "I will fight again. It's all that matters."

She wasn't sure she understood the words, but the meaning was clear, and it filled her with fear.

Perhaps it was because she was tired beyond belief. Or perhaps it was because she had seen her mother in the crystal, the mother she had longed for and mourned, and her emotions were raw. Whatever the reason, she felt an impulse to beg Valéry Chirac not to return to the war. It made no sense. He wanted to fight again, and she had no right to prevent him. She had no right to fear for him any more than she feared for any of the other soldiers in her care. It was as if her efforts to save him had created some sort of bond between them.

But Valéry Chirac would never know what she had done. He would never be aware that she regarded him differently from her other patients. She would make certain of it.

5

Wartime erased formality at Sweetbriar, and Veronica no longer believed the old customs would return. She and Lord Dafydd took all their meals in the morning room now, which was simpler for the staff. They gave up dressing for dinner. Veronica cropped her hair short for convenience. Breakfast was a spare meal, just coffee and toast, a boiled egg if one was available.

One morning in early December, she sat in silence across from her father, twisting her engagement ring and worrying. Phillip was flying sorties over Germany. They believed Thomas to be in France. Valéry would soon be well enough to fight.

A bomb had fallen on the Home Farm, destroying the old stone house and setting the wooden barn ablaze. When Veronica trembled at the thought that Jago might have been killed, Oona, lying beneath the table, tucked her little whiskered muzzle over her foot, and Veronica reached down to stroke her head in gratitude.

Lord Dafydd laid aside his newspaper. Veronica read the dour headline upside down: TERROR RAINS FROM THE SKY. "It's bad, isn't it, Papa?"

"Terrible," he answered. "I can't imagine celebrating Christmas with this going on."

"No." Veronica folded and refolded her napkin to stop herself from turning her ring. She frowned, looking at the lines of pain around her father's eyes and mouth. "I think you're suffering as much as our patients are."

"Nonsense!" He pushed back from the table and reached for his cane. "I'm going with Jago to the Home Farm, see if there's anything we can salvage."

"I'll go to the shops," Veronica said.

"Why can't Cook do that?"

"Papa! She's working night and day trying to feed the men, the staff, and us. She has trouble managing the ration books, too. I have to help her with that."

"Jago and I will have a look at the fields while we're down there, decide what to plant in the spring. Dig for Victory, and all that."

"No digging for you, Papa," Veronica said firmly. She was about to say more, but Honeychurch interrupted, coming in with the post on a silver tray.

Lord Dafydd leafed through it, tossing most of it aside. When he came upon one small cream-colored envelope he paused. He held it up between two fingers, giving his daughter a curious glance. "From Buckingham Palace. Were you expecting something?"

"No! Is it addressed to me?"

He handed it across to her. The return address was engraved, and the paper was thick and smooth. Her name was handwritten in elegant script: "Lady Veronica Selwyn, Second Drift, Sweetbriar, Stamford." The envelope was embossed with the royal seal.

Wondering, Veronica slid her thumb under the flap. The note was handwritten, too, in the same script, with strong capitals and disciplined lines:

Dear Lady Veronica,

We beg the pleasure of your company at Buckingham Palace on Tuesday, the 10th of December, at four o'clock, for a private talk. Please come. We will regard it as a personal favor.

Elizabeth Windsor

Veronica stared at it for long moments. Finally she breathed, "The queen wants to see me, Papa. Privately! What can that mean?"

"I have no idea. I suppose you'll have to go and find out."

"I think I must! But can you manage?"

"I have Honeychurch. And Jago."

"Perhaps Jago should move into the house."

"That's a good thought. I'll suggest it to him this morning. When are you off to London to visit the queen?"

"That sounds like a nursery song." Veronica smiled, distracted from her worries by the mystery. "Tuesday's the day, in the afternoon. I'll take the morning train."

"Take your gas mask."

She rose, smiling at him. "I will, dear Papa. I always do."

❧

Veronica, since her presentation, had seen Queen Elizabeth only from a distance. Her Majesty was always, it seemed, accompanied by various men and women looking serious and attentive. The Selwyns had no connection with the Windsors, and although Lord Dafydd served in the House of Lords, he had met the king only once or twice, and never the queen. Veronica didn't expect a "private talk" to be truly private. She expected at the very least a butler, or perhaps one of the ladies-in-waiting, certainly a maid to serve the tea.

In the event, she learned that Elizabeth had written precisely what she intended. A butler escorted Veronica up the stairs to a small parlor, where he left her alone. A maid appeared with a tea tray, then also disappeared. A moment later, hurrying in with a little clatter of high-heeled shoes, came Her Majesty.

Veronica leaped to her feet and curtsied. Elizabeth put out her hand—ungloved—to be shaken, and said with a smile, "Lady Veronica. Thank you so much for coming. I know how busy you and Lord Dafydd are with the convalescent hospital."

"Yes, ma'am," Veronica said. "Naturally, since you asked to speak to me, I wouldn't dream of refusing. It's an honor."

"Still, it's kind of you. We're all at sixes and sevens these days, aren't we?" Elizabeth, with a small sigh, sat on a brocaded divan, and waved Veronica to the matching one opposite. "This is something I couldn't write in a letter." She leaned to reach the tea service and poured out the tea with her own hand, saying absently, "Milk? Sugar?"

It had been months since Veronica had taken her tea with sugar. There simply wasn't enough of it, and she and her father saved what there was for the soldiers. She hesitated, and Elizabeth glanced up, a twinkle in her startlingly blue eyes. "It's all right," she said. "We're quite careful about rationing here at the palace, but we do indulge in a little bit of sugar. Please take some."

"I will then, thank you, ma'am."

When they both had their cups in hand, Elizabeth settled back and took a sip. "Ah. I needed my tea. It's been a trying day."

"You've been touring the bombed neighborhoods, I believe, ma'am."

"Yes. It's ghastly. So many people have lost their homes, and far too many their lives."

"I know. From Sweetbriar we can see the explosions, and last night a bomb fell on our Home Farm. The house was destroyed."

"No one injured, I hope?"

"No. Our staff there had already moved up to the house to help with the hospital."

Elizabeth nodded. "England is in peril."

"I fear so, ma'am."

"We have to do everything we can to help the war effort."

"Is there something more I could do, ma'am? You have only to ask—" She broke off at the expression on the sovereign's face. The bright blue eyes darkened. Elizabeth's round, pleasant face appeared to sharpen, her lips to thin. Her chin even jutted, just a bit.

Veronica froze with her teacup halfway to her lips. Her Majesty's face reminded her of the faces she had seen in the crystal, fading in and out of the light as they gazed back at her. She gulped and lowered the cup carefully, lest it slip from her suddenly chilled fingers.

The queen said, "You must have wondered why I wanted our talk to be private."

Veronica nodded.

"I have—let's call them friends—in some strange places, my dear. One of those places is a rather unusual bookshop on Museum Street. Atlantis Bookshop. I believe you know it."

Veronica's heart skipped a beat, and her next breath trembled in her throat.

"I see you understand me." Elizabeth, looking nothing at all like the smiling monarch the English public adored, set her teacup firmly into its saucer. She fixed Veronica with a gaze of blue steel. "I dare not say too much, Lady Veronica, in case I'm mistaken. I think, however, having been alerted by my friend in that bookshop, that you and I may have something in common."

"Ah—ma'am, I don't see—"

Elizabeth clicked her tongue. "We must save time. Let me put it this way," she said. Her eyes grew even darker, until they were nearly black. "Do you have a grimoire?"

Veronica, staring at her queen, felt a rush of gratitude so powerful it left her shaking. Someone knew! Someone else knew, and understood. She wasn't alone after all.

She said, in a voice rough with emotion, "Yes! Oh, ma'am, yes, I do!" Then, realizing suddenly that the queen had confessed to her just what she had been forbidden to reveal to anyone, she said, "Does that mean—ma'am, I hardly dare—that is, are you—"

The darkness of Elizabeth's gaze began to abate, and the habitual softness to return to her plump face. "Yes, Lady Veronica. I am."

"Oh, I can't believe it," Veronica cried softly, forgetting the formal mode of address. "I've always wondered—longed so much to meet someone else—"

"I'm sure you've felt terribly lonely."

"Truly, I thought everyone else—everyone like me—was dead."

"Happily, no." A faint twinkle softened Elizabeth's eyes. It was a relief to Veronica to see her looking like herself again. "I'm not entirely certain of your lineage, though I've heard of it. My own, of course, is known to everyone, for better or worse. I don't know if you understand how the craft is passed down."

"I know very little."

"Handed on mother to daughter, if at all. Not everyone inherits the power, but enough do that the craft survives, if the practitioners aren't discovered. We take a terrible risk."

"Still? But surely no one believes, in this day and age..."

"Let us pray we never find out." Elizabeth gave a delicate shrug. "One of my Glamis ancestresses was burned as a witch in Scotland, in 1537. Others have been suspected over the years. When I was a little girl, a gypsy walked up to my mama and me and announced, rather loudly, I'm afraid, that I would be a queen, and mother to a queen. It was obvious she recognized us for what we were. No doubt she was one herself."

"*Your* mama was a . . . ?"

"We will say the word, my dear, but very quietly. We need to understand each other perfectly." Elizabeth glanced at the door, which remained firmly closed. "Yes," she said. "My mama was a witch. I am one. Evidently so was your mama, and now you." She nodded toward Veronica. "I am of the Glamis line. Do you know yours?"

"Yes. My mother left instructions with someone she trusted. It's the Orchiére line."

"It's a great tragedy your mother didn't survive to teach you. I'm so very sorry. That's why you ordered the books, isn't it?"

"Yes, ma'am. There was little enough in them to help me, and I wouldn't have tried, except . . . well. There was a need."

"There always is." Elizabeth, returned now to the image of the gentle royal known to her people, picked up the teapot and poured fresh tea into her cup. She held the pot up in question, and Veronica nodded, holding out her cup so Elizabeth could refill it. "Never more need than now, I fear. The evil being visited upon our people is beyond anything I could ever have imagined. We need every one of our kind to come together to do what we can."

"There are others?"

"A few. It's so terribly dangerous to reveal ourselves. Can you imagine the effect on the monarchy if I was even suspected of such practices? They say enough about me as it is, and such exposure would make my life unbearable, and poor Bertie's. It could bring down the monarchy." She gave a delicate shudder. "It's unthinkable. And of course it makes it difficult for women like us to connect, one to the other."

"What do you wish me to do, ma'am?"

"Move to London, Veronica. Bring your grimoire and take a room with us, at Windsor Castle." Elizabeth gave her a narrow look. "You're not afraid of the bombs?"

"No, ma'am. I mean yes, of course I'm afraid, but then, isn't everyone?" Elizabeth nodded. "I have something else," Veronica added. The queen raised her brows. "I have a stone. A scrying stone. It was my mother's, and my grandmother's, and her grandmother's, very far back. Farther than I can trace."

"You can use it?"

"Yes. Yes, it seems I can."

"Then that," Elizabeth said, "is the best news I have heard in a long, long time."

⁓❧

"Her Majesty," Veronica said, using the words she and Elizabeth had decided on before she returned to Sweetbriar, "remembered me from my presentation. She needs someone she can trust to carry messages to the princesses."

"Surely she has staff for that sort of thing," Lord Dafydd said. He had met Veronica at the station, with Jago driving the Daimler. "Why does she need you?"

Veronica couldn't meet his eyes, and she felt Jago's attention as acutely as if he had stopped the car and turned around in the driver's seat to listen. "The royal family has the same problem we do, Papa. Many of their usual staff have gone to fight."

"But we Selwyns...the Windsors...This doesn't make sense."

Veronica managed a laugh. "Papa, I could take offense, you know! Queen Elizabeth *remembered* me. She *likes* me, and I'll be helping with the war effort."

"But London," Lord Dafydd said mournfully. "It's dangerous."

"It's dangerous everywhere, Papa. Even the princesses are working, you know."

"But where will you stay?"

Veronica took a deep breath and relaxed. It seemed there was to be no serious argument. "We'll work during the day mostly at Buckingham Palace, then go by car to Windsor Castle, where there will be a room set aside for me. I'm allowed to take Oona, also."

Her father took her gloved hand in his. "You must write me every day," he said.

"Of course." She leaned to kiss his cheek. "And you, too, Jago," she added. Without taking his eyes off the road, Jago touched his fingers to his cap.

⚶

Just before moving to the palace, Veronica went to see Phillip, who had a short leave. He was staying at the Strand Palace Hotel in London. She took the train down, and when he met her at Charing Cross, he looked authoritative and striking in his uniform, his hair very fair beneath his dark cap. She hugged him, and kissed him with enthusiasm, glad to be one of the throng of dashing officers and lovely young women. Phillip, as always, stood out from the crowd, tall, handsome, polished. She was proud of him, and proud to be seen with Squadron Leader Paxton.

They drank champagne that night, and danced in the club of the hotel until four in the morning. Everyone was giddy with the awareness of being young, of being alive when so many had died, of stealing a few precious hours from the terrors of war. The old rules of behavior were far from their minds.

When it was time to say good night, Veronica and Phillip embraced in the corridor outside her room. She whispered, "Come in with me, Phillip. Stay."

He stiffened and pulled away. "Veronica! You can't mean that. It wouldn't be—"

"Honorable," she finished for him, giving him a wry look.

"Exactly! I could never—I mean, Lord Dafydd—your father trusts me."

"Phillip, this war! Anything can happen. We should make the most of every moment!"

"I'm a gentleman, Veronica. You're a lady. We don't do things this way."

She let it pass. She knew Phillip and his ideals too well to be surprised, and as it happened, when she woke in the morning, alone and lonely in her single bed, she was grateful he had refused her impulsive gesture. There was risk there, as he had clearly understood. What he didn't know was that she had work to do, important work with her queen. It would be foolish to let anything interfere.

❧

The night before she left for London she went through the hall saying good-bye to the nurses, the doctors, and a few of the patients who had been there for a long time. She found Valéry Chirac on his feet, leaning on a cane, but dressed in a shirt and trousers instead of hospital wear. "Valéry," she said, putting out her hand. "I understand you're moving up to the dormitory."

He shook her hand and gave a courtly little bow over it. "I am if I can manage the stairs," he said. "It is a miracle, is it not?"

"It does seem that way."

The change in him did seem miraculous. He had gained weight, though he was still lean. He was taller than she was, which she hadn't known before, and his hair had grown back, black and thick and straight. Almost the only things she recognized were his dark eyes and long-fingered hands. His face still bore the marks of the suffering he had endured, and, she feared, grief.

In these days of so much death and loss, she supposed there was nothing to be gained by avoiding the topic. "I mailed your letter, Valéry. I don't suppose you've had a response."

He shook his head as he released her hand, and turned to folding his few belongings into a canvas bag. Veronica recognized the bag as one that had belonged to a British officer, one who had not survived his injuries. They kept a little hoard of such things in a storeroom, putting them to good use when they could.

Valéry pulled the drawstrings and tied them before he answered. "I thank you very much for your efforts, *mademoiselle*, but there will be no reply."

"Why do you say that?"

His voice was hard. "The news from Drancy is very bad, many deaths, little food. And—" He turned his head away and said softly, "You may not believe, but I dreamed of my mother, and she told me. She did not live long in that place."

"Of course I believe you," Veronica said. A girl who saw faces in crystals could hardly deny the power of a dream. "I'm so sorry."

He lifted the bag and slung it over his shoulder. "They came to the school," he said. "They asked which ones were Jews, and which were Gypsies, and then they took them, tiny children screaming for their parents."

"That's unspeakable."

"The dead are the lucky ones at this time, I think."

"What a terribly sad thought."

"I am sorry to say I am without hope, *mademoiselle*."

"We have to find something to hope for, don't we?"

"I hope only for revenge."

"There has to be more than that," she said. "I was thinking of the miracle of Valéry Chirac getting well." She put out her hand to him and offered a tentative smile.

He took her hand, and though he didn't quite smile, his expression lightened enough to show her the handsome man he must have been before war stole his youth.

Her youth had been stolen, too, she thought, as they shook hands and said their good-byes. In a different time, she and this intense man might have been friends. Might have been more.

As she left the hall, she twisted and twisted her heavy engagement ring.

6

"First," Queen Elizabeth said, as she poured tea for Veronica, "we will take a few days to establish your position here." She twinkled at her as she added three lumps of sugar. "The princesses are coming to meet you in a few minutes."

"Do they know, ma'am, what I—what we—are?"

Elizabeth shook her head. "I don't see any evidence that either of them has inherited my gift, I'm afraid. It could still happen, especially for Margaret, but all too often it doesn't. I fear modern life depresses the power, diverts it."

"Are there any others of your line?" Veronica accepted her tea-cup, amazed that these were her sovereign's fingers grazing hers, as if she were any usual hostess. "Your sisters, perhaps?"

"Only one. Mary Frances, Lady Elphinstone." Elizabeth sipped her tea calmly, but Veronica saw the telltale darkening of her famous eyes. "She has a bit of a gift for simples. When we were children, she used to do something with sugar water so that birds would sit on her hand." She shrugged. "It wasn't much. I have hope for her daughters, but of course, I can't ask."

"Your mother taught you, then."

"Yes, thank goodness. I can't imagine what it's been like for you, Veronica." She smiled. "But my friends and I will see to it that you learn what you need to know."

"Friends?"

"You'll meet them soon. You left the stone at home?"

"Yes, as you suggested."

"I think it's best. There are so many servants here. We wouldn't want anyone to discover it in your room and have questions. We will establish you first as my special assistant, and prepare for the work ahead. For now—" She glanced up as a discreet knock sounded at the door. "Ah. My daughters."

Veronica jumped to her feet and curtsied to each of the princesses as she was introduced. The two of them could hardly have been more different from one another. Princess Elizabeth seemed already somber with the weight of the responsibility that would one day fall on her slight shoulders. Princess Margaret was gay and voluble, even now, discussing the responsibilities of the royal family in wartime.

"Lady Veronica will be my personal courier to the two of you," Queen Elizabeth said.

"How kind," was Princess Elizabeth's comment, with a nod to Veronica.

"What fun!" exclaimed Princess Margaret. "Are you allowed to drive? Perhaps we could take a spin one day. And is this your dog?" She crouched to stroke Oona, who lay beside Veronica's chair. Oona responded with a thorough face licking.

Veronica smiled at the younger girl's enthusiasm. Margaret was only twelve, and though she was second in line to the throne, that apparently did not concern her. She chattered throughout the tea, winning indulgent glances from her mother and a forbearing expression from Princess Elizabeth.

For a week Veronica and the queen kept up the fiction that she had come from Sweetbriar to be Elizabeth's courier and companion in troubled times. She worked at the palace during the day and rode home to the castle at night, where she had been given a private room with an en suite bath. She was comfortable there, but achingly lonely. She missed her father, and Jago, and Mouse. And, of course, Phillip and Thomas. She worried over them both. Whenever a messenger appeared, which was often in the palace, her shoulders hunched with tension, and didn't release until she knew the message was not for her.

She dreamed once of Thomas, a dark dream in which he was cold and frightened and hungry. She woke feeling fearful and restive.

She dreamed of Phillip, too, a dream of memory. Thomas was in the dream, too. They were all young, the three of them playing croquet on the lawn of Sweetbriar, laughing, teasing each other, running in the sunshine. It wasn't the romantic dream of an engaged girl. It was the dream of a lonely and anxious one.

She told herself it would be sorted out, in time. When she was less worried, less frightened, she would feel what she was supposed to feel. She would be able to look forward, instead of back to easier days. She would feel desire as well as affection, would be excited over becoming a bride, would be enthusiastic about her future as Lady Paxton.

In the meantime there was the war to fight.

At the beginning of her second week in London, the queen herself knocked on her bedroom door, at an hour when Veronica was already in her dressing gown. Veronica opened it and hastily curtsied.

Pleasantly, as if it were the middle of the day instead of the middle of the night, Elizabeth said, "Could you dress, dear? My friends are here. Oh, and do wear something warm."

Veronica dressed hurriedly in a skirt and a heavy sweater, then followed the queen down three flights of stairs to a narrow basement corridor. In a small room, which Elizabeth opened with a key she drew from beneath her dress, two elderly women waited. They were both shrouded in long coats and wearing thick-soled shoes with old-fashioned black stockings. Neither, Veronica noticed, curtsied, though they both inclined their heads to Elizabeth.

The queen locked the door from the inside, and used only given names as she presented the two to Veronica.

One, a wrinkled woman called Rose, was tiny, with a small, foxy sort of face, and thin, perpetually pursed lips. She greeted Veronica with a nod of acknowledgment.

The other woman, named Olive, was tall, lean, and leathery, with a deep voice and a trick of holding her head very high and looking down her long nose at whomever she was speaking to, even Elizabeth.

Olive and Rose were the witches of Queen Elizabeth's coven.

Olive showed little sympathy when Elizabeth explained that Veronica was an apprentice, and that her mother had died in childbirth. "No grandmother?" Olive demanded in her rough baritone.

"I never knew her."

"Shame. Always better to learn from your own line. Still, better late than never."

"Yes, Miss—Mrs.—I apologize. I don't know how to address you."

"Olive will do. The less we know about one another, the safer we are."

Rose, in a high, creaky voice that reminded Veronica of a hinge in need of oiling, pointed to Oona, who was pressed close to Veronica's calf. "Familiar?"

"What?"

"Your spirit familiar."

Olive said, "We all wish for one, you know."

"I don't know if that's what she is."

Olive emitted an impressive sniff drawn through her long nose. "Yes, you do. Foolish to deny it."

Veronica almost laughed aloud. She was unused to being called foolish by anyone, much less a woman clearly of lower rank than herself. She was prepared to dislike this tall, mannish woman. She soon changed her mind.

Olive and Rose had been practitioners for decades. The vocabulary and techniques of the craft seemed to come as naturally to them as walking did to Veronica. Olive, despite her abrupt manner and evident lack of sympathy, took it upon herself to become Veronica's instructor.

There was a great deal to learn. Olive explained each detail of the rites as they worked.

"We use a new candle to prevent contamination by any earlier intention," she said. "Salt water is for protection, because salt is necessary to our survival, and is therefore strengthening. It's important. We make ourselves vulnerable to evil elements when we cast."

She made a gift to Veronica of a white silk scarf to drape over her head. "It has no practical meaning, but tradition is part of the craft," she told her. "In another place, at another time, we could go sky-clad, but—"

"What's sky-clad?"

"Naked."

"Oh."

"Yes, that practice goes back a long way. To quote Leland:

And ye shall all be freed from slavery,
And so ye shall be free in everything;
And as the sign that ye are truly free,
Ye shall be naked in your rites."

"Bit silly, really," Rose said in her creaking little voice.

"Why?" Olive snapped.

"Cold."

Olive repeated, with a bite in her voice, "*Tradition*, Rose." Rose pursed her wrinkled lips even tighter and didn't answer. Veronica suspected it was an old argument.

It was all a bit like being back at school. Veronica sometimes felt as if her head would burst with the information Olive poured into it, expecting her to remember everything, but she welcomed the intensity. When she had free time, she pored over the grimoire in her room, trying to understand its secrets. On the days when there was no coven, she ran errands for Elizabeth, sometimes accompanying the younger princess to the park with Oona bounding alongside, or carrying private correspondence to the elder princess, who was learning to repair motors as a member of the Auxiliary Territorial Service.

She was so busy, at all hours of the day and night, that she lost track of how long she had been in London. She wrote her father often, as she had promised, but she had to make up stories about lovely luncheons with the princesses, tea with the queen, outings to libraries or museums. She was shocked to realize, one morning, that she had been away from Sweetbriar nearly two months.

It was another dream that reminded her. It had been weeks since she dreamed. She had been, she thought, too tired, and too distracted by all that was happening. But this dream—this dream was so real, so vivid, that it was as if it had actually happened.

She dreamed of Valéry Chirac, in the brown uniform of a French soldier, holding a fearsome-looking rifle with a bayonet attached to it. In her dream they were saying good-bye, not as a nurse and her patient, but as sweethearts, with kisses and a lingering embrace. She woke with tears on her face, and an ache of parting in her chest. But not, she realized with shame, a parting from her fiancè. She hadn't seen Phillip in weeks, yet it was a Frenchman she barely knew who made her cry in her sleep.

It was the bloody war, she thought. Or the bombs. Or even just the strangeness of being away from home, lonely despite the people around her. She reminded herself how grateful she was to have found others like her, to be doing good work, to be able to serve her queen. She showered and dressed in haste, and refused to think of the dream again.

She was breakfasting alone in a small dining room of the castle when the queen appeared. Veronica jumped to her feet and curtsied. "Ma'am?" They had had a very late night in their basement room, and she had expected the monarch to have a lie-in.

"Yes," Elizabeth said, with a distracted air. "Something's come up. The king will need me today, and tomorrow as well—the rest of the week, in fact. He has a terrible cough, and I'm going out to Sandringham with him, try to get him to rest."

"Yes, ma'am," Veronica said. "What would you like me to do?"

"Get word to Rose and Olive—you know where they live, don't you?"

"Yes, ma'am."

"Drive yourself. No one must know." Elizabeth ran a hand over her face, and had she not been the queen, Veronica would have gone to her, patted her shoulder, tried to offer words to ease her anxiety. But she was the queen, and such an action was impossible.

"Anything else, ma'am?" she asked quietly.

Elizabeth gave her a sad smile. "Go home for a few days, Veronica. You've worked hard. Your father will be glad, and a rest will be good for you, too."

❧

Veronica set out on the train that very afternoon, happy to be on her way home, even briefly. Jago met her at the station, giving her a broader smile than was his custom. Despite his objections she put Oona in the back seat and sat beside him in the front. She savored the familiar sights of the lanes leading to Sweetbriar, and the chance to talk to Jago. "How is Papa?"

"Well enough, I think," Jago said. "I can't help him with his pain the way you do."

"I know. I worry about that. But you've been able to manage the rest of it?"

"In my way," he said. "Not as well as you do."

"Mouse?"

"Mouse will be happy to see you. He could use a gallop."

"As soon as possible! Ynyr?"

"Much the same."

She found things just as she had left them, in the private rooms of Sweetbriar and those of the hospital. She toured them with her father, and then left him resting in the morning room with his tea as she went out to the stables to see Mouse. Oona was overjoyed at being in the country once again, and dashed here and there, barking at squirrels and birds.

Veronica stood in Mouse's stall, letting him nibble a carrot from her palm. She rested her cheek against his mane to breathe in the comforting and comfortable scent of horse.

"He's a beauty," came a deep voice from the door of the stables.

Veronica gave a little start, and Oona, who had been nosing in the corner of the stables in search of mice, lifted her head. "Valéry!"

"Lady *Véronique*," he said. She smiled at the sound of her name in French, and at the color in Valéry's lean cheeks, the fullness of his hair brushing his forehead. He leaned on his cane as he walked toward her, but lightly. He said, "You have come home."

"There was a break in my—in my work," she said, giving Mouse a last pat and stepping out through the stall door. "You look well."

"Well enough. I leave in three days."

Veronica paused, one hand still on the stall door. Oona trotted toward her, sensing a change as Veronica's dream came rushing back to her.

Valéry said, "Are you all right? You look tired."

"I'm fine," she said, but her hand trembled a little as she put it out to shake his. His skin was warm and smooth, and the fineness of his fingers sent a thrill up her arm. He wore a thin gold ring on the little finger of his right hand, and she felt the scratch of its pale stone—a peridot, perhaps—against her palm. "Where are you going when you leave?"

"Somewhere I can fight," he said.

"Yes." She withdrew her hand, but slowly. He seemed equally reluctant to relinquish the contact. They gazed at each other for a moment, and though neither moved, something flashed between them, unspoken but intense. Veronica felt her engagement ring drag at her left hand. Hardly knowing she did it, she hid her hand in her pocket.

"And you?" he said. "How long do you stay?"

Her heart began to thud so loudly she thought he must hear it. She said, "The same. Three days."

"How fortunate we are to see each other one more time, then."

She breathed, "Yes."

He broke the moment by smiling. The expression took years from his face. "I am sorry," he said. "I should have told you how lovely you look in your city clothes. My manners have left me."

"Oh no!" she laughed. "Wartime manners follow different rules."

"Perhaps." He offered his elbow. "But let me escort you back to the house."

She took his arm and tried to resist the *frisson* it gave her to walk with him, their shoulders touching, back over the lawn to the house. They parted at the hall, Veronica for tea with Lord Dafydd, Valéry to assist in repairing a broken wheelchair.

She promised herself, as she made her way toward the morning room, that she wouldn't think of him again. Probably, she told herself, he wasn't thinking of her at all.

~❧~

Her three days passed all too swiftly. She spent them mostly doing small things for her father. Jago had the other tasks of the household more or less in hand, with Honeychurch to help. She conferred with Cook, and was pleased at how she had managed on her own, with Jago to run to the shops for her. She rode Mouse down to the Home Farm, with Oona trotting alongside. The destruction there made her heart sink. She feared it would never be rebuilt, that old house where she and Thomas had enjoyed so many pleasant afternoons. Thinking of it made her miss her brother with a physical pain.

She saw Valéry occasionally, but at a distance. She smiled at him, but made no effort to speak privately. The hospital beds were full. The work seemed to grow heavier each day. Veronica promised she would speak to the queen about more help when she returned to London, but while she was at Sweetbriar, she threw herself into the effort alongside everyone else.

On the night before her final day, she dreamed of Valéry again, the same dream of parting, of embraces and tears, with the same pain upon waking. Early in the morning, hoping to shake it off, she set out for the park with Oona. They had just reached the protection of the trees when she saw Valéry step out of the hall and onto the terrace.

Veronica stumbled to a halt. Valéry was wearing the exact uniform she had dreamed of.

He lifted his head and caught sight of her beneath the branches of an ancient yew tree. He gazed at her for a long, still moment, then started toward her. His cane was gone. The uniform was crisp and clean. Her heart thumped as she stood where she was. She wasn't capable, she thought, of moving.

When he reached her, Valéry seized her hand. "I dreamed of you," he said.

Without thinking, she breathed, "And I of you." There was a weakness in her belly. Her lips parted as she gazed at him. "You found a uniform," she said in French. It felt more intimate, somehow daring, though she suspected her accent was atrocious.

"*Oui*," he said. "It belonged to someone else, but he has no further need of it."

She knew what that meant, and she saw, now that he was close, that there were carefully mended tears in the jacket. "Be careful, Valéry. Promise me."

"I'll try."

They had forgotten, somehow, to unclasp their hands. Veronica looked down at their entwined fingers. She knew they were standing too close for propriety, but she couldn't bring herself to move away. The warmth of his body met her own warmth, and the beat of his heart synchronized with hers.

She didn't stop to think. In fact, she didn't think at all. She tipped up her chin.

He pressed his mouth to hers, lightly at first, as if unsure of his welcome, then more and more firmly, pulling her to him until the two of them were wrapped in each other's arms, lost in the yearning power of a long, sweet, impossible kiss.

Even as they drew apart, remembering who they were and where, their lips clung until the last possible instant.

"Valéry," she began, but stopped. What could she say? She wanted to throw herself back into his arms. The war, her engagement, a dozen obstacles loomed, but it was very, very hard to think of them at that moment.

"*Véronique, je suis désolé—*"

"Don't!" she whispered through an aching throat. "Don't be sorry. I'm not! I could never be sorry."

"It's not fair to your fiancé." Misery dragged at Valéry's eyes and mouth. "He's off fighting, and I'm here with you."

"But you're going to fight, too."

"I must." He caught up her hand again, and pressed her fingers to his lips, to his cheek. "*Je t'aime, Véronique,*" he said, very low. "*Toujours, je t'aime.*"

"*Moi aussi,*" she murmured. She might have said more, but voices sounded, approaching from the drive. Abruptly she pulled away her hand, turned, and hurried away into the park, Oona trotting behind.

Veronica's pleasure in her sojourn at home dissipated that morning. The day labored on, and though she tried to make the most of it—a last visit to Mouse, a private chat with Jago, luncheon and tea with her father—there was a persistent ache beneath her breastbone. "All right, you?" Jago asked, and she had to pretend that all was as it had been.

Was this love? If it was, she wasn't sure she liked it.

The day dragged to an end at last. She didn't see Valéry again, which was probably for the best. After dinner she hugged her father, made arrangements with Jago to be taken to the station in the morning, and climbed the stairs to her bedroom.

Once she had changed into a nightgown, she turned off her light and pulled back the blackout curtains before she climbed into bed. There she lay awake, listening to the distant thuds of the bombs dropping on London, watching antiaircraft fire glitter in the night sky. Her body would not let her rest.

She hungered to touch someone, to be touched. She wanted

Valéry. Amid the death and destruction and fear, the deprivation and worry, there was something warm, something hopeful. It seemed bitterly unfair to let it slip away.

She tried to think of Phillip, but it did no good. It was Valéry's face that haunted her, Valéry's deep voice, even the grim determination in his eyes. He was here, in the house, on the floor just above her. She would in all likelihood never see him again. The waste of this moment was more than she could bear.

In the dark she rose and pulled the Fortnum & Mason hamper from her wardrobe. She didn't bother with a candle, or salted water, or herbs. She unwrapped the crystal, set it directly on the floor, and knelt over it.

Oona watched from her basket, her eyes glowing in the darkness, as Veronica passed her hands over the stone. The others had helped her in the past, her forebears, wielding their power on her behalf. This time she would have to manage alone. If the power of her need was not enough, then it was never meant to be.

The words came to her in a rush. She didn't know their source. She didn't pause to think about them, or edit them in any way. She spoke them with her hands on the crystal, her gaze focused on its smoky depths.

Mother Goddess, hear my plea:
Bring my one true love to me.
Caution and fear forgotten be
Heart to heart in ecstasy.

The stone began to glow, lighting the dark room. Sparks flittered through it, randomly at first, then spinning closer and closer together until they gathered into a pulsing center, bright within bright. Veronica gazed into it, her heart fluttering. When his faint knock sounded on her door, the light dimmed and disappeared as if it had been waiting for the signal.

Veronica covered the crystal and rose from her knees. She thrust the stone back into her wardrobe, then, still in her night-gown, she hurried to open the door.

7

When Veronica returned to London, the queen was waiting at the palace. She met Veronica in her private parlor. Veronica thought she looked preoccupied, but Elizabeth gave her a gentle smile. "Good, Lady Veronica. You're back. You brought the stone?"

"Yes, ma'am." Veronica had her valise with her, and the stone buried beneath two sweaters and a chemise.

The queen said, "Excellent. Let us take it straight down. It will be safe there. No one has a key to that room except myself."

They settled the crystal in the very center of the altar, hidden beneath its silk coverings. Elizabeth locked the door as they left, and rattled the handle to make certain. "They're coming tonight," she said. "Go and have a rest. Eat something. I'll come for you when I can."

Something had changed in the queen. Veronica suspected it, but was certain when Elizabeth came for her at midnight. There was tension in every line of her small body, and she walked quickly, as if in a hurry to begin their work.

The coven met in the basement hallway, and Elizabeth unlocked the door to their room without saying a word. When they were inside, and the dim light was burning, she said, "Veronica has brought her scrying stone."

"Oh, how lovely," Rose said vaguely.

Olive said nothing, but strode to the altar and whipped off the silk wrappings of the crystal. She grunted, a sound that might have indicated approval. In her gravelly baritone she demanded, "Whose was it?"

"I don't know," Veronica said. "I believe it's very old."

"It's magnificent." Olive gestured to the stone, asking permission. Veronica nodded, and Olive said, "Thank you," before she spread her leathery fingers above the crystal. She closed her eyes and whispered a phrase of command.

The air in the dank basement room began to crackle with energy, stirring the hairs on Veronica's arms. Elizabeth and Rose gasped and moved closer to the altar, eager to be part of the magic. The light in the stone grew swiftly, a steady glow that brightened the room, illuminated Rose's wrinkled cheeks, glowed on Elizabeth's round ones. Veronica pressed her fingers to her lips in wonder.

Olive opened her eyes, and her deep voice rumbled in the small room.

"Show us the Orchiére witches."

Veronica barely breathed as she watched her own stone respond to the other witch's power. Before, the faces had tumbled pell-mell through coruscating lights. Now they came and went in measured fashion. Each appeared out of the glistening mist, paused long enough for Veronica to make out its features, to know she would recognize it when she saw it again, then faded to make way for the next. Veronica's heart quivered as she watched the parade of faces, of dark hair and eyes, smooth cheeks and wrinkled ones, all of them her ancestresses, mothers and grandmothers and great-grandmothers, a line that stretched beyond memory. At length the procession ended with a face she knew.

"Mama," Veronica breathed.

"Is that Morwen?" Olive said.

"Yes."

"Hmm. Good." Olive lifted her hands from the stone, and the light glimmered and died.

"How did you know my mother's name?"

"Didn't know for sure. There were stories, but we feared your line was at an end."

"Oh." Veronica sighed. "Oh, Olive. You must teach me how to do that."

"What I'm here for," the older witch growled. "That, and a war to win."

Veronica thought they had worked hard before, but now their labors intensified to a level she couldn't have imagined. She marveled at how disciplined the older women were, how staunch their efforts. The coven met almost every night, holding their rites around the makeshift altar in the basement room, and drawing upon every tradition the four witches understood. They invoked the Goddess. They called upon their ancestresses. They implored the forgotten gods of the British Isles, Andraste and Mabon and Britannia herself, names Veronica barely recognized. Each of the women composed spells derived from her personal grimoire, and recited them as they swayed amid fragrant smoke and flickering candlelight. Oona lurked in a corner, her dark eyes glistening in the gloom, her ears following the women's voices.

Olive taught Veronica that her ancestresses were connected to the stone, that they had developed its resonance over the centuries, creating a portal to their descendants, the women of their line who would practice the craft after them. She showed Veronica how to concentrate, and trained her to listen with her mind's ear. She explained that the craft was both a tool and a practice, a religion of sorts, though without the dogma attached to most organized faiths. She taught her how to wield her power to influence fate, and to accept failure when it came.

Olive also brought books to warn her of the peril of exposure. They were awful books, badly written and with hideous illustrations, all meant to point out the evils of witchcraft. They were full of stories of women, and sometimes men, being burned on the slightest pretext. Most of the victims, Olive said, were probably not witches at all. Many were herbalists, whose simple remedies frightened the ignorant. "They're afraid of us, Veronica. Never forget that. They're afraid, and that makes them dangerous."

"Why should they be afraid?" Veronica asked.

"Think about what the craft can do. Women like us heal illnesses doctors can't, and though I don't recommend it, we can cause illnesses, too. We can hide ourselves when we don't want to be seen. We can change the weather, or change a man's mind. We live our lives the way we want. We don't need men to take care of us, which many men, and some women, too, think is unnatural. They find it terrifying." She looked up from her task of brushing ash from the altar. An enigmatic smile eased the lines of her long face as she added, with satisfaction, "As they should."

They studied the war reports in the daytime, and made their petitions at night in response. At first Veronica was not sure they were having any effect, but she began to understand, over time, that what they did in that cold basement room had real power. The challenge was in knowing what to ask for.

They knew the German bombers were coming, a wave of airplanes escorted by fighters. "Bring down the leader," Olive demanded. The candlelight accented the lines of her face, making her look like one of the elderly gods they called upon.

Olive never bothered with rhymes. Her only rule was to pronounce what she wanted three times three times. No one could argue with her method. Her power was made clear when the first of the enemy bombers caught a round of antiaircraft fire and crashed into the sea before it could reach its target.

A giant bomb fell on Bristol, but didn't detonate. Such bombs were particularly dangerous because they could explode at any time. Rose discovered the Germans had named the thing Satan, painting the word on its gray fuselage. She composed a spell of avoidance, and the witches spent most of one night working it to prevent the bomb from blowing up. They succeeded. It never did explode, and the bomb with the name of Satan became a public symbol of German failure and English determination. For the witches it was a sign of hope.

They invoked protection for cities, for naval vessels, for airplanes. They begged inspiration for the code breakers, and summoned good weather for the convoys. They were unlikely warriors engaged in a secret battle, and they fought with every weapon and talent they had. Occasionally a neighborhood was destroyed despite their efforts to divert the bombs. Too often a battle was lost no matter how hard they worked to disrupt the enemy's plans. Such failures were heartbreaking, but they persevered. Like those on the battle lines, they could not give up.

It all left Veronica very little time to think of herself, to miss her home, her father, Jago, and Mouse. Most importantly, she had little time to yearn for Valéry.

She had relived their night together a hundred times. For days afterward she'd felt a new magic in her body, an ancient power she had never been aware of. It had lain dormant, she thought, now roused from its slumber by Valéry's kisses, by the sweetness of his breath against her cheek, his mouth on her breast, his hands beneath her thighs, hard, demanding, thrilling.

She couldn't hold back her tears at their last embrace. It was exactly as she had dreamed it. As she watched him walk away from her, off to whatever fate awaited him, she felt as if something had been ripped out of her chest, a fragment of her heart that could never be replaced.

At the last moment, as their lips and arms and, finally, their hands had released each other, Valéry had pressed something small and cool into her palm. She curled her fingers around it, and he kissed her closed fist before he strode away down the corridor. He didn't glance back.

She had closed her door and rested her forehead against the cold wood for long minutes before she opened her hand to see what he had given her. It was the ring, the slim gold band with the small greenish stone he had worn on the little finger of his right hand. She pressed it to her heart for a moment, then straightened, set her jaw, and went to pack for London.

From London she set herself to write more often to Phillip. As she did in her letters to her father, she composed cheerful notes to Phillip about happy times with the queen and her staff, of the princesses devoting themselves to the war effort, of the courage and optimism of the Londoners.

The truth was quite different. The people of London, though certainly courageous, were not so much optimistic as resigned. Princess Elizabeth seemed to enjoy her work as a mechanic, but Princess Margaret chafed at the restrictions of wartime, begging to go shopping, to go riding, to go to parties. Queen Elizabeth, though she smiled and waved, and made brave little speeches whenever she went out, was soberly realistic when she was out of public view.

Veronica barely noticed the calendar other than to note dates associated with military actions. Rising late on a cold, drizzly morning in March, she thought her fatigue must be the result of so many nights spent with the coven. Certainly the queen was looking weary, and her own eyes looked hollow when she glanced in the mirror. She felt a little queasy, as well, and she wondered if she had somehow contracted flu. She ran a warm bath, hoping it would restore her.

As she lay in the tub she looked down at herself, and a chill gripped her despite the warmth of the water. She sat upright, staring at her altered silhouette. She couldn't have gained weight. No one could, living in London on rations. They were meticulous, even in the palace, about rations. Her arms had grown so thin she never wore sleeveless dresses. Her ankles looked as fragile as a foal's. But there was no denying what she saw as she gazed, horrified, at her body. Her stomach curved outward, delicately, but definitely, a graceful and damning convexity beneath her ribs.

She began to shiver. It couldn't be true. It couldn't be happening. She pressed her wet hands to her face, covering her eyes, as if by not seeing the evidence she could change the reality.

She knew, even behind the shelter of her palms, that the terrible fact was not so easily wished away. Countless girls had no doubt felt just as she was feeling, terrified, trapped, aghast at what had happened and what it meant. They, like her, had had to face the truth.

She dropped her hands to look at herself again. Desperation shook her. It was unfair! She had spent all her energy on her work with the coven, on learning what she needed to know, on fighting her hidden war. Her preoccupation had made her oblivious.

She felt suddenly both hot and cold, as if she really did have flu. Her hands began to tremble, and she climbed out of the bath with exaggerated care, fearing her knees might buckle.

Her father would die of shame. Phillip would be terribly hurt. Valéry would never know. Perhaps worst of all, she had betrayed her queen at a time when she was needed.

This couldn't continue. She would have to take action.

Lady Veronica Selwyn, daughter of Lord Dafydd Selwyn, assistant to Queen Elizabeth and engaged to an RAF officer she had not seen in months, could not be pregnant.

❧

Deciphering the venerable French of the grimoire had gotten easier with practice. Veronica had gone all through her French textbook again in order to converse with Valéry, and she had spent hours in search of the protection and disruption and distraction spells needed for her work with the coven. She took the grimoire out again and began to turn the crackling pages, scanning the faded texts and drawings for what she would need.

She found it with astonishing ease. She could guess that the book had been opened to this particular page many times before. At the top, in a spidery hand, was the title *La fausse couche*. The list of herbs was long, but Elizabeth had ordered an entire apothecary's shop of herbs to be stored on shelves next to their basement room. With a small torch in her hand, Veronica slipped down the back stairs and made her way to them.

Raspberry leaf was easy. Cinnamon, too. Black cohosh was an herb she had never encountered, but with the help of the torch, she found a packet of it at the back of a shelf, still with its Canadian source label attached. Pennyroyal, tansy, kelp—they were all there. Cautiously she slipped a bit of each into a sack and tied it around her waist, beneath her dress in case she encountered one of the servants.

Oona watched her every move as she mixed her potion on the low parquet table in her bedroom. When she began to measure out leaves of tansy from her sack, the dog began to whine, and to lick her chops.

"Don't fret, Oona," Veronica said, without pausing in her work. "I know it's dangerous."

She ground the tansy leaves in a mortar and pestle, and crumbled pennyroyal into the mixture. Oona shifted on her hindquarters, giving little groans of anxiety. "Oona, quiet," Veronica pleaded. "We don't want anyone coming in to see what's wrong with you."

The dog subsided, though she still looked unhappy. She shook herself once, then lay down with her head on her paws so her gaze could follow Veronica's every movement.

As she lit her candle, sprinkled water, then passed her hands over the crystal, Veronica refused to allow herself to think about what she was doing. She could not afford to feel regret, or sadness, or shame. She didn't dare. She had a job to do. Her feelings didn't matter. Her path was clear, though it was tragic. It was an act of war.

She placed the cup of her potion on the table next to the crystal, and proclaimed the words of the necessary spell.

Mother Goddess, hear my plea:
Touch these fruits of land and sea.
Root and leaf full blessèd be,
And from this burden set me free.

Three times three times she repeated the chant. When the rite was completed, she blew out the candle, covered the crystal, and picked up the cup. In the darkness she put it to her lips. She gagged at the taste, but she choked it down, and pressed her hand over her mouth in hopes it wouldn't come back up. Oona sprang up and pressed against her ankles, whimpering and licking at her shoes with anxious laps of her pink tongue.

By the time Veronica heard the maids beginning their morning work in the corridor outside her room, the cramping had begun,

the mockery of labor. Oona was making circles around her, whining. Veronica lay down, still in her clothes, and pulled a quilt over
her legs. Oona jumped up onto the bed next to her and lay licking
her hand, whimpering when she whimpered, groaning when she
groaned. A maid knocked on the door, but Veronica called out that
she wasn't feeling well. When the maid asked if she needed a doctor, Veronica answered that she just needed to rest. The maid went
away, and Oona pressed her small body closer and closer, as if she
could share Veronica's pain, absorb some of the misery into herself.

At the worst moments Veronica clung to the dog, gripping her
muscular little body with her hands and pressing her forehead to
Oona's flank. Oona twisted her head to lick her face. It was an
odd sort of comfort, but it was all there was. For hours the two
of them lay on the bed together. When the pains in her body
peaked, Veronica staggered to the bathroom. Oona followed,
never leaving her side.

Not until it was all over, and Veronica had bathed and put on a
fresh frock, did Oona trot down the stairs to go out into the back
garden. Veronica followed more slowly, her body sore and aching. Two gardeners watched her with curiosity, but they didn't
approach her. She sat on a set of stone steps that wound through
the shrubbery, holding her overheated face up to the cool sunshine. Only then did she allow herself to contemplate the gravity
and the import of what had just happened. Of what she had done.

She had committed a sin, she supposed. Indeed, a great deal of
what she had done in the past months might be considered a sin.
Fornication. Deception. Witchcraft. Now abortion.

A cloud settled over her soul, dark with implication, thick
with guilt. She shivered under its shadow, and wondered how she
would find the strength to go forward. For a long time she sat
there, hugging a sweater around her tender body and trying to
discern her way.

She didn't rouse herself until Oona nudged at her ankles, asking for food. Veronica expelled a breath. Moving gingerly, her belly hurting and her head buzzing with exhaustion, she came to her feet. This was a time for discipline.

What had happened was bad, but the world at this moment was inundated with bad things. It was sad, but there was sadness all around her. She had done what she had to do. She hadn't been detected. She would have to be grateful for that, and carry on.

She must. If she succumbed to remorse, she would never recover.

Phillip needed her, and Thomas, and her father. Her queen needed her. Her country needed her. There was work to do. She dared not think about anything else.

8

The war had taxed everyone. Queen Elizabeth still smiled gallantly in public, but in private she was a different person entirely, bone weary and grim. Rose and Olive had already been old when the coven was called by the queen. Veronica guessed them to be in their seventies. Elizabeth was forty-four, but she looked twenty years older.

Veronica supposed she, too, looked older than she should, but she wasted no time thinking about it. The coven shared one certainty: if England lost this war, they and others of their kind would end up in the death camps with the Jews and the Gypsies. Olive had seen the possibility in the stone one night when the witches were trying to foce the commander of a panzer division to lose his way.

With a look of horror on her craggy face, Olive described what the crystal was showing her. "It's divided in two, like an egg with two yolks. I've never seen this before. On one side is victory, a free England, but on the other—on the other we have lost. The wrong king is on the throne." Her deep voice dropped even lower, and it made Veronica's skin prickle. "It's King Edward... and his Queen Wallis..."

Elizabeth spit on the floor, as a man might have done, and gritted, "Over my dead body."

"Oh yes," Olive said dully. "Many dead bodies, too many to count. There's a camp, right here in England. They're burning people—oh Goddess, I can't watch anymore!" Olive pulled back from the stone and turned her back on the altar.

Veronica cried, "It doesn't have to be, does it? You saw two scenes!"

"Yes. Victory is possible, of course." Olive's shoulders slumped as she turned back, very slowly, to face the other women. Between them the stone roiled with ominous, muddy mists. "The danger is far greater than we have realized."

Rose said, in her thin voice, "What can we do?"

"I can tell you," Elizabeth said, "that the next weeks are vital. We will end this war soon, if we're going to end it at all."

"Invasion?" Olive said.

Elizabeth hesitated for a fraction of a second, then nodded. "Yes."

Veronica said, "Our strongest tool is our weather spell, ma'am. We can affect the weather over the Channel, if we know the dates."

"I'll get them. Be ready. It's coming soon."

❧

It wasn't easy, with such knowledge weighing on her mind, but Veronica did her best to muster a smile for her fiancé when he came on leave to see her. They met in a café, with other couples around them embracing, laughing, chattering as if they hadn't a care in the world. Phillip smiled, too, and kissed Veronica's cheek, but the air was electric with tension. She was certain he no more felt gay than she did. Phillip, too, had aged beyond his twenty-nine years. Squint lines had appeared around his eyes from flying. His fair hair, worn short and combed straight back, had begun to gray, and he was whip thin.

No one spoke of the coming invasion, but everyone knew it had to happen. The country couldn't survive another year of bombings, losses, food and medicine shortages. Even the Americans were running low on resources. The occasional glimpse of spring sunshine only served to accentuate the looming threat of defeat.

They found a table in a corner where there was relative quiet, and Phillip helped Veronica out of her coat and pulled out a chair for her. She said, "You're so thin, Phillip."

"We all are, I'm afraid." He set his cap on the table. "But it will be over soon." He spoke with the confidence they were all pretending to feel, but weariness emanated from him, as distinct as a cloud of cologne.

Veronica sighed, sensing it. "I can't believe you're still flying sorties. Surely you've done your bit by now."

He gave her a tight smile and covered her hand with his. "Mostly I instruct," he said, squeezing her fingers.

"You're just telling me that so I won't worry."

"It doesn't help if you worry."

"I know."

She did worry, though. She worried all the time, especially since the ghastly news had come about Thomas.

She expected no word of Valéry. They had agreed, before they parted, that there would be no letters. She couldn't help, though, dreaming of him at night, when the self-control she exerted during her waking hours relaxed. She dreamed of Valéry, and woke to a fresh pall of guilt and shame. Occasionally she thought of giving away his ring, or burying it somewhere she couldn't find it again, but she couldn't bring herself to do it. She had tucked it into a small silk bag, and kept it with her other modest accessories. Sometimes her fingers encountered it when she was searching for a pair of earrings, and her body shivered anew, in memory.

Phillip Paxton had been her friend all her life. If she didn't feel the passion for him that she felt for Valéry, she still cared about him very much. She hated to break the news to Phillip, but she knew she must. She hadn't wanted to tell him in a letter, but now, faced with the difficult task, she could almost wish she had.

"Several weeks ago," she began, "the queen sent me home to recover from—from a brief illness."

"Thoughtful of her."

"Yes. She's very kind." Veronica hesitated, toying with her ring once again. "It was a blessing I was there, Phillip. We received the worst possible news."

"God, no. Not Thomas."

She bowed her head. "We were at luncheon, Papa and I. The maid brought the telegram on a tray, the way she might bring the post."

"I suppose she didn't know any other way to do it."

"I'm sure. Papa turned so white I thought he would faint, and his hand shook so badly he couldn't open the envelope."

Phillip covered her hand with his, and she gripped his fingers, grateful for his strength. "I had to read it to him, and I—he slumped forward as if he had lost consciousness. I didn't know what to do, so I sent for the doctor, but—it was the worst day of my life, Phillip."

"Of course it was. My poor darling."

She didn't tell him, of course, that the vision of Thomas that had troubled her for so long had returned in force. She knew exactly how her brother had died. She had seen it far too many times. She asked Olive about it once, after a long session in their secret room.

They were trudging up the stairs, whispering so as not to wake the servants in their bedrooms. Veronica murmured, "Do you have visions, Olive? Premonitions?"

"Naturally," Olive had answered. "All our kind do, if they practice the craft."

"If I stopped practicing, would they go away?"

Olive cast her a sidelong glance. "Do you want them to go away?"

"Sometimes. Sometimes I don't want to know what's going to happen. It doesn't help to know, does it? Not when there's nothing I can do."

"It's part of who we are, I'm afraid." Olive spoke more gently than usual. "You mustn't repress such things. They're part of the gift."

"And the burden," Veronica sighed.

"Yes. Power is a burden. It's the price we pay."

It was, Veronica thought now, gazing at Phillip's war-weary face, a terrible price. Her heart twisted, and her eyes began to sting. She blinked hard to make them stop. She couldn't show her true feelings. It would be a betrayal.

All of them—civilians and soldiers alike, all the men and girls in this room—worked hard on the appearance of confidence. They kept a stiff upper lip. They held their chins up. They joked and laughed and danced, denying their dread of what might come.

Veronica lifted her head. "Phillip. Let's get married now. As soon as possible."

He gave a startled laugh. "You can't be serious! What brings this on?"

"I know you want the wedding to be in your family church, with your sisters there, your parents. But this war has dragged on five years already! Our engagement is—it's *ancient!*"

Phillip laughed again, but his expression lightened a bit. "It's a crazy thing to suggest."

"Why? Everyone's doing it!" she said. "Besides, it's not as if we could find enough sugar for a wedding cake—or enough satin for a bridal gown!"

"Perhaps you're right, but I wish it could be different. I want you to have the wedding you dream of."

"I don't dream of a fancy wedding, Phillip. I never did."

"The one my mother dreamed of, then! I suppose that wedding will never happen now. Certainly we've waited long enough."

And time is running out.

Veronica didn't speak that thought. She wasn't even sure she believed it. She wished it had not come into her mind.

Lady Veronica Selwyn married Squadron Leader Phillip Paxton in a civil ceremony that was brief and businesslike, as if even the registrar felt the rush of the war. They didn't tell anyone, not even their families. Phillip placed a narrow gold band on Veronica's finger, and kissed her briefly before they signed the forms and shook hands with the registrar and the two witnesses who had left their desks for the purpose.

It all seemed terribly anticlimactic until they got to the Palace Hotel, where Phillip had arranged a room for the one remaining night of his leave. They had just reached the door to their room when the air raid siren went. They dashed down to the shelter below the hotel, hand in hand. When the thump of a bomb reached them, Phillip put an arm around Veronica's shoulders and kissed her forehead. "There's your organ music," he said.

"And fireworks," she answered, with a fierce smile. "Just like a royal wedding!"

Around them were other officers, a few girls, and a number of hotel staff. Everyone was talking and joking as if they had simply brought the party down with them. No one seemed to be afraid, and in truth, the bombings rarely reached the city anymore.

Phillip cocked his head for a moment, listening. "There go the fighters," he said.

Veronica closed her eyes, trying to sort out the sounds, but she couldn't distinguish which airplanes were English and which were German. She could feel, though, the tension in Phillip's body as he strained his ears to follow the battle above their heads.

The all-clear sounded before midnight, and the shelter emptied swiftly. Phillip guided Veronica back up the stairs, through the lobby, and into a crowded lift. When they reached their floor, Veronica felt a sudden reluctance to go into the room, to be alone with her new husband, to do the things that were expected of her. She had to force herself to walk swiftly down the carpeted corridor, pretending to be as eager as he.

She was startled, when Phillip unlocked the door and held it open for her, to see a bottle of champagne and a slender spray of white roses waiting for her on the dressing table.

"Surprise!" he said softly.

"Why, Phillip! However did you manage?"

"The Americans have ways of making things happen. I know a lot of Americans, and I called in a favor."

He opened the champagne, and they each drank a glass. She put the roses into a tooth glass, then opened her small valise, which contained little but her sponge bag and a nightgown. When she had washed and changed, she found the bed already turned down, the lights dimmed, and Phillip waiting for her.

It wasn't easy. There was none of the aching need that had drawn her to Valéry, no trace of the desire that had made every touch, every movement, every intimacy a precious experience, something to be savored. But Phillip was not only her friend, he was now her husband. He was a hero many times over. He was a good man, and a brave one. She loved him as she loved her queen, and her country.

Veronica put her arms around Phillip and held him close. She couldn't give herself to him as passionately as she had given herself to Valéry, but she did her best. She hoped and prayed Phillip wouldn't know the difference. He deserved everything she could offer, and more.

⁂

Rumors of the coming invasion swirled through London. The bombing raids had dwindled almost to nothing. The Germans had been routed in North Africa, and the Allies had taken Italy. Though ordinary Londoners couldn't know the exact dates, or the scope of the plans, the sense that something big was approaching pervaded every square, every shop, every street.

The king confided the plans to his queen, and she carried them to the basement of Windsor Castle, where the four witches of Elizabeth's coven planned their own, quite specific kinds of sorties.

It took a long time and stretched over several nights. Olive asked for a storm over the Channel, with a lull in the pounding rain and rough seas that lasted just long enough to allow the landing craft to reach shore. Rose added a request for deception of Herr Hitler. Elizabeth concocted a spell of confusion for the German meteorologists, as well as one for accuracy for the Allied scientists. It fell to Veronica to try to cast the light of protection over the soldiers and fliers of the Allies, but even as she did it, she felt how enormous the task was, too large for a small coven to accomplish.

In many ways the coven succeeded. They confused the German weather forecasters into believing the storms in the Channel would continue well into the month. Herr Hitler was persuaded the invasion would come through Calais rather than Normandy. The Allies believed the weather would change enough to allow their landing craft to reach the beaches.

The witches burned baskets of herbs and boxes of candles.

They stood by the hour, chanting in the smoky room, all through the first days of June. They took breaks only for food and sleep, and only when they could no longer work without them. On the final day, they emerged rumpled and exhausted from their labors, almost too weary to climb the stairs.

Elizabeth broke her habit of caution that one time. She took the three women to her private parlor and ordered the best breakfast the kitchens could produce. They sat together, too tired to talk, too tense to listen to the wireless. The crystal was wrapped and stowed away in its hamper behind Veronica's feet. They gazed at each other with tired resignation as they waited for their meal. There was nothing further they could do.

They had to wait with the other citizens for details of the invasion. They learned, in time, that though the weather was hardly clement, it had eased enough to allow the Allies to land at Utah Beach and Omaha Beach, and to take Pointe du Hoc. They heard the stories of how Gold, Juno, and Sword Beaches fell that first day, and other targets on succeeding days. They read accounts of the German commanders dining and dancing, drinking stolen French wine, secure in the certainty that the invasion had been postponed. It took longer to discover that Hitler himself, the great evil, slept late on what would become D-Day, in happy ignorance that his vicious reign was near its end.

Veronica was crushed by the casualty figures. She felt she had let the others down, that her efforts had been less successful, her power less effective than theirs. The loss of life appalled her. Elizabeth reminded her that though it had been a cruel day, it marked the turn toward final victory. Veronica did her best to accept her sovereign's reassurance, but her heart broke under the weight of the nation's grief, and soon, just as she had feared, under the weight of her own sorrow.

Halfway through the battle, Squadron Leader Phillip Paxton's Bristol Beaufort, flying inland from Omaha Beach, took a direct hit from the guns of a Heinkel He 51. Phillip was dead before his airplane struck the ground. His bride of three weeks, now his widow, was drinking coffee with the queen.

9

Veronica's war ended with D-Day. When word arrived of Phillip's death, Elizabeth ordered her home to Sweetbriar. "You've served gallantly, my dear. The king and I are grateful." The queen's small body was as erect as ever, though her cheeks were shadowed by fatigue, and new lines, delicate as the seams on an oak leaf, fanned from her eyes.

Veronica protested, but weakly. "Ma'am, won't you need me?"

"We can manage the work that's left. I'm told surrender will come soon. You've suffered a terrible loss, and you should be with your family."

Veronica was too weary to argue. While the battle for France raged on, she packed her things and said her good-byes to the coven. Rose shook her hand. Olive regarded her with a hard gaze and said, "Don't turn your back on the craft, Veronica."

"I thought I would leave it be, now that our work is done."

"That never succeeds."

"What do you mean?"

"You'll find out, in time, and I hope you'll have someone to teach in your turn. A daughter to carry on your line. There aren't enough of us left."

Veronica nodded without committing herself. Olive startled her with a stiff embrace that marked the end of their service together.

Carrying the Fortnum & Mason hamper and a small valise, with Oona at her heels, she boarded the train at Charing Cross. She sat in her compartment with the dog at her feet and the hamper in her lap, and watched the ruins of London pass as the train wound out of the city and clattered into the countryside.

Jago met her at the Stamford railway station. He insisted on taking the hamper from her as they walked to the Daimler, though she protested it was too heavy. "Think I'm too old, you," he said cheerfully.

"Of course not," she said.

She did find him aged, though. His hair had gone white and thin. She could see his pink, vulnerable scalp through the silvery strands. He had developed a slight stoop, and he walked awkwardly, as if his legs hurt. She felt an urge to hold his arm as they moved through the station and out to the car park, but she restrained the impulse.

She settled her things in the boot and opened the back door of the Daimler for Oona to jump in before she settled herself in the front next to Jago. "How are things at Sweetbriar?" she asked, as he maneuvered the car out into the street.

"Proper to sit in back, you," was his first response.

"Who knows what's proper anymore, Jago? The war has changed everything, even at Buckingham Palace."

He admitted this with a shrug. "Certainly Sweetbriar is changed."

"It will be over soon, they say."

"Never thought it would last this long."

She glanced at his profile and saw with sadness how his cheeks and chin sagged, how ropy the muscles of his throat looked. She had no idea how old he was, and she didn't dare ask. She blurted instead, "Jago—do we know how old Ynyr is?"

His mouth curled at one side, and she squirmed in her seat. He probably understood how she had arrived at her question. "Well," he said good-humoredly, "Ynyr is uncommonly old for a horse. He was two when he came to Morgan Hall, with your grandmother. That would make him over fifty."

Veronica turned in her seat to stare at him in shock. "Jago, that's impossible!"

"Think I've lost my memory, you?"

"Well, no, but…" She turned back to watch the hedgerows flow by.

"A long life," Jago said calmly. "Perhaps you can understand that."

"Because he was my mother's familiar," she said.

"As Oona is yours."

Veronica blew out a long breath and dropped her head back against the upholstery. "You're the second person to say that to me."

"Obvious."

From the back seat Oona emitted a single yip. Veronica and Jago both chuckled. She said, "I didn't know there were such things. There were so many things I didn't know."

"You do now."

"Yes. Knowledge, though, Jago—it's not always a blessing."

"A hard truth. Some things we'd rather not have learned."

Veronica had been relieved to find her father, although now confining himself to a wheelchair, otherwise unchanged. Using the chair had relieved some of his pain, and he was clearly delighted to have her home again, though he said little about it. He had made a shrine to Thomas in the morning room, arranging his army portrait, his ribbons and medals, and a framed copy of his commission. Veronica, before she went up to her room, stopped before it.

Lord Dafydd rolled his chair to her side. "Thomas was a sweet boy. A good son. He should have been a vicar, or a professor."

"It breaks my heart, Papa."

"And mine." He took her hand. He held it for a moment before, in an uncharacteristic demonstration, he raised it to his lips. She glanced down in surprise and saw unshed tears glistening in his eyes.

She wanted to kneel beside him, put her arms around his shoulders, kiss his forehead. She did none of these things. He would never forgive her if she broke his reserve, and those tears escaped.

Instead she said, "I'll take my things up now, Papa. Shall we have a sherry together afterward? We can toast Thomas, and then you can show me how things are with the hospital."

He nodded without speaking, and without looking up. She knew he didn't trust his voice. They hadn't even spoken of Phillip yet. She trudged up the staircase, feeling as if she had aged twenty years in the four she had been away.

She wasn't prepared for the onslaught of memory that met her when she opened the door to her old bedroom. She stepped inside and set her valise and the hamper on the floor. Oona watched with her head cocked to one side as Veronica walked to the bed and sat on the edge. She smoothed the coverlet with her hand, recalling how she had felt that long-ago night.

So much had happened since she and Valéry lay here, while the bombs fell on London and the world they knew crumbled into ruins. So many had suffered. Too many had died. And she herself—she had done many great things, and one that was terrible.

Yet she could remember how it felt to be young and innocent, in the throes of her first love. She remembered how strong Valéry's hands had been, how sweet the touch of his skin. Her body had melted in his warmth, and rebelled when she tore herself away.

Poor Phillip had known none of that passion, and now he never would.

She was certainly not the only young Englishwoman to face the prospect of lifelong widowhood. She supposed she could take some comfort in that. They would be a sisterhood, the war widows. They would recognize each other when they met. They would know how many of them lived in the villages and in the towns, childless and solitary. They would find occupations to pass the lonely years, good works perhaps, or teaching other people's children.

Veronica sighed, smoothed the coverlet again, and got up. She had promised to have a drink with her father, and to inspect the hospital. There was still work to be done. The war wasn't over yet. She had enough, for the moment, to think about.

As if he had only been awaiting her return to Sweetbriar, Jago died that night. Ynyr, the great horse who had lived long past his normal life span, lay down in his stall at the very same time, and breathed out his last. It fell to Veronica to find them both.

It was Oona who alerted her that something was wrong. Veronica was having coffee in the morning room, and Lord Dafydd was immersed in his paper, when Oona began a long, skin-tingling howl. Veronica put down her cup and hurried outside. At first she didn't know where the dog was, but then she saw her, a blur of black and brown running back and forth between the stables and the garage.

"Oona! Oona, quiet!" Veronica called. Jago had declined to move into the big house, and still lived in the small apartment above the garage. With anxiety fluttering in her chest, Veronica dashed up the stairs.

Despite her nursing experience in the Sweetbriar hospital, it was a terrible shock to find Jago still and cold in his bed, his lifeless eyes fixed on something she couldn't see. It was no less a shock to find that Ynyr had followed him.

When Veronica had closed Jago's eyes and drawn the curtains over his window, Oona led her to the stables. There she found the big horse, still beautiful with his dappled coat and shining mane and tail, lying on his side in his stall, peaceful and unmoving. His eyes, too, were open, and resisted all her efforts to close them.

With the discipline instilled in her by five years of war, Veronica straightened, smoothed her skirt, and started toward the house to inform her father of the two passings, and to begin the arrangements that would need to be made. For Jago, of course, an undertaker and a service. And for Ynyr...

Suddenly she found herself spinning about, running back into the stable to fall to her knees in the horse's loose box. She circled his neck with her arm. Oona, beside her, tried to lick the tears from her face. Veronica lifted her other arm to snuggle the dog close, and she held both as she cried. For a long time she stayed there, weeping out her sorrow, her shame, and her exhaustion over the cold, intractable fact of death.

It seemed impossible that life at Sweetbriar would go on more or less as usual, yet it did. Veronica persuaded her father to allow her to step into Jago's shoes, and to take on the greater share of the duties of running the house and administering the hospital. Both needed supplies, provisions, and staff. The house itself had begun to fall into disrepair, but there was no one available to paint or plaster or replace fallen bricks. The Victory gardens needed tending. There was the post to answer, and telephone calls to direct. The work never ended. Veronica, thinking of Queen Elizabeth's brave and steady smile, put one on her own face each morning as she left her bedroom, and tried to maintain it until she closed her door at night.

A tentative air of hope brightened the atmosphere at Sweetbriar. The wounded officers were cheered by the news from Europe. Fewer and fewer soldiers arrived, and the number of patients began to dwindle. The nurses brought a wireless into the main ward so those still bedridden could listen to encouraging pronouncements from the king and the prime minister. A fragile sense of relief was growing by the time autumn leaves swirled over the drive, but Veronica couldn't feel it.

When she had the time or energy to feel anything, she felt sadness and confusion. She wrestled with a feeling that all her losses—Valéry, the little life that might have been her daughter, her brief marriage, poor Phillip, sweet Thomas—that all of them had served no purpose.

When she lay in bed, staring at the ceiling with disconsolate tears running down her temples, Oona would jump up to lie beside her. If she made the dog get down, Oona just leaped up again until Veronica finally conceded. She fell into the habit of letting Oona curl over her ankles as she slept, surprised by the comfort it gave her. Oona's breathing soothed her restlessness, and the little node of life and warmth reminded Veronica that although she was lonely, she was not alone. Oona's loyalty brightened the long succession of dark days in which Veronica fought the conviction that her life, at the age of twenty-four, was over.

10

Lord Dafydd Selwyn, maimed by the First World War, died on the day the Second ended in Europe. While the prime minister spoke, everyone in the hospital gathered around the wireless, their cheers echoing through the halls of Sweetbriar.

Lord Dafydd remained in his room, too ill to go downstairs, and refusing to let Honeychurch summon his doctor. Veronica sat with him in his darkened room, the curtains drawn, but the door ajar so they could hear the news.

When the cheering began, she patted her father's hand. "It's over, Papa. The Germans have surrendered."

His eyes didn't open. He muttered, "Again."

"Yes."

He took a long, rattling breath, while Veronica held hers. She jumped when he spoke again. He croaked, "Japan."

"Yes, I know, Papa. But for us, for Europe at least, we have peace. Japan will fall."

His fingers moved weakly in hers, and she squeezed them. He took another noisy, shallow breath before he said, "Morwen?"

"No, Papa, it's me. It's Veroni—"

"Morwen!" he cried, his voice louder than it had been in days. His eyes opened, just for a moment, and fixed on the door to the bedroom. Involuntarily Veronica turned to see what he was looking at.

She saw nothing. She was still holding his hand, and she felt a sudden slipping sensation, as of water running through her fingers. With a gasp she turned back. Her father's eyes were still on the doorway, but the light in them, the light of consciousness, of awareness, of life, had died. He was gone.

For an hour or more Veronica sat, dry eyed, beside her father's body. She held his hand, though she knew he could no longer feel the contact. She imagined her mother had come to fetch him. Theirs had been a real love, a lasting one. It had been far more powerful than the affection she'd felt for Phillip.

She looked around at Lord Dafydd's spartan bedroom. His abandoned prosthesis was gathering dust in a corner. The wheelchair with its folded woolen blanket rested beside the bed. His dressing table was almost bare except for the miniature of her mother he had allowed no one to move. It all felt abandoned. Empty.

Who would sleep in this room now? Her father's death made her the mistress of Sweetbriar, but she couldn't imagine moving into this room with its four-poster bed and its tall windows overlooking the park. It was not a room for a solitary woman. She would be lost in it.

At length she released her father's hand and laid it on his chest. She closed his eyes for him and pulled his blanket up to his chin, though that could hardly matter now. His face was smooth in death, with the trace of a smile on his lips. Before she went out to alert the staff to his passing, Veronica bent and placed a kiss on his cold forehead. "You were a good man, Papa," she said. "I think you must have been a fine husband. I know you were a good father, and a brave and faithful soldier. I'm proud of you."

Dafydd Selwyn had been spared learning what his wife was, and his daughter. That, Veronica thought, as she closed his bedroom door, was a mercy.

The next night the inhabitants of Sweetbriar gathered on the south terrace to watch London alight, not with bombs this time, but with fireworks and bonfires and a rainbow of red and green flares dropped by three Lancasters soaring above the city. The king had addressed the nation. The wireless announcer described the royal family emerging onto the balcony of Buckingham Palace, and the cheering crowds waving Union Jacks and dancing in the streets.

Veronica had spent a dreary day making funeral arrangements and receiving condolences. She didn't go down to the terrace, but remained in her bedroom to watch the fireworks from her window. She pictured Elizabeth smiling down at the cheering throngs. Olive and Rose might be in the happy crowd, looking up at the queen, celebrating her triumph in the secrecy of their shared knowledge.

Veronica wanted to feel triumphant, too, but she couldn't summon that emotion. She would have to settle for relief.

She wondered, without much energy, if there was any chance Valéry had survived the war. She doubted she would ever know.

꧁

Fireworks still bloomed in the night sky when Veronica fell into an exhausted sleep, curled on her bed with Oona beside her. She woke when the night was far gone. The sky was beginning to lighten, but ribbons of smoke still wavered against the faded stars. She lay drowsily watching the drifting spirals and wondering why, now that the noise had stopped, she was awake.

She rolled onto her back and realized Oona was no longer on the bed. She sat up, rubbing her eyes, and looked around.

Oona was perched directly in front of the wardrobe, ears pricked forward, gazing at its closed doors. Every few seconds she whimpered. From inside the wardrobe, piercing the dimness of the room, a light shone, as if a lamp were burning among the dresses and coats.

Veronica was out of bed and halfway across the room before she realized there was no lamp in the wardrobe. It was the crystal. The stone had lain neglected in the Fortnum & Mason hamper for months. It was trying to get her attention, and had captured Oona's instead.

Olive had said, "That never succeeds," and "You'll find out." This must be what she meant. Olive had no scrying stone, but she was descended from a long, rich line of witches who had passed on their history and their stories. Grandmother to mother to daughter, generation after generation. She knew what she was talking about.

With a sigh Veronica knelt beside the dog and opened the wardrobe doors.

The light that poured out from beneath the lid of the hamper was neither soft nor gentle. It was white and harsh, and it pulsed angrily, blistering through the woven rattan, past the hems of garments, and glittering in Oona's eyes.

Oona's whimpers became a growl, a long, uneasy rumble. "It's all right, Oona," Veronica said, as she reached through the hanging clothes to pull the hamper out. "I know what to do."

She set the hamper on the floor, and Oona jumped to her feet, watching warily as Veronica lifted the lid and began to fold back the layers of silk.

"You see, Oona. Olive was right. I should have known she would be. The craft has its own power."

Ritual, in this case, was not required. The moment the crystal was free of its covering, images began to tumble through it, a jumble of scenes half-obscured by glimmering lights and shifting shadows, flowing at such a dizzying pace Veronica had to brace her hands on her knees to keep her balance.

Face after face peered out at her, dark eyed, dusky skinned, sometimes with black hair, sometimes gray, one haloed by a mass of silver curls. The faces appeared, gave way to others, reappeared, disappeared again in a stunning procession, and she was connected to all of them.

When she had seen the faces before, she had not understood, but thanks to Olive's instruction, she now understood who they were, and why they had come.

These were her ancestresses. They were her predecessors in the craft. She had become an adept. She had learned how to listen. She had only to watch, and wait. She knelt beside the hamper, unaware of the rising light beyond her window, of the stirring of the house beneath her. Energy thrilled through her body and her soul. The old ache in her body was welcome, hinting at a return to the vitality she had lost.

In her excitement she forgot one of Olive's crucial lessons, and Jago's, too. She forgot the peril that hung over every witch, in every age. She neglected to lock her door.

The succession of dim faces slowed, after a time, and settled into a single, wavering image. Veronica leaned closer to make out what it was. There was a row of what looked like cots, covered in white sheets, with people in them. Sleeping people, she thought—no, not sleeping, ill. These were hospital beds, a room full of them, very like Sweetbriar's hospital at the height of the war. This wasn't Sweetbriar, though. The walls and the ceiling were unadorned, and the cots were crowded together, with barely enough space between them for a person to move.

The patients were men, some in bandages, some in casts, some with their eyes closed and their hands folded on their breasts as if they were waiting for death to relieve them. And one...

Veronica leaned closer. He had black hair. A bandage covered half his face. He turned his head in her direction, as if he sensed her attention. She could see only one eye, the fine straight shape of his nose, the lean jawline she remembered.

Valéry.

She gripped the crystal tighter. Something terrible had happened to him, some awful wound, but he was alive! She couldn't make out details, but she could see the movement of his head, the lifting of a hand as he pushed back a lock of hair from his forehead. He was alive!

At the very moment of her realization, a knock sounded on the door to her bedroom, and a second later the door clicked open.

Veronica was on her knees on the floor, her hands on the scrying stone. The crystal was as bright as if it were on fire. The lights must reflect on her face, even shine in her mirror. She drew a breath of alarm as she realized morning had come while she knelt here.

"Lady Veronica?" It was Honeychurch. "Cook wants to know—"

Of course! It was the day of Lord Dafydd's funeral, and there would be guests.

The door was opening wider, the butler in full expectation of his welcome. Veronica shot to her feet. The lid of the hamper was an arm's length away. Even if she could have reached it in time, the light from the stone would coruscate through the rattan. A dozen ways of hiding it shot through Veronica's mind in an instant, but none of them would be quick enough, and she couldn't think—

Oona burst into a sudden frenzy of barking and threw her small body at the door. Honeychurch exclaimed in alarm, and though the door swung wide, poor Honeychurch stumbled backward, into the hall, away from Oona's onslaught.

"Oona!" he said helplessly, as she nipped at his toes and worried his trouser legs, barking and growling as if he were the devil himself. He fell against the wall opposite, swinging at the dog with the empty tray in his hands. "Oona, what's wrong with you? What's the matter?"

Veronica strode into the corridor, her nightgown swirling around her ankles. She shut the door firmly behind her, and made a great show of seizing Oona's scruff and scolding her.

The moment the door was closed and the scrying stone out of Honeychurch's sight, Oona fell silent. She sat down beside Veronica and began to beat her tail cheerfully against the carpet, the very picture of a well-disciplined canine.

"I'm so sorry, Honeychurch," Veronica said in as matter-of-fact a voice as she could muster. "I can't think what got into her."

The old butler scowled. "Terriers are unpredictable. Always like a nice spaniel, myself."

"Yes, I know you do. But she was a gift, you know. From Jago. I couldn't part with her." Veronica gave the dog a pat and released her. Oona lay down, gazing up at Honeychurch without a trace of guile.

Veronica put a hand to her throat, where her pulse beat a mad rhythm. Her voice, she was proud to notice, revealed nothing. "Such a ruckus!" she said in an offhand manner. "Now, tell me, Honeychurch, what is it Cook needs to know?"

❧

Veronica rarely made use of her title, nor had she ever intended to take advantage of her private relationship with the queen. Just the same, in this case she felt it was necessary. She wrote a cryptic note to Her Majesty, and received one just as cryptic in reply. She made a day trip to London and was treated to a private interview with Elizabeth that yielded a sincere promise of help. On the way out of Buckingham Palace, she met the king coming up the stairs, and she curtsied with care.

"Ah," he said cheerfully. "Lady Veronica, isn't it? My wife's wartime assistant. I th-thank you for your special help. She t-tells me you have been invaluable."

"It was the greatest honor, Your Majesty," Veronica said with sincerity. He smiled charmingly at her and went on his way, innocent, she supposed, of any knowledge of the true service she had rendered. Unescorted, she hurried down the stairs to the private door. Soon she was back on the train, eager to be at Sweetbriar to await the promised information.

Elizabeth did not fail her. Two days later a note arrived from the palace, listing several hospitals that, according to the War Office, were caring for wounded American soldiers, with some French and British casualties among them. The queen closed her note with "Happy hunting."

Veronica wasted no time in collecting maps, traveling money, and papers. She packed only a small valise, though she didn't know how long she might be gone. If she went to the right place first, she would soon be home again. If she had to visit them all, it could be weeks.

When Honeychurch learned of her plan to go into France, he fussed at her for a full fifteen minutes, until she put up her hand to stop him. "Honeychurch," she said firmly, "we're at peace now. The war is over in Europe."

"There are still dangers, Your Ladyship," he said dourly. "Land mines. Prisoners of war. Unexploded bombs."

"We have those right here in England," she said.

He acknowledged this bitter truth with an inclination of his head, but he wasn't finished protesting. "At least take someone with you."

"Who? Everyone's gone!"

"Don't you have friends in London? At the palace, perhaps?"

"I'm going to be fine," she said. "My French is much improved. I will need you to watch over things while I'm gone."

"I don't like it, Lady Veronica. You're the heir to Sweetbriar. You're needed here."

"I'll be back, Honeychurch. Please don't worry."

She had written out detailed instructions, just in case, and placed them in her desk, but she thought it best not to mention that. She hadn't told Honeychurch precisely why she was going abroad. She had implied there was an old friend wounded and lying in hospital, but she hadn't spoken a name.

It was an odd sensation to realize there was no one who could forbid her going. She was her own mistress. She was the lady of Sweetbriar, the last of her line. If she didn't return, for any reason, Sweetbriar would pass to her father's brother's grandson. She couldn't remember his given name, but at least his surname was Selwyn.

She wondered, idly, who would care if she resumed her maiden name. She couldn't see that it would matter much either way. The aristocracy was on its last legs, she was sure of that. The Great War had dealt it a nearly fatal injury. The second war had been the death blow.

❧

The night before her departure, Veronica locked her door, opened her wardrobe once again, and pulled out the Fortnum & Mason hamper. She lifted out the crystal and set it on her little table with a new candle, a posy of herbs she had gathered from Sweetbriar's park and woods, and a vial of salt water. She had more confidence in her ritual now, and as she began, she silently thanked her instructresses—Elizabeth, Olive, even Rose—for their guidance.

Mother Goddess, hear my plea:
Show what lies ahead for me.

It was a simple prayer, but a clear one, as Olive had taught her. The answer she received might be unclear just the same. It might be one of warning. Worse, it might be one of danger. She had decided that if the stone showed her some threat, she would do her best to prepare for it, but she wouldn't be deterred. Valéry's child had become one of millions of war casualties. She would not allow its father to be added to the lists.

She knelt in front of the stone of her ancestresses, with fragrant smoke floating about her head and tremulous candlelight dancing across the crystal's surface. She chanted her prayer in a low, clear voice, three times three times, while Oona sat nearby, watching and listening.

The succession of faces was familiar to her now, like those in a recurring dream. The images peered at her, each in turn, half-obscured by the mists of time. The sequence spun rapidly at first, too fast for her to pick out individuals. After a time it began to slow, to allow features to become distinct. There was the old woman in a long, shapeless robe. There was the one with a cloud of silver hair. The final one to appear was her mother.

The mists receded enough for Veronica, for the first time, to see Morwen's face clearly. It was the face of the portrait, and yet it wasn't, quite. The portraitist had worked hard to make her into a beauty, shortening her nose, softening her jawline, widening her eyes, making her cheeks unnaturally rosy.

The face Veronica saw was subtly different. It was better than beautiful. It was a face of character. The eyes, smaller than the painting showed, tilted at the corners, ready for laughter. The nose was longer, stronger than the painter had shown, the chin more pronounced. Veronica leaned forward to cup the stone with her palms, and she whispered, gazing into her mother's eyes, "Oh, Mama. Could you show me..."

Morwen's smile was one no painter could ever replicate. It was full of love, full of mystery, the tender expression of a mother for her child. It vanished swiftly as her image dissolved into the mist, as if she had taken a step backward to make way for another.

Veronica had been too occupied, in recent years, for vanity. She spent as little time looking into a mirror as she could, and almost none improving her appearance. She had cropped her hair short when the war started, and she never bothered with cosmetics beyond a dash of lipstick when she thought of it. So when she saw her own face in the crystal, for a disorienting moment she didn't recognize it.

Even when she realized whose image it was, she was distracted by the infant this slender, dark-eyed girl held in her arms, snuggled close under her chin in the age-old posture of mothers and babies.

The image trembled before her for what might have been mere seconds, or long minutes. The girl—herself, Veronica realized at last, though she would check in the mirror when she could—didn't look up. She was absorbed in the child. Her child.

A daughter, of course. A girl, to carry on the craft.

All anxiety about her upcoming mission fell away. Whatever was to come in the next days and weeks, Veronica's prayer had been answered. She had a future, and there was a child in it. Someone's child, in any case.

With fresh energy she brought out the grimoire and began to turn its pages.

11

The American nurse, dressed in practical khaki trousers and a loose shirt, walked ahead of Veronica, leading her up a set of wooden stairs that creaked alarmingly as they climbed. The hospital at Mirecourt had once been a psychiatric facility, but the Twenty-First General Hospital of the United States Army had transformed it into a sprawling medical facility, the largest of its kind in the war zone. The entryway had become a triage room, though it was quiet now. Rows of cots, most of them empty, filled every room Veronica could see.

"Most of our men have been shipped home, you see, Mrs. Paxton," the nurse said over her shoulder. "We still get an occasional accident, or infection. Sometimes leftover munitions go up, and people get hurt." She passed the second floor and headed to the third. That staircase was steep, and creaked even more loudly. "Long-term cases are up here, in what used to be the attic. These patients are waiting while someone figures out where they should go."

"No one knows where they belong?"

The nurse sighed. She was a squarish sort of woman, a girl really, with short brown hair and wide shoulders. "The non-American ones. We have two who can't speak at all, and their identity disks are gone. I think they're Russian, but it's hard to tell. It's sad, but they probably won't make it anyway. There are several French soldiers, all of them too sick to go home on their own. Some of them aren't sure they have homes anymore."

"That's terrible."

They reached the top floor, and the nurse paused outside an unpainted door. "You English had the worst of it, I guess. The bombing and all."

"Not worse than the French."

"No."

"And there were the camps."

The American girl shuddered. "I can't look at the pictures," she said. "I see enough here without putting those horrors into my mind."

She reached for the door handle, but still she hesitated, eyeing Veronica doubtfully. "It can be shocking, seeing these men."

"My home was converted into a convalescent hospital. I nursed wounded soldiers, too."

"Oh. Sorry. It's just—the way you speak—"

"Oh yes?" Veronica wished she would just open the door.

The nurse grinned. "You sound just like the king! I listen to him on the radio. Can't imagine him nursing patients, can you?"

Veronica tried to smile back, but she was tempted to reach past the nurse and open the door for herself.

It had been a hot and uncomfortable trip to reach Mirecourt from Southampton. A summer storm had made the crossing rough. The train journey had been long, often interrupted, and short on amenities. She had come first to Mirecourt, but she had several other hospitals to visit if Valéry wasn't here. They were scattered all over France, meaning more frustrating travel, overlaid with the constant worry that he might be gone at any time.

She had transformed the little silk pouch where she kept Valéry's ring into a sort of charm. She sprinkled blessed salt inside it, and needles of rosemary. She added a fragment of silk from the scrying stone's wrappings, carefully removed with her nail scissors. She wore the bag on a thin ribbon around her neck, and as she steeled herself to step into the ward, she touched it beneath her frock.

The attic was a dim room with a slanting ceiling and exposed roof beams cutting the space in half. As in the other wards, cots lined the walls. Perhaps a dozen patients reclined or sat on the beds. A nurse working at the far end looked up and left her desk to meet the visitors. Veronica put out her hand with automatic courtesy, but she was already looking past both nurses, scanning the men in their various bandages and splints, searching.

She had anticipated this moment for days as she traveled. Her imagination had served up anxious possibilities. Of course she feared she might visit every hospital on her list without finding him. Or she worried she might find the right place, but find him already discharged to some unknown location. She knew he might have died, but she tried not to let that thought linger in her mind. She was terrified, too, that when she saw him, she might not know him. It had been more than four years. She knew she was greatly changed, perhaps beyond his recognition. He must be even more altered. He had been wounded twice, and if the scrying stone had shown her truly, his face was half-hidden by bandages.

She excused herself to the two nurses and started slowly down the room, looking into each bed in turn.

When she found him, her legs began to tremble so that she had to grip the foot of the bed's iron frame to steady herself.

If he had been gaunt after Dunkirk, now he was skeletal. The laugh lines around his mouth showed gray against the darkness of his skin, and his eye, the one left unbandaged, was hollow and unfocused. Even his hair was different, shot through with gray and shaved here and there to allow his wounds to be dressed. Only his hands, long, fine fingered, looked as they once had.

Yet she knew him. She knew him as her heart's companion. He was the one chosen for her. Sent to her. Saved for her.

She gazed down at him, her palms pressed together beneath her chin. His eye opened. He gazed at her, unspeaking, for a long moment.

She said, very softly, *"Valéry. Est-ce que tu me connais?"*

For a moment he didn't answer, but then, as the nurses came up behind Veronica, about to interrupt, the corner of his mouth curled, ever so slightly. His voice was hoarse, but she remembered its deep timbre, and the slow, sweet way he had of speaking. *"Bien sûr,"* he said. *"Bien sûr. Tu es Véronique. La belle dame de Sweetbriar."*

⁓⚶⁓

It was shockingly easy to persuade the Americans to discharge Valéry Chirac into the care of Veronica Paxton. She had no need of magic to accomplish it. She suspected the officer in charge of the hospital was glad to see his burden diminished by at least one.

The nurses waved good-bye as Veronica and Valéry settled into the taxi that came to take them to the Nancy train station. Valéry, who had leaned heavily on a cane as they walked the short distance from the hospital to the taxi, put his head back and closed his good eye. When Veronica took her seat beside him, she felt the trembling of his body. She wanted to take his hand, to reassure him, but he had already made it clear such gestures were unwelcome.

"I can manage," he had said repeatedly, when she tried to help him down the stairs, or pick up his cane when it slipped from his hand, or even carry the small bag of toiletries the nurses had packed for him. Veronica had seized the package of bandages and ointment before Valéry could reach for it, and she settled it on her lap as she gave orders to the taxi driver. As the taxi pulled away, she waved a distracted farewell to the hospital staff.

She thought Valéry had fallen asleep, but after a few minutes of jouncing down the rutted road, he said, "I hope you won't regret this, Véronique."

"I will not." She patted his hand where it lay on his knee. His right hand—in fact, all his right side—was relatively unscathed. His injuries afflicted his left side, where the grenade's explosion had caught him. "How could I regret finding you, Valéry? It seems a miracle."

The truth she wouldn't admit was that doubts did flicker at the edges of her mind, shaking her faith in herself and in the future. She feared he might never fully recover. She worried Honeychurch and Cook and the rest of them at Sweetbriar might not accept him. She didn't know what might be required to heal a man who would never see again from his left eye, whose left arm and left leg had been torn nearly to shreds, whose heart and mind were so shaken by the horrors he had witnessed that it was a wonder he still had the will to live.

There were so many things she didn't know about Valéry Chirac. She didn't know his family background. She had no idea if he had a girl somewhere. She didn't know where he had gone to school or if he had any money of his own.

The taxi chugged through the wounded countryside, where thick hedgerows gave way here and there to fields that had once been green and lush and were now scarred by the passage of tanks and trucks and the marching feet of the Third United States Army. Gay summer sunshine poured its nourishment onto pastureland that would yield no crops this year, or perhaps even the next. This country was as injured as the man sitting next to her.

Veronica put her hand to her breast, and through the cotton of her frock she cupped the medicine bag with her palm. Warmth flowed from it into her hand, and she sighed.

Valéry said, without moving his head, "Are you wearing an amulet?"

"What?" Veronica started, and dropped her hand. She had never heard the word he used, *amulette*, but it was enough of a cognate that she thought—even feared—she understood him. She turned to him, her face flushing uncomfortably. "What is— what do you mean?"

The side of his mouth that was unencumbered by bandages curled in that old, charming way she remembered. For that moment he was the young officer he had been when she fell in love with him. "Véronique," he murmured. "I am from Brittany, you know. My people were Romani. *Gitans.*"

This word she knew. *Gitan* was gypsy. She gazed into his good eye and tried to fathom what he was telling her. She didn't dare ask.

He closed his eye, as if the effort of talking had wearied him. Fearful for him, fearful for herself, painfully aware of the listening taxi driver, she turned her face back to the window. The hedge- rows had given way to the proper road, the one that would take them to the station. They passed a bombed-out house, little more than a chimney and a portion of roof, but with an intact barn a few yards behind it. A stone church appeared behind a low rock wall, and then a village with an assortment of houses in various stages of destruction.

How long, Veronica wondered, would it take for the coun- try to rebuild? Or for her own country to rebuild? She planned to reconstruct the Home Farm. She envisioned it restored to its former comfort, the haven it had been for Jago and for her and Thomas, but the project would have to wait until building mate- rials were available.

She shivered suddenly, strongly, chilled by revulsion for war and for those who waged it.

Beside her Valéry shifted, and his eye opened. "Are you all right, Véronique?"

"I'm sick to death of all of it," she said in a bitter undertone, and realized a moment later she had spoken in English.

"*Non, ma chère*," he said. His hand fumbled for hers, and when he found it, he held her fingers with only a slight tremor in his own. "We are alive," he said in careful English. "We must be glad."

She drew a slow breath and returned the pressure of his hand. "Yes. I know."

"We will talk more," he said. He released her hand and lapsed into silence again.

Veronica turned her head to look at him. She had seen him in the hospital, of course, but she had not been so close. Now, with his face only inches from hers and his eye closed, she searched his features for the man she had known. Would she love him again? Would he love her? She couldn't predict it.

They were no longer young lovers, full of idealism. They were youthful enough, but bruised by war and tragedy. Their romance might be beyond their ability to rekindle.

It wouldn't change her intentions. She would coax him back to whatever state of health lay in her power. She would make Sweetbriar his home for as long as he wished. If the romantic love she remembered no longer existed, perhaps that was what was meant to be.

She touched her silken bag once again. She could feel the outline of his ring there, in its nest of herbs and salt and fabric. Perhaps she should return it to him. Perhaps the young man who had given it, and the young woman who had accepted it, no longer existed.

12

The journey to England sapped the last of Valéry's strength. When they reached Southampton, Veronica took him first to a hospital, where he remained several days until the doctors decided he was strong enough for the train ride to Stamford. She wired ahead to Sweetbriar to explain, and Honeychurch sent the Daimler to carry them home from the station. Between them they assisted Valéry up the staircase to the big bedroom, with its view of the park and the woods beyond. He didn't leave that room, or speak to anyone but Veronica and Honeychurch and Dr. Mountjoy, for more than a month. He was unable to eat anything more substantial than Cook's beef tea. It didn't seem possible he could get any thinner, but he seemed to be disappearing before their eyes.

Every night of that month, Veronica locked her bedroom door and set the crystal on the table that had become her altar. She took care with her rituals, consulting the grimoire often to choose which herbs to use, raiding the pantry for new candles when Cook wasn't looking, collecting the purest rainwater she could with a beaker set on her windowsill. Despite all of it, Valéry grew weaker and weaker. Veronica felt helpless. She continued her nightly efforts only because she didn't know what else to do.

Searching through the grimoire, as July wore on in a succession of hot, windless days, Veronica came across a recipe for a Lammas ritual. It was one Olive had never mentioned, a ceremony dating back to medieval times. Veronica could see that the page in the grimoire had been written out a very long time ago. A good bit of it had faded to smudges, but she could decipher enough to see that there was something called Lammas bread, which was to be broken into four pieces to set at the cardinal points. After the ritual, those fragments of bread would have special influence, blessed as the first fruits, meant to nourish and strengthen the community for the winter ahead.

At least, that was what Veronica hoped the page said. It wasn't specific about the kind of bread, but she supposed anything Cook baked must be satisfactory. She waited until the morning baking was done, on the eve of Lammas, then slipped down to the kitchen to pilfer a small loaf.

She took the greatest care that night, observing every tradition, every ritual practice she had been taught. With Oona watching, and with the four pieces of bread arranged on her altar, she chanted the simple prayer from the grimoire:

The work is done,
The harvest home;
Blessèd be the weary ones.

She thought the old rhyme was perfect for Valéry. Surely the work he had done, to which he had given so much, was worthy of blessing. She recited the prayer three times three times, as Olive had always done. When she was done, and the hour of midnight had passed, she crept down the corridor with three pieces of Lammas bread in her hands. Making as little noise as possible, she set one piece in the corridor outside Valéry's door, and another in the dressing room attached to his bedroom. There was a little sitting room to one side of the bedroom, and she deposited a piece of the blessed bread there. She tucked away the last piece in the hamper with the crystal, first crumbling off a fragment to add to her charm bag.

The sky was brightening by the time she fell into bed, and Oona jumped up beside her.

As she drifted off, Veronica touched Oona's scruffy head. "I've done everything I can, I think," she whispered. "But I wish I could have called on the whole coven." Oona licked her fingers once, then wriggled close and settled down with a sigh. The two of them fell into a sound sleep, and didn't wake until the maid came in with morning tea.

Veronica hurried to dress so she could go down the corridor to Valéry's room. She was so startled to see him sitting up in bed, tucking into a breakfast of bread and butter, a grilled tomato, and a boiled egg, that she laughed aloud. She was rewarded by seeing a smile ease his weary face. His voice was thin but steady. *"J'ai faim!"*

She crossed to his bedside. "You look so much better, Valéry! I can hardly believe it."

He scooped the last bit of egg out of the shell, ate it, then settled back against his pillow. "I'll get up today."

"Perhaps. Let's see how you feel."

He smiled again, wider this time. "I feel like getting up!"

❦

His recovery after that was so swift Veronica worried Dr. Mountjoy would be suspicious. As it turned out, there was no need. The doctor considered the victory to be his own, and she didn't mind that. Perhaps he needed a win. He removed all bandages except for the one over Valéry's left eye, and he encouraged his patient to be up and about as much as he liked. First Valéry was allowed to sit on the south terrace to take the summer sunshine. By the middle of August, leaning on a cane, he was walking in the park with Veronica beside him. The two of them took long rambles through the woods, with Oona tagging along, snuffling under leaves, digging beneath tree roots in search of vermin.

By Samhain, Valéry was working alongside the gardeners, spending long hours digging in the kitchen garden that had flourished since the early days of the war. Veronica said, "You don't have to do that, Valéry. We were lucky. Our gardeners all came back, and the rest of the staff, too."

"I don't like to be idle," he said. "It feels good to have my hands in the dirt. I was accustomed to working in my mother's garden."

They were on the terrace, watching the red disk of the harvest sun settle into the west. Veronica said gently, "Do you want to talk about your mother?"

He gazed into the dusty twilight for several minutes before he spoke. "I've been afraid to talk about her, Véronique."

She was about to ask why, but she saw him catch his lower lip between his teeth, and she realized he was choosing his words with care, the way someone with a sore foot walks across gravel, cautious of anything that will cause fresh pain. Haltingly, he said, "After I left Sweetbriar, I went to my home. The neighbors told me—" He paused, and in the gloom Veronica saw his eyes glisten.

Since he had gotten out of his sickbed, she hadn't touched him except in passing. Now, though not entirely sure it would be welcome, she took his hand between both of hers and held it. The memory of the night before they parted flooded back, and just as he had that night, he turned his hand so their fingers intertwined.

He said, in a low voice that vibrated with pain, "When I asked if they had heard from my mother, they said no. My aunt was gone, too." His fingers tightened on hers. "Just women, sweet women who loved to cook and sing and laugh. They would never hurt a soul."

Veronica didn't try to offer words of comfort. What could she have said? The depth of the cruelty and evil visited upon his family, indeed upon the world, could never be plumbed with words. They sat on together, hand in hand, as the night darkened around them. It seemed to Veronica that the years dropped away as the stars pricked the darkness above them, as if the time of their being apart, the time of sacrifice and loneliness and fear, rose like mist into the night sky and dissipated in the warm autumn air.

She didn't know if Valéry felt the way she did, and she didn't find out until after they had eaten their dinner, read for a time beside a small fire in the parlor, then climbed the stairs side by side. Valéry was still using her father's old room, having stayed on out of convenience. When they reached the landing where they would turn to their respective bedrooms, he caught her hand again and turned her to face him.

"I told you, Véronique," he said, "when we said farewell, that I would love you forever."

Her lips parted, and a butterfly sensation tickled the base of her throat. She looked up into his eyes. "Valéry, I..." He bent before she could finish, and kissed her, searchingly, for so long she had to pull back for a breath. Gently he pulled her head toward his chest and cradled it there. He smelled wonderfully of sunshine and sweet earth and the port wine he had drunk after dinner. He whispered into her ear, "I meant it then. I still do."

She must have answered him, though later she couldn't remember what she had said. She also couldn't remember how she found herself in his bedroom, then in his bed. Oona settled herself outside the closed door, where Veronica found her in the cool gray hours of early morning. She hastened back to her own room, fearful of being seen by the housemaids. Oona padded silently behind her.

⁂

They married in December. The wedding invitations said "Christmastime," but to Veronica, though she could tell no one, it was Yule. Since the war, weddings tended to be modest affairs, even for the aristocracy, so Veronica was surprised and pleased at how many people in the neighborhood and from London attended. Olive and Rose came, bearing a gift of an embroidered cloth. Veronica pretended it was meant for her table, but she knew its true purpose was to be an altar covering. She sent the queen an invitation, out of courtesy. She didn't expect Elizabeth to attend, nor did she, but she sent a beautiful silver candleholder, another addition to her altar, with a note of congratulations in her own hand.

"This is really from Queen Elizabeth?" Valéry asked wonderingly when he saw it.

"I worked wi—for her. During the war."

Valéry raised his eyebrows. "Am I expected to converse with royalty? I fear I will be a disappointment to your lords and ladies."

Veronica laughed. "I don't think you'll be meeting the queen, Valéry. You would like her, though. And no one could be disappointed in you." He shook his head, chuckling.

They devoted themselves, after the wedding, to restoring Sweetbriar's grounds and farms to their prewar state. They took back any worker who had gone to fight and now wanted his old position back, even two who had been so badly wounded their jobs were all but impossible for them to perform. Veronica spent her days putting the great hall and the parlors to rights, seeing to repairs of scratched and cracked woodwork, broken light fixtures, stained carpets. Valéry worked outside, spending so many hours at the surrounding farms that Veronica teased him she thought he had changed his mind and returned to Brittany.

Veronica had not touched the scrying stone since Valéry's return to health, but it comforted her to have it nearby. She let it lie in its usual resting place, hidden well back in her wardrobe. Valéry had moved into her bedroom, since she'd told him she could never be comfortable sleeping with her husband in the room that had been Lord Dafydd's. They brought in an extra wardrobe and installed a larger bed. At night they lay gazing out her window on the peaceful starry sky, remembering how it had once blazed with explosives.

The only sign that Valéry still thought about his family and his old home was his perusal of the French newspaper he had delivered each morning, which Honeychurch laid beside his breakfast plate. He pored over the pages, studying each report of refugees and reparations.

Once Veronica asked, "Darling, are you searching for your students? The little ones? Shall we go and look for them?"

"There is no point, Véronique."

"How can you be sure?"

For answer he put his sun-browned hand over his heart and shook his head. Since it was the way she herself so often knew things, she didn't question him. She left her place, though, to go and kiss his cheek. "So many losses," she murmured. "I suppose we will always grieve."

"Do you still grieve for Phillip?"

They had spoken very little about her short marriage. She left her hand on his shoulder and gazed out the window, remembering Phillip's widowed mother, who had accepted his photograph and the family ring back with tears in her eyes. She had embraced Veronica, holding her tight for several moments and wishing her well in her new marriage. Veronica's throat had contracted, and as she kissed her former mother-in-law, she'd found it hard to speak.

She told Valéry now, "I do grieve for Phillip. I grieve for him as I do for so many friends who died. As I grieve for my brother, and my father."

The photograph of Thomas in his uniform, with his medals laid beside it, remained in the morning room, arranged just as her father had left it. That would never change, not so long as Veronica lived at Sweetbriar.

"I wish," she said sadly, "that you had pictures of your family."

"The house was destroyed. Bombed to nothing. Burned to ash."

"I wish I had known your mother."

He stroked her hand on his shoulder. "So do I."

Their lives were full and busy. They longed for only one thing more. When it didn't come, Veronica couldn't help feeling it was a punishment. Valéry asked once, carefully, "You do want a child, Véronique?"

She never told him what she had done. She couldn't. He had suffered enough pain, and she knew how it would hurt him. She put her arms around him, and pressed her cheek to his strong shoulder. "I do want a child," she whispered fiercely. "Of course I do." But the longed-for pregnancy didn't happen.

The problem was not a lack of passion. Despite the long hours they worked every day, they often went early and eagerly to bed, remaining in the parlor after dinner just long enough so the staff would not be embarrassed. They made love nearly every night, and slept curled together, their bodies touching, loath to be apart.

Like true country people, they loved watching the countryside change with the seasons. They savored the trees turning green in the spring. They saw the summer flowers blossom, fade, and drop. They exclaimed over the autumn colors, gold and red and rust.

They watched the leaves fall, and the fields turn sere, to be puri-fied by winter. The wheel of the year turned once, twice, three times. They were happy enough.

One clear winter's night, when stars glittered over a frostbit-ten landscape and the windows were rimed with ice, Veronica shivered, chilly despite their thick comforter and Valéry's warmth beside her. He slid out from beneath the blankets. "I'll get you something to put on."

"My dressing gown is hanging inside the door of the wardrobe."

He padded barefoot across the room. She snuggled deeper beneath the quilt, waiting for him to return. When a minute passed and he had not come back to bed, she sat up.

Valéry was standing in front of the wardrobe, both its doors pulled wide. She said, her voice catching with a sudden anxiety, "Can't you find it? It should be right—"

"Véronique. What is this?" He stepped a little aside so she could see for herself.

The light, seeping through the cracks of the wicker hamper behind its barrier of hanging clothes, was subtle, but in the deep winter darkness unmistakable. Veronica pressed her hands to her mouth. Valéry thrust aside the dresses and coats to reveal the Fort-num & Mason hamper glowing steadily through the shadows.

He bent to pull it out. "Valéry, don't," Veronica began, but then stopped. What could she say? The crystal was speaking with its own voice. Its own power.

Valéry lifted the lid of the hamper, and the light intensified. He folded back the layers of silk, and when the stone was revealed, he crouched, gazing into it.

Veronica threw back the quilt and went to kneel beside her husband. She trembled now with fear as well as the cold, but he surprised her by putting an arm around her shoulders.

She leaned against him. Together they looked down at the old,

old crystal, round and smooth on top, its base jagged and rough. Inside the stone, lights flickered, gold and bronze and ivory. Veronica could think of nothing to say, no way to explain that would be safe. Resigned, she waited for Valéry to say something.

He spoke in French. "I know what this is."

She started, and jostled his arm free as she turned toward him.

He let his hand fall to his knee, his eyes still on the coruscating lights inside the crystal. He said softly, "You must have a very great power for it to wake on its own."

"Valéry!" she breathed.

"My aunt had one. It had been my grandmother's, my great-grandmother's—I don't know how far back the history goes. It didn't look like this. It was small, and smooth all around, an almost perfect sphere. I only saw it once. My aunt made me swear never to speak of it."

"What happened to it?"

"The Nazis no doubt stole it, as they stole anything they found. It was the only object of value my family owned. We will probably never know what became of it." He turned his dark gypsy eyes to her, the eyelids heavy with worry. "Do you use this, Véronique?"

"I have," she said, so softly she wasn't sure he heard her.

He turned away and began covering the stone, then lowered the lid of the hamper. As he did, the light faded and disappeared, leaving the bedroom lit only by starlight. Veronica was shivering in earnest now, clenching her teeth to stop them from chattering. Valéry got to his feet and took her dressing gown from its hook. As he draped it around her, she looked up into his face. Even in the darkness, she could see that his mouth was set and hard.

Veronica stood up, too. She shrugged into her dressing gown, and thrust her feet into the slippers waiting beside the bed. Valéry still didn't speak. She walked to the window, her arms folded against the cold, and gazed out. "I'm also sworn to tell no one," she said. "But I will tell you this, Valéry. My crystal—which belonged to my grandmother, and hers, and hers before that, just like in your family—my crystal was a great weapon in the war. I don't apologize for that. I feel no shame over it."

"Do you think I would want you to feel shame?"

She turned her back to the cold glass and gazed at him. "You appear to be angry."

He crossed the room in three long strides and wrapped his arms around her, holding her tight to his chest. "No! My darling, no! I'm not angry, I'm—I'm *afraid*."

"Valéry!" She wound her arms around his waist and clung there. "Why?"

"If anyone else were to find this...If they knew..." He crushed her against him, burying his face in her hair.

"Valéry, I have kept my secret." Her voice was muffled against the fabric of his nightshirt. "No one but you will ever know."

He loosened his grasp enough to take her chin in one hand and lift it gently so he could look into her eyes. "Véronique, you must listen to me. You, my aunt, our grandmothers—they were women of power. Men fear such women. They might not put you to the flame, as they once did, but they will not hesitate to harm you in other ways, ways that can make your life unbearable."

Veronica closed her eyes, remembering Elizabeth saying that very thing.

"You could lose Sweetbriar."

"I would never let anyone see the stone..."

"Anyone could have found it," he insisted. "A maid, your butler. It's not safe for you. Promise me you won't use it again, Véronique. Put it away. The war is over. There should be no need."

"There is some reason it called to me tonight, Valéry."

"What reason could there be? Promise me. Please."

She opened her eyes and met his with as frank a gaze as she could muster. Though her heart quaked with unease, she whispered, "Very well, Valéry. I promise."

He blew out a breath and kissed her forehead. "Thank you, my darling. We'll put it someplace not so easily discovered."

"All right. *D'accord.*"

But even as she promised, something stirred in her, sparking like the ember of a banked fire. She had not meant to lie to him, but there was some part of her—some secret part of her soul—that resisted. It was, she thought, her power. Her power, which would not be denied.

As he led her back to bed and drew her into his arms once again, she struggled not to recognize the rebel taking cover behind her submissiveness.

13

Oona's muzzle and beard had gone gray, but she frisked ahead of Veronica just as she always had. At another time Veronica might have felt like frisking herself on such a day. The sunshine had the golden tint of autumn, slanting through the turning leaves onto the freshly mown lawn around the Home Farm. Veronica paused on the flagged pathway to look up at the house, which was taking shape with remarkable speed.

Valéry had found most of the original stones of the cottage piled behind the barn. One of the farmers had organized that effort while Veronica was in London. The locals either hadn't known the stones were there, or cared enough about Sweetbriar not to help themselves to the rubble. Only two truckloads of fresh stones were needed to rebuild the walls. They had decided to replace the slanting stone floor in the kitchen with wood. Valéry said it would be level now. He also suggested central heating. Veronica agreed to that, with the proviso that the big hearth, where she and Thomas and Jago had spent so many contented afternoons, should remain.

A workman in coveralls and a flat cloth cap came down the path. When he saw who she was, he snatched his cap from his head and held it in front of his chest. "Lady Veronica," he said, dipping his head. "Come to see how we're getting on?"

"I did, Mr. Longstreet. Good weather for the work, isn't it?"

"That it is, milady. Perfect." He turned and made an expansive gesture toward the house, which already had the framing and floors in, with the walls growing steadily skyward. "This will look just as it did in His Lordship's day."

"That's marvelous. You should be proud of this job."

"Oh yes!" He grinned at her and replaced his cap. "Good to see the old place restored."

"How is your daughter? Phoebe, isn't it? Just starting school now, I think."

"Yes, thank you, milady. She's at the village school, happy as a rabbit in clover. Loves her books!"

"Does she? That's wonderful. Please tell her she's welcome to borrow from the library at Sweetbriar."

"Very kind of you, Lady Veronica. Very kind indeed. The wife will appreciate that." He pointed to the side of the house. "If you're looking for your husband, I think he's back there sorting a load of planks just delivered."

"Thank you. Keep up the good work, Mr. Longstreet."

"A pleasure, milady."

With Oona at her side, Veronica made her way around stacks of wood and stones to the side of the house. Where the barn had once stood, only four foundation blocks were left. She thought perhaps they would rebuild the barn. With the old Shire gone, it hadn't seemed important, but they might want to keep horses again.

"Véronique."

She crossed the litter of sawdust to reach him. His deep voice still had the power to make her heart beat a little faster, even with the sad news she carried. He pushed back the battered hat he wore and bent to kiss her, carefully, because he was covered in dust and what looked like plaster. His lips were warm on her cheek.

She put up her hand to brush grime from his chin. "You're making such progress," she said. "It's hard to believe how fast it's going."

"We have hard workers," he said. His English was nearly perfect now, but it still had a French flavor she loved, a slight angle to the vowels, a rhythm all his own. He had steadily gained weight, despite some food still being rationed. He always said he had no need of sweets, but he absolutely refused to touch margarine, and Veronica agreed with him. They and their staff coped well, though, with butter from the farms, and the bread Cook baked each day. Now, working outdoors as he so often did, Valéry's skin was gypsy-dark. His hair shone blue-black in the sun, starred with silver at the temples.

Clothes rationing had only just been lifted, but since they almost never went to London, or out to social events, neither of them cared much about that. Today Veronica wore a tweed skirt she had owned since her school days, and a light sweater that had been darned countless times. Valéry wore a pair of stained coveralls exactly like those Mr. Longstreet had on. They fit Longstreet better. Valéry's ankles showed between the too-short trousers and his workman's boots. His eye patch was as dusty as the rest of him, and she made a mental note to see that he had a supply of clean ones.

"You're a sight, Valéry," Veronica said.

He touched his hat brim and sketched a bow. "Milady," he said.

"Pfft!" She poked him with her finger, and he put an arm around her.

It was a source of amusement to both of them that she was invariably addressed by her title, no matter who was speaking, but that no one knew how to address Valéry. He could not be, of course, "Your Lordship." "Sir" made him sound like the king. He was not even Mr. Selwyn, although Veronica had returned to the name for the sake of Sweetbriar's history. Many noble families hyphenated their names, but Chirac-Selwyn, or Selwyn-Chirac, just seemed too much of a mouthful. Valéry, technically, was Mr. Chirac, but he never heard it used. The household staff called him Mr. Valéry. Most people in the neighborhood didn't use his name at all.

"I've brought sandwiches," she said now, freeing herself and digging into the satchel she carried over her shoulder. Oona, at the mention of food, wagged her tail and pressed against Veronica's legs. Valéry, too, looked ready for food. "Shall I offer some to Mr. Longstreet?"

"Of course."

Valéry settled himself on a plank set on two blocks, and she handed him a sandwich, then sat gingerly beside him, wary of splinters. She took a sandwich for herself, and broke off a small bit to offer to Oona.

Valéry took a huge bite of bread and ham and cheese, and began chewing with the appetite of a man who had labored long hours without refreshment.

"I have something to tell you." Veronica held her sandwich in her lap, untouched except for the fragments Oona was eagerly licking from her fingers.

"What?" Valéry spoke around a second big mouthful.

"I saw Dr. Mountjoy this morning."

Valéry swallowed and watched her, his thick eyebrows raised. "What does he say?"

"He says—" She paused, hating to say it aloud. "He says," she tried again, "that there is something wrong with me. That I probably won't ever conceive." She saw the way he lowered his sandwich, only half-eaten, to his lap. He averted his gaze, and she knew he was trying to hide his disappointment. "I'm so sorry, Valéry. *Je suis désolée.*"

He responded in English, as he sometimes did when he was trying to control his feelings. "It's not your fault," he said, laying aside his sandwich, and putting out his arm to draw her close to him.

But it was her fault. It was what she had done, during the war, and she knew it. She had done it to herself, and her body had never fully recovered. She drew back a little, fearing that the guilt she felt would radiate through her, and he would recognize it.

He released her and looked into her eyes. "We have each other, Véronique."

"Yes. But I know how much you want a child."

"I want many things." He leaned close to her and kissed her forehead. "You must not worry," he said. "Perhaps it was never meant to happen." He picked up his sandwich again, but without relish, as if his appetite had subsided.

Except that it had happened. It had happened easily, that first time. It had come about perfectly, but at a perfectly impossible time. There had been no other choice for her to make.

But now...

She stood up, her own sandwich uneaten. "Come, Oona," she said. "We'll take a sandwich to Mr. Longstreet. Then—" She glanced at Valéry, and they gazed at each other for a painful moment. He started to speak, but she shook her head. "I'll see you at dinner."

"Véronique..."

She gave a brief wave, and turned away before he could see the tears shining in her eyes.

She noticed, as they moved away, that Oona no longer frisked ahead of her. The terrier's ragged tail drooped to the ground and she plodded without energy beside her mistress. Veronica thought that if she herself had a tail, it would also droop.

☙

She slipped out of bed when the stars told her it was well past midnight. Valéry, with the exhaustion of physical labor, was sleeping hard and didn't stir as she and Oona crept out through the door and along the corridor to the attic stairs. The servants' rooms at Sweetbriar were mostly on the main floor in the back, giving them access to the gardens, the garage, the kitchen, and the tradesmen's entrance. Only Honeychurch had a room on the second floor, and it was well to the back, where he could keep an eye on the younger staff.

At Valéry's request Veronica had moved the Fortnum & Mason hamper to the attic, settling it behind a stack of steamer trunks, cartons tied together with twine, discarded bits of furniture, and aged valises. She trod lightly on the attic stairs, and didn't turn on a light until she and the dog were inside. When the door was securely closed, she pulled the string of a single bare bulb beside the door that barely illumined the dusty, crowded space. She jammed a chair under the latch, then turned to cautiously slide the hamper out of its hiding place.

She had nothing with which to work a spell, neither water nor herbs nor salt nor candle. She hadn't dared try to collect such things, not when she had promised Valéry. She hadn't celebrated the Sabbats, major or minor, in a very long time. She hadn't looked into the stone since the night he had discovered it.

The crystal would answer her, or it would not, but she had to try.

She uncovered it and set it on the bare wooden floor. She knelt before it, cupping it in her palms, and spoke very low, with Oona watching from the shadows.

Mother Goddess, hear my plea:
Let my fault forgotten be,
And let there be a babe for me.

She spoke it three times three times, peering into the stone for any response.

There was none. The crystal, which usually flared to life when she approached it, which sometimes glowed of its own accord to get her attention, which had shown her the spirits of her ancestresses and guided her uncertain steps when there was no one to teach her, would not answer her. Its dull gray surface was opaque in the dim light, with no spark in its depths.

She let her prayer die away, but she stayed where she was, gazing disconsolately at the stone. "I didn't mean to turn my back on the craft," she murmured. "Valéry begged me, and he has had so many losses. So much pain. I thought—I just wanted to reassure him. He was so worried..." The thin, whispery sound of her voice threaded through the dusty attic. She wasn't sure whom she was addressing. All of them, perhaps, all the women who had handled this stone, who had called on it, relied upon it.

She thought of Olive, and Rose, and Elizabeth, and the way the stone had blazed inside the circle of the coven. Of course, they had done things properly. They had herbs, and salt, and new candles, everything the grimoires prescribed.

She didn't know what to do. Surely the grimoire had spells for fertility, but did she dare take it out? It was difficult to read at the best of times, and in this light it would be impossible. She couldn't risk carrying it to her bedroom, or any other place where Valéry would see it, and know she had broken her promise.

She glanced at the small dormer window set into the peaked roof of the attic. The stars were beginning to fade. The early sun would rise soon. Valéry might wake, and wonder where she was. It was obvious she was wasting her time here, but it hurt to give up.

"Maybe," she said mournfully to Oona, "I'm not meant to have a child after all. Maybe that girl I saw, the image Mama sent— maybe it wasn't me. Perhaps I am the end of my line, the last of the Orchiéres. The line of Valéry's family died out, and unless one of the queen's nieces has inherited the power, the line of the Glamis witches will also die out."

She sighed and got stiffly to her feet, pausing to rub her knees. She bent to replace the wrappings on the crystal. When she lowered the lid of the hamper, she let her palm rest on the wicker top for a moment. She closed her eyes, feeling this was a final farewell. She wondered who might one day come across the old Fortnum & Mason hamper, and open it out of curiosity.

"Well, Oona," she said aloud, as she opened her eyes. "I suppose I made a terrible mistake, but I did it for love. You and I know that. Everything I've done, I did for love."

It was true, she thought, as she picked her way through the clutter of trunks and boxes toward the door. Love of family, of friends, of country, of her queen, of her house and her husband—these were what mattered. If it was the end of the practice of the craft for her, she could at least feel content with the knowledge that she had offered the best she had.

She was just reaching for the string to turn off the light when Oona emitted one short, sharp bark.

Veronica glanced back, a command for the dog on her lips. It died unspoken.

Light pierced the woven wicker of the hamper and cast an unsteady lattice pattern on the slanted ceiling. The stone had come alive.

With a soft cry Veronica hurried back to it. She barked her shin on the corner of a trunk, and nearly tripped over a cast-off floor lamp, but in the space of a breath she was crouched beside the hamper again, throwing open the lid, tearing off the silk covering.

They were all there, the faces appearing and disappearing through the glowing mist inside the crystal. It was, as it had always been, like dreaming of them, the crone with the stone in her hands, the sharp-faced woman, the old woman with the wild mane of silver hair, and the beautiful one. Her mother. Morwen.

"Mama," Veronica breathed, and the whirl of faces ceased.

Morwen gazed out at her, a faint, sweet smile on her lips. In her mind Veronica heard her mother's voice. *All will be as it's meant,* Morwen told her. *You have the greatest gift already. Love him. Let him love you. Nothing else matters.*

A heartbeat later she was gone. Other faces took her place, curious faces, laughing ones, some that scowled as if finding their descendant unworthy. Veronica stayed where she was, meeting their gazes, smiling even at the frowning ones.

The sky beyond the windows of Sweetbriar was already turning rosy when she left the attic, and she and Oona hurried down the stairs and along the corridor to the bedroom.

She opened the door as quietly as she could. Valéry sat up as she came in, peering at her through sleep-heavy eyelids. "Where have you been?"

Veronica said, without a twinge of guilt, "Oona needed to go out."

Yawning, Valéry threw back the covers and patted the sheet. "You must be cold."

"I am." She crossed to the bed and slid beneath the blankets, snuggling close to Valéry's warmth. He put his arm around her and she tucked her head against his shoulder, just beneath his chin.

"I was thinking, Véronique," he said. She felt the rumble of his deep, sweet voice against her cheek. "No matter what *le docteur* has said, we should keep trying."

Veronica turned up her face and kissed his cheek. A bubble of happiness rose in her breast, and she chuckled. "Were you thinking that, darling?"

"Ah, oui." He turned his head to kiss her lips, long and hungrily. He rolled on his side so he could take her in both arms, pull her close, and nuzzle her throat. "At the very least, my dear love, it will be great fun."

Acknowledgments

In the writing of this complicated book, I am indebted to a number of talented and generous people. The independent editor Michele Whitehead provided a critical eye when I needed it; my faithful friend Catherine Whitehead advised me on French; the excellent writer Rosemary Edghill gave me advice on contemporary Paganism; my great friends and wonderful colleagues Kay Kenyon and Sharon Shinn provided support and guidance and often inspiration.

I can hardly thank Lindsey Hall, my editor at Redhook/Orbit, warmly enough for her vision, her eye for detail, and her painstaking and perceptive editorial style. Peter Rubie, my agent at FinePrint Literary Management, has all my gratitude for his energetic support of this book and this writer.

I felt my mother's spirit with me as I worked on this book, and I'm deeply grateful for her influence.

The entire experience of creating *A Secret History of Witches* has been magical.